DEAD SHOT

"Compelling."   —*Publishers Weekly*

"The [plot] propels the pages forward, but this one isn't all about action: Swanson proves a surprisingly complex character . . . *Dead Shot* suggest[s] a hardware-heavy story that only an armed-services veteran could love. Surprisingly, it's completely the opposite. Readers will be compelled . . . and will look forward to another Swanson adventure."   —*Booklist*

KILL ZONE

"Stunning action, excellent tradecraft, insider politics, and the ring of truth. Just about perfect."   —Lee Child

"Tight, suspenseful . . . Here's hoping this is the first of many Swanson novels."   —*Booklist*

"The action reaches a furious pitch."   —*Publishers Weekly*

SHOOTER

The Autobiography of the Top-Ranked Marine Sniper

"One of the best snipers in the Marine Corps, perhaps the very best. When I asked one of his commanders about his skills, the commander smiled and said, 'I'm just glad he's on our side.' "

> —Peter Maass, war-correspondent and
> bestselling author of *Love Thy Neighbor*

"The combat narratives here recount battlefield action with considerable energy . . . A renowned sniper, Coughlin is less concerned with his tally than with the human values of comradeship and love."

> —*The Washington Post*

"Coughlin is a sniper, perhaps one of the most respected and feared in the Corps, and his memoir, *Shooter*, offers a uniquely intimate look into the life of one trained to live in the shadows . . . some of the most poignant action ever recorded in a modern Marine memoir."

> —*Seapower* magazine

ALSO BY JACK COUGHLIN

Shooter: The Autobiography of the Top-Ranked Marine Sniper
(with Capt. Casey Kuhlman and Donald A. Davis)

Kill Zone (with Donald A. Davis)

Dead Shot (with Donald A. Davis)

Clean Kill (with Donald A. Davis)

An Act of Treason (with Donald A. Davis)

ALSO BY DONALD A. DAVIS

Lightning Strike

The Last Man on the Moon (with Gene Cernan)

Dark Waters (with Lee Vyborny)

RUNNING
THE MAZE

GUNNERY SGT.
JACK COUGHLIN
USMC (RET.)

WITH
DONALD A. DAVIS

St. Martin's Paperbacks

This is a work of fiction. All of the characters, organizations, and events portrayed in this novel are either products of the author's imagination or are used fictitiously.

RUNNING THE MAZE

Copyright © 2012 by Jack Coughlin with Donald A. Davis.
Excerpt from *Time to Kill* copyright © 2012 by Jack Coughlin with Donald A. Davis.

For information address St. Martin's Press, 175 Fifth Avenue, New York, NY 10010.

Library of Congress Catalog Card Number: 2011041348

ISBN: 978-1-250-01639-3

Printed in the United States of America

St. Martin's Press hardcover edition / March 2012
St. Martin's Paperbacks edition / December 2012

St. Martin's Paperbacks are published by St. Martin's Press, 175 Fifth Avenue, New York, NY 10010.

10 9 8 7 6 5 4 3 2

1

Five-minute break. Dr. Joey Ledford sat on the shaky remnants of a wooden chair, smoking a Marlboro and sweating while monsoon rains slammed the tin roof of the makeshift medical clinic of United Nations Refugee Camp Five. Somewhere, doctors and nurses were performing surgeries in antiseptic, air-conditioned rooms that were packed with every conceivable device of the medical arts, with storage areas nearby bulging with vital, lifesaving medicines. They were listening to Bach or Norah Jones or Latin jazz as they performed meticulous cuts and closed wounds with care, taking all the time they needed to do it right. Somewhere, the magical art of medicine was a smooth choreography conducted by well-educated professionals in offices and clinics and hospitals. Somewhere, but not here.

Ledford exhaled, and twin streams of cigarette smoke flowed from his nostrils. The rain was not a gentle and sweet thundershower like back in Iowa. Instead of giving life to crops, this was unrelenting and fell in great sheets, as if some angry demon had ripped open the bellies of the fat black clouds. He looked out at the sprawl of the camp, where thousands of people were hiding under whatever shelter they could find. Armed guards were at the clinic door to keep them out. They had been driven out of their homes by overflowing rivers and leaking dams and were still being pursued by water. *Poor creatures*, Ledford thought. *Poor, damned souls.*

Sweat caked his T-shirt and khakis, and when he dropped the cigarette and ground it out, he noticed the bloodstains on his black rubber boots had become deep, splotchy layers during the day, and he could not recall the individual patients from which the blood had come. He would wash it off later. Break over, Ledford ducked back into the tent, back into the world of misery.

He sloshed his hands in a basin, slid gloves on, and put on a surgical mask and a fresh apron, then walked over to what once had been someone's kitchen table but now served a higher purpose as an operating room surface. It was covered by squares of disposable white paper on which a baby girl lay screaming as a nurse inserted an IV needle in her arm to start a drip. The mother shrieked nearby, echoing and amplifying the suffering of her one surviving child.

"It looks like another cholera," a nurse replied. "Once you set the broken arm, we will begin the antibiotics."

Ledford nodded. "We have any patient history or X-rays for her?"

"No. She's about six months old, has a one-oh-one fever and coughing. Cries are weak. The mother just arrived this morning and said a big rock banged into the child during a mudslide two days ago."

The doctor wasted no time complaining about what they didn't have, because they could only work with what was available. He was thirty-one, an even six feet tall, had longish dark hair that reached his collar, and possessed impeccable credentials: University of Iowa for premed, then the Carver College of Medicine there, followed by a three-year internal medicine residency at the Mayo Clinic in Minnesota. He'd been ready for the next step toward a successful career when he decided to take a holiday from his studies and go see the world. He did not like what he found out there. He had a rugged, handsome face, but the eyes were those of a combat veteran, for he had seen horror after horror in refugee camps from Haiti to Africa. The emergency calls for help from Pakistan when the floods struck had come as he was wrapping up an assignment in Bangladesh, and he did not hesitate. This was who he was now, at least for as long as he could stand it.

"OK," Ledford nodded to the anesthesiologist, David Foley, an irreverent Canadian from Ottawa. "Let's put the kid to sleep so we can move her on down the assembly line. We've got a lot of other customers waiting. Raining like hell and the drinking water is filthy because we can't store it. No excuse for waterborne diseases here."

There was a soft hiss in a plastic mask over the baby's mouth and nose, and she immediately began to calm. "Hey, Joey?" asked the gas-passer.

"What, David?"

"Five years from now you will be doing nip-and-tucks for rich ladies in your own fancy clinic. I will be driving a red convertible. We will tweet and play Fantasy Football and date supermodels." He looked at his instruments. All good. "OK. She's down."

Ledford let his fingers gently probe the left arm of the infant and explore the fracture. "Stay focused, Dr. Foley."

"Joey?"

"Be quiet. I'm trying to concentrate." He found the break and tried to picture in his mind how it looked. With luck and a few years, if the child beat the odds and lived that long, her limbs might one day be strong again. Babies are resilient.

"Doc Yao says we can have some time off. Sort of."

Ledford's hands were working smoothly now, and the nurse stayed with him, putting another damaged little human being back together. He let her do as much of the work as possible to improve her skills. "What's the catch?"

"We go up north and visit some of the flooded villages where the water is receding. Pick a site for a new UN facility upcountry. I think we can carve out some serious downtime in the process. Actually get some rest. We about done with this kid?"

"Just a few more minutes." As the nurse finished the bandaging, he gave the rest of the body a quick examination. No other breaks, but she was malnourished from being sick and unable to feed. He could clearly see the rib cage. He gently pinched, and the skin did not quickly resume its shape. "The arm will be fine, but the cholera is going to kick her little butt." He made a note to admit the child as a patient and try to get her cleaned up, inside and outside. If she survived all of that, then all she would have to worry about would be measles and malaria and land mines and machine guns and mortars and a long menu of infectious diseases and the questionable privilege of growing up in a third-world country in which women were second-class citizens. Thankfully, Ledford thought, the strict Islamic religious zealots had not invaded the camp yet, or he would not have been allowed to touch or even look at the naked female baby.

"What did you tell Dr. Yao?"

"I volunteered us."

"Humph," Ledford grunted. Might be interesting.

The team of nine medical workers headed out the following morning, in a convoy of three United Nations trucks, carrying just enough supplies to establish a base camp that could expand rapidly to help meet the flood emergency. Fifteen hours later, after grinding through brutal, washed-out roads, they reached a camp that was run by Doctors Without Borders, where they spent the night before pushing on deeper into the wasteland in the dusty gold of the new dawn.

"My ass is completely broken," complained David Foley by radio as the sun reached its zenith. He was in the third truck, and Ledford was riding as the only passenger in the lead vehicle.

"Take two aspirin, put it in a sling, and call me in the morning," Ledford joked.

"Better idea would be to just stop and have some lunch. Get our bearings," Foley replied.

Ledford thought that was a good idea, for the road had smoothed out a bit for the last few kilometers as it moved through some small hills. A side road branched off to the right and downward, and he told the driver to follow it to a spot where they could have a break. In a moment, they were on the back side of the hills and following an old road that sloped down into a valley, edging onto a flat plateau. "Here," he said. The trucks pulled up, nose to tailgate, and the team got out and stretched.

Foley walked up to join Ledford. "Why the grin? This place looks like the dark side of the moon." The flood had laid waste high up the banks before receding.

"I think we can set up the camp here," Ledford said. "Water is down quite a bit, and there is plenty of room to spread out. And look up at the other end of the valley, Dave. That big bridge is new; hell, they're still working on it. Traffic, people, and supplies could feed over it and down to us without a problem. The valley is perfect for air resupply drops, too. Maybe the bridge people could lend us a bulldozer to carve an airstrip."

Foley had a pair of binoculars. "There are big machines at work up there, but I see trucks, too. So maybe it is in operation. You're right."

They joined the others, who had spread some blankets under stunted trees and laid out a lunch. Having some time off from the misery of the camps was reinvigorating. Afterward, some of them stretched out in the shade for quick naps, while Ledford took a walk farther down the road, alone. Although the driver, who carried a pistol, was the only member of the team with a weapon, they felt safe; medical workers helping people in need, no matter what their politics, were usually immune from any severe threat.

"Well, I'll be damned," he said with a loud laugh. He had come across an old steel trestle bridge that had been taken out by the flood, and the eastern end was canted down into the water. It reminded him of home, of an almost identical bridge where he and his sister, Beth, once played. He found his cell phone, snapped a picture, added the text message REMEMBER THIS? and sent it to her.

The group was stirring again when he got back. "Come on, everybody. Let's go for a walk and get a feel for the valley as our possible refugee camp site, then pay a visit to the big bridge at the other end. They will be our new neighbors, so we might as well pay our respects to whoever is in charge." There was a path along the western side of the river, and they followed in line. The afternoon was sunny, and a wind pushing through the valley cut the heat. This could be a good place.

2

U.S. Marine Gunnery Sergeant Kyle Swanson was in the Mixing Bowl, punching without much success through the clogged web of highways around Washington, D.C., getting away from the Pentagon parking lot, inch by inch, heading for a shootout in the Ghost House. The tinted windows of the gray Taurus rental were closed tight, and the air conditioner fought bravely against the thousands of exhaust pipes in the rush hour traffic and the stifling heat of late August. There was a reason that politicians and lobbyists abandoned Washington to the tourists and the nation to its fate in the teeth of the brutal summer, and he was happy to be leaving for a few days as the highways, monuments, and stone government buildings sucked up the hard rays of the burning sun and cooked. The TV weather people had showed their maps and grimly explained that it was unseasonably hot, as if it hadn't happened every year since the government moved here from Philadelphia a couple of centuries ago. A taxi probably headed for Dulles swerved in front of a white SUV, which braked hard, causing a tailgating sedan to swerve into an adjoining lane, and traffic in two lanes died a temporary honking and swearing death. Swanson stopped, found a sports talk radio station on the Sirius, and waited for a report on the close of training camp for the New England Patriots or the pennant race for the Boston Red Sox. In three minutes everyone was lurching forward again.

He rode the I-395 southwest and gradually put the District of Columbia in his rearview mirrors. Across the Beltway, traffic thinned out around Springfield. Things weren't as bad when the highway turned into I-95, and he was able to speed up, although he had plenty of time. His destination was Virginia Beach, where the Naval Special Warfare Development Group was headquartered, and the shoot with SEAL Team Six was scheduled for 0700 tomorrow morning. The only hitch was that Senior Chief Richard Sheridan had asked him to come down early for a private talk over a pitcher of beer. The Navy senior chief and the Marine gunnery sergeant had known each other for fifteen years and had worked together in some unfriendly places that had funny names. If Rockhead wanted to chat, that was cool.

Sheridan was waiting in a waterfront bar that specialized in serving military personnel. The whole Tidewater area was a huge sprawl of current and former military men and women and their families, from all branches of the service, but predominantly Navy. Kyle thought the squids could probably dig up a crew for a battleship just by posting a note at the nearest 7-Eleven.

They sat at a table on the deck away from the crowd, beside a wooden rail that had been split by the sun and rain. A huge anchor jutted from the sand of a little garden, as if dropped off by a passing ship. Nets and old buoys and military memorabilia passed for decoration, and bare bulbs hanging overhead painted the place with light.

After trading insult greetings and catching up on old friends while the server brought beer for Rockhead and ice water with a slice of lime for Kyle, then took their orders for steaks, Rockhead got to the problem. "You still got security clearances all the way up to God, right?"

Kyle nodded. He was the key operator for the deep black unit known as Task Force Trident and answered directly to the president of the United States. "What's up, Senior Chief?"

"I need your professional assessment on one of my guys. Not a damn thing wrong with his performances; in fact, he's top of the heap in Team Six."

Swanson raised an eyebrow. Six was the elite of the elite, the guys who finally nailed Osama bin Laden. Nobody got into that secretive, handpicked bunch without exceptional skills.

"Petty Officer First Class Ryan Powell is maybe the best shooter we've got. He can punch holes in the ten-ring with either hand, and even while holding a weapon upside down. We picked him for the Special Warfare Development Group a few years ago because of exceptional performance. He is still sort of young, twenty-seven, but is just the kind of pup we love to groom for better things. He's got all the skills: powerful, can swim forever, and has the reflexes of a cat after a bug. His teammates call him Captain America."

"Sounds like your typical Team Six Superman. What's the problem?" Kyle sipped the water.

Rockhead ran a palm across the bristly hair on his tanned scalp as ropy muscles worked in his forearms. "My gut is the problem, Gunny. You know how Superman has problems with that kryptonite shit? Well, I'm looking past the fitness reports. There's something missing with Powell, and I can't put my finger on it. I want you to work out in the Ghost House with him tomorrow, get up close and personal, put him under pressure, and give me a personal reading."

"What will I be looking for, Rock?"

"I'm thinking Superman has turned coward."

Kyle let that comment sit undisturbed for a while, but it was if a small elephant had just taken the third chair at the table. Swanson considered SEALs to be among the best fighters on the planet, so the Rock worrying that one of his best boys might be cracking up came as a shock. Some electric country music filtered out to the deck from the bar inside. "So, why me?"

"I want an outsider's unofficial viewpoint that can be kept between the two of us. If you think he's fine, he stays. I don't want to ruin his reputation and career and usefulness, but not everyone is cut out for this work, and I can't put other lives in jeopardy because this guppy has lost his nerve."

"So how do we go about this . . . unofficial . . . examination?"

"I've paired you up to go into the Ghost House with him tomorrow morning. Put him into some unexpected pressure situations that go beyond the fixed scenario and parameters. He will be expecting it just to be another training exercise that he can coast through on sheer physical ability. You make it something else. Force him. Press him hard."

Swanson thought a bit, then nodded. "You can dial up any scenario you want in the Ghost House, right?"

Rockhead smiled. "Almost any exterior or interior except your sister's bedroom, and they may have that, too."

One thing that Kyle Swanson really enjoyed about training with SEAL Team Six was its seemingly limitless budget. The squids always got first crack at the experimental stuff that was way out on the edge of the combat curve, and they burned money faster than a Wall Street banker figuring his annual bonus. Trying to determine how best to fight tomorrow's wars was what the Special Warfare Development Group was all about.

The Ghost House represented a quantum leap in close quarters battle training. Usually, CQB houses were crude mockups in a desolate environment so the SEALs could regularly blow them apart with bullets to practice moving through a tight, hostile environment. Those were static environments, except for pop-up targets. The Ghost House, by contrast, was almost alive. It sat inside a weathered airplane hangar in an area generally used for storage, out of sight to everyone but those directly involved with it, and it bloomed with electronics and computerized graphics.

Stacks of tires and other retardants were still used to soak up the spent rounds, but instead of just plywood, the interior walls were green screens on which different worlds were projected. Automobiles and taxis and buses moved, smoke hindered vision, people were shopping in stores, and sounds and motion were constant. Or the setting might be the interior of a quiet suburban American home, or the cars of a train, or the bowels of a ship or an oil platform or a nuclear power plant. Foam cutouts were used to represent furniture and obstacles, also colored by the computers. The jackpot was the unknown opposition force, which was no longer merely stiff pop-ups but full-sized, three-dimensional holograms that responded to the moves of the trainees. Their weapons would blink to fire simulated bursts, and the updated MILES gear worn by the attacking good guys would shriek if the computers scored a hit. The holograms did not necessarily die with the first hit, unless the computer judged it as a kill shot. The controllers guided the fight from racks of computers in a safe blockhouse outside of the hangar.

"Then let's start by using that *Mayberry R.F.D.* innocent street scene. There's no information on it about who the tangos might be. I want Powell concentrating on having to make careful decisions so that he doesn't shoot Floyd the Barber by mistake because he steps outside the shop carrying a razor."

"Everybody hates the *Mayberry* set," Rockhead said with a laugh that sounded more like a growl. "That old TV show has a built-in wild card with Deputy Barney Fife running around with an unloaded gun. What about weapons tomorrow? Normally, they armor up and use MP-5s for these scenarios."

"No. In my line of work, there is seldom a submachine gun around when you need one. I want this guy stripped down to get him out of the protective bubble and make him feel more vulnerable, almost naked, from the start. Jeans and T-shirts and sneakers. One pistol of his choice, no silencers. The story line is that we are on a fishing trip near Mayberry and the closest responders when Sheriff Andy calls for help because his police station is under attack. Terrorist on Main Street and lots of women and kids."

"What about comms?"

"Standard headsets, but I want the controllers to jam the frequency just after we go in to help throw him off balance. And send word to him tonight not to wear a jockstrap."

"Why? We don't wear jocks anyway."

"Part of the mind game. I just want him thinking about his groin. Vulnerability."

"Put him under some real stress, Kyle."

"All right."

"So what are you going to do?" Rockhead finished off his beer and wiped a plash on the table.

"Scare the shit out of him."

"How?"

"I have all night to plan it."

Boatswain's Mate First Class Ryan Powell readied his weapon and growled at the man who would be going with him into the Ghost House. "Don't get in my way, old man. We're using live ammo today." Powell was somewhat pissed at being paired with this over-the-hill Marine. Dude had to be way into his thirties, about ten years older than Powell, which meant he was going to be slow. Some kind of hotshot sniper, back in the day.

Swanson said nothing as he studied the rangy SEAL: less than six feet tall, shaggy brown hair, wide shoulders, and corded muscles that flexed through the strong forearms like ropes. Even in jeans, he had the stiff look of a Transformer robot, as if he were about to turn into a pickup truck. Swanson looked beyond the taut, healthy body. The weight was evenly distributed but back on his heels, and the eyes were black dots, twitchy. The fingers drummed lightly on the Heckler & Koch SOCOM pistol in the belt holster. *Anxious, or just normal jitters in facing the unknown?*

"The fuck you staring at, Pops!" Powell barked. He was confident that he would master the Ghost House again and put the old Marine to shame while doing so. Then he would ride the jarhead mercilessly, and try to pick a fight just to have the pleasure of whipping his butt. Youth, strength, ability, determination, and pride were all on his side. It still bothered Powell that he had not been part of the bin Laden hit. The Marine had nothing. Powell gave Swanson a mean grin, like a pit bull eyeing a kitten. "I'm gonna kick your jarhead ass."

"Ready on the range?" called the range safety officer. Swanson racked a round into the chamber of his reliable Marine Corps .45 ACP pistol and clicked off the safety. "Ready," he said.

"Ready," echoed Powell, bringing out his pistol and getting into his stance.

"Stand by," ordered the range safety officer. A double door swung apart to let the shooters enter the target zone and closed behind them. "The range is hot."

Swanson and Powell were alone on Main Street, guns up. Aunt Bee was looking at them from a window, her eyes wide with fear. The bodies of two children lay dead in the street, and people were running into houses for safety, away from the rattle of automatic weapons down the street at the sheriff's office. Smoke poured from the windows. Powell stepped forward, pistol grasped in two hands while his eyes probed the surroundings and the shadows. Swanson was five feet away on his right, matching his advance. There was a crackle in their earbuds; then the radios went silent.

"Control?" said Powell, and heard no reply. He pushed the microphone closer to his mouth. "Control?" He glanced at Swanson and tapped his ear. Something was wrong. The Marine ignored him and took another step forward, ducking into cover behind a foam block that looked like a Dumpster. Powell got his eyes back on the street scene. Part of the scenario assumed that the area behind them was already cleared. A little girl in a doorway stared at them as if they were interplanetary aliens, and a dirty pickup truck suddenly sped out of an alley and dashed across the street into the grocery store parking lot, where the driver bailed out and ran inside. Civilian. A misty smoke snaked along the ground.

Powell was tense, beginning to sweat. First the radio glitch, and now he had almost pulled the trigger on the dude in the pickup. He slowed down to ease his breathing. Where was the damned tango?

Then came a thunderclap of two fast shots almost in his right ear as Swanson fired twice right over Powell's head, missing him by no more than six inches. Powell flinched, took a knee, and yelled, "Cease fire! *Cease fire!* What the fuck are you doing?" He safed his weapon and put it away, but nothing changed. The rules were that anybody on a range could stop an exercise if he saw something going wrong. The Marine bounded across a sidewalk and into a doorway, heading for the sheriff's office. A flicker of computerized tracers shot out of the target zone, slashing past Powell, who hit the deck hard, prone and with his hands over his head. *"WHAT THE FUCK IS HAPPENING? CONTROL! CEASE FIRE! STOP IT!"* The Marine fired three times at a hologram that appeared in the street with a gun, putting two in the chest and one in the head. The pictured man crumbled to the ground.

A loud horn honked inside the Ghost House, and the images dissolved and the doors opened, letting in the sunlight as the smoke poured out. Ryan Powell jumped to his feet as the Marine ambled back toward him, his weapon on safe and hanging loosely from his hand. Powell was furious. "You almost killed me," he yelled, balling up a big fist. "This was a live-fire training drill, and you deliberately shot right over my head. I'm going to have them write you up, then I'm going to kick your scrawny ass."

Swanson looked calmly at the warrior and saw worry painted on the young face. Death had come near. "I was part of the test today, Bos'n Powell. It was negative training to snatch you out of your comfort zone and not let your muscle memory and practice kick in. You froze at the critical moment. As soon as things started south, you shut down. Your job was to finish the mission, not pussy out." Kyle returned his own pistol to the holster in the back of his belt and lowered his voice. "You can't call cease fire in real combat, Powell. You just can't. There are no second chances out there, buddy, and my opinion is that you don't want to be here, not really. Something has taken the heart out of you and has left only your natural talent. It's time for you to get on with your life."

"You are full of shit. Who the fuck do you think you are?" The raging Powell felt the touch of Rockhead on his elbow. "Who is this asshole, Senior Chief?"

"Somebody you would not want to meet in a dark alley, Powell. Let's you and me go have a talk, son."

Rockhead Sheridan met Swanson back at the same watering hole that evening. This time they sat inside, at the bar. A news report was on the TV about the upcoming launch of the first mission that would eventually lead to a Mars landing. A cut of cool ocean air had moved in to drop the temperature, and rain was blowing onto the patio. Neither man was in a good mood.

"Had to be done," Rockhead said. "Powell has already departed for a thirty-day leave to try to get his act together. Turns out he had some serious home problems and a set of new twins, both of them real sick, so he was at a personal crossroads. I told him to go home and do what was really important, take care of his family."

"So he's done with Team Six?" Kyle folded a wet napkin, just to be doing something. He had not enjoyed taking part in the collapse of Ryan Powell.

"Yep. If he wants to stay as a SEAL, we'll rotate him into being an instructor in the BUD/S training. He'd be close to home and probably be pretty good at the job." Rockhead shrugged. "Life sucks sometimes."

They went silent for a little while. Then Kyle asked, "You gonna let me have another run at the Ghost House tomorrow? By myself?"

"That was the deal, Gunny Swanson. You should get two, three more chances to shoot some holograms before you go back to the Puzzle Palace in Washington."

Their attention was drawn to a breaking news banner flashing on the television set that hung from the ceiling, a fragmented report about the slaughter of an international medical team in the northern part of Pakistan. Nine dead and no survivors.

"Tough," observed Rockhead, signaling the bartender for another beer. "Bunch of tree-hugging do-gooders out hiking where they don't belong."

Kyle agreed. "Plenty of places in this screwy world where they could be helping, and they chose Pakistan. Not that the refugees don't need all the help they can get. That flooding is a mess."

"My only real beef is if those doctors and nurses start crossing over and give training in first aid and medical treatment to the terrorists. Maybe even treat their soldiers. Helping keep the enemy alive, no matter how noble, is bad karma. We want to kill them and some liberal medics want to patch them up? No way."

Kyle thought for a moment as individual photographs of some of the medical team passed on the screen. He agreed with Rockhead. "Well, at least that one is over and done with. Doesn't involve us."

3

A Pakistani army patrol had found the bodies but knew little more than that most of the victims were foreigners. Wallets and identification cards had been stolen, but the corpses had been scattered around a truck that wore the blue symbol of the United Nations painted on its doors.

The bare details were quickly passed along to a Doctors Without Borders outpost that the medical team had visited the night before it set out on its final journey. The unofficial grapevine that binds the various relief organizations soon got the news back to UN Refugee Camp Five, allowing Dr. Lin Yao, the director and chief administrator, to place a direct call to the UN Headquarters in New York and pass along the tragic news. A general press announcement was dispatched, but the identities of the murdered doctors and nurses were withheld pending the notification of family members, no small task since the victims had been an international group.

Dr. Yao, a small and precise man, needed an entire

day to confirm who had volunteered to make the trek north. His eyes misted, and he had to remove his glasses to wipe them as he determined the names of the nine dedicated medical personnel who had been senselessly murdered. Their loss was going to be a significant blow to ongoing operations at Camp Five.

There had been only one American, the team leader, Dr. Joseph Ledford, the gentle and dedicated physician who had trained at the Mayo Clinic. Two Canadians, two Chinese, and one more each from Venezuela, Fiji, South Africa, and Jordan. Yao realized his mistakes: The group did not include enough Muslims to go out into the countryside on their own, and the Fijian nurse openly read her Christian Bible every day and protested the subservient position of women in this rigid society. *My fault,* thought Yao, blaming himself for a tragedy that could not have been predicted. *I should have paid more attention before giving permission.* There was just so much work.

Once his list was complete, Yao found their personnel folders and sent the names to New York, where workers set about contacting proper authorities around the world to carry the worst news possible to the affected families. The U.S. delegate to the United Nations was given the name of Dr. Joseph Ledford, whose home address was in the state of Iowa, and the State Department sped the information along to the office of the governor of Iowa in Des Moines, which steered it over to the state police, which passed it along to the Kossuth County Sheriff's Office in Algona.

Towns and villages dot the farmland in the middle

of Iowa, and many miles separate them. As a result of
a shrinking tax base, road patrol units covering the 974
square miles of the largest county in the state are
spread thin. The dispatch officer checked his computer,
saw that the nearest deputy was about thirty miles east
of the Ledford Dairy Products spread, and assigned
him to personally go to the farm. The call was made on
a cell phone to keep it off the police scanner frequencies that were monitored by the media.

Margaret Ledford was sweating in the August heat
as she helped a hired hand fit a repaired chain to the
screw of a broken conveyor belt, and she stepped away
from the job when the sheriff's car pulled in behind a
tractor parked near the barn. She lifted the broad brim
of her straw hat and wiped her forehead, recognizing
Deputy Bill Turner, who had once attended the combined junior-senior high school with both of her kids,
Joey and Beth. Everybody knew everybody out here.
He seemed slow to get out of the car as a dust cloud
settled about it, giving Margaret a moment to wonder
what in the world he was doing out here in the middle
of a Thursday afternoon. She waved.

Turner gave a nod and reluctantly stepped onto the
dirt, looking like a cop, not an old friend. Mrs. Ledford
was not someone with whom he could postpone getting
to the point. Best to get it done professionally but kindly.
Turner had great respect for her. Her husband, Stephen,
had died of a heart attack three years ago, their son,
Joey, had left long before that to become a doctor, and
their daughter, Beth, was overseas somewhere with the
Coast Guard. Margaret refused to move and had

continued to run the big farm with hired help, losing her grief in the grind of pulling a living out of the rich Iowa dirt. Against the odds, and with a pair of full-time hands, she successfully ran about four hundred acres of corn, wheat, and soybeans, and at least a hundred and fifty head of cattle and a dozen horses. The fog of working from dawn to dark every day had slowly eased the burden of her husband's passing; she would never forget him but had accepted things as they were. The kids came back to visit now and then, and that's just the way life was. Her hair was going gray, but Deputy Turner knew that Maggie Ledford was one tough lady, and that she would need that strength now.

"Hey, Bill," she called, walking over to him. "You wearing sunscreen today?"

"Yeah, Maggie." He did not engage her in the banter, and his face was serious. "Can I get a glass of water?"

"You tell me what you're doing here. Then you can have water, milk, or a beer of your choice." She put the hat back on but stripped off the heavy gloves and crossed her arms, looking up at the tall deputy.

He hooked his thumbs in his belt and bit his lip, then sighed. "No way to make this easy, Maggie, so I'll just say it: Joey's dead. He was killed with his entire medical team by the Taliban over there in Pakistan." The deputy looked straight up, unwilling to make eye contact, and when he glanced back down, he saw that the color had drained from Maggie Ledford's face and she was collapsing. He caught her. "God damn them," Bill Turner whispered to himself, taking the weight of the woman before she fell. "Damn 'em all straight to hell."

Inside the cool house, once Mrs. Ledford recovered from the initial shock, she asked Deputy Turner if her daughter had been notified. He didn't know. Maggie went to her little desk in the kitchen, pulled open a drawer, and found a special telephone number that she was to call in case of a personal emergency; the American Red Cross would contact Beth, who was on classified duty somewhere overseas.

"Prepare to take the shot, Gunner."

"Aye, aye, sir. Think you can hold this flying machine steady for a moment? You're bouncing around so much I might not be able to even hit the dang ocean." The voice in his headset was totally calm.

"I have my own problems, Gunner," Lieutenant Commander Arvis Taylor replied. "You thinking maybe you can pilot this extremely complex MH-68H helicopter better than me?"

"You think you can shoot better than me?"

"No, Gunner. I do not. So stand by to slam a round into that boat, if you please. He didn't get the message from your warning shots. I'm steadying up now. If you see anybody with an RPG, take 'em down without waiting for my order." Taylor studied his instruments closely as he worked to bring the bright white Coast Guard helo with the bold orange stripe to a midair standstill.

"Ab-so-lute-ly, sir." At the open side door behind Taylor, the sniper also was running through mental geometry to sight in on the engine compartment of the speedboat below—relative speed, angle of attack, bullet drop over distance, the effect of the powerful downdraft on the shot. Adjustments were made. These pirates had met their match but didn't understand that yet. The sniper had ripped a few warning bursts from the M-240 machine gun around their boat with no effect. Now that weapon was pushed aside, and a thirty-seven-pound M-82 Barrett .50 caliber rifle was in position instead, dummy-corded with a D-ring to the harness. The powerful scope brought the engine compartment at the rear of the target boat into a tight, clear view.

The Coast Guard helo was flying the unfriendly skies of coastal Somalia as part of the international naval effort to interdict the prowling seaborne pirates who preyed on merchant shipping. The target vessel, long and wide and slow, had attacked a freighter, but it swerved away when the helo, which had been returning from another mission, heard the distress call from just forty miles away and heeled into a smooth turn. It was overhead in minutes. Luck is always an advantage in combat.

The sniper saw that the boat was hauling the combined weight of ten men, who stared up at the helicopter. One had an AK-47 at his shoulder, pinging away ineffectively, far out of range. "I'm ready, Skipper."

The pilot and the sniper had worked together for a long time as members of the U.S. Coast Guard's Helicopter Interdiction Tactical Squadron (HITRON) and were experienced in taking down much tougher targets, such as the go-fast boats of drug smugglers in the Gulf of Mexico. Lieutenant Commander Taylor had seen the sniper shoot those quick, dancing speedboats with such precision that often only one shot was needed, because the bullet would penetrate the engine and blow it apart. Without power, the go-fasts became wallowing hulks that would stay where they were until a ship arrived to arrest the crew and seize the cargo of marijuana or cocaine. Taylor was confident that his sniper was as good as they come.

He settled the helicopter into position, and the dials were right where they should be. The big problem in flying over water was not to be fooled by a smooth, mirrorlike surface and fly right into it. "Commence firing," he said.

The sniper shot on the command, and the web of straps bracing the Barrett took the recoil. There were two big Mercury outboards on the rear of the pirate boat, and the one on the left exploded in a shower of metal shards that wounded several pirates. With practiced ease, another bullet was chambered and fired, and the second motor was torn from the stern. The impact of the powerful shots sent the long boat into a lazy, powerless turn.

"You finished yet, Gunner?" asked Taylor.

"Yes, sir," replied the sniper, pulling the Barrett back into the helo and securing it. As Taylor radioed the results to a French navy frigate that was heading to the scene, the sniper pushed the goggles up, took off the helmet and ran both hands through her blond hair, then pulled on a blue baseball cap with gold lettering. Beth Ledford took a drink of water and waved to the drifting Somali pirates, who began to shout and shake their fists in futile anger when they realized that they had been attacked, and thoroughly beaten, by a woman.

Once the French warship was in sight and heading for the disabled vessel, the helicopter spun out of its holding pattern and was soon making its final approach to the landing area on the broad stern of the National Security Cutter *Stratton,* a 418-foot-long white vessel that looked friendly to allied maritime units but overwhelmingly threatening to potential enemies. Petty Officer Ledford was looking forward to a quick debriefing, cleaning her weapons, then some hot chow and a shower, clean sheets, and sleep.

"Oh-oh." Taylor's voice cut into her daydreaming. "Hey, Ledford. You still awake back there?"

"Yep. Sir."

"Look at that welcoming committee just beyond the platform. You got better eyes. Who is it?"

Beth shaded her face from the sun with the palm of her hand. Three officers in pressed khaki uniforms and blue hats were in line, watching the helo come in. "It's the skipper . . . chief of the boat . . . and the third one is the chaplain. They aren't smiling."

Taylor spoke again on the aircraft's internal network. "Listen up, everybody. The doom and gloom squad is out to meet us. The only time those three ever get together is to play poker or deliver bad news. I did not get an alert about it, so we'll just have to wait and see. Don't spaz out."

The helo shifted into a smooth hover, then edged slowly forward to match the speed of the *Stratton.* Petty Officer Second Class Beth Ledford thought, *Dang. Wonder what they want?*

4

Kyle Swanson stood at the general's window in the Pentagon, looking out over the serene park at 1 Rotary Road while the Lizard gave the office a final electronics sweep before the meeting. The crepe myrtle trees were showing signs of maturity as their roots dug deeper into the soil, a visual marker of passing time, like a child's growth measured year by year on the sill of a door. People were strolling on the gravel and sitting on the cantilevered benches. More than a decade had elapsed since American Airlines Flight 77 was hijacked a short time after takeoff from Washington on September 11, 2001. Its captors had turned the fully fueled Boeing 757 jetliner around and flown it straight into the west wall of the Pentagon at 345 miles per hour. There were 184 benches out there now, one for each of the 59 passengers and crew and 125 military and civilian Pentagon personnel who died that day. The same day, the Twin Towers fell in New York, and the United States went to war against terrorism.

Reconstruction of the charred and gutted section of

the huge building went fast, for the Pentagon had been in the middle of a renovation program. The emphasis on secrecy and going to war against terrorists also brought along a gloves-off approach, and several special offices were included in the new Pentagon, offices that were almost impossible to find on any diagram or directory. These would be home bases for warriors who prowled the dark side. One of those areas was assigned to Major General Bradley Middleton of the U.S. Marine Corps, the commander of Task Force Trident, a special operations unit that reported only to the president of the United States.

The glass through which Swanson was watching the solemn tourists was two inches thick and blast resistant. Structural steel beams encased the few rooms, the doors had combination locks and retina scans, and a polymer-mesh-reinforced fabric covered the walls. The electronics suite was state-of-the-art. Swanson was pleased that he worked right at the aiming point for the terrorists. Time might pass, but coming to work here hardened his resolve every day. His job was to fight the enemy, wherever they might be, and no one in Trident believed the death of Osama bin Laden meant the war was over. Rival sects in the Middle East were trying to seize bin Laden's mantle of mysterious leadership. Terrorists don't sign peace treaties.

Neither did Task Force Trident. It had only five members, but Middleton could draw as many people as needed from other services and agencies to accomplish a mission. The two-star general was the commander, and the operations officer was Sybelle Summers, the youngest female lieutenant colonel in the Marine Corps and the only woman ever to make it through Marine Recon training. Her clandestine exploits had earned her the nickname "Queen of Darkness."

Navy Commander Benton Freedman was Trident's communications officer, an electronics genius with a round face, round glasses, and such an incredible intellect that he had been called "the Wizard" in the submarine service. The Marines in Trident altered that to "Lizard" to get under his skin, and the nickname stuck.

Senior Master Sergeant O. O. Dawkins was the administrative chief, the behind-the-scenes operative who kept the ship running, no matter what the obstacles. A huge man with a deep voice, he wore his uniform crisp and starched, his short hair high and tight, and was one the few men to hold the Marines' highest enlisted rank.

The final member of Trident was Marine Gunnery Sergeant Swanson, the never-miss trigger-puller, considered by many to be the best sniper in the deadly game.

"You finished yet, Lizard?" General Middleton asked loudly. He was seated at his desk, with a stack of folders before him.

"Just now, sir. We're clean." Freedman tapped a final key on his laptop, and the automatic sweep of the office for listening devices came to a halt. He hit one more key, and backup dead bolts slid home in the outer doors. Swanson drifted over and took the last seat in front of the desk.

The general looked at the four of them, his big brows narrowing toward the broad nose as he laid a palm on the folders. "All right, people, let's get down to business," he said. "We've got a Green Light package." He handed out four of the five folders, keeping one for himself and opening it to lift out an eight-by-ten glossy photograph of a man in white robes, smiling through a bearded face. "Recognize this guy?"

"It's that fuckin' Charlie Brown." The gruff voice of Senior Master Sergeant Dawkins rumbled.

"Score one for Double-Oh," the general confirmed. "Abdullah al-Mohammed, born as Charles Peter Brown in Lawton, Oklahoma, thirty-five years ago. He's our target. Most of the rest of the papers in your folders are a compilation of what is known about him, current locations, that sort of thing."

"How good is the information, sir?" Sybelle Summers asked as she fanned quickly through the pages. "They include newspaper clippings, for God's sake. That's not actionable information. Got to be some snip-and-paster over at CIA."

"It indeed is pretty sloppy work for a Green Light, but I will do a full workup." Commander Freedman antici-pated that within a few days, he would know everything possible about Charlie Brown and could put it into co-herent form. His mind was already at work, and he un-consciously started to hum the old rhythm and blues song "Charlie Brown." *Fe-fe, fi-fi, fo-fo, fum.*

"Stop that," the general snapped.

"Sorry, sir. The Coasters, 1959. King Curtis on the tenor sax."

"Why is everybody always pickin' on me?" Dawkins drawled the song's most memorable line.

"All of you. Shut up. You are not a doo-wop group!"

They smiled. The tense atmosphere that usually came with an assassination assignment was broken. Now it was just a job.

"Where is he?" asked Summers.

"Looks like Yemen," said the Lizard. "There's a country that is going the wrong way in a hurry on terrorism."

The general leaned back and folded his hands on his chest. "The little bastard crossed the line. It was bad enough that he went through al Qaeda training and then began those broadcasts in English to try to recruit more Americans, but now he's really gotten big in operations. Buddies up with fanatical American kids and prepares them to return to the U.S. as his moles, just waiting for his command to blow up some shopping mall and create mass casualties."

Summers asked, "So our leaders have decided there will be no due process or fair trials or that other stuff for him. We're going to execute an American citizen?"

"Yes, Colonel Summers. That is exactly what we're going to do. Several presidents have had the authority to do so. You have a problem with not giving Charlie Brown a jury trial back in Oklahoma?"

"Oh, none at all, sir. He forfeited that right, as far as I'm concerned. Just another terrorist bum now. Before, he was just an annoyance, but now that he wants to be a real player, he has to pay the price." There was a murmur of agreement in the room.

"Well, gang, he likely is not going to be coming to

us, so we will have to go after him. High-value target. Gunny Swanson, you have anything to add?"

Swanson was the sharp point of the Trident spear. "No, sir." His eyes drifted to the window, and the memory of September 11 came back. "No questions at all."

The general closed a briefing folder. "Right. Get to work. I want a plan within a week, and to have Swanson on the ground over there in two. Figure out what and who you need, and pull whatever resources are required. Keep it simple, because we're not planning an invasion of Yemen, just a cleanup job on a stupid asshole terrorist. Send any questions to me."

The Lizard shut down the security measures, the big dead bolts slid back to unlock the doors, and the five members of Task Force Trident drifted away. As soon as Sybelle Summers returned to her desk, her cell phone buzzed. She looked at the screen with a small frown, not recognizing the number of the caller. "Summers," she answered with no inflection in her voice.

"Lieutenant Colonel Summers? This is Petty Officer Second Class Beth Ledford, the Coast Guard sniper?" The voice was hesitant and carried an undercurrent of worry. "When you lectured our special ops class about a year ago, you gave me this number to call if I needed some extra help?"

Sybelle remembered the meeting. She had felt an immediate affinity for Ledford, the lone little blonde trying to fit in among a classroom filled with tough-guy warriors from all branches of the armed forces. Everybody in the room had seemed at least a foot taller than Beth Ledford, who stood five-six and weighed about

115 pounds soaking wet, but the records revealed the young woman had the best shooting scores in the entire class. Summers had taken her out for a coffee afterward, and a sister-to-sister talk about succeeding in careers dominated by men.

"Well, hello there, Petty Officer Ledford. Sure I remember you," Summers said, changing her tone from distant to neutral. "This is a surprise. What's going on? You quit the military and joined the circus yet? Little Sure Shot?"

The offhand compliment did not bring the laugh that Summers expected. "I have a problem, Major. It's not a glass ceiling thing, I would never call you for something like that, and I can't discuss it over the phone, so can we meet up for lunch today? Please? It's important." The briefest of pauses. "National security kind of important."

Sybelle sat up straight and snapped her fingers a couple of times, and Kyle Swanson looked over. "Lunch, then, Beth. Since we will be in public, drop the rank thing and come in casual civvies. I'm bringing someone else along." She gave the name of a pub in Crystal City. "See you there in forty-five minutes."

Swanson had wandered over to her desk by the time she finished the conversation and hung up. "Go put on some real-people clothes, Gunny. I'm taking you out to lunch with somebody I want you to meet, another sniper."

"Who?"

"You'll see." While Kyle went to change, Summers briefed General Middleton on the conversation and the planned meeting. His eyes twitched when she said the words "national security," and he nodded silent permission to meet the source.

THE UNITED NATIONS,
NEW YORK

The clatter of silverware against good china was drowned out by the polyglot of voices in the Delegates' Dining Room on the fourth floor of the United Nations Headquarters in Manhattan. Men and women in business attire that would be acceptable back in their home countries helped themselves to the cuisine served at the long buffet, which today featured a mildly spicy menu from the lower Pacific Islands. Sunlight bathed the huge room where the administrative staff workers from the 192 member states that made up the United Nations frequently had their lunches. Although the dining room was open to the public, the dress code of no jeans, shorts, or sneakers usually frightened away American tourists.

There was normally a steady flow of people during the lunch hour, and the volume of the conversation, although subdued, was enough to cover the private talk being carried on by two men seated at a table beside the glass wall that reached from the floor to the high ceiling and overlooked New York's East River.

"You don't enjoy the hot food?" James Doyle shoveled another fork of lamb curry and rice into his mouth, chewed thoughtfully, and felt a bead of sweat pop out on his forehead. He smiled. Bliss. The lanky and nondescript midlevel diplomat was enjoying the trip to New York, getting away from Washington for a day.

"Not today. I drank too much at the Danish ambassador's party last night," responded the heavyset Mohammed Javid Bhatti, a cultural attaché of the Pakistani Foreign Office. "In about a half hour, you'll be sorry for eating that stuff."

Jimmy Doyle knocked back a deep draft of cold beer. "No way, Javid. Next to a Nathan's hot dog, this is my favorite food."

"You should learn moderation in all things."

"Javid, you're the one with the hangover, and you're fatter than me. Moderate yourself, pal." He took another sip of beer, glanced around and saw the area around their table was clear, and lowered his voice. "So, do we have this medical team thing buttoned up on your side?"

Bhatti nodded. "We think so. My contacts assure me that, contrary to local rumors, the Taliban slaughtered them—an act of pure banditry. What probably started as simple robbery escalated when a Bible was found in their belongings."

"Escalated, you say? Escalated? They killed them all!"

Javid waved away the protest, as if brushing away a fly. "It's over, Jimmy. Over and done. Our army tracked down the raiders and destroyed their camp, killing four of them. We took care of it. Wars have unintended consequences."

Jimmy Doyle pushed away his plate and put his elbows on the table to lean in closer. "But this wasn't war,

Javid. It was a group of trained medical professionals trying to help your country's flood refugees in the middle of a disaster situation. Our country is pouring in aid, and we don't like our people shot for delivering it."

"Save the moral outrage, Jimmy. My countrymen don't enjoy having our people attacked by Predator drones, but it happens almost every day. You didn't even give us advance warning on the Osama bin Laden raid, and that also was on our territory. Remember that?" Javid Bhatti folded his napkin and put it beside his plate of half-eaten salad. "Anyway, we don't want this new incident to gain any more traction in the media. There is too much at stake."

Doyle nodded. "That is exactly what my boss in the Bureau of American-Islamic Affairs thinks, so we are in agreement. We have sent word up and down the diplomatic food chain that this was a most regrettable incident and that our Pakistani allies have taken prompt and appropriate action."

"No American military intervention?"

"No. The sooner this goes away, the better."

Bhatti agreed. "As a gesture of thanks to the international community for all of their sacrifices and help, we have given permission to construct a new refugee center not far from the area of the ambush, and will provide army protection."

"You mentioned local rumors. What about?"

"The usual. Evil spirits were responsible. Some villagers take comfort in quaint superstition instead of uncomfortable fact."

"Evil spirits with AK-47s and sharp knives. Let's

leave that out of any report. It would just clutter up the findings."

"Agreed."

"We bullshit pretty good for a couple of minor functionaries," said Jimmy Doyle.

"Indeed we do," agreed Javid Bhatti. "Indeed we do. Are you going to the party at the Colombian ambassador's residence tonight?"

CAPE CANAVERAL,
FLORIDA

Test pilot Buck Gardener and his astrophysicist wife, red-headed Erin Tyne-Gardener, had a wedding made in heaven and a marriage made in hell. The two attractive young people, who had met after they had been selected for astronaut training, had somehow found time for romance among the rockets. The wedding, which was widely publicized by the NASA public relations department, took place within a year, and the couple walked beneath crossed swords and into the cameras. Four years later, they hated each other but endured living together rather than ignite a divorce scandal that might jeopardize both careers. It had worked, to a point. Erin had been picked for the first Mars program shot, but Buck had been left behind in the wake of his superstar bitch wife. He wasn't going to Mars, or to the moon, or even back to the rattletrap space station. Buck, once a hot jet jock, wasn't going anywhere.

His current assignment was as a member of the

support crew for the Mars shot, which was the backup for the backup crew and did the scut work for the real astronauts who were assigned to fly. This was his third time on a support crew, and would be his last, for three strikes meant you had been passed over, for reasons that were never explained. Worse, Buck knew that his wife was screwing around with Colonel Dan Merrill, the mission commander. During their continuing domestic arguments, Erin had recently told Buck she would file for divorce as soon as she got back to earth. He thought about pulling out the .38 revolver and shooting her right there and then, then driving over to Colonel Merrill's house and blowing him away, too, but that would just send Buck to prison for the rest of his life. There had to be a better way.

Maybe he had gotten drunk one time too many, complained in public once too often, and gone too far outside the program for sympathy and understanding, because his sour attitude had drawn attention. NASA told him to get his shit together, or he would be canned. There was a mission to fly, he was told.

The United States space program had always been a target for intelligence agencies from other nations, because of the technical innovations that were constantly being developed. Even during the International Space Station years, spies hung around the Cape and Houston as thick as flies at a cookout. A nice-looking woman named Linda had found him and become very friendly, and they pillow-talked long into the nights.

In turn, she introduced Buck to another new friend, a man who said he had gone through something similar. He was from the Middle East, where women were not allowed to treat a man so shabbily; his own wife had an affair, and he had killed them both, and nothing was done about it, for it was proper. Just because Erin Tyne-Gardener was now a celebrity, she should not be allowed to make a fool of Buck. Suppose, the man said, just suppose that you could get rid of her and her lover without leaving a trace, get away with it, have the sympathy of a grateful nation—and earn five million dollars, to boot?

Buck thought it over for a couple of days and decided, why not? A rich future was much better than having to spend another minute with Erin.

5

ALEXANDRIA, VIRGINIA

They were late, and she was early. After making her telephone call, Beth Ledford had ducked into a Washington Metro station, swiped her card through the turnstile, descended the smooth escalator, and reached the platform just as a Blue Line train whooshed to a stop. The doors slid open; a crowd got out, a sea of determined faces, important people hurrying to government offices. Another crowd with faces set with equal firmness got on, and the train eased forward and accelerated. No one spoke; a long tube filled with VIP strangers. In minutes, Beth got off at the Crystal City stop in Arlington.

She linked to Google on her iPhone, typed in the restaurant name, and received explicit directions through the busy and stylish underground grid of shops that lay below the glassy towers of government offices, apartment buildings, and private corporate headquarters. The pub was about half filled with customers, since it was after the lunch hour rush, so there was no waiting. The rusty decorations gave it the look of a working-class saloon in Pittsburgh rather than a trendy spot in the power orbits of Washington. She took a stool at the far end of the bar, facing the frosted glass door, and ordered an iced tea. A *Washington Post* had been left on the next chair, so she paged through it. The flooding and relief work in Pakistan had already fallen off the front page, and there was no mention of the murdered international relief workers. She sighed with sorrow and bit her lip in silent anger.

They came in like a pair of cats, haughty and unapproachable, totally aware of their surroundings but not seeming to care. Beth had not even realized they were inside until the door closed behind them and they were walking her way. She immediately recognized Sybelle Summers: dark hair styled collar-length short, faded jeans over low-heeled soft black boots, and a dark blue summer top, with minimal makeup because she did not need much. Summers had made it big in the men's club of special operations but retained her femininity. Beth Ledford raised her hand and gave a little wave. *That's what I want to be when I grow up. If she can do it, so can I.*

She did not recognize the man only a step behind Summers. He moved with athletic smoothness, but was not really very big, about five foot ten and 175. The clothes looked expensive, a lightweight linen jacket over dark trousers with sharp creases. He was clean-shaven, with sun-bleached brown hair worn slightly long. A frown pulled at the corners of his mouth for no apparent reason. As they approached, she could see him better and was gripped by the greenish, no-nonsense eyes. She judged Summers's bodyguard to be a stone killer. *Sundown eyes*: the last thing an enemy would see as life blacked out. Those eyes would seldom laugh or hold joy for more than a few seconds.

"Beth! Hello, girl!" Sybelle increased her pace over the last few steps and put her hands on Beth Ledford's shoulders, pulling her close for an air kiss. She whispered, "Make this look normal." Then she pushed away with a big smile and slid onto the stool between Beth and the paneled wall.

"Sybelle! I'm so glad you could make it. I didn't want to leave Washington without saying hello." She had turned to face Summers, and when she turned back, the man was already seated to her left, elbows on the bar, looking at her. "Who is this?"

"A guy who specializes in the kind of thing you mentioned, so I brought him along to pay the taxi fare." Summers kept the smile playing on her face.

Beth studied the man for a moment. "You look familiar. Do I know you?"

He shook his head. "No." A silent, one-word conversation.

The bartender came down and rolled her eyes when they ordered only a tonic with a slice of lime, and a glass of water. "Can you afford all that?" she joked. "I mean, along with this lady's iced tea, the bill is going to be horrendous. Maybe four bucks."

Sybelle reacted first. One sure way to draw attention is to be too cheap. Bartenders remember slights. "Bring us a couple of menus, too. We just want to catch up on some things before we order." The bartender drifted away, happier.

"Really," Beth continued. "You look familiar."

The man cleared his throat. "Get to business. Why are we here?"

Beth Ledford looked over at Sybelle. "Is this Kyle Swanson?"

"Damn," said Swanson.

"Told you she was sharp," said Summers. "Pay up."

Swanson laid a hundred-dollar bill on the bar.

"Wow," Beth said. "Summers and Swanson both. The A-List. Pleased to meet you, Gunny. You're a legend in the community. I've seen your picture several times, including when you got the Medal of Honor." As she shook his hand, the drinks and menus arrived.

Summers spoke, the voice dropping to a lower tone that would not go beyond the three of them. "Beth, I heard about what happened to your brother. It was horrible. I'm very sorry."

"Thank you. My mom is all torn up about it. Joey was special to all of us, and the closed-coffin funeral was difficult. I've seen what bullets can do to a human body, and my imagination ran wild." Softer, she said, "He was my brother!"

Kyle Swanson leaned closer. "I'm sorry he got killed, too, Ledford. But just to be clear, he should not have been running around a war zone with just a box of Band-Aids."

Beth Ledford felt as if she had just been slapped. In the three weeks since Joey had been killed, nobody had said such a thing to her, although it had been implied. Anger surged through her, and she turned to Swanson, their faces no more than eighteen inches apart. "You can go to hell, Swanson. I don't care who you are."

Sybelle placed a hand on Beth's forearm. "Ignore him, Beth. Kyle is as subtle as an Abrams tank. Apologize, Kyle."

"Right." He took a sip of water and scanned the mirror that spread across the wall behind the bar.

Beth crossed her arms and leaned back, doing a slow exhale to keep her temper. *Asshole.* "Joey discovered something important, and that's why he was killed. I can prove it." Her eyes drifted away from them. "I may have made a mistake here. I thought you might help, but nobody in Washington listens to me. I'll just leave."

"Who's the 'nobody' in your 'nobody will listen' scenario?" Kyle had changed neither his voice nor the set of his face.

Ledford answered, "I've been in D.C. for the past week, trying to get somebody to take me seriously. First, my own people, the Coast Guard, turned me down. Then the State Department, and the FBI. Even my own congressman. Nobody will touch it." She brought her cell phone out of her purse. "I've got the pictures right here."

Swanson's frown lifted slightly. He did not want her to show any cell phone photos in a public place. "Put that away and settle down," he ordered. "If you're claiming a matter of national security, this is not the place to discuss it."

Summers leaned in. "When does your emergency leave end?"

"I have to be back in Jacksonville in six days."

"Not anymore. As of right now, you are now on temporary duty as my special assistant. You and I are going directly back to our offices in the Pentagon and do the paperwork, get you a higher security classification, and have you sign an unbreakable national security secrecy oath. Kyle will join us a little later." She flicked a glance at Swanson, who nodded.

"I got it."

"What?" Beth asked as she slid off the chair. "Got what?"

"Keep smiling. You're being followed."

Swanson remained at the bar, and when the bartender wandered over, he apologized for skipping out on the lunch order but handed over a big tip. He kept his eyes over her shoulder on the long mirror, where rows of liquor bottles sat on shelves. As he spoke, he watched the reflection of a woman at a table near the door. Her auburn hair had been swept back in a tight bun, but she was shaking it free so that it reached her shoulders. From her purse, she took out a pair of dark-rimmed Sarah Palin glasses and put them on. A white plastic shopping bag with the logo of a shoe store also had been folded inside the purse, and she shook it open. The wide-knit lightweight pink sweater around her shoulders was whipped off and stuffed into the shopping bag, along with the purse. In less than thirty seconds, her hair, eyes, and expression had all been changed, resulting in a brand-new look that someone as unaware as Beth Ledford would never have picked up.

Sybelle and Swanson had noticed her because it was their business to look for anything strange and out of place. Across from the restaurant's front door, they had seen a young guy in old jeans, worn-out Nikes, and a green baseball cap loitering outside, reading a newspaper. A guy like that should have been busy playing a video game on his cell phone, not reading about current events, and the two Marines immediately recognized that he was doing surveillance.

Then the woman came in alone, out of breath, took the empty table beside the door, and buried her nose in a glossy big magazine about weddings and brides, studiously avoiding looking at Ledford at the bar.

Swanson admired her swift disguise change. Whoever she was, she was a pro. The guy with the green hat was also a watcher, waiting just outside to tail Ledford upon leaving. This woman was now able to switch back into the rotation. Kyle estimated there would be at least four of them to keep the subject in a visual box at all times. Make that six, because someone would have been stationed to cover the rear door of the restaurant, and a spare would be roaming in the area. Plus there would be cars waiting upstairs in case the target had wheels. Then there also would be a couple of people running the show. That added up to a lot of assets to deploy to watch Beth Ledford, who believed nobody was paying any attention to her.

He sipped his water and chatted aimlessly with the bartender for a minute so the woman left the restaurant first. By the time he left a minute later, she was already lost in the crowd, and Mr. Green Cap was also gone. *This is no mom-and-pop operation,* he thought. *It's being run by an alphabet agency like the CIA or FBI, or maybe Homeland Security.*

Swanson headed back to the Pentagon. Ledford had not mentioned pestering the CIA or the Department of Homeland Security, but she had talked to the FBI. It did not matter how many people the Feebs had on her, because Sybelle was taking her to the Pentagon, into the secret offices where the watchers could not follow. Kyle decided that it would be good for Ledford to drop totally off the grid for a while.

THE BRIDGE
PAKISTAN

The two boys, not yet in their teens, were skinny from the food shortages but had sinewy muscles from hard work just like almost everyone they knew. Ahmad and Ali were the best of friends, and late at night they liked to leave the familiar streets of their village and get out from beneath the eyes of the adults who were always watching them. They were always back home before morning, sleepy but able to work.

As all boys of that age do, they thrived on tales of great adventure. In the mountains of Pakistan lived clans of fighters who had battled invaders like the Russians and the Americans and other soldiers from other countries over hundreds of years. There were Taliban fighters, and Pakistani army troops, and fierce troops loyal to warlords, and all had exciting tales that fascinated impressionable boys. Ali and Ahmad could not wait to grow up and join the ranks of some fighting corps. They did not understand, or care, about politics or the religious aspects woven into it. They just wanted adventure.

So, not for the first time, they had slipped into the forbidden territory to explore at night, each daring the other to go a step deeper into the shadows. At the destroyed bridge, they decided to rest a while before heading home and made themselves comfortable in amid the angles of the steel girders on the fallen span. They ate some nuts and a few dates and kicked with bare, callused feet at the water flowing beneath them.

From where they sat, the boys could easily see the bright bubble of light at the new bridge a mile upriver, where trucks and construction equipment were always on the move, building the biggest thing the boys had ever seen. The new bridge, seeming to be a mountain itself, was already allowing some traffic to cross, but the construction never slackened. The boys heard the clanking of metal machines and the faint shouts of the crews.

"They are doing more work tonight on the left column," Ali noted, chewing. "I hope they will use explosives."

From the woods along the riverbank came the growl of a dog, followed by an angry bark, a brief burst of snarls and snaps, a cry of agony, then sudden silence. The dog had caught whatever it had been chasing.

"We could go and find it." It was another dare from Ahmad to box his friend into a corner. Both knew they had to leave in the next few minutes to be back home on time. Even bravery has its limits, and they understood that in the early morning hours, this area was said to belong to the Djinn. Too many strange things had happened in this low valley beyond the bridge for the boys not to at least pay attention to the stories that an evil spirit roamed the area. That made their daring adventures even more frightening and fun. As they talked and splashed, they never noticed that danger was approaching.

Ahmad was knocked senseless when a club smashed into his head, and then he was toppling off the bridge and into the water below, his right arm cracking on a big rock before he was swept downstream. He heard a distant cry from Ali, then just the rush of the water. His right arm would not work, but he flailed and kicked as he gasped for air. He managed to get out of the main flow of the river, and a whirling eddy pushed him to calmer water, where he dragged himself ashore. He struggled to turn over, coughed up some water, and flopped onto his back to catch his breath.

Ahmad struggled to his feet, cradling his hurting arm, knowing it was broken. He had been taken down the river, but not too far. As his thoughts cleared, he called, "Ali?" Steered by the lights on the new bridge, he saw the tilted beams of the collapsed old one and broke into a run.

He could not find Ali at first and thought that maybe he also had been thrown into the river. He stepped onto the span and edged forward, feeling the rusty steel beneath his feet and reaching for handholds. Something was at the far end. "Ali?"

Ahmad took one final step, then stopped in shock and horror. The body of his best friend hung from a steel beam, hoisted like a goat for butchering. A rope was looped over the brace and tied around Ali's ankles, with the arms hanging straight down, as if pointing toward the pool of blood on the deck below the body. There was no head.

Ahmad gripped a big girder with all his might as his aching head reeled, and he heard a man shouting from the darkness on the far side of the river.

"Go home! Tell everyone what you have seen tonight. Tell them what the Djinn does to those who intrude in his valley."

Ahmad ran.

6

THE PENTAGON

What are we looking at?" Major General Brad Middleton had unfolded two blurry photographs and spread them flat on his desk with his palms.

Beth Ledford fought her anxiety at being in the general's presence, and at the whole operation in which she had become so unexpectedly involved. "Those are blown-up versions of the last two pictures that my brother sent to me from his cell phone. They lost quality when I downloaded and made those prints. Sorry. I don't have the technology to get better pictures."

Middleton arched his heavy left eyebrow. "I know they are photographs, Petty Officer. But of what?"

"Sir, the one on your left is of an old steel bridge that has fallen into a river in Pakistan, maybe washed away by the floods, or even earlier. Joey attached it to a text message that asked, 'Remember this?' "

"Why would he think that? Were you ever in northwest Pakistan?" The general reached into his desk drawer and scuffled around until he found a large magnifying glass. He bent closer to the photo, studying it.

"No, sir. My brother was referring to an old abandoned bridge near our family's farm in Iowa. It once was part of a spur rail line, but that closed in the fifties, and eventually, the bridge fell down. We played on it when we were kids. The skeletons of the two bridges are remarkably alike."

Middleton grunted. He saw nothing of interest. He pushed it aside and ran the magnifying glass above the second picture. A huge new bridge was under construction, a colossus that looked more like a dam. "And this one?"

Ledford shifted, and her hands drew into fists on the arms of the chair. "I think that's why he was killed."

Middleton lifted his eyes to meet her gaze. "Tell me."

"Here's what the text message on this said." She helped herself to a pen and a yellow legal pad from the gerneral's desk and wrote N TRBBL RUNNING CC. He passed it around without comment. "That was the last contact anyone had with the team. Since I never take my phone or personal effects off base during a mission, I didn't receive these until we finished a multiday patrol in Somalia. By then, it was too late."

The general grunted and slid the pictures aside. The photos had already been examined by Summers and the Lizard, and they would not have passed them up the chain of command to him unless they thought the information was worthwhile. "I still don't see anything."

"You probably won't, sir, not in the picture at least."

Ledford was more certain of her ground now. At least the members of Task Force Trident, including its commanding general, were listening to her. "It's in the message itself, sir, not only the photographs. The 'CC' initials. Our father was an Army infantryman in Vietnam, and since he was small, he sometimes was assigned as a tunnel rat. He used to tell us stories about being underground with a flashlight and crawling through these amazing networks of tunnels, like an anthill. One place he worked was around the town of Cu Chi, not far from Saigon. Joey and I were too young to take it all in, but when we would find some exciting place to explore, we would call it Cu Chi. Then we shortened the name to just CC."

"Your conclusion, then, is what, Petty Officer Ledford?" Middleton pushed back in his chair and was watching her for signs that she might be lying, or making it up as she went along.

"Sir, I think—I know—that my brother's medical team stumbled into somewhere they were not supposed to be and discovered something that reminded him of Cu Chi. Somehow he figured out they were tunnels, and probably for military use. The Taliban chased them down and killed them to keep it secret."

"You informed your superiors and people in here in Washington of everything you just explained to us?" The other four members of Trident had sat by without comment as the general addressed Ledford.

"Yes, sir. Nobody listened." She hesitated. "Nobody cared."

Middleton glanced at Swanson. "Now she is being followed by the FBI?"

"Best as I can tell, although I didn't ask to see their badges. It's a total surveillance package."

"But the FBI did not confiscate your cell phone when you spoke to them?"

"No, General. The two agents showed no interest in me, or my story. They listened politely and told me how sorry they were that my brother had been murdered by jihadist fanatics." The memory of the brush-off made Ledford's lips tighten. "I don't understand it."

The general examined her quietly for a few moments, and the room fell silent. "Well, Petty Officer, I frankly don't understand it either, and I don't like it." He unfolded from his chair and walked to the window, looked out, then turned back, having made his decision. "Lieutenant Colonel Summers, I want you to set up Petty Officer Ledford with a lawyer and take a sworn statement, and get a polygraph so we can start a file on this. Names, dates, and places of the people she talked with. Lizard, take her cell phone and go do some of your electronic magic. See if it has been hacked, get the call history, and enlarge those two photographs, as clear as you can get them. Gunnery Sergeant Swanson, you find out what's going on with our friends at the FBI. Everybody be back here at six o'clock for a briefing."

Master Gunny Dawkins cleared his throat loudly to get the general's attention. "Sir, we already have a Green Light project under way."

"I am aware of that," Middleton said. "We just have

to juggle two balls with one hand for a little while. Dismissed. Get out of here."

Special Agent David Hunt of the Federal Bureau of Investigation met Kyle Swanson in a Starbucks near the National Archives, where they each bought a coffee and walked the two blocks to the Mall. The tourists were not as thick in August, with schools around the nation getting ready to start and vacation time drawing to a close. Hunt had been with the Bureau for almost twenty-five years, and somewhere along the way, the burly special agent had become a bureaucrat. He didn't even remember when it happened. He thought more and more about life after the Bureau, retirement, slowing down and rebuilding the family time that had suffered for his job for so long. Maybe even learn how to fish. No, not that. Fishing was worse than playing golf.

"Here," he said and handed a plain manila file folder to Swanson. "Didn't need any private face time for this, Kyle. I could have sent it by bike messenger. Nothing to it. We offered to help the Pakistani ISI investigate the ambush, give them access to Bureau forensic resources, and they almost laughed out loud. These raggedy-ass pictures of the scene are already on the Internet, and it's all we've got."

Swanson led them to a park bench beneath the shade of a big tree that broke the heat. "Pretty thin stuff,

Dave," he said, studying the half-dozen photographs. Nude bodies on the ground, swelling due to the heat. An empty truck. Just a normal slaughter of innocents. He had seen similar atrocities in different places all around the world.

"Well, after we got slapped around by our pals at the ISI, the State Department also decided to shut us out. I got a memo that the Pakistani government had taken appropriate action, found and disposed of the murderers, and that it was officially all over but for the burying. It was all very terse, very convenient. Since WikiLeaks, they're scared shitless over there at State about writing anything down."

Swanson drank his coffee. "I thought we were all supposed to be working together these days. The War on Terror ring a bell?"

"Yeah. Well, it ain't happening. Why are you guys interested in this little scrape, anyway?"

Swanson handed the folder back to Hunt. "Some Coast Guard chick that knows Sybelle Summers came to town to shake some bushes because her doctor brother was among the victims. She's got a lame story that he saw something that is possibly militarily important over there in Mudville, and that's what got him shot. When she took her story up the chain, including to your FBI shop, she was ignored."

Hunt shook his head. "I didn't hear anything about any inquiry from a relative, but it's a pretty routine situation. Some family members always see conspiracy in the violent death of a loved one. Did she have any proof?"

Kyle said, "A couple of messed-up cell phone photos that her brother had sent, along with a cryptic text message that she claims refers to the Viet Cong tunnels in Vietnam, back in the day."

Hunt grunted. "Humph. And you think my file is thin? You've got nothing there."

"I agree, but General Middleton has one of his feelings that something isn't right and wants it checked out. We'll keep it all in-house for the time being until we see if there's anything worth following. I ain't betting on it. The kid may just be a flake."

Hunt flipped his empty cup into a trash can, then adjusted his glasses and leaned forward, planting his hands on his knees. "She may not be such a flake, Kyle. In fact, she may be onto something. My opinion is, this thing deserves some investigation but is being stonewalled by somebody over in Foggy Bottom."

Swanson looked hard at his old friend. Hunt was getting on in years, but he was still part bloodhound and part street cop. "Why? You having some old jealousy vibes because State won't let you guys into a party?"

"Look at the pictures carefully, Kyle," said Hunt. "Take them back and let your guy the Lizard work on them, make them clearer. Something important is missing."

"What's missing?" Swanson opened the folder again and studied the pictures more closely.

"The story is that they were shot up and robbed by some Taliban loonies, right? These photos supposedly represent the positions in which the bodies lay when Paki army troops found them."

"Yes." Kyle looked closer. *What don't I see?*

"If their trucks had been stopped and they were forced out and murdered on that spot, then where's the blood? There is blood around the bullet holes in their clothing but not around the bodies, Kyle. The guy with his head blown apart should be resting in a big puddle of brains. Get it now?"

Swanson did. Hunt was right. He knew from personal experience that nobody ever gets badly shot and keeps all of the blood inside. It leaks, gushes, oozes, sprays, drips, and floods, and it keeps coming out until the heart stops beating. In the photos, the ground around each of the bodies was trampled but unstained. "Maybe the rain washed it away?"

"It had stopped raining in that particular area two days before, and the sun dried it out. The floods had never reached that high ground. The dirt, the side of the truck, the foliage, those logs near the bodies—all devoid of blood."

Swanson closed the folder. "You're saying they were killed somewhere else, then moved to this place and dumped."

"Exactly. Those bodies bled out, then were transported to this spot to be found, away from the actual murder scene. One other thing. Look at the ankles we can see. They're all without shoes, which is not abnormal in a place filled with thieves. But those dark stripes look to me like rope burns, which had to be made while they were still alive. Our people down at Quantico say the bruising is consistent with a victim being hung upside down."

"I thought you didn't investigate."

"Just called for a few observations by friends." Dave Hunt grinned. "Nothing official. Your people will find the same thing. I think these poor people were captured, hung up like sides of beef, and shot to hell, and the blood emptied out by the barrel. Then they were brought to this place and dropped. Why? I have no idea."

"Weird," said Kyle.

"Indeed," said Dave Hunt. "We may be stymied on our end, but you and Trident can go around the normal rules. Kick over some rocks on this one, Gunny Swanson. See what crawls out."

The six o'clock meeting in General Middleton's office at the Pentagon was a tense session that seemed to be taking them down a road they did not want to travel. Sybelle Summers reported that Beth Ledford had passed the polygraph examination and had been interviewed by a Marine Special Ops lawyer, under oath. Middleton had copies of the polygraph results and the legal statement.

Commander Freedman had produced a slick set of eight-by-ten reproductions from the grainy photographs that Ledford had brought, but they showed nothing more than the fallen railroad bridge, with one end sticking in the river, and another shot of a valley. He had examined her cell phone and said that it was clear. No one had hacked it.

Then Swanson gave a debrief on his talk with Special Agent Hunt of the FBI and added his photos to the growing stack of paperwork.

Middleton spread all of the photos side by side on his desk, the pictures the Lizard had enlarged next to the gruesome forensic-style pictures from the Pakistanis. "It's not the same location. Both of Dr. Ledford's pictures are from a low area, and the bodies are on dry ground, with completely different foliage," he said. "Better if you not look at these, Petty Officer Ledford."

"It's all right, sir. I just want to know everything about what has happened. My whole theory is based on Joey having seen something that I would recognize. I have to look at everything if we want to figure it out." She carefully took the pictures, forcing herself to stay calm. Joey would still be dead, no matter whether or not she saw the ugly pictures of his ravaged body.

Master Gunny O. O. Dawkins pulled at his cheek as he thought. "The fuckin' State Department is covering this up?"

"We don't know that for sure, Double-Oh," replied Swanson, "but according to my Feeb, that is where the information funnel narrows. That way, the incident is moved out of reach of any investigating arm and disappears into the diplomatic arena. Cables will be exchanged saying it was a tragic situation. No fault to be assigned beyond the Taliban gunmen who are also now dead and cannot challenge any official version."

Middleton gathered the photos and returned them to the stack and straightened the corners. He closed his eyes for a moment before speaking. "All right. Here's what we're going to do. I want a plan to put some boots on the ground over there. Lizard, you get some overhead images of the area. Swanson will take Petty Officer Ledford in to see whatever it was her brother found. Go in, then get the hell out quick. Stay out of trouble, if you can. Should be a piece of cake, since the Paki army swears they have control of the area."

"Sir!" Kyle almost came out of his chair in surprise. "All due respect, general, but Petty Officer Ledford isn't qualified to do a special ops mission."

"I don't recall asking for your opinion, Gunnery Sergeant. You will take her in there, find what needs to be found, and then bring her out again. Are we clear?"

Swanson gave up. No use arguing with Middleton, who wore two stars on each shoulder. He knew the general was already thinking several moves ahead. "Aye-aye, sir. We're clear."

Beth Ledford was out of her chair in an instant, standing at rigid attention. "Sir. May I speak freely?"

Middleton's brow furrowed. "Go ahead."

"Sir, I do not feel that Gunnery Sergeant Swanson is the right man for this job. I don't trust him. He is condescending, and if he does not believe I am up to the mission, he will be distracted and could get us both killed."

Swanson jumped up to attention, too. "Sir!"

Middleton slammed his desk so hard that it sounded like a gunshot. "Sit down! Both of you! Jesus H. Christ on a shingle. What's the matter with you two? This is not some junior high school hayride, nor is it a democracy. I make the decisions around here. I gave an order and you will obey it. You don't have to like it; you just have to do it. *Now . . . are we clear?*"

"Yes, sir," said Swanson.

"Yes, sir," said Ledford.

"Good. A warning for both of you. You will get your shit together and work as a team. Put your differences on the shelf, because I don't care whether you like each other. But you screw up this mission over something that minor and I'll put you both in front of a court-martial. If my estimation is correct, Dr. Ledford stumbled on something that may be of great importance for our country's security. Master Gunny Dawkins, we will give this priority over the Green Light on Charlie Brown. He gets to live a few more days."

7

The morning sun came up like a bright ball over the Atlantic horizon. First there was a hint of the coming dawn, then the first bars of sunshine hit the black water, and in only a few minutes, it was daylight at the Unknown Distance Range on the Marine Corps base in Quantico, Virginia. Chilly. Kyle Swanson was sitting on a fender of a Humvee, watching the dawn and drinking coffee from a thermos. He was still angry at Beth Ledford for saying she did not trust him. He was right in the argument, because the woman was not spec op trained. Freakin' Coastie. There was an old ditty about their motto: *Semper Paratus is a laugh, they join to dodge the draft*. He snorted and dumped the rest of his coffee onto the grass of the firing range.

Turning to the Humvee, he saw Ledford sitting in the passenger seat, still huddled in a jacket, arms crossed, obviously as miffed with him as he was with her. "Ledford, I would be very much obliged if you would begin, if you please." Exact, phony, politically correct politeness.

"I told you earlier, Gunnery Sergeant Swanson. I don't do exhibitions. You want to see trick shooting, go to a carnival, put down a dollar, and I'll win you a teddy bear."

Swanson stalked to the back of the Hummer and lifted an M-14 with a scope from the cushioned carrying case, then an ammunition clip. To hell with polite. His voice hardened. "Listen, Ledford, the general and I agree that we're not going anywhere until I can figure out what kind of skills you have. That information is pertinent to this mission."

She had her own cup of steaming coffee and was still drinking it slowly. A black watch cap was pulled low on her forehead, low enough to touch her eyebrows. "How can you lead us anywhere, when you don't know where we're going? You're just along for the ride, Swanson—my personal bouncer."

He thrust the rifle at her and dropped the ammo clip in her lap. "I don't know what world you're living in, woman. You bring nothing to the mission but possible geographical recognition. You're just a GPS tracking system; no more, no less."

"I'm a sniper," she said. "OK?"

"No, Ledford, that is not OK. You are a Coast Guard sniper, which I personally rate as being at the level of a designated marksman, the guy who is the best shot in any Marine squad. The Coast Guard may be great for rescuing dogs off rooftops and stopping sailboats carrying weed. It is not, in my opinion, a combat arm of the United States military."

"Screw you, jarhead. Marines are antiques and

should be dissolved into the Army and Navy. It would save a lot of money and be a big relief to everyone that has to put up with your constant bragging."

Kyle ignored her and walked away carrying a large heavy-paper target, the black silhouette of a man's torso and head. Except for Ledford and Swanson, the range was empty at this time of early morning, a wide swath of carefully prepared ground that was graded specifically for firing weapons and soaking up the bullets. He heard the choppy sound of a helicopter, normal around any military installation. The bird was flying high, dipping down and climbing again, orbiting. Probably a pilot logging some stick time for his flight pay.

At the five-hundred-meter marker, Swanson secured the target to a post. When he looked back, Beth Ledford was out of the Humvee, standing at the firing line, resting the butt of the M-14 on her hip, checking it, and adjusting the sling. "That weapon had better be unloaded, Ledford!" he shouted. "You saw me downrange. Didn't the Coast Guard even teach you range safety procedures?"

"Oh. Gee, mister. I am so sorry. Is that how the Marines do it? I didn't know that." She waved the clip of ammo in her free hand. "This bullet-holder thingie is, like, way cool. And there's even a cute little telescope on the top of this gun."

Kyle huffed a deep breath and returned to the Humvee to get the monocular spotting scope. As he reached into the vehicle, he heard the crisp mechanical snap of the ammo clip being slapped home and the sharp *rap-rap-rap* of the M-14 being fired fast, but on single shot.

Rap-rap. He turned and yelled, "Cease fire! Cease fire! Cease fire! What the fuck? Why didn't you wait for my command?" *Rap. Rap-rap-rap.*

She casually tucked the rifle under her right arm, picked up her coffee cup, and drank while staring at him with the malicious look of a naughty child. "Oops. Was I supposed to wait? You weren't standing in front of the target anymore, so I thought you wanted me to shoot. Sorry again. My bad."

Swanson felt the anger growing from the back of his neck. She was giving him a headache. Ledford was violating every rule of procedure. He exhaled, but it was a fight to keep himself under control in this battle of wills. With the spotting scope in his hand, he walked back to the line and focused it on the target, until it loomed large and clear. It was grinning at him—two holes for eyes, one for a nose, and three in a tight V for the mouth. For good measure, she had put three more holes right in the in-center mass-ten ring. *Damn. Shots like that from a standing position.*

"Keep watching, cowboy," Ledford said. He glanced over and saw that she had picked up the rifle again, this time locked into a standing position but without using the sling, which drooped beneath the weapon. With two more quick shots, she gave the target ears, then lowered the weapon, keeping it pointed downrange, smoothly removed the clip, and popped out the bullet in the chamber.

"You want to test me, then OK, but test me with something worthwhile. I could do this five-hundred-meter crap all day long and never miss. You understand that, Gunny? Never. Same thing at a thousand. I can shoot the lights out with pistols, rifles, shotguns, it doesn't matter. I've been able to do it since I was a kid, and I love to shoot. Won my first turkey shoot while I was still in pigtails. Somehow, I was born with this peculiar skill in my genes, and the Coast Guard, bless 'em, taught me the technical side. I understand that you needed to see my capabilities because our lives might someday depend on my being able to take a shot, and now you have. I promise you that if I must, I will, and I won't miss. Are you satisfied now, or do you want to see me pop an ace of clubs, or maybe you flip a quarter into the air?"

Kyle looked hard at her. The new sun was heating the area enough that she had removed the watch cap and shaken out her hair. Her bright blue eyes were large and questioning. She looked like a schoolgirl and shot like an assassin, and the way she had stood up to him and the general was proof that she had no fear. He nodded his head. "I've seen enough. Put the weapon back in its case, Ledford, while I police up the brass. We're done here, so let's go get some breakfast. We need to talk."

They drove away, leaving the shredded target hanging there, smiling to greet the Marines who next used the range. The distant helicopter circled in the morning sky.

The International House of Pancakes was seven miles away, a boxy building with a blue roof, and a cluster of vehicles in the crushed-rock parking area. A sign on the door read OPEN, and they went inside. A booth was available by a window overlooking the parking lot, and they slid into it, facing each other. The menu was as thick as a book and as confusing as a nuclear launch code, with every possible combination of pancakes and eggs and potatoes. Three small bottles of syrup stood beside the fake sugar packets, and the laminate table-top was still damp from being wiped down after the previous customers.

Swanson and Ledford were the only military uniforms in the place, but a large man with a bristly high-and-tight haircut was gobbling eggs and waffles at a single table, his back to the room, reading a morning newspaper. He had not looked up. Ledford ordered eggs over easy and sausage, with blueberry pancakes. Kyle blanched at the amount of fat implied in that order and went instead for his usual fruit and cereal. Mugs of coffee soon appeared. Kyle adjusted his jacket and slid his M-1911 .45 caliber Colt pistol free, putting it beside his leg.

"You made me start rethinking things, out there on the line, Ledford," he said. "I know what you mean about being able to shoot and not knowing why you're so good at it. I barely got through high school in South Boston because I was no good at math and science courses. Never had fired a gun in my life. Then in the Marines, when they issued me a rifle and took me out to the range, they discovered that I was a better than average shot. All those hillbillies who grew up hunting couldn't touch me. In the classroom, all of the equations and formulas and explanations and tables suddenly made sense. I didn't question why; I just ran with it. Sound familiar?"

Beth Ledford looked at him steadily, and a tentative, relaxing smile came to her. "At first, I thought I was weird; a little girl who liked guns instead of Barbie dolls. People would come out to the farm just to watch me plink targets. Then a local TV show did a bit about me, and the news media tried to make me a celebrity. Mom and Dad, thankfully, stopped all that in its tracks when they saw what was happening. No more exhibitions, no special appearances, and plain ol' Beth Ledford who stayed in school, ran track, and was afraid of the popular cheerleaders. My gun work was kept strictly private. Dad worked with me, and eventually hired a coach to see if I was material for the Olympics or a military shooting team. I kept improving, but then Dad died and I lost interest in the fancy stuff. Had no desire to go to college, so I joined the Coast Guard."

"Why not the Army or the Marines?"

"Coast Guard was the only available path for a woman to become a sniper. You guys run a closed shop. I am dying to find out how Colonel Summers did it."

"You ever have that strange moment, when you're shooting, that you actually can see the bullet?"

"Uh-huh. I can watch the disturbed air behind it."

"What about your brother, the doctor?" Kyle saw a gray pickup track pull into the lot, and a medium-sized man in blue coveralls got out and made his way inside. Dark hair, dark complexion, physically fit. Swanson adjusted his pistol beneath the table as the new customer was taken to a booth.

"Joey was a genius. He always wanted to be a doctor. When we were kids and I'd get a cold, he would write me a prescription for two aspirin from the medicine cabinet. Before we knew it he had a first-class medical education. He told me that he went on the humanitarian missions to balance the guilt he felt for being so blessed. His real love was research." She leaned toward him. "I think he was going to do great things . . . What's happening, Gunny?"

The big man who had been sitting alone was on his feet, and Kyle slid out of the booth, the big Colt against his leg. They arrived at the new customer's table at the same time, and Chief Master Sergeant O. O. Dawkins jammed in beside the surprised stranger while Kyle eased into position across the table, letting the man get a glimpse of the weapon before it disappeared.

"What the fuck?" the man stammered.

"Keep both hands on the table," Double-Oh ordered. "Try to pull that gun in your overalls and I will break your arm."

"Who the hell are you?" the man demanded.

Kyle tapped the pistol against the bottom of the table. "I'll ask the questions this morning. We're a detail assigned to protect Petty Officer Ledford over there. You and your people are following her. Why?"

"I don't know what you're talking about," the man said, settling in and growing calm.

"Look, buddy, your surveillance has been busted for two days now. I saw your helicopter this morning; now you show up. You have a partner outside who is probably listening to this conversation, so invite him in. I'm putting my weapon away now." Swanson stuck the pistol back under his windbreaker. Within two minutes, another man appeared at the door and ambled over. Jeans, boots, stained blue sweatshirt, and graying hair. He looked at Ledford, then dropped into the booth beside Swanson.

"My name is Fred Watson, and that's Hector Holmes." Watson flipped open a leather folder with a gold badge and a laminated identification card and put it on the table. "Counterterrorism Division of the Diplomatic Security Service, State Department. And you are?"

"Samuel L. Jackson and Brad Pitt. Task Force Trident. Pentagon." Double-Oh produced some identification.

Kyle said to the man across from him, "Holmes and Watson. Not very original."

"Better than movie stars." Watson flashed a crooked grin. "I don't make these things up. I just carry the plastic."

"Yeah, I know the feeling. Well, here's what is going on, Special Agent Watson. Petty Officer Ledford is currently on extended temporary duty with Task Force Trident, we're not going to let her go, and we're not going to let anything happen to her."

"It's a terrorism thing with us," said Watson. "Nothing was going to happen to her."

Dawkins replied, "Your appearance here just underlines what we already know: that the State Department is somehow involved in those medical team murders in Pakistan."

Watson scratched his cheek. "I wouldn't know about any of that. Our instructions were just to follow Ledford and see who she contacts. She met you, Mr. Jackson, and Mr. Pitt. And I never heard of Task Force

Trident, so since the quiet surveillance has been blown, you boys are just going to have to get out of the way now and let us have Ledford for some questioning."

"Not gonna happen, Mr. Watson. Call your boss and tell him or her that it's over." Kyle's words were emotionless. An order.

"Well, I hate to tell you, Brad Pitt, but your Task Force Trident, whatever it is, does not outrank the State Department. I can have a dozen agents in here in five minutes." He pointed toward the table where Ledford sat.

Dawkins took a cell phone from his pocket. "No, we don't, but the White House does, and they will back us. We already have four more guns in this place right now, and none of us wants a firefight. But when Ledford leaves, she's going with us. Want me to make the call?"

Watson looked over to where Ledford was staring at them. Sybelle Summers, wearing the black pants and white blouse of an IHOP waitress, was leaning back against the table, facing them, with her right hand holding a pistol that was barely visible beneath a white dishcloth.

Watson waved his hands slowly. "OK. OK. Make that call, Mr. Samuel L. Jackson, and tell whoever it is to set up a meeting between all the right people. Then both sides here know what's what. This is obviously some kind of fuckup, and I don't want to get shot over a stack of pancakes." He winked good-naturedly at Summers. "Say, miss, could you put away the artillery and get us some coffee over here?"

Summers smiled sweetly and said, "Fuck you."

8

He dreamed of great ropes of shining steel hanging in the sky, double-deck trusses, towering monopoles, and H-shaped pylons standing tall, probing into the clouds above wide bodies of water, and supporting wide carriageways and pedestrian footwalks, all illuminated by lights hidden in the ribs. Asleep, his brain amused itself by solving the mathematical and technical riddles of the complex Tsing Ma Bridge in Hong Kong, the majestic sweeping curve of the Øresundsbroen, between Denmark and Sweden, and the impossibly beautiful Rion-Antirion over the Gulf of Corinth in Greece. All were works of art in his opinion, classical outdoor statuary that would serve mankind for ages. In the dreams, each bridge had an engraved stone that hailed the name of the greatest Islamic builder of the twenty-first century—Mohammad al-Attas: Chief Engineer and Architect. Then he awoke in his wide, soft bed and lay still. Just dreams. Someday, Allah willing, such miracles could come to pass for him.

For now, instead of building a sky-piercing colossus,

he seemed to be working in the opposite direction, creating a smooth, single-arched bridge of rock across a flood-chiseled chasm in northeastern Pakistan. His task was to make it utilitarian and strong, unremarkable in every way, so that the casual eye would pass right over it instead of lingering and applauding the ingenuity involved. Al-Attas rose and went into his private bathroom to wash his face. This was not to be one of the great bridges of the world, but it might become one of the most important: the first of many along a highway of enlightenment being created for the New Muslim Order, and a protected secret refuge for its leader.

He stared into the mirror above the porcelain sink, and his intense black eyes peered back. He ran his fingers through his long hair and was disgusted when loose strands clung to them. Even as he shaved, more mathematic calculations unscrolled in his mind, a precise march of equations.

And his skin! He was becoming pale from the lack of sunlight and the constant work underground. The physician had given him a large bottle of vitamin D to help maintain his health, and al-Attas made a mental note to install more ultraviolet lights. If it was happening to him, it would happen to anyone spending much time in this self-contained underground fortress. That could not be allowed. *Make it a point,* he told his reflection, *to get topside more. Every day.*

He pulled a fresh white towel from a cabinet and stepped into the shower, letting the hot water, soap, and shampoo fully awaken him. A hot breakfast would be waiting in the canteen; then he would put on his hard hat and take the elevator that was used to move freight up to the surface. An hour at least in the morning sun, and even a brisk walk to the little village that had sprung up at the west end of the bridge. Then back down in time for the noon teleconference and working on the computers. He checked his fingernails carefully and found them clean. His teeth got a hard brushing. He pulled his hair back into a ponytail, which he bound with a rubber band. Mohammad al-Attas was not a mole or a termite, and this bridge job was only a step toward greater things. He would endure. Why was the bathroom such a mess?

As he left his little apartment one hundred feet belowground, his silent manservant was already busy cleaning the bedroom. The man had been especially chosen because his tongue had been cut out as a child to make him a better beggar, and he could not talk. Al-Attas ignored him and left the room, dressed for the day in the Western style of blue jeans and loose shirts, with a billed cap turned backward.

The servant stopped his work and pressed his forehead to the burgundy carpet on the chill stone floor, giving thanks to Allah for letting him survive to see another morning. He was terrified of his young master. The man was very smart, the smartest the servant had ever met, smarter even than the elders in his home village, but the man's mind was bent like a horseshoe. The servant entered the bathroom and found a stack of blood-soaked towels and clothing that had been flung into a corner. The shower would have to be scrubbed hard to remove the streaks of blood on the floor. Sandals crusted with thick mud needed to be cleaned. The weapons would be cleaned and sharpened, and put away in the cabinet. His young master was not what he seemed, and the servant could not, would not, ever tell a soul.

"The man is a lunatic," said Major Najib Umair of the Pakistani Directorate for Inter-Services Intelligence, the ISI. He had read the reports and seen the videos made by his agents at the bridge about the engineer running about in the night, killing people and cutting up bodies. They had even documented the cleanup and subsequent cover-up after the engineer slaughtered and brutally violated the entire team of doctors and nurses who had somehow stumbled into the most secret tunnels.

"A very useful lunatic," reminded Lieutenant General Yahya Gul, the director of the ISI, who also had examined the latest reports. "Your agents say that because of his activities, the area is believed to be haunted. People in the villages speak of the Djinn and are afraid. That is not a bad thing for us."

"A minor benefit, sir. He went crazy with bloodlust for a few hours. By killing that medical team, al-Attas put the entire operation at risk. He is not an evil spirit, just a very deranged man."

General Gul lightly tapped his fingers together, then pushed up the rimless eyeglasses that had slipped down his sharp nose. He had seen many things in his time with the ISI, but the Djinn was unique. An ISI psychologist had concluded that the man was mentally unstable, perhaps having collapsed beneath the weight of being a scientific savant. He was embedded with an unknown number of different personalities; there was the gentle, brilliant engineer of the daytime, and the bloodlusting Djinn at night. The agents that watched him had heard him howl and bark. The psychologist had predicted other personalities could be lurking just below the surface, waiting to break out. Truly psychotic.

"Do you have him under control?" the general asked.

"Control? No, sir. That would be impossible. We do have him under constant observation, when he changes and becomes the fanatic. He leaves through what he believes is his own secret door in a bridge abutment. Three agents with night-vision goggles triangulate him but stay back unless he drifts too far afield. Then they capture and sedate him and haul him back to his apartment at the bridge. When he awakens, he does not remember that anything unusual has happened, because it happened to the Djinn, not to his dominant personality, the chief engineer."

The general nodded approval. "Very well, Major. We will let him continue with his hobby for the time being. His value to this project far outweighs the lives of a few unlucky people. Al-Attas is building a fortification that stands in the open but is almost invisible. When he completes this first one, we will have all of his plans and inventions to build more, and can do so without his help. After what happened with Osama bin Laden, creating this safe haven for Commander Kahn is a very high priority with us. For now, we must keep al-Attas working to complete this bridge."

"I have taken one more step, sir. I am assigning one

of our best men to be his personal bodyguard, his keeper. The chief engineer has a huge, but fragile, ego and will willingly believe a cover story that a bodyguard is needed now that the infidels have issued a reward for his death because of his brilliance."

"Good. Keep him safe. Should his insanity increase beyond our ability to handle him, we will adjust to the situation. It would be good to have the bodyguard close by to do the job quietly, but I want to be the one to make the final decision."

"Yes, sir. I will make that clear to Hafiz."

"You are giving this to Hafiz? Excellent choice."

Mohammad al-Attas put on a pair of wraparound sunglasses when he emerged from the mouth of a shaft and stepped to the side of the busy roadway. The sunlight was brash and hard and made him squint. He flipped his blue Los Angeles Dodgers baseball cap around so the long bill would provide some shade. A mix of bossa nova music pumped a Latin beat into the earbuds of his iPod. People on the road looked at him strangely but said nothing.

Giant yellow Caterpillar bulldozers, Komatsu graders, and Firmengruppe Liebherr crawler cranes with long lattice booms roared and snarled as if in competition as they rearranged the earth. Heavy conveyor belts brought up dirt and stone that would be carted away by a convoy of waiting trucks, and a dome of dust covered the work area. Al-Attas made his way to the operations platform to confer with the shift foreman and gave him a few instructions after doing the numbers. Everything topside was going well. Every ton of dirt hauled away was one less ton of dirt below, steadily opening areas available for new tunnels, living quarters, work spaces, and the defensive positions. He told the foreman to check the steel bracing in tunnel four, which seemed to be out of plumb.

Now he had some time, and he put his hands in his pockets and strolled away to visit the collection of huts and vendors who had set up merchandise beneath sagging canvas at the western end of the bridge, which was much closer to completion than the east end. Al-Attas waved to some workers gathered in a group, then strolled the narrow aisles of makeshift shops. Where would he find some vitamin D? The best source was fish, and there were none. All of that floodwater, but no fish. He couldn't believe it. He eventually found a woman who had several boxes of medicines, and she said she could get some vitamin D tablets from the staff at the refugee camp. They bargained a little bit and struck a deal. He would return tomorrow to get the pills.

He bought a pear and munched it as he headed back to the work zone, with plenty of time before the teleconference. His mind was on the reports he needed for supplies and equipment, and what progress had been made in the past twenty-four hours, those thoughts wrapped around the beat of the strange South American music. A strong shoulder rammed into him and Mohammad al-Attas was sent sprawling onto the hard ground and the pear he had been eating bounced away.

A swarthy man with a long spade of tangled beard and wearing loose tribal garments stood over him, shouting insults about the way al-Attas was dressed, about how he was offending the Prophet. An AK-47 dangled from his shoulder. The engineer was startled and afraid. *Taliban.* The man raised his arm as if to strike the engineer, but suddenly another figure was there, kicking the Taliban fighter in the back of the knee and pulling his head backward, throwing him to the ground. The second man made a swift move and straddled the Taliban's chest, with the gleaming point of a knife resting just below the right eye. Al-Attas could not hear what was being said in a harsh whisper, but the struggle was over in an instant; then the bigger man rose, helped the Talib to his feet, and sent him on his way.

Then the man extended his hand to al-Attas and easily pulled him up from the dirt. "Are you all right, sir?"

"Yes." The chief engineer brushed at his shirt and jeans. "Thank you."

The big man laughed. "He did not know who you were, sir, and apologized for his action. That will not happen again."

The chief engineer adjusted his cap. His new friend was over six feet tall, rippled with muscles, and wore a trim military uniform of some sort. Al-Attas did not see a rank insignia, but he did not care much about military things. A holstered pistol rode on the man's hip, almost like a toy. "Who are you?"

"Sergeant Hafiz of the ISI at your service, Chief Engineer. Come, let us walk and find some privacy. I will explain."

"What is going on?" The engineer felt strangely safe in the presence of the large sergeant as they walked along the road.

"I have been sent here by Islamabad, sir, and bring the compliments of General Gul. Our intelligence service has picked up reports, information the general believes is valid, that the Americans and Jews want to assassinate you. We are worried about your safety, and I have been sent to protect you."

The engineer shook his head. "I cannot do my work with a bodyguard underfoot."

The big laugh came again, accompanied by a smile. "I have done this sort of thing before, sir. I know how to stay out of the way. I will be nearby when you come aboveground to prevent unexpected incidents such as the one that just happened, but down below, I will be able to organize effective security so that you will soon forget that I am even around."

They reached the main shaft heading down, and the conveyor belt on one side continued to rumble. The chief engineer took off the sunglasses and again flipped the baseball cap backward. "They want to kill me? Do they know about the Commander?"

"We don't think so. What they do know, sir, is that you are one of the brightest thinkers in the world today. It would definitely be in the interests of the infidels to snuff out such a great mind of our religion and culture."

They were deeper in the shaft, nearing a solid door that branched off into another brightly lit tunnel. The explanation was startlingly clear; the enemy was afraid of his ideas and abilities. "You can stop them?"

"Yes, sir. I can. Be at peace about that."

"Well, Sergeant Hafiz, I would like for you to join me tonight for dinner. I wish to know more about you."

"With pleasure." Hafiz stopped, and the chief engineer walked on, immediately lost in other thoughts. Soon he was gone. *This was the Djinn? Incredible.* Hafiz had been an operative for more than twenty years, spoke four languages, was expert with numerous firearms and demolitions, and had killed men with his bare hands. Surely there were missions that would be more of a match for his skills. However, General Gul and Major Umair had made it clear that guarding the preoccupied young man was only part of his overall assignment; he also had to assess the overall project, which not only would anchor a high-tech defensive line but would house and protect the most important treasure in modern Islam, Commander Kahn, a person of utmost and growing importance.

So Hafiz would be content to be a sergeant for a while and keep an eye on things. It would be interesting to see if the little engineer really did transform into a monster after dark, and he was eager to explore the fascinating maze below the earth. Hafiz went back up top to call Islamabad and report that he had made contact, and to pay the rest of the fee to the Talib soldier hired to stage the bumping incident.

9

The day had grown hotter, and there was little relief in the shade of the steamy, humid forest that surrounded Beth Ledford and Kyle Swanson in the map and endurance exercise. Both were in camouflaged battle utilities, with light packs, and carried no weapons other than Kyle's Ka-Bar knife. They paused on a thirty-degree hillside while Beth took another map reading and matched the heading with her compass. "We're at grid coordinates six-two-one-two, four-two-one-two, Gunny. The third point."

She sucked in a deep breath, exhausted. From the first step, this exercise of reaching a precise point by an exact time had been like climbing a wall. She reached for her canteen.

"No," Swanson said. "This is a forest, Beth. There's plenty of water around. We have to hydrate, but save the good stuff for emergencies. Just over to your right, see that rock ledge? There may be some water pooled there. It rained last night, remember? Watch everything. Listen to everything. Remember everything."

Beth moved to the outcropping and found a bubbling little stream of fresh water dripping over the sharp edge of the rock, pushing by a pool about four inches deep that was gathered from the downhill movement of the water in the hill. Gravity at work. She lowered her mouth, but Swanson stopped her again. "Examine the source first. Is it murky or stagnant? Does it smell rancid? Is there a dead animal in it?" She looked it over and then gave it a tentative taste. The water was cold and delicious, and Beth drank her fill.

Before setting out from the Humvee, Swanson had given her a plastic laminated one-to-one-hundred map and marked the place they were standing, and she copied a half-dozen more grid points that he read from his own map, each with eight numerals. "In Pakistan, we will be using a GPS, but a computer in the field is always liable to break at the worst possible time. So today, I want you to use only the basics. You should be able to navigate to within ten meters of your objective." He pointed uphill. "Go that way."

Beth pointed her compass and shot an azimuth from magnetic north, then followed the map key to convert it, plus or minus, onto the chart. A little thin plastic protractor no larger than a postcard was used to draw straight lines between points, and she stretched a piece of string to mark the distance between the locations, pinching the exact point between her fingers. The length of string, placed on the measuring bar on the bottom of the map, gave her the distance. So far, she had been accurate.

"I'm not used to the physical labor part of the job,"

she admitted, massaging her thighs in hopes of easing the burning muscles.

"I understand. I don't expect you to be. But you have to put in your own time over the next few days doing PT, things like running, pull-ups, and sit-ups. Hell, just walk for distance. Any cardio exercises will help. The more it hurts today, the less it will hurt when we go into Taliban country. For now, just get up this hill to that next set of coordinates. And don't make so damned much noise breaking through the brush. Up and at it, Ledford. Push."

He had been given less than a week to get her through some rudimentary training. She could shoot but would need as much knowledge about working in the wild as he could cram into her during that short time. He had decided on using a basic escape and evasion exercise today to help her at least to recognize some of the possibilities, both good and bad.

As they climbed, he wondered if General Middleton was having any progress in his meetings with the politicians and diplomats. The State Department had promised to stop the surveillance, but refused to explain why the CT/DSS had been following Ledford in the first place. You don't put a full-scale tight net over somebody without a good reason. For Middleton, the State plea that they were just following orders wasn't good enough. Orders from whom, and why?

Then Commander Freedman had pulled a series of overhead satellite shots of the bridge area in Pakistan and pointed out that the heavy equipment clustered at the site was far out of proportion for simply building and improving a road. Nothing much was visible beyond a giant construction site, and the extensive flat surface of the bridge and its side apron. There was a village a mile away to the east, a bazaar to the west. Middleton was uncomfortable with the whole thing, and when the general was uncomfortable, he made sure everyone else was, too.

After Swanson completed Ledford's workouts, they were to get over to London immediately, with next stop Islamabad. Kyle had the familiar feeling of some unseen hand increasing the tempo of events, speeding things up ever so slightly, pulling him forward.

Another quarter mile of struggling up the incline, and he gave Beth a three-minute break. She flopped down on her back, breathing hard. "I'm glad I joined the Coast Guard," she said. "This marching and climbing sucks."

"Well, when you finish with this little hill, you get a treat. Sybelle has arranged for a Coast Guard helicopter to pick us up. So we'll go out over the water and I can watch you shoot from the bird, see you operate in familiar surroundings."

"Really? Great. Do you know what kind?"

"She says it is your usual ride, an MH-68H, piloted by your buddy Lieutenant Commander Taylor, who got chopped from regular duty down in Jacksonville just to come up here and taxi you around."

"Wow. You guys can do that sort of thing?"

"Yep. Here's the catch. Taylor is to do a touch-and-go at the landing zone, just the kind of situation we may face in extracting from Pakistan. He will not wait.

You have to have us at that landing zone, the map mark, at exactly fifteen hundred hours, or we miss our ride."

"That's less than forty-five minutes from now!" She was already on her feet, ignoring her aching legs and back. "Why didn't you tell me sooner?"

"Welcome to the world of special ops, Ledford. You'll be told what you need to know, when you need to know it. Just follow the map and keep going. You can do this."

"Five minutes, Ledford. The LZ is straight ahead. You can see it from here. Go!" Swanson barked in a drill sergeant voice.

The toes of Beth Ledford's boots were at the edge of a sharp gully that bisected the path, and stones crumbled down a thirty-foot drop. She hesitated, knowing she could never get all the way down there and climb up the other side in time for the pickup. "What do I do, Gunny?" Her question was urgent.

"You will never know exactly what is on the ground from reading a map," Swanson said carefully, now in a quieter, instructive tone. "If you hit an impassable obstacle like this, don't come to a complete halt. Do a ninety-degree offset, left or right, for about one hundred meters, counting your steps for distance, and bypass the problem. Then turn back to your original line and keep going. Now, go!"

She spun to the right and made her way along the edge of the gully. After counting one hundred and seventy-eight steps, she found a narrow point that was only about eight feet wide. Backing away, she got a running start and jumped the gap, yelping when her blistered feet hit the hard dirt on the far side, and she lost her balance and tumbled into the brush, face-first.

The thudding sound of an incoming helicopter did not allow time to catch her breath. She jumped up, but instead of going back the way she had come, she decided to cut off some distance by angling up the hill, as if drawing the hypotenuse of a triangle. In the sky, to the east, she could see the white and orange helicopter coming on fast and shedding altitude.

Swanson was on her heels and did not correct her, because she was already realizing her mistake. A thick tangle of thorny growth blocked her path, and it only got thicker as she fought through it. She looked up and saw Arvis Taylor smiling down at her. He shook his head, and Beth knew that she was not going to make it.

The helicopter landed with the engine at full throttle, but the bird never stopped. Had Beth been there, she could have just flopped through the open hatch. She wasn't, though, and Taylor's orders were to make it a touch-and-go, never coming to a full halt. Just as Ledford fought her way free of the clinging thorns, he finished the touchdown less than a hundred feet away and was lifting off, unwilling to wait an instant longer than ordered, even for one of his closest friends.

Beth Ledford's shoulders sagged in disappointment, and she sat down hard on the dirt. Unscrewing the canteen, she drank some water while she listened to Swanson on his radio, reporting failure. The blades of the bird overhead were beating retreat.

"Ferrybird One. Ferrybird One. This is Swanson, over."

"Swanson, this is Ferrybird. Send your traffic."

"Roger. Looks like our girl missed the pickup. Divert to LZ Two."

"Roger that. Ferrybird out."

She bristled at hearing him call her a girl and was about to say something when Kyle was in her face. Drill sergeant time again. "You've blown the LZ, Ledford. Now the enemy knows where you are, so you just added three kilometers to the day and are in escape and recovery time. Get off your ass and read your map. You've got ten minutes to cover three klicks to the alternate LZ. This time don't go wandering off course."

Beth pushed herself erect, checked the map, blew out puffed cheeks in determination, and set out for the listed grid coordinates of the new LZ. The blades of the departing helicopter were still loud in the air.

Swanson did not let up but stayed right in her ear, yelling. "Move out, Petty Officer. It pays to be a winner, Ledford. Because you screwed up, now we may have to walk back. I wanted to eat some Greek food in Q-Town tonight, but if you mess up getting to the alternate LZ, I will be stuck on this damn little hill with you walking around lost in the dark."

A bright flash drew their attention, and the smoky white trail of a surface-to-air missile lanced upward from the far treeline and drove straight for the low-flying helicopter. There was the shaking clap of a loud explosion as the missile struck the brightly colored helicopter, blowing off the tail rotor section. The front of the bird hung momentarily motionless in the air, then was engulfed in a massive fireball as another explosion ruptured the fuel tanks. It crashed to the ground, burning.

"Oh my God!" Ledford screamed and started to run toward the crash site.

Swanson saw a glitter of sunlight flashing on glass, thought *scope,* and tackled her in midstride just as a bullet banged overhead. He pushed through the tackle, driving them both forward and down to the ground. "Ambush, Ledford. For real!" Kyle slithered forward on his stomach, with Beth at his heels. A cluster of boulders provided some temporary protection.

"Let's flank him," Beth said. "Split up, circle around, and come in from the sides." She was breathing hard, her mind still reeling from seeing the helicopter destroyed and then being shot at almost simultaneously. Her hands were raw from skidding through the gravel and dirt as she had broken her fall.

"Negative. This is no coincidence, Beth. You were supposed to be on that helicopter, and the shooter was backup in case you were not. We're unarmed out here, and we don't know how many guys are after us. My job is to get you out of danger." He grabbed his radio and tuned it to an emergency frequency as the *crack* of another rifle shot was followed by a whining ricochet of a bullet off the edge of the rocks. It showered them with splinters.

"Quantico Tower. Quantico Tower. This is Gunnery Sergeant Kyle Swanson. Mayday. Mayday. Mayday." Kyle had his radio at his lips and fumbled his map open with the other hand.

The calm voice of an air traffic controller responded immediately. "This is Marine Corps Air Facility Quantico Tower. I read you, Gunny. What is your emergency?"

"A Coast Guard helicopter was just shot down by a SAM missile on a training exercise," he said, reading off the coordinates. "Now my partner and I are under fire in an ambush by at least one individual and are evading. Send anything you have in the air to buzz this site to keep their heads down."

"Roger that, Gunny. Be advised we are diverting a fast-mover for a flyover, and it's on the way. A Cobra should be right behind him. The Quick Reaction Force is being alerted."

Kyle responded, "We're moving at one hundred ninety-eight magnetic azimuth. Swanson out." He stuffed the radio into a pocket and turned to Ledford. "We're heading for that clump of trees about fifty meters down the slope. It will take between six and seven seconds to get there, with minimal cover. I will go first, at an angle to draw his fire, then you run like your life depends on it, Beth. Somebody wants you dead real bad." With that, Swanson broke from cover and headed downhill, dodging sharply to his left. Ledford raced out a moment later, her arms windmilling for balance on the treacherous slope.

Major Charles Marshall Jones saw the spiraling black smoke from the downed helicopter, then the bald spot of the landing zone. He had been only a few miles away, approaching the air station in his Lockheed Martin F-35B Lightning when the controller issued the emergency orders. Instead of setting up for a slow vertical landing, Jones peeled away and punched the Pratt & Whitney turbofan engine into afterburner. The stubby wings and the speedboat lines of the latest generation fighter jet had him climbing and turning at five hundred miles per hour in seconds.

He had no idea what was going on down there. Incredibly, someone was attacking American troops inside Quantico, one of the nation's premier military installations. The tower only wanted him to buzz the LZ, which was good because he had no missiles on the hard points, nor anything in his cannon. As a Marine aviator, he had been trained to fly low and fast in support of the ground troops, and he coaxed the Lightning down to two hundred feet above the deck as he sped into the area.

Jones saw two figures running down the hillside on the same azimuth he had been given, scrambling away from the LZ. They had to be the people he was to cover, and he scooted lower as the terrain rose up higher. The Lightning passed with a sonic boom, and a concussive wave of displaced air churned the LZ into a noisy dust storm. The major hauled hard back the stick and bored a hole straight up into the sky, bent his plane into a 5-g turn, and came back in for another run from the opposite direction. Another sonic boom slammed the hillside.

That ought to let whoever is fucking around down there know that we're watching, he thought, as he listened to the radio calls. Jones carved high to fly tight circles around the LZ in plain view of anyone below as a Cobra helicopter came hurtling in from the west for an even lower sweep. The QRF was no more than five minutes out. Soon, the place would be crawling with combat-ready Marines.

Beth Ledford and Kyle Swanson hustled downhill on parallel courses through the pine trees, their boots crunching the carpet of brown fallen needles, twigs, and cones. Her lungs were on fire, and her legs were barely under control.

Swanson ran closer and called, "Twenty meters straight ahead. Into that ditch." He watched as she jumped into the depression feet first; then he did the same and immediately rolled back over to see if anyone was chasing them. At least, they were no longer alone. The F-35's two passes, plus the Cobra that was now nibbling around the LZ, had been more than enough to warn off the attackers, but he would not take that chance. Whoever had been smart enough to penetrate deep into a Marine base might still be lurking around up there, or worse, still following them.

There was a roaring growl behind him, and a Humvee came bursting up a nearby dirt road. Kyle ducked down again. *Good guys or bad? Probably good, but maybe not.* The powerful vehicle continued charging toward the LZ.

He clicked his radio and raised the tower again, which acknowledged the call and transferred it to the commander of the Quick Reaction Force. The QRF was only a minute out, and Kyle could hear the rotors of their helicopter. Beth Ledford raised her head, and he shoved her back. "Stay put," he ordered.

After receiving the new coordinates, the helo changed

course and slowed until it was directly overhead. Then it came to a hover and Marines were coming out of the bird, sliding down thick ropes, landing on the narrow road. Weapons ready, they automatically formed a perimeter, and a sergeant major was barking orders. A captain in full battle gear walked over to the ditch in which Kyle and Beth had taken shelter, his pistol drawn.

"You Gunny Swanson?"

"Yes, sir," he replied, panting and out of breath. "This is Petty Officer Ledford."

"Sir," she said. Beth struggled upright. Her face and hands were bleeding from scratches from the dash through the pine forest.

"What the hell is going on?" asked the captain.

"Don't know, sir. It's a complicated national security matter that I'll explain later, but we need to get Petty Officer Ledford to a secure location ASAP. Alert your people that this is no drill. A helicopter has been blown out of the sky by a SAM, there is a terrorist shooter running loose around here, and she's the target."

"OK. Both of you stay in that ditch until we get a medevac chopper in here and a gunship to fly cover." The captain sent ten men up to comb the LZ and pulled the rest of his force into a tight circle around Swanson and Ledford. He looked over at Swanson. "Terrorists? At Quantico? They'll never make it off the base alive."

Kyle said, "They made it in okay. They have some plan for egress, and a Humvee just went tearing past us, heading up the road. My guess is it was their ride. Your QRF is dealing with professionals."

10

The Bureau of American-Islamic Affairs was less than two years old, a new bureaucracy within the U.S. Department of State, with the onerous portfolio of trying to chart a stable diplomatic course in the fractious Muslim world. Career workers who were specialists in the field had been culled from other sections to take up duties in a heavily guarded and secure office complex outside of the Washington Beltway, but the heartbeat of the bureau was a remodeled three-story Victorian building at Thirty-fourth Street and Massachusetts Avenue NW, on the grounds of the United States Naval Observatory. In that ornate building, Arab princes and Persian potentates and the bewildering array of leaders in the volatile Muslim world were welcomed and entertained almost on a daily basis. In its short existence, the mansion had become an important back door to power.

From his lavish office on the third floor, Undersecretary William Lloyd Curtis could look over the treetops and see the groomed front of One Observatory Circle, the stately official home of the vice president of the United States. While the White House was the most visible point of government in Washington, hardly anyone even knew where the vice president lived. It was therefore easy to arrange private sessions between Muslim leaders and U.S. government officials without drawing undue attention. The American representatives would say they were visiting the home of the vice president; the Muslim representatives would declare they were in private meetings with Undersecretary Curtis. In reality, they could all be in a secure conference room on the second floor of the BAIA.

Curtis was a tall and broad-chested man who wore tailored suits that were obviously cut from cloth rich enough to denote private wealth, as did the patrician Massachusetts accent. Deep gray eyes matched the thick brows and carefully barbered hair that was thinning but was still full for a sixty-year-old. A closer look at the calm face would show hard lines that had been etched at the corners of his eyes from staring into the desert sun too much. His scarred hands also gave away his true past, for although the nails were manicured, the fingers were gnarled and the palms hardened from decades of working in oil patches and construction projects all over the world. His nose had been broken several times, leaving it with a curious bent shape that added to his look of experience. Bill Curtis had grown from being a mining engineer to becoming a one-man equipment hauler and eventually to creating Curtis Construction, a multinational corporation.

By the time Bill Curtis decided to retire from the

business, he had contacts all over the globe and was
friends with most of the powerful men in the Middle
East. Those contacts, and his easy ability to juggle
business, political, and personal favors, had led to him
becoming the American ambassador to Kuwait, and
then he was given the plum prize of Egypt.

Curtis was there to steer U.S. interests when Egypt
fell apart under the tidal wave of revolutionary upheaval
that was beginning to sweep through the Muslim world,
and the old regimes toppled and fell so rapidly that it
was often difficult to determine which side the American government should support. There were no good
options in some of the uprisings.

The overwhelmed State Department decided to
bring the entire troubled region beneath one tent, so it
created the BAIA, and Big Bill Curtis was deemed
uniquely qualified to be its leader. The paint was hardly
dry on the walls of the new offices when the American
SEALs staged the assault in Pakistan that killed Osama
bin Laden and created a leadership vacuum in the terrorist world. The charming and tough Curtis was the
man who would have to ride the tiger of Arab revolution, and he was more than happy to do so, for he had
spent several years pushing the idea that bin Laden and
his al Qaeda organization had become obsolete.

For more than a decade, since the attacks of 9/11,
there had been the feeling that bin Laden and al Qaeda
were in charge of the entire Muslim revolution, for he
had struck the biggest blow ever against the Great Satan. The Saudi was revered for that, but almost before
American sailors wrapped his body in a white sheet

and dumped him overboard from an aircraft carrier, internal bickering erupted within the terrorist community over who would carry that violent legacy forward. Bin Laden's old friend Mullah Omar was too worried about being the next on the list for Seal Team Six to step forward. The egocentric Sayyid Muqtada al-Sadr in Iraq spoke loudly, but no one listened to him. Dr. Ayman al-Zawahiri from Egypt inherited the official role as head of al Qaeda but could not control it. Even an American Muslim cleric in Yemen derisively known as the "big-headed little man" due to his likeness to the cartoon character Charlie Brown made a pathetic attempt to be seen as the ultimate leader. The Palestinians were never even in the game.

Curtis felt that Osama bin Laden's death marked the passing of the flag. Hezbollah, the Muslim Brotherhood, Hamas, and the inevitable lone wolf terrorists were scrambling for wider pieces of the pie and their own agendas, but none was succeeding, and he blocked them all whenever possible. Iran bankrolled revolution but cared only for itself. The only real success was being shown by the New Muslim Order and its leader, Commander Kahn. Bill Curtis had long ago decided that Kahn was to be the one and used his position as undersecretary to nudge things in the proper direction. He had a dog in the fight. The Commander was no stupid outlaw but a friend and ally from years gone by.

Which was why Curtis was angry as he stood beside the big office window. In his hands was a handwritten note that had been delivered by a private courier, folded and sealed in two envelopes. His lips had drawn into thin lines when he read it, and the eyes darkened. Failure! The girl still lived!

The undersecretary sighed and fed the note and envelopes edge-on into the office shredder, which cross-chipped the paper into microscopic pieces that would be impossible to ever reassemble. At the end of the day, they would go into the burn bag and be incinerated. During the Iranian revolution that toppled the shah from power back in the 1970s, the U.S. Embassy in Tehran had shredded all of its important documents. Those thousands of strips had been reassembled and pasted back together by Iranian students and today could be read verbatim. The WikiLeaks scandal made security even chancier. William Curtis preferred for his secrets to remain secrets.

There had been no mention of the Quantico action in his morning briefing, which was gratifying. The Marine Corps was keeping it bottled up while its investigators tried to determine exactly how the breach happened and who was involved. Curtis was confident that they never would. The mission that day to which the girl had been assigned was a simple training exercise, and all preparatory communications were handled through normal open channels. The people at Task Force Trident had contacted the Department of Defense with a request for technical support, and DoD went through the Treasury Department to get a particular helicopter and its Coast Guard crew. Orders were cut from departmental operations to base ops and squadron ops, specifying exact times and coordinates. It had all been available in various military mailboxes, easily monitored by outsiders.

Curtis had had a rogue private security company monitoring the system for information ever since the CT/DSS terminated surveillance of Petty Officer Ledford, declaring that she was no threat. That depended, the undersecretary thought, on who, or what, was being threatened. The target wasn't even in the United States but in Pakistan, where the huge new bridge project was under way, with funding flowing in from the oil fields. Front companies of Curtis Construction, in partnership with similar Muslim businesses, were lost in the organizational maze. He could not afford to have that link exposed.

When Beth Ledford had first begun making inquiries, Curtis managed to blunt her requests and employ State Department resources to track her under the guise of a potential terrorist threat. When the DSS pulled out, he had resorted to his very expensive friends in the private sector who specialized in unusual assignments, professionals that he had used before.

For them, infiltrating the Quantico base had been easy. Distant fences that were bare of infrared sensors or cameras could have been scaled easily, since guards were posted only at the choke points of entrances and exits. That would have made getting away more difficult, however, so two uniformed Marines in a Humvee bearing the proper stickers on the windshield drove up to the gate and merited no more than a wave from the guard who allowed them in. They drove to the landing zone coordinates, where one had taken his long rifle and found a comfortable hide on the side of a hill overlooking the LZ. The driver hid the Humvee nearby and took up position with a reliable Stinger ground-to-air missile. Afterward, they simply drove off the base, right before security was heightened.

It should have worked. Now the message stated the mission had failed, the hundred-thousand-dollar fee was nonrefundable, and the girl had dropped out of sight. The only good news was that his team had acquired the name of the Marine who had been her training escort. A second operation was being assembled to snatch him and squeeze out the information on the whereabouts of prime target Beth Ledford.

THE FRANCIS SCOTT KEY BRIDGE
WASHINGTON, D.C.

Sleep did not come easily that night for Kyle Swanson in his apartment near Georgetown University, so after midnight, he went out to walk and think. There were few people around, except those lingering at the doorways of bars and pubs to smoke their cigarettes before going back inside to the beer and laughter. Some were students, but most of them were government workers and young lawyers and lobbyists pawing through the bureaucratic victories and defeats of their day on Capitol Hill like witches divining a purpose from a scattering of bones.

The unexpected catastrophe at the landing zone had

left everyone in Trident, including him, also searching for meaning. There were no answers, and General Middleton was pissed, shaking the trees hard. The counterterrorism people at the State Department were equally bewildered and adamant that they had nothing to do with what had happened. For Kyle, how the daring ambush was done was less important than why it was even attempted. What did Beth Ledford have that was so damned important?

He meandered down M Street, heading east. The buildings all around were relatively small by the standards of other major urban areas, because skyscrapers did not exist in Washington. Nothing was taller than the Washington Monument; buildings were instead spread out, or excavated to create space underground. Swanson paused. Just ahead, M terminated as it crossed the Potomac River into Rosslyn on the Virginia side. With the heat of the day finally gone, a slight mist was rising from the water. A well-used pathway led to the boathouses clustered under the Francis Scott Key Bridge, named in honor of the writer of the "Star-Spangled Banner." He followed it down to the water's edge, giving plenty of space to a young couple making out in the shadows.

Bridges, he thought. *What is going on with bridges?* His Nikes padded silently along the board of the dock where the long canoes were stacked and secured. Sailboats. Motorboats. Sculls. Jet Skis. Why wasn't there a big river going under that big bridge in Pakistan? The mist was thicker on the water.

With his hands in the pockets of his jeans, Kyle turned toward the lights of the city downriver. The upper part of the monument could be seen, with small red lights at the top blinking to warn pilots of its presence, as if the big floodlights that bathed the obelisk at night did not provide enough of a clue. To his right were the elegant lines of the Kennedy Center, and closer was the stack of concrete-and-glass pancakes of the Watergate Complex. He went halfway up the grassy bank, found a dry spot of grass, lay down, and fell asleep just after seeing the faraway sparkle of a falling star.

He heard an oar sluggishly moving against the Potomac water and instantly knew it was not some sculler out for a midnight row. The smell told him so: dried tears, dead flowers, fresh blood. Swanson let out a groan. The Boatman had arrived. He knew the ragged figure emerging from the fog was nothing but a dream, a character that had a habit of showing up in his mind when there was a crisis. Invariably, death followed in his wake.

> *Hello.*
> *You're on the wrong river. The Styx is underground somewhere, down in hell. This is the Potomac.*

A slender thread of crooked laughter made Kyle look up. Charon was still in his boat, the long oar over the stern bumping ever so lightly against the boardwalk.

> *We will be doing more business soon. Carry plenty of gold coins to put on their eyes or beneath the tongues, Gunnery Sergeant. I give no free passage from this world.*

Swanson looked across the river to the Virginia shoreline, which was being eaten by a churning wall of fire.

> *I will never pay you to take a man to hell.*
>
> *But you are the one who sends them there. It is only fair that I be paid if I am to further your work.*

The silent laughter rose again, and the Boatman pushed back the hood of his rotten cloak. A bald bone skull seemed to grin, and the black holes of the eyes had seen an eternity of life and death.

> *Why are you here, you decayed piece of trash?*
>
> *Why is there a bridge in Pakistan, in a place with little or no water?*
>
> *There was a huge flood. Thousands died. Don't you watch the news?*
>
> *Yes. I have been busy there, and with paying customers. Their friends and relatives do not want the souls of their loved ones stuck on this side of the veil, to loiter around as unwanted ghosts. If the flood collapsed dams, no mere bridge would have held back such water. So the bridge is over a tributary waterway, not a major river. And why is a bridge needed at all now that the flood has receded? I can hardly paddle my little boat in that trickle.*

Kyle waited a minute before speaking again.

I have known you many years.

Yes.

This is the only time you have ever made any sense.

Do not forget the gold coins. And take two for your own eyes, and two more for those of the girl. She also will be on this voyage.

Gold is too expensive. Copper pennies will have to do. How about I pay you a dollar in advance? Give me room to work.

The skull turned upward and looked toward the sky, and the skeletal arms were raised wide.

You would bargain with death?

Yes. And I will cheat you every time.

The laugh turned into a shriek from the gaping mouth, and the Virginia inferno climbed higher, licking the bottom of the night clouds. Kyle's nostrils seemed clogged by the thick scent of charred, dead bodies. There was a flash of light, and the Boatman vanished with a final hiss: *"It begins now . . ."*

Swanson snapped awake, with all senses alert, although he kept his eyes closed and his body immobile. He picked up the sound of cars going across the Key Bridge, but there was something else, a slight movement in the stillness, weight being gently pushed against the heavy grass on the slope where he lay, and he heard a man breathing, moving closer. With one approaching cautiously, there was probably another nearby. He heard the creak of a board from the dock, so the backup was down there, about fifteen feet away beside the water, to cover his partner.

As soon as Kyle opened his eyes, the nearest man made his rush, holding a thin, extended steel baton high above his head and ready to slam it down. He leaned in to make the strike, which made him slightly off balance on the gentle slope. Swanson dug his left foot into the soft dirt and pushed over into a roll hard to his right toward the attacker, and the baton swished harmlessly through the air. It smacked the ground at the same time Kyle rammed his shoulders into the man's ankles.

The unknown assailant fell forward and hit the ground facedown with a loud grunt, stunned. Kyle finished the roll and smoothly came to his feet, drawing the .45 Colt from the shoulder holster beneath his jacket. The downed man wore a gray sweatshirt and straight-leg jeans, was probably about six feet tall, and had enjoyed too much fried chicken and pizza. Kyle stomped hard on the spinal column at the base of the skull with his left foot and felt and heard the C-2 neck vertebra give way with a loud snap as it forcibly parted from the C-3 under great force, in a classic hangman's break.

He swiveled to face the second threat and saw the man charging from the dock, a dark figure moving fast but from lower ground. He was shorter and even wider than the other one and had Asian features. The blade of a knife flashed in the subdued lights below the bridge. Kyle raised his pistol and fired point-blank into the face, and the man jerked to a halt as the back of his head blew off in a spray of blood and bone. The body fell backward and landed on the grass with a wet sound. The double-tap of gunshots echoed wildly beneath the arch of the bridge.

Kyle held his Colt in both hands and methodically quartered the area around him. The choice of a baton and a knife instead of guns meant the two men were not expecting to be unsuccessful in the attack, and therefore they were likely professionals. It was unlikely that they had brought along even more support. Two tough pros would normally have been more than enough. When Swanson was certain no one else was there, he holstered his pistol and made a quick search of the pockets of the dead men. Neither had a wallet, nor any identification. Pros, for sure. Swanson for a moment considered dialing 911 on his cell but decided it would be better to just move on out of there. Let someone else report the sound of gunfire.

He walked up the hill and back into Georgetown. This whole thing was out of control. It was time for Trident to go black on it, and for Kyle and Beth Ledford to vanish. He was tired of people knowing where the fuck he was at.

11

They were on Interstate 95 only a few hours after the attack. Glowing strands of headlights marked the commuters flowing into the Washington corridor. Within an hour, the traffic would thicken in the southbound lanes to bind the cars trapped on it into a slow-moving parking lot. Swanson and Ledford were going the other way, as Kyle glided a big Land Rover north, heading for a small airport just outside of Providence, Rhode Island, that served private passenger planes. He would have preferred something less conspicuous than the big SUV but was thinking defensively, and the specially equipped vehicle was rigged with bulletproof glass, heavy-duty bumpers, tires that would resist gunfire, and interior weapons storage areas. It also had the advantage of sheer weight in case somebody tried to ram it, and its enhanced four-wheel drive would take it almost anywhere. The Land Rover had been part of the FBI fleet until earlier that morning, when Special Agent Dave Hunt checked it out in his own name, then handed the keys to Kyle with the warning that it was lousy on gas mileage. The wipers clicked methodically against the windshield as they drove through a light rain.

"Why don't we just use a military flight out of Andrews?" she asked, leaning back in the big comfortable seat. "The general could clear it, right?"

"There is a hole somewhere in the comm net, Beth, and we don't know where. We cannot trust normal operating procedures," Swanson said. "What happened yesterday at Quantico, and then last night with me, could only have been planned with advance intelligence. Too many people had access to what we were doing. So from now on, we're dark. Only the four other people in Trident know our plan, plus a few on the other end, along with the two of us—not even your mother can know what's going on. Nothing is being written down, entered into any computer, or spoken on any open comm line or channel. We intend to keep this new loop as tight as possible."

She thought that over. It still felt like they were running away. "Gunny, I think we should stay here and fight whoever they are. Instead you have us going on a cruise? It's like we're scared."

"Just the opposite, Beth. We're moving toward the real fight. The cause of all of this trouble obviously is in Pakistan."

"The bridge."

"Yes. The bridge."

"And Task Force Trident is able to lay on a private jet and a yacht to get us there?"

Kyle pressed a button on the console to activate a device that showed no radar was painting them, then accelerated. The Land Rover jumped forward in response.

"The yacht is just a way station for us, a secure position where we can get ready in private for the final move. The plane is owned by the same corporation that is providing the yacht."

"Your General Middleton has some pull, huh? He trusts the civilian owners?" She looked quizzically at him and saw the flicker of a smile.

"He should. It's my family."

After a hearty dinner, Chief Engineer Mohammad al-Attas took Sergeant Hafiz along on his final inspection for the evening. They buzzed through the big central tunnel in an electric cart, dodging around workers and technicians. In a subsidiary corridor, the engineer halted the cart and led Hafiz into what looked to the sergeant like the pictures he had seen of America's space mission headquarters in Houston, Texas. Tangles of wiring hung loose from the false panel ceiling, and the temperature was a comfortable sixty-five degrees. Al-Attas stepped onto a raised platform and took a seat in a cushioned high-backed swivel chair, wrapping his hands around a pair of computer joysticks that rose one from each arm. He faced an array of flat computer screens mounted side by side and stacked in rows on wall brackets. Hafiz stood beside him, silently impressed, keeping his arms crossed. The colors on the electronic devices were crisp, the resolution perfect, and the largest single monitor in operation was divided into four sections, each showing an identical room.

The only furnishing in any of the narrow rooms that

were featured was a slender Type 85 12.5 mm heavy machine gun, a belt-fed, gas-operated, air-cooled weapon that was a staple of the Chinese army and could fire up to six hundred rounds per minute. The long tubular weapon did not rest upon the usual tripod in their special caves but on a sturdy articulated arm of lightweight titanium that reached out from thick cylinders bolted into position in the stone floor. The barrels faced what appeared to be a blank rectangle of painted steel.

The chief engineer explained, "From my position here, a controller will be in command of a dozen separate weapons systems, a mix of machine guns, rockets, and missiles." Al-Attas nudged the joystick in his left hand, then squeezed a green button, and one of the steel walls before a gun slid open to reveal a section of the valley facing south. The engineer eased the joystick straight ahead, and the robotic arm obediently moved forward, pushing the nose of the machine gun through the firing slit. Another control movement and the image of the machine gun dissolved into a wide view of the area it covered, directly ahead of the open window.

"Certain adjustments have been made to the machine gun, including replacing the manual trigger and spade grips." Al-Attas shifted the angle to point the gun at another area. "It will be fired from here, and will continue firing as long as the trigger is depressed, or until the belt is empty. You can use it against a single target or sweep a sixty-degree sector. Then you pull it back in and shut the blind, which is camouflaged on the outside."

The machine gun automatically pulled back into its

original position with the smooth assuredness of a robot doing an assigned task. "Forgive me, Chief Engineer, but that does not seem particularly threatening," Hafiz observed. "A single man gets close enough and takes this whole thing out with a grenade or a handheld missile."

Al-Attas laughed. "A lone soldier may be lucky enough to get that close only if his unit is sacrificed. Our controller will be fighting with all of his other weapons at the same time, or he can slave the systems to the computer to fire automatically at targets picked by sensors and cameras hidden in the valley. Interlocking fields of crossfire will force the enemy into mined areas. When the gun is empty and retreats, and the chamber sealed and safe again, a loader who services several weapons will put in a new magazine, check the gun, and then leave to service another. Then it becomes part of the battle again."

"Maximum firepower with minimal human loss potential," Hafiz said. "Still, if the enemy starts hitting this place with smart bombs and cruise missiles, this gun will be gone."

"True, but that would take a number of direct hits, and I have an automated air defense system that will make even that almost impossible. Jamming devices will turn the space above and all around into an electronic wasteland: Their pilots' radios won't work, false returns will replace real targets on their displays, lasers cannot lock on, cruise missiles will fly off course, and all the while, our own antiaircraft guns and missiles will be shooting down enemy aircraft to panic the remaining crews. I understand, Sergeant Hafiz, that no defensive system is totally immune to attack, but a few trained technicians at the video control stations here can put up a terrific fight—I estimate that one controller and a half-dozen loaders can hold off at least an entire battalion for three days of hard fighting, and we are planning twenty control stations. When all of the weapons are finally silenced, most of the operators will have survived and should be able to leave safely. When our wireless system is perfected, the controllers will not even have to be on-site. They can guide the action from miles away. Any sort of attack—by ground or by air—is going to be a very long process, and extremely costly for the attackers. My cameras will capture the carnage and feed it to the cable networks."

"You *expect* the bridge and all of these fancy defenses to be overrun?"

Mohammad al-Attas rose from his seat, turned off the display, and shrugged his shoulders. "We must face reality. Put yourself in the mind of the enemy commander. After a week of hard fighting, nothing seems to work and you have suffered horrendous losses of men and materiel. Is that a victory? So your troops finally make it in, wading through more mines and booby traps and the occasional sniper or counterattack at designed choke points. They will think they are in the devil's toilet, sergeant. Then, just when the general thinks it is over, that he has won, internal bombs explode, and it all collapses around his ears."

Hafiz had been told little of this when he was given the assignment of watching over the engineer. He said, "Nuclear bombs?"

"Possibly, but those would not really be necessary, and the radioactivity would create a wasteland for centuries. This land belongs to us, and might someday be transformed into a fertile breadbasket. Anyway, there are things worse than a nuclear bomb."

"What could be worse?"

"Breaking the will of the enemy. Our most likely attackers would be the Americans, and maybe some of their European allies. The Pakistanis will never try to take this fortress, because they are helping to pay for it. Let us not be coy, Hafiz. Important lessons were learned from the tragic death of the grand martyr Osama bin Laden, and I won't make those mistakes. There were no real defenses at the house in Abbottabad, and it was too easy for the Americans to take him out with an extremely small force. That could never happen here."

Hafiz pondered that statement. "So you are confident that Commander Kahn would be safe in this futuristic cave dwelling? Would you bet your own life on that?"

"I deal in facts, Sergeant. Anything is possible. But let's look at the scenario in which they try to come after the Commander. After suffering staggering losses, the infidels would be under immense pressure from their governments to stop the slaughter. Remember, I will be televising the images of dying Americans. Generals would be replaced, elections could be influenced, politicians ruined. Commander Kahn would be totally safe during the attack and have plenty of time to be safely evacuated to another prepared position, and the enemy would understand that now they will have to do it all over again; take out the next bridge, and the one after that, and on and on, all with equally abhorrent body counts. Airpower and cruise missiles simply will not do the job, and the Americans always stop short of using nuclear weapons.

"Eventually, when the Americans leave Iraq and Afghanistan, they will focus even more on Pakistan. We will be ready. In the coming years, we are going to have a long road across the top of our country, Sergeant Hafiz. There will be a lot of bridges and tunnels, and each of them will be a sharp fang in a gigantic death trap. Would you want to fight that fight?"

Hafiz shook his head. "No," he said. "I would not."

The chief engineer settled back in the big chair. "Neither will they."

A private Hawker 800XP Execujet with the gold emblem of Excalibur Enterprises gleaming on its white skin descended through a deck of low clouds and kissed the paved 4,500-foot runway of Flores Island, one of the smallest of the Azores, with only a single bump. The elegant aircraft had effortlessly jumped the Atlantic Ocean in just under five hours, cruising the 2,261 miles in a direct flight from Rhode Island and bypassing the air traffic hub in Lisbon. Officials at the small airport expedited the passage of the vice president of the well-known multinational corporation and his friend through the customs procedures and cleared them for immediate departure aboard a waiting helicopter that also was the property of Excalibur. As a courtesy to the minister of defense, the officials respected the couple's privacy and no names were recorded. The modernization program of the Forças Armadas Portuguesas had forged a very friendly relationship between Excalibur officials and the government of Portugal.

A little more than another hour of comfortable flight in the sleek helicopter put Kyle Swanson and Beth Ledford on approach to a luxurious yacht that was cruising straight toward a brilliant sunset. "That rowboat down there is the *Vagabond*," Swanson said.

"That's huge. It's as big as a Coast Guard cutter," she said, astounded at the obvious richness of it all. She estimated the airplane alone had cost almost four million dollars. The yacht would carry a much higher price tag. "It must be two hundred feet long."

"Only one-eighty," Swanson replied. "Twenty-nine feet wide."

"This all belongs to your family?"

"Take the comfort while you can, Ledford. We won't be here long."

He had dodged answering her question, so Beth tried again, much more forcefully. "So just who the hell is your family?"

Kyle looked at her and smiled. "I'm kind of the adopted only child of Pat and Jeff Cornwell, a British couple you've probably never heard of."

Beth gulped, startled. "You gotta be kidding. You are related to Sir Geoffrey and Lady Patricia Cornwell?" She unconsciously touched her hair. "God, and I look a mess. Dammit, Kyle Swanson, I hate you more every day. How did that come about?"

"I don't talk about my private life."

"So I have noticed. In fact, you never explain anything, but now you've dropped this bomb in my lap, and I need to know some background before you let me make a fool of myself." How was she supposed to greet a lord and lady? Shake hands? Curtsy? Little-girl fairy tales swam to mind.

"The short version is that Jeff retired out of the SAS and got into weapons development, then started his own company. The Pentagon lent me to him as an expert adviser in developing the Excalibur sniper rifle, and we all hit it off from the very start. I had grown up as an orphan and they had no children, nor any other living relatives. We just sort of found each other."

"So it's not a blood relation?"

"Oh no. Much better than that. We actually enjoy each other."

The helicopter swept in closer and circled the vessel, then approached the helipad on the stern and set down. Crewmen dashed forward and lashed it to the deck as the pilot powered down and the spinning blades slowed. A hatch opened, and the fresh salty air wafted in. A short stairway folded down, and a suntanned man in a white uniform trotted up and inside the chopper. "Welcome aboard, Kyle," he smiled, extending his hand. "You, too, Ms. Ledford. I'm Michael Berryman, the captain of this barge."

"Hello, Mike. Good to be back, even if we are just passing through."

"You always are, mate. Come along now. I'm to fetch the both of you immediately to the main salon." They all stepped onto the deck, feeling only a gentle roll underfoot as the *Vagabond* surged through the calm sea. "We'll have good weather for the next few days. Maybe an overnight squall, but that's all."

"How's the old man?" Kyle asked.

"Irritable. Still thinks he's the indestructible Special Air Services colonel. The legs give him trouble, but at least he's no longer wheelchair-bound: It's a miracle he even survived that terrorist attack on the castle in Scotland, much less that he is walking again."

"What's that about?" asked Beth, as they entered the central corridor of polished paneled wood that ran the length of the vessel and looked like the entranceway of a five-star hotel. "What terrorist attack?"

Kyle said, "Jeff and Pat were damn near killed when some tangos blew up a reception they were hosting for the signing of a peace treaty between Israel and Saudi Arabia. The Muslim fanatics did not like that idea, so they tried to kill everyone involved."

"Of course! I remember that. Can I stop off at a restroom before we go in? I'm a frump."

Captain Berryman chuckled. "Please be at ease, miss. You look quite exquisite, particularly after such a long journey. Now, here we are." He tapped on a wooden door, opened it, and stepped away.

A slender, middle-aged woman with traces of silver glistening in her blond hair was on the other side and threw herself on Swanson, burying her face in his shoulder and embracing his neck. He picked her up in a bear hug, spun her around, kissed her cheek, and said, "Hey, Mom. Can I stay here tonight?"

She held him at arm's length and stared at him, cocking her head to one side. "Maybe. We'll see." She turned from him. "You must be Miss Ledford. I'm Patricia Cornwell, but I insist that you call me Pat, and I will call you Beth because . . . well, just because I want to. Come in, come in, my dear. We are so very happy that you are here."

Swept up by the woman's charm, Beth was barely able to speak in a normal voice. "Hello," she said. "Please pardon my appearance, Pat. I wasn't expecting this."

Lady Patricia still had the slight figure of a fashion model and wore an elegant pale green blouse-and-slacks outfit that matched her eyes. She linked her arm through Beth's and led her into the salon, where Swanson was locked in another hug with an older man who was leaning on a knobbed wooden cane. The man pounded Kyle heartily on the back.

"Beth, let me introduce you to my grouchy old bear of a husband," Pat said. "Jeff, say hello."

Sir Geoffrey Cornwell turned from Swanson, bowed, and took Beth's hand to give it a light kiss. "Welcome aboard, Petty Officer Ledford. Please consider yourself among friends on the *Vagabond*. You will be safe here, and we can brew up a nice little war."

12

Sergeant Hafiz jogged along in lightweight exercise gear through the tunnels, disguising his inspection as being nothing more than a regular evening workout. His running shoes thumped a steady tempo, and his breathing was easy. During the past few days, the workers, engineers, and technicians had grown used to seeing the big man doing his routine and ignored him as he loped and dodged through the work areas. Some nodded a greeting, but he did not interrupt their work to chat. Hafiz wanted to be regarded as unimportant as he accumulated more knowledge each day, exploring each cavern and cave and tunnel in turn—miles of them, some illuminated only by bare bulbs hanging from a spider's web of overhead wiring, with idle machinery covered with protective plastic lining the walls. Much of it smelled dry and dusty.

Midway through one of the broader tunnels, down several levels from the surface, he slowed to a walk and leaned over, hands on knees, to catch his breath. The hallway was pale yellow and bore a bright red cross

with the word INFIRMARY printed neatly in three languages, including English. He entered a large door that
gave way to an airlock and then to a central chamber
with several small side rooms. The smell changed to
the antiseptic aroma of a functioning medical center,
more like a hospital than an emergency field infirmary.
Current medical needs were served aboveground in a
medical trailer. Men seriously injured on the job site
were transported out to hospitals by helicopter. As far
as Hafiz could determine, this clinic, with its specialized hardware, was ready for its very important role of
serving any medical need of Commander Kahn. All it
needed was an increased staff of doctors and nurses.

As Hafiz walked through the room, his shadow slid
along the smooth walls and tiled floor, all the way to
the far side, where another large door was closed and
locked. Hafiz gave the handle a hard jerk, and there
was no give. Good. *We need to post a guard here.* Beyond that door lay the living chambers, which he had
visited often. The underground suite, complete in every
respect, was served by a private entrance and had a
unique design that provided all the amenities for a
comfortable life: filtered, pure air and controlled air-
conditioning and heating, soundproofed walls, adjustable lighting, expensive furniture, and cushions and
pillows stacked on lush carpets and rugs. A full kitchen
was attached to one side, as were guest rooms for important visitors. A door in an outer wall led to a sheltered stone patio that overlooked the valley.

Down a short hall was a modern studio from
which the Commander could record broadcasts to be

transmitted to the world. There would be audio only, for the Commander never allowed his picture to be taken. Hafiz had been given a demonstration of that facility only yesterday.

He would report his conclusion to General Gul at the ISI headquarters that the place was ready for occupancy, pending final inspections. Hafiz trotted back into the corridors to finish his daily run, mentally composing his account. The strange little chief engineer had done a magnificent job.

That would be another matter to be enclosed in the confidential report: Mohammad al-Attas, the brilliant designer whose delusional personality was putting the project at risk. By the chief engineer's own estimate, construction was more than 80 percent complete, and specialists to man the battle stations were still to be trained elsewhere, so his unique skills were still required.

Things were reaching a critical stage, and Hafiz planned to ask for a full security detail, at least a platoon of regular soldiers, which would allow him to establish patrols, overwatch positions on high ground, put automatic weapons in bunkered positions outside, and patrol the road.

The tales of the evil spirit haunting the valley were balloons of illusion, waiting to burst, and no deterrent at all from a tactical standpoint. Even some foreign civilians had managed to accidentally penetrate the chief engineer's digital battle space with ease before they were captured. The chief engineer had been so enraged by that breach that he had fallen into his ferocious per-

sonality in the room where they were being held prisoner and slaughtered them. The bodies were then quietly
trucked away and dumped elsewhere. Still, the killings
had drawn unwanted attention from the outside world,
almost as if a bright golden arrow were flashing for the
world's intelligence services to follow. The secret was
at risk. Had al-Attas outlived his usefulness? Could
other engineers finish what had been started? For the
moment, Hafiz believed, the strange young man should
be allowed to continue his work.

Several hours later, night swept into the undulating
valley, and pale moonlight painted the trees, rocks,
and water through scudding clouds. Workmen on the
road and in the tunnels toiled on, wary of venturing beyond the edges of the racks of spotlights fixed along the
construction zone. They had heard stories of men who
had gone alone into the darkness and met their deaths
somewhere out there; the Djinn roamed after midnight.

"Post Three reporting." The voice of an ISI sentry
came crisply into the earpiece worn by Sergeant Hafiz.
"He's outside. I saw movement at the base of the western bridge abutment."

"Close on that area," Hafiz ordered. He pulled his
night-vision goggles down over his eyes. Would the
Djinn go afield tonight, or try to pick off a straggling
workman? "Don't let him see you."

"Post Three. Confirming that he exited through the
hatch closest to the river."

"Stay with him, Three," Hafiz said. "We're moving
toward you." With an exact location, the three outposts

could triangulate on the moving figure so that some-body always had him in view. Hafiz scrambled down the slope, his boots sliding on the loose rocks and scree while his hands grabbed branches.

"Post Two reporting. I see him now. He's apparently heading back to the old bridge. I'm too far away to be certain."

Hafiz had been spending time at each outpost every night since he had arrived. Only once during those four nights had he seen Mohammad al-Attas leave his resi-dence to hunt, almost invisible in a loose black robe. That first night, they had watched, but done nothing, as the Djinn crept into a small dwelling at the edge of the workers' camp. He remained there for almost an hour before leaving and making his way back to the hidden entranceway, staggering like a drunk. The following morning, the mutilated body of a murdered woman was found in a blood-soaked hut.

"Post Three here. Sergeant, how close are you?"

"About two hundred meters from your position. Why?"

"My eyes must be playing tricks. It's the Djinn, all right, but he is naked."

"Say again, Three." Hafiz picked up the pace, and the soldier with him matched his stride.

"He is walking around without any clothes. He has a dagger in his right hand and is slashing at the empty air. Wait. He's at the old bridge now and is working out toward the middle."

Sergeant Hafiz stopped. He could see the man standing on a slanted steel beam, totally nude, dancing and spinning. The knife moved fast, and a howl of pain rose from the thing on the bridge, rattling the nerves of the watchers.

"Everybody move in!" Hafiz ordered, breaking into a run when he saw a gush of blood spurt from the arm of the crazed man. "Get in there now! He's cutting himself to ribbons. Take him down."

Mohammad al-Attas's eyelids fluttered as he rose into consciousness. At first, there was stillness all around, cool air, and a terrible taste in his mouth. Then he made out vague figures and felt a gentle hand on his chest. When he tried to move his arm, he could not, and when he tugged harder, panic overtook him. He heard some talking far away, then more people speaking close by. His other arm was also immobile, and his feet refused to obey his mental commands. A doctor peered into his eyes, then adjusted the drip in an IV tube, and a warm sensation of weightlessness consumed al-Attas, dropping him back into unconsciousness.

He came out of it again four hours later while someone was spooning chips of ice into his dry mouth. He groaned and coughed and opened his eyes to find himself in a white room. A slash of pain hit him when he tried to move. The first face he recognized was that of Sergeant Hafiz, standing at the foot of the bed, looking concerned. "What's the matter with me?" al-Attas said in a thick voice. "Why am I here?"

Hafiz smiled. "Ah. You're back. Very good." The

big man came around and pulled a plastic chair close to the side of the bed. "Don't worry. Everything is under control. You must remain still, sir."

A nurse was busy unfastening the straps that had held him immobile. The IV tube remained connected to a small needle that was taped in place on the back of his right hand. He noticed that bandages wrapped his left arm, his chest, his stomach, and his left thigh.

"You had a very close call, my friend," the sergeant said. "An assassin attacked while you were asleep. You somehow woke up enough to fight back, but by the time we reached your room, you were a bloody mess, rolling around on the floor, fighting the attacker. You prevented him from slitting your throat or puncturing your vital organs. Well done, Chief Engineer." Hafiz patted the uninjured arm and smiled. "Maybe I could make a soldier out of you."

"Please, can I have some water? My throat is as dry as the sands." The nurse came with a jug and a glass of ice. She put a straw into his mouth, and he sucked in the chilled liquid. "An assassin? In here?"

"Yes. Of all people, it was your servant, the mute. Obviously he had been put in play by our enemies to spy on your work. Now that you are nearing completion of this magnificent project, his paymasters decided to stop you before you could finish."

"What happened to him?"

"I killed him." Hafiz shrugged. "Piece of filth. The ISI is going through his past history now to determine who he worked for. It looks like the work of the Zionists."

Al-Attas sagged against the pillows. "I cannot believe it. The man was a termite, a nothing, merely someone to clean my living quarters. I hardly ever noticed him. He could not even speak."

Hafiz said, "Exactly. What a clever fellow, eh? Who would ever have suspected him? We will find someone more trustworthy to perform those duties. But that's over, so don't worry about it. Here you are with about a half-dozen good cuts, some of them deep, and the doctors had to spend some time sewing you back together. You lost quite a bit of blood. It was good fortune that you had built this wonderful medical facility, for by doing so, you helped save your own life. Allah was merciful." At a nod from the sergeant, the nurse opened the morphine drip again.

"I am tired." Al-Attas's pain receded into a mild throbbing, and then went away.

"Then sleep, Chief Engineer. All is well now, and you will be back to work in no time."

Sergeant Hafiz sat back in his chair and stared at the bandaged young man. He had changed his mind. *What am I to do with you?*

Undersecretary William Lloyd Curtis of the Department of State's Bureau of American-Islamic Affairs received a copy of Sergeant Hafiz's report to General Gul, which was hand-delivered by a member of the Pakistani Embassy with diplomatic immunity. Curtis dismissed the messenger, so he could read and consider the message in private.

The near-suicide by Mohammad al-Attas did not

exactly come as a surprise, for the man had been known for some time to be somewhat mentally unstable. The peculiarities of his personality were far outweighed by the value of his ideas and his work.

Curtis had known him a long time, since he had personally recruited the young engineer ten years ago, while al-Attas was still a semester short of obtaining his master's degree in electrical engineering at the Massachusetts Institute of Technology. The brilliant student had been not much more than a boy, only nineteen years old, but Curtis believed that al-Attas had an innate talent and could probably build a cathedral from a child's set of plastic LEGO bricks. Further specialized education had followed MIT, with field assignments on major projects in Brazil, Arizona, Germany, and Indonesia. It was in the mosques of the teeming capital of Jakarta that al-Attas's latent Islamic beliefs bloomed into serious study of the Koran.

Curtis had applied gentle pressure to ensure that the youngster embraced the fundamentalist pull of the religion, for it was an opportunity. As if he were the owner of a sports franchise, Curtis traded the rising-star engineer to his good friends at the largest construction company in Saudi Arabia, and when the boy proved to be more comfortable in the Middle Eastern environment, his extraordinary skills continued to improve.

When the international consortium of giant building companies needed a special man to head the secret new project in Pakistan, Curtis had suggested al-Attas for the job, for it dovetailed with his other interests.

Now it appeared that the unique usefulness and

skills of Mohammad al-Attas might be coming to an end. The report from General Gul had been a courtesy alert of possible danger.

The undersecretary did not object, for the engineer knew too much and was a direct link back to Curtis, and that could not be exposed. Although his company was being run by a blind trust during his tenure in public service, Big Bill Curtis still kept a close eye on his empire. His friends trusted him to do that, and not to make mistakes.

Disappointed, Curtis prepared a reply for General Gul. The overall task and protecting Commander Kahn were of far more importance than the life of young al-Attas, or anyone else, and keeping the Curtis name out of the affair was mandatory. The ISI had his approval to do as it thought best.

13

The summer squall came on the starboard quarter, from out of the northeast, just before sunset. Swirling, steady winds increased in strength, and the *Vagabond* altered course slightly to nose into the rising sea. With plenty of depth, and no land nearby, the ship had room to maneuver, and there was no schedule to keep. Solid-state inertial sensors fed digital processors that automatically positioned stabilizing fins to keep the yacht running smoothly at twelve knots with only a minimal roll. Grim clouds moved in and loosed cascades of raindrops that broke hard against the windows before sliding harmlessly away into the scuppers. Beth Ledford was comfortable. "It feels good to be back on the water again," she said.

"How does *Vagabond* stack up against your big Coast Guard cutters in this sort of little blow?" Sir Jeff was beside her, one hand on his cane and the other holding a glass of whisky.

"We would be feeling the change worse than this,

humping along and busting wave after wave. But look at this." The surface of the sweet white chenin blanc in her stemless Reidel crystal glass hardly rippled with the motion of the yacht. "Your ship sails like a dream, Sir Jeff. Our cutters aren't designed for personal comfort, but they can handle anything any sea can throw at them."

"As good as a Navy ship?"

She laughed. "Better. We have much more control of our vessel, with highly trained crews in every compartment, and we are more mission oriented. Innocent lives can be at stake every time we're out. Entirely different animals."

Jeff sipped the amber liquid. "Kyle says you can shoot."

"Yes, sir. I'm a qualified sniper."

"He says you're even better, that you have a special gift for it."

"He never said that to me."

Jeff grinned. "No. He wouldn't, would he? Well, my dear, this weather will clear soon. Tomorrow morning, I'll give you a tour of our armory and you can test some of the experimental weaponry we have aboard, if you wish."

She was charmed by the old man but had to bite back her normal reaction when she felt somebody wanted to test her. He was not patronizing, however, but speaking as one professional to another, and as a host to a guest. "You know, I think that might be fun," she said.

"Excellent," he said. "Now if you'll please help an

old man over to the table, I see that Kyle is done with all of the homecoming greetings and wants to make us work before dinner."

Swanson had spread out computer photographs, overhead satellite imagery, maps, and relevant paper and was standing there staring at them, with his hands on his hips. "I don't know how it happened, Jeff, but someone has been either one step behind us or one step in front ever since we got involved in this thing. That's why we came out here. Whatever we decide must be off the reservation."

"Just what is it that you're planning?" Jeff settled into a soft chair and rested his arms on the table. Adjusting his glasses, he riffled through the papers. "This is forbidding country, Kyle, and that big bridge looks as strong as the mountains around it. Your options are limited. No sane commander would go in there with less than a regiment and a month of planning. Terrain sand tables and such."

"That's why it has to be just me and Coastie. I think that if we go in quick, then we can see whatever there is and get out before anyone knows we're there."

"That's your plan? You're dreaming, lad."

"Which is why I am picking your brain, old man. You must have learned something during all of those years with the SAS."

Sir Jeff placed his fingertip on the bridge location on the map and studied the contours. "At least we should assemble a team of professionals to back you up on the ground, with adequate air cover. It's quite a distance from a safe base."

Kyle shook his head. "I don't like the situation either, but right now, nobody on the ground is expecting us. Whoever is chasing Beth and me does not know where we are. We can use this window of secrecy to our advantage, if we can put something together fast."

"Does General Middleton know what you're up to?"

"Hell, Jeff, I don't even know what I'm up to. All we have is a target zone and a lot of questions. Shouldn't take more than twenty-four hours to scout the valley and find the tunnels. The Lizard told us that security in the area is almost nonexistent. The floods cleared everybody out, and although the water has gone down, not many people have returned. They're still in the refugee camps."

Lady Patricia had been listening. "Why not go into the area disguised as part of a medical team, just as Beth's brother did? One of these briefing papers said the Pakistanis were opening the area for an inspection and were ready to establish a new refugee camp there. Since you both have undergone some medical training in the military, you could be part of it."

Kyle looked up at her. "Possibility. Beth, you have enough training as a medic to get by for a couple of days in a camp? We could be like volunteers, then drop off for a day and go into the valley."

Beth glared at him. "Remember how you insulted my brother for doing humanitarian work? You could wear sheep's clothing, Kyle, and carry the supplies, but you would never fit into a staff of doctors and nurses. Never. As soon as you opened your mouth, your hostile attitude would spill out."

"Hey—"

Sir Jeff interrupted. "She's right. You have too much of an edge about you to blend into their work, Kyle. Some covers work, some don't. What else have we got?"

"Zip. Nada," Kyle said, letting their remarks slide. "No personal identification paper, lack of assets, unfamiliarity with the target area, and no backup."

"Very well, then. As Sherlock Holmes famously advised, one should never overlook the obvious."

Beth asked, "What is obvious about this?"

"Are you jump qualified?" Jeff asked her.

"Yes. I got my silver wings at the Army's Airborne School at Fort Benning."

"Somehow, that is exactly what I expected from you," Cornwell said with a chuckle. "Anything beyond that? HALO?"

"No, sir. I wanted to, but my Coast Guard superiors saw no need for me to qualify for high-altitude, low-opening. Heck, they didn't even want me to go airborne with the basic five jumps, but I took up skydiving as a hobby and learned on my own until I could get my captain's permission. Don't worry. I can handle myself in the air."

"There's no need for a HALO on this one anyway," Kyle said. "It's a well-used air traffic corridor out there, everything from F-16s to cargo birds, even passenger jets. I doubt that anyone even looks up at the sound of a passing plane."

Jeff tossed his glasses on the papers. "So the two of you jump at night. If you don't break your legs or backs, or get captured, you should be able to secure a hide before daybreak, then lay up until you can finish the reconnaissance."

"We jump in at night?" Beth was having difficulty keeping a glow of excitement from her eyes.

"Twenty-four hours maximum," Kyle agreed. "With minimum gear, not a combat load."

"Sounds good," she said.

Jeff rose stiffly to his feet. "By damn, I wish I could go with you. Just to jump out of a sturdy aircraft again would be a perfect tonic for these old bones."

"Well, you cannot." Lady Pat hooked her arm around him and kissed his cheek. "You would splatter yourself in some treetop in the middle of Nowhereistan, and I would have to go to all the trouble of getting your body back and burying you. It would ruin almost an entire week."

"She Who Must Be Obeyed has spoken," Jeff said in a grumpy *Rumpole of the Bailey* stage voice. "Enough of this for now. Dinner beckons."

With authority in hand from General Gul of the ISI, Sergeant Hafiz was free to act to impose order on the chief engineer's chaos.

Everyone was in agreement that Mohammad al-Attas should be allowed to continue his work, but under much stricter control. An experienced ISI psychiatrist arrived at the bridge to assess al-Attas and prescribed a regimen of antipsychotic medication. Al-Attas, recovering from his wounds, participated in the interviews willingly and took the new pills without hesitation. Although his body healed rapidly from the ugly but superficial wounds, his mind was being put on a loose pharmaceutical leash. The psychiatrist promised that the chief engineer would be able to work all day long, without the wild avalanche of ideas that usually accompanied his thoughts. At the evening meal with the doctor and Sergeant Hafiz, he was given what he was told was extra vitamins and a mild narcotic to help him sleep, thanks to this carefully balanced chemical stew. An hour later, the chief engineer would be so tired and woozy that he would be happy to climb into his bed and sleep there like a dead man for the next nine hours. The Djinn had been tamed, but at what cost to the valuable brain of the chief engineer? They would just have to wait and see.

Hafiz was topside when the first truckload of his new temporary security team rolled in. Although a regular army platoon was being readied for extended duty at the bridge and would soon be on the way, for now Hafiz had to make do with Taliban irregulars. General Gul had granted only a half a loaf, but it was better than nothing.

A sweat-stained man with a grizzled beard climbed from the passenger's seat in the cab, wearing the normal soiled and patchwork clothing of a Taliban fighter. He paused to sling an AK-47 over his shoulder, then called out for the men in the back of the truck to get out and line up. Workers shied away from the vehicle, leaving them in the middle of an empty circle. They were a wild-looking crew, all beards and arrogance, wearing long baggy trousers, a hodgepodge of robes and shirts, sloppy turbans, and cartridge belts across their shoulders or around their waists. The men slouched against the truck or sat cross-legged on the ground and started to talk and smoke, ignoring everyone else. Within a few moments, they had established themselves as a nest of snakes, best to be avoided.

The leader approached Hafiz but did not salute or offer to shake hands. *"Allahu Akbar,"* he said. *God is great.*

Hafiz gave a curt nod. If the fellow wanted to be rude, that was fine. Keep it all business. It would not matter in a minute anyway. "How many did you bring?"

The man looked back. "We are nineteen in all. Seven in this truck, plus weapons, and the others will be here before nightfall. All have been in successful actions against the infidels." He removed the automatic rifle from his shoulder and cradled it comfortably in his arms, almost pointing it at Hafiz.

"Are you their leader?"

The man stiffened. How could there be any question of his authority? This sergeant was a stupid man. "Yes. I am Sayyid, and my leaders have ordered me to secure this place. I will now take control. Are you Hafiz . . . Sergeant Hafiz?"

Hafiz looked down at his boots for a moment, studying the ground, the bowed head indicating subservience. Why couldn't this have been easy? Why did these people refuse to cooperate? *"Insh'Allah,"* the sergeant said. *God's will.* He reached behind him and pulled the modified Makarov 9 mm pistol from the belt holster, swung it up, and fired directly at the nose of Sayyid.

The back of the man's head blew off in a crimson curtain of bone, brains, and blood, and Hafiz fired again before the body hit the ground.

He looked over at the Taliban fighters. Suddenly, they were paying attention. Hafiz held up his left hand, palm outward, to signal them to remain still, then planted a boot on each side of their fallen commander's body and methodically emptied the remaining ten shots of the magazine into the corpse. Streaks of crimson glistened on the ground as Sayyid's body bled out. Turning away from the bullet-riddled corpse, Hafiz walked over to the waiting group, clapping a new clip of ammo into his pistol as he moved, his eyes killer cold.

"*Allahu Akbar,* you motherless pieces of dung," he snarled. "You work for me now. Get in line."

The rain had passed over during dinner, and Lady Pat and Beth went for a slow turn around the deck so Pat could smoke one of her little cigars. The doctors insisted that Sir Jeff be in smoke-free environments, and the portable oxygen tank that was always near him made it necessary for her to smoke outside. The women had put on sweaters against the chill. The clouds were breaking up, and moonglow found openings to color the moving water as the *Vagabond* cruised along northeasterly.

"Your brother, Joey, sounds like a dedicated man," Lady Pat said. "I'm sorry things ended so badly. Your mother must be devastated."

Beth looked up but could not see any stars. "It was almost his destiny, his karma, as the Buddhists would say. He preferred to help the helpless in some of the world's worst cesspools instead of making a lot of money and living well anywhere in America. He measured himself against the evil of the world, and that led him into trouble more than once."

"Still, it is a sad thing." Pat exhaled a puff of smoke that was surprisingly fragrant, like flowers. "Now you have been pulled into his world. Are you certain that you want to go on this adventure? I would advise you to leave it to the professionals."

"Pat, I have no choice. Joey saw something in that valley that only I would recognize, and I'm not even sure what it is. Kyle says the job is doable, with minimal risks, and I am a professional, too."

Lady Pat threw back her head and laughed. "Kyle and Jeff would consider fighting a saber-toothed tiger with their bare hands to be a piece of cake. They live for the rush of it all. You're not really like them, Beth. Very few people are, even within the special operations forces. Still, if I have to see you go off on this errand, I prefer that you have Kyle as your partner. He's the best, and he even admits that you're pretty good. That is a very high compliment."

"I work hard at it, Pat. Always trying to break through the glass ceiling, you know? Because I'm petite and pretty, men won't treat me as an equal."

"The eternal story, my dear." They paced on in silence until they reached the stern, then looked back over the churning wake behind them, glowing with green phosphorescence. "You haven't asked the question."

"What question?"

"About Kyle and Jeff and me." Pat smiled. "You must be curious why someone as sophisticated as I, a lady of the realm, would have anything to do with a foul little mongrel like him."

"He gave me a synopsis on the way in, Pat, but it's really none of my business."

Patricia threw the remains of the cigar overboard. "Do you know how hard it is to find a true friend in life? What started as a simple business deal, when Kyle was sent over to advise Jeff on a new weapon, unexpectedly grew into a deeply personal friendship among the three of us. As you said about your brother, maybe it was our karma. No one was trying to make it happen, which is probably the only reason it worked. We did not really need him, and Kyle didn't need anybody. Yet he slowly filled a gaping hole in our lives, and we acted as surrogate parents to him. As the company grew over the years—Jeff turned out to be an even better businessman and financier than he was a soldier—so did our relationship, until we became quite the odd family. Kyle is invaluable to us now, and we love him to death. We always try to lure him away from the Marines, but he refuses. The Pentagon stays happy because it gives the U.S. special access to the Excalibur products, and as you see, we provide the occasional spot of help for some operations."

"Are you telling me that Kyle can choose between being a jarhead gunnery sergeant and living in this sort of luxury, and he stays in uniform?"

"Yes. Someday, he will retire and come into the business as a full partner. In the meantime, he is a member of the board of directors and a vice president. When Jeff and I die, Kyle inherits the company." Lady Patricia looked sideways at Beth. "Did I mention, darling, that he is extremely rich?"

Beth thought in silence for a moment. "I don't care about his money, or his private life," she said. "From the moment we met, he has been an insufferable enigma. We're barely friends, Pat. He can be cold and abrasive and rude one minute, and the next encouraging and understanding. All I want from Kyle Swanson is to get me into that valley in Pakistan and then get me out again."

14

Sergeant Hafiz tried not to overthink the task. The Talibs were unimpressive substitutes for real soldiers. They were courageous if untrained jihadists, but tribal. He divided the remaining eighteen men into three groups of six and assigned each team to be led by one of the ISI regulars who had been watching the Djinn at night. Since the man who was the evil spirit would now be sleeping soundly during the dark hours, those few soldiers could be switched to lead the new irregulars.

One group would be on patrol, and the second in reserve, while the third rested. They would rotate every six hours. Sleep pulled at his eyes, and Hafiz went to the basin and washed his face, forearms, and hands clean of the fine grit that caked into every crease and wrinkle. A final radio check with the new squad leaders told him that all was quiet outside, so he headed for his bunk and a few hours of rest. He had learned long ago that sleep deprivation dulled a leader's abilities. The inspectors from the New Muslim Order were due to arrive tomorrow, and he had to be alert.

Just as Hafiz was drifting off, Mohammad al-Attas snapped awake. He was in his own bed, wearing only boxer shorts and bandages, and the lights were off. He smiled broadly into the darkness and got up, as if pulled by a friendly hand. Fools! Did they really think the Djinn would be an easy prey? He clicked a switch on the wall, and the room filled with such brilliance that he bent double to cover his eyes, moaning with the pain until he could reach out and turn it off again, plunging the room back into restful, familiar darkness.

Why was he so sore? Oh, yes. Ghostly images slashing at him emerged as a real memory; evil creatures with sharp claws and teeth had tried to devour him until he fought them off. Then he remembered the hospital and the drugs, and coming back to life behind the masquerade of being a mere human again, the weak little engineer who was liked and respected by everyone, feared by none. The Djinn could withstand pain; it had a delicious taste that proved he was real, that he was alive. The thick dreams induced by the morphine had been a tumble of terrifying characters that loyally followed him as they scourged the earth with fire and blade. Once he had rested enough to move beyond the grasp of the heavy narcotics, the Djinn pretended to take the pills offered to him in his weak body, then threw them away.

His own laugh comforted him, and he felt for the edges of the cloth and adhesive bandages and tore them away, baring the stitches and the wounds. Where were his clothes? The knives and his scimitar? No matter. Naked and pure, he left the room, sauntered down the empty hallway, and scaled a short ladder that led into a gun pit. The push of a button opened the wide firing slot, and he wiggled through, leaving a trail of blood.

Once outside in the night, he could hear the songs from the stars as he breathed deeply in the rain-cleansed air. Voices called for him to hunt, and to answer them, he squatted on a rock beside the river, cupped his hands around his mouth, and loosed a single, screeching howl.

The sound ricocheted down the still valley to where the Taliban patrol was slowly working along a muddy path. The ISI soldier who had been manning Post Three prior to becoming the shepherd for this herd of stumbling goats had just told them for the fiftieth time to shut up and keep moving when he heard the familiar cry, and he stopped everyone in their tracks. He grabbed the radio on his belt and raised the command post in the tunnel. "Get Sergeant Hafiz for me right away. Tell him the Djinn is loose outside; position unknown."

Lieutenant Colonel Sybelle Summers and Master Gunny O. O. Dawkins of Task Force Trident caught a ride from a special operations base in North Carolina all the way to Afghanistan aboard a Lockheed Martin C-5M cargo hauler. The Galaxy, affectionately called a FRED by its crew—the acronym for Fantastically Ridiculous Economic Disaster—was the most expensive flying machine to operate in the U.S. Air Force.

Thousands of pounds of equipment, from cargo pallets of food and ammunition to helicopters and howitzers, were buckled down in the cavernous lower-deck cargo bay. Five dozen troops rode in the rear upper-deck troop compartment, with seats to spare. Sybelle and Double-Oh occupied positions on the forward flight deck that was reserved for dignitaries.

The flight had been a long, droning, boring crossing of the Atlantic that required alternating flight crews, and twice they made the slow rendezvous with refueling tankers and then roared on. The dull whine of the four new General Electric engines was quieter on this updated model of the Galaxy, but it was always there, burrowing into the eardrums.

Sybelle played her tunes, tried to nap beneath a light blanket, or immersed herself in an almost indecipherable textbook on international economic theory that was part of her program with the Lejeune Leadership Institute. As she studied some arcane charts, she wished she were down in the dirt, chasing bad guys, but to punch another notch on the career belt, the warrior had to rest while the student finished her master's degree. The constant droning in her ears was maddening. How could people really sleep on any airplane?

Across the aisle, Double-Oh snored. He was a Marine, by God, and slept when he was told to, anywhere, anytime. In his pocket was a little black notebook in which he had been jotting reminders about the best way to throw Kyle and the little Coastie out of an airplane over Pakistan in about twenty-four hours. Getting them to the target area would be the jobs of the pilot and copilot of the small jet, but as jumpmaster, it would be *his* plane, and he would personally handle everything else. Swanson and Ledford would face enough risks on the ground without having to worry about just getting out of the damned plane OK. Nothing would be left to chance.

Upon entering Afghan airspace, the Galaxy crew activated the Pacer Snow onboard defense system of flare dispensers and the antimissile warning system. Everyone straightened up, scratching and yawning, as the giant aircraft began its descent, then settled easily onto the runway at Kandahar and was guided to its parking ramp. Unloading began immediately after the clamshell doors spread open in the back, and the nose of the plane swung up and out of the way. The two Trident Marines walked down the rear ramp into the night chill and found a Humvee waiting to take them into the heavily guarded special operations section of the base.

Once in the building, Summers dialed a secure private number on her sat phone to give a coded confirmation of their arrival to the Lizard in Washington. Only code names were used. "Queen and Knight are in place."

"Roger that, Queen," replied Commander Freedman. "Shaky and Coastie arrive your location approximate twelve hundred."

"Queen, out."

She terminated the call. No names had been used, even on one of the most secure frequencies available. "Shaky" was an old nickname of Swanson's that referred to his unusual habit of physically quaking after a particularly hard and heated battle, his way of releasing the self-imposed total lack of emotion during the fight. "Coastie" now applied to Beth Ledford.

"They are on their way and will be here by midday tomorrow," Sybelle told Dawkins.

Double-Oh grunted approval. That gave them the rest of the night and all of the next day to prepare for the drop. "Let's get some chow, then catch a few hours of sleep. I'm bushed."

"How? Why? You didn't do anything for the last twelve hours but sleep. You're getting old, Master Gunny," Summers said. "I was thinking more about going for a run. Stretch out the kinks."

"You do what you gotta do, Ms. Lieutenant Colonel, ma'am. Act like some fool *hoo-ah* butter-bar second lieutenant if you want to. I, however, am wise beyond your tender years and am no longer tempted by such foolish things. I'll meet you at our little plane at oh six hundred, well fed and fresh as a daisy." He walked away.

The Djinn growled contentedly, feeling strong and happy out in the air. He heard distant shouts and saw pinpoints of light flashing in the valley coming his way. Kneeling, he slathered mud over his naked body, from the top of his head to his toes, and the camouflage allowed him to slowly disappear into the blackness. Then he ran away, into the trees.

The valley seemed to be coming to life, with yells and brilliant cones of flashlight beams slashing the darkness, and he giggled as he circled onto the higher, rocky ground. The patrol went by below him. They were shouting and disorganized, strung out along the path and losing sight of each other, panting with effort. He descended behind them and followed unseen, picking up a short, thick tree branch for a weapon.

The last man in the Taliban column was fatter than the others and labored on the slippery slope, panting and falling farther behind until at last he gave up and slowed to a walk. As the patrol moved on, he called out that he had hurt his ankle and would catch up to them later. He sat on a smooth boulder to catch his breath, laid the AK-47 to the side, and lit a cigarette, drawing the harsh smoke into his lungs and exhaling with pleasure.

The Djinn was a few feet behind him, hidden in some brush and studying his target. The creature he was stalking was totally relaxed, immobile, and unaware. Rising in the shadows, the Djinn took two steps forward and swung the club as hard as he could. It slammed against the fighter's ear so hard that it carried him off the big rock, and the Djinn leaped onto the dazed man and beat him to death. *This is good.* He stripped the victim. Warm clothing and a good weapon, and even some food in a pocket, with water in a metal container. Best of all, a dagger with a broad, curved blade in an elaborately decorated scabbard that hung from the ammunition belt around the blubbery waist alongside two hand grenades. He dressed, slipped on the sandals, and wiggled his toes. Much better. The rifle was undamaged, the knife sharp. *Now I can really hunt. Where?* More lights were pock-marking the valley, coming down from the crest and spreading out. He cut the throat of the corpse for good measure, then headed up toward the lights.

The patrol leader had finally stopped and counted his men, finding only five instead of the six. "Who is missing?" he asked.

The Taliban looked at each other, and one finally spoke. "It is Akhtar again. He can never keep up on a climb. Too old and fat."

"Then you go back and get him. We will wait for two minutes. When you come back, you had better have the fat fool with you."

While the other four Taliban fighters plopped down by the side of the path to rest, the one picked to fetch Akhtar stared hard back at the patrol leader, his insides burning with hatred at being told what to do by a worthless Pakistani. He finally obeyed, cursing beneath his breath.

He walked back down the trail for thirty seconds before he saw the shadowy shape coming toward him, the eyes cast down to watch his footing. "By your mother, Akhtar, you are a useless dog! Come on. The rest of the patrol is waiting for us." He turned on his heel and started back.

The Djinn slammed the stock of the AK-47 into the man's head and heard a satisfying crunch. He fell on top of the stunned man, with the dagger already out and plunging into the neck, and he was rewarded with a shower of thick arterial blood as he sawed off the head. He picked it up by the ears and smiled at the dead face, then tossed it away, watching it bounce down toward the river. He wiped the knife clean on his own tunic, slid it back in the scabbard, and snapped off the rifle's safety.

He came upon the others gathered beside the dirt pathway, and he ran at them, screaming and pulling the trigger, spraying out bursts of automatic gunfire. The surprised fighters attempted to roll away as the maniacal figure went charging through their midst without breaking stride, and they did not notice the bouncing grenade he left behind until it exploded.

The patrol leader got off some rounds that hit nothing, then grabbed his radio, just as Sergeant Hafiz came on to demand a status report. "He just came out of nowhere and went straight through us, Sergeant. We have unknown casualties. I'm leaving these people and going after him myself. It makes no sense, but he was headed your way, right into our strength."

"Very well," Hafiz responded. "We will clean up the guard detail after we catch him. Fire your weapon into the air, and drive him toward us."

The Djinn heard the gunshots and saw the lights and stopped to drink some water from his canteen. Then he emptied the remaining liquid over his head to clear his eyes. A sudden weariness struck him like a wave, along with dizziness and nausea, and he leaned over to vomit. He brushed his hand across his sour mouth, his thoughts tumbling about, his muscles aching from so much unaccustomed exercise and running. He needed to rest for a time. Not long. Then he would resume. There was excellent hunting tonight. He put down the rifle, the ammunition packets, and the remaining grenade and staggered away, singing a little song from childhood.

The faint voice of his mother spoke in his head, telling him that safety was not far away: a door into the ground, his entrance to the underworld. It took five struggling minutes for him to reach it, and fatigue had an iron grasp on his legs as he dragged along. He pulled the hidden door open, then closed it carefully behind him.

A cavern gaped before him, and a map appeared in his mind in flashes of memory. Safety lay down one corridor, up one level, and around two corners. The passages were empty as he plodded through, leaving a track of muddy footsteps and, where he brushed against the walls, dark bloodstains. A doorway that he recognized appeared, and he pushed it open, almost ready to fall. The bed was so far away, across miles of floor, but was so welcoming that he managed to stagger to it; then he lay down and closed his eyes, exhaled twice, and was asleep.

15

Kyle and Sir Jeff stayed up most of the night as the *Vagabond* worked its way through the sea. Neither was happy, because the target in Pakistan presented more questions than answers. The bridge stood there like a monolith, silent and brooding, and the mission to check it out was unlikely to resolve all of the riddles.

"There has to be something else in play, Kyle," Jeff said. "There obviously is some connection between the structure and the multiple attempts on the lives of you and Beth. I like her, by the way. Do you?"

"I'm not taking her out on a date, Jeff. In answer to your point—the damned bridge—from what I can tell, it is just another pile of rocks and steel. We suspect there is a network of tunnels under it, but so what? Could be just for supplies and stuff." Kyle had his shoes off, and his feet were propped on a low table.

Jeff shook his head. "That cannot possibly be the reason. If so, the medical team would just have been detained, maybe roughed up a bit, and turned over to the authorities. Instead, they were butchered. There remains some unknown linkage between all of that unpleasantness and a dangerous leak somewhere in Washington, someone who can summon professional killers."

Kyle puffed out his cheeks, thinking. "Still have to go look at the place, so Beth can see whatever it was her brother saw."

"So why don't you ask her for a date? The recon mission will be over in two days. You can celebrate with a nice private dinner somewhere."

"Like the Kandahar mess hall?" Swanson laughed. "No, Jeff. I tell you, though, that I have been impressed with her ability. She's got a future in this game. Just needs some more training. Any relationship between us is going to stay professional."

"Quite right. Your track record with women is abysmal. They fall into your hands, and you let them slip through your fingers like gold dust."

"Bad things seem to happen to women I like," he said. "Better to keep them at arm's length."

Jeff flipped the cover of his laptop computer and logged in to check his private mail. Pat and Jeff had known all of the serious women in Kyle's life, and some sad times had indeed shadowed them, including some who had been killed or maimed by terrorists. What woman in her right mind would want to enter such a zone of danger? This little one, though, Beth, might prove to be the exception: She seemed to thrive on danger. "Confirmation here on the plane that will fly you from the Azores straight to Kandahar. All squared away."

"Amazing what money and contacts can do, isn't it?"

"Not really." Jeff gave a low laugh. "That combination pretty much works every time."

"Have you come across anything really unusual about the bridge, Jeff? Your people find anything?"

Jeff opened a file. "Not really. The engineering is quite sophisticated, and it is a sturdy bloody thing. That was shown when the floods hit. Although the power of that much water was an immense force, the bridge was still standing after the waters went down. Needed a bit of repair on the exterior, but the anchoring held, and the span itself survived untouched. Some fine work, that."

Kyle drank some juice while he thought about it. Dams burst, thousands of people were dislocated, entire villages were swallowed, and this structure had held its own. Maybe they were using it to try out better building techniques so that thousands of Pakistanis would not die every time there was some natural disaster. "Who built it?"

"There we have a bit of a problem. This has been a hugely expensive and technical operation, millions of dollars, with an international consortium involved. With front companies and subcontractors and the foreign banks, it has created a financial thicket that is hard to penetrate. Haven't figured out yet where it started, or where it leads."

"Well, it must go somewhere. Have them stay on the money. I have a feeling that it may be important." Kyle looked at the clock on the bulkhead of polished wood. Time to leave. The helicopter on the fantail was warming up, and Coastie was out there with the deck crew, talking about helicopter things. "We'll take the first step and see what happens."

As Sir Jeff started to get up, a leg muscle tightened in spasm and a flash of pain was painted on his face. He sat back down. "Go on, Kyle. I'll see you when you get back. Take care of that girl."

Where are they? Undersecretary Curtis rolled the thick glass in his hand, and good Scotch whisky swirled with the ice cubes. Beth Ledford and her Marine sidekick had disappeared so thoroughly that nothing was showing up in the databases. The need to find and dispose of both of them had increased, because they were not giving up. Maybe they were just hunkered down in some safe house on the outskirts of Billings or Tampa, waiting for the storm to clear. Curtis could not afford such a wait. He drank deeply, walked to the standing bar, refilled his glass, and resumed pacing the living room, half-watching a television documentary about the space vessel *America,* the first ship of a series that would eventually land astronauts on Mars. He paid little attention, for he already knew the rocket would never reach orbit; it would travel more than a hundred thousand feet straight up, then *boom,* and another space catastrophe would invade the placid worlds of television watchers.

Curtis still burned about being lectured by the director of the Diplomatic Security Service, who had snapped and threatened consequences if Curtis ever again attempted to use the DSS for his own purposes. Curtis had kept calm during the tirade, although his stomach had churned. Prison? Abuse of power? The man carried a pistol in a shoulder holster and made certain that Curtis had seen it.

Bill Curtis had carefully explained that he had acted fully within the law, as stated in the Patriot Act, and in his official capacity. Any citizen could be investigated on a whiff of suspicion of terrorist activity. No proof was needed. Beth Ledford had been acting very suspiciously, even disobeying direct orders in a politically charged situation that fell within the interests of the Bureau of American-Islamic Affairs. Her interference could further impede the already weak diplomatic relations with Pakistan.

That grain of truth had saved him, along with a contrite admission that he had overstepped his authority by ordering the full surveillance of the Coast Guard woman. Curtis promised never to do so again. The DSS man had not wanted the involvement of his own office exposed any further and chose to drop the matter. The book was closed with the security service, and Curtis would not reopen it. It was well that the man had not known the other half of the story.

He had arranged for the DSS only to track Ledford around the Washington area. For the direct attacks on Swanson and at Quantico, Curtis had turned to his contacts within a renegade element of the private security community, but the mercenaries had failed, and two of them had been killed. After that, the private firm was no longer interested in the job, no matter what the pay.

Curtis drank the sharp whisky and felt the burn go down into his stomach. *So am I alone in this now? No.*

*I have powerful friends all over the Middle East, many
more than the U.S. government knew, and those friends
have friends in the United States.* Some would be more
than willing to help track down this loose end. Unsaid
was that Curtis, as the head of the BAIA, had granted
favors before, and would do so again. No. All was not
lost. This was just a temporary setback, and he would
never be alone.

He emptied the glass, washed it in the sink, and set
it on a towel to dry.

Curtis climbed into bed, turned out the light, and
again weighed the entwined issues carefully: revenge
against the possible charge of treason, and protecting
the most wanted man in the world.

Before turning off the light, he picked up a framed
colored photograph from his nightstand and set it up on
a pillow beside him, as if the paper images could look
back at him, maybe even talk. It showed a beautiful,
young Iraqi woman with flowing ebony hair and penetrating eyes, clad in ski clothes and seated in a comfortable chair beside a roaring fire in a lodge in Aspen,
Colorado. At her feet was a grinning boy who had inherited his mother's good looks. He was missing a tooth.
Bill Curtis had taken the photograph while the family
was celebrating the child's fifth birthday. He drifted off
to sleep with the picture still propped up beside him.

Curtis had met Raneen at a garden party in Baghdad
in the old days, when he was running an oil exploration
operation for the Iraqi government and spent a lot of
time there. Life had been quiet and enjoyable in the
big polyglot city during those times, because Saddam

Hussein kept religious extremists on a tight leash. Raneen was the daughter of one of the dictator's reluctant generals, a professional soldier, and it took Curtis months of careful maneuvering to win the family over enough that he could marry his dark-eyed beauty. A year later, they had a child, a boy, and they named him Cane. Life was golden, and stayed that way until 1990, when that fool Hussein decided to invade Kuwait.

Curtis was in Taiwan on business, and his family was visiting the grandparents in Baghdad. They were caught on opposite sides of a sudden and vicious war, and for the first time, Raneen and Cane were beyond his reach. When American bombs struck Baghdad, one landed squarely on the general's home, killing the entire family, including both Raneen and their son. The picture on the pillow was all that was left, and Bill Curtis cherished it.

THE BRIDGE

The search of the wide valley below the bridge did not find the madman who had single-handedly wiped out the entire patrol of Taliban fighters, leaving four men dead and two more wounded. Only the ISI soldier who led the group had escaped the attack unharmed.

Sergeant Hafiz had taken command and organized the hunt all the way down to the fallen steel bridge, clearing it grid square by grid square on his map, but found nothing. He was disgusted with the Taliban. Not only were they poor soldiers, but after learning what happened to their comrades, some of the others were spreading a story of how an evil monster that dwelled in the darkness was chasing them. Hafiz would never be able to trust them. Real troops were needed to secure the area so he could send these mountain men back to their rocky wastelands. He sent out a replacement patrol but desperately wanted regulars here, now.

As dawn approached, a cleaning worker found Chief Engineer Mohammad al-Attas sound asleep in the bed of his underground apartment, still wearing the bloodstained clothes from his night of rampage. Sergeant Hafiz brought in three other large men and slapped al-Attas hard across the face, snapping his head to one side. The engineer awoke to a streak of pain, a scream ripping from his throat as he was snatched from the bed and roughly carried back to the infirmary, where he was lashed again to the metal rails of a bed with thick restraints.

"What are you doing to me? What is happening?" he yelled. The men left the medical center, and Hafiz appeared. "Sergeant . . . What is going on? Why am I being treated like this?"

Hafiz brought a chair forward and sat beside him, quietly studying him as if trying to see who was really inside the shell of flesh and bone. The face and other exposed areas were all covered in dried mud, which stuck in clumps between the toes and proved he was the Djinn. The eyes, however, were startlingly clear and free of guile, indicating that he was also the engineer. The split between the two personalities was sharp and complete. "Who are you?" the sergeant asked in a conversational tone.

"You know very well: Chief Engineer Mohammad al-Attas. Let me go. I demand that you set me free and explain yourself."

"I'm afraid that is not possible right now. Where were you last night? What did you do?"

Al-Attas struggled against the restraints, which squeaked with the strain but held him firmly in place. "I was asleep, you fool. That is why I was in bed when your men assaulted me."

A long period of silence stretched between them before Hafiz said, "You really don't know, do you? Look down at your clothes, Chief Engineer. Tell me where all of that blood came from."

Al-Attas managed to lift his head to stare down at his chest and legs. Huge caked splotches of maroon covered the long shirt, which was filthy. He could feel the stiffness of the dried blood on his skin. "What has happened? Was I in some kind of accident? I remember nothing like that. Am I going to be all right?"

Hafiz had heard enough; he pushed back the chair and stood up, crossing his arms. "I doubt it." He pushed a button on an electrical cord, and a doctor came to the bed. "Give him a sedative to calm him, and keep him hydrated. I don't want him completely unconscious, because I have more questions. Others will need to see him. Tend to this personally, Doctor. Then have him cleaned up and lock him back down tight."

"Yes. I understand," said the doctor, a small man with a well-trimmed beard. "Please leave a guard in the room with us."

"Of course."

"Why are you doing this? Why have I been taken prisoner?" The face of the man on the bed was twisted in confusion, and tears tracked down the sides of his face. He was sobbing like a baby, his body shaking in growing despair.

The doctor busied himself at a cabinet, tearing open a plastic bag to prepare a sterile syringe.

Sergeant Hafiz had moved to the foot of the bed. "I know you cannot understand this, Chief Engineer, but the reason that you are being restrained and kept under guard is very simple—you are one of the most dangerous men I have ever met. You are a ruthless and merciless and ingenious killer. Now go back to sleep while I decide what to do with you."

"No!" The shout was hard and came from deep within. "No! I am the chief engineer! I am in charge here!"

"Not any longer, my friend. Now you're just one more piece of paperwork for me." He grabbed al-Attas by the left arm and held it steady while the doctor swabbed the skin clean with alcohol, found a vein, and worked the needle in. Within a few seconds, the heart distributed the strong liquid throughout the body, and al-Attas's eyelids fluttered, then closed as the body went limp.

"I'll send in the guard," Hafiz said and left, looking at his wristwatch on the way through the door. Time was short, and he had work to do.

Al-Attas was not only a fiend but had been a well-protected one during the long months while the bridge and the complex of tunnels were constructed. Hafiz would not summarily dispose of him without first getting permission from General Gul of the ISI, a routing of messages that would take hours. Eventually, the result would be the same, a bullet in the head, but Hafiz wanted the execution order in writing before he murdered this peculiar genius. Otherwise, his own head might also be on a pike.

Even with all of that in progress, the advance team from the camp of Commander Kahn would be arriving within a few hours to inspect the facility, and Hafiz would provide the full tour. He understood that the inspectors would question the presence and condition of al-Attas in the infirmary. It would be best to simply tell the truth, including that the death warrant was in progress. The man had been crazy long before Hafiz ever arrived at the bridge. It wasn't the sergeant's fault. Better to prove that the lunatic was in custody by simply showing him off like an exhibit and letting the inspectors confirm his actions. The man was weak, tied down, drugged, and harmless.

Hafiz anticipated a pressure-filled few days of face-to-face meetings but was confident that the inspectors would approve the overall project. He would report that all of the important work was on schedule. The Commander could transfer to his new home before the first snows fell and closed the high passes.

16

"Time to gear up, boys and girls." Master Gunny Double-Oh Dawkins was at a long table in a large hangar in the special ops area of Kandahar, and his deep voice echoed in the emptiness. The table was strewn with equipment, each piece neatly arranged in its own space after he had double-checked every item. "Let's get this show on the road."

Sybelle Summers grinned at the boyish enthusiasm of the big man, who would have preferred to be heading into action himself rather than consigned to the supporting role as jumpmaster. She took over the briefing. "Less than a dozen people know what's happening tonight, and six of us are standing here. Because of the leaks back in the States, everything has been kept mission specific and names have not been used. There's nothing in the system. So, let me introduce the two gentlemen who will be doing the flying for us. We will just refer to them by their family names, Major and Captain."

Both of the slender men nodded. They wore standard olive green flight suits, with no identification patches. "Sir Jeff, who is bankrolling this little adventure, helped keep things outside of the U.S. information chain by getting us that slick ride over there, and its pilot team. These guys are from 47 Squadron, the special ops flight of the Royal Air Force. Each is a former fighter pilot who now specializes in flying low, fast or slow, and at night. Questions?"

Kyle acknowledged the fliers. "Good by me. Nobody flies for 47 Squadron by accident." When there were no further questions, the pilots left the little group and went to the plane to start the preflight checks.

"Neither of them knows details of the mission. Only that they are to fly to exact coordinates and slow down enough for you to jump, then return to Kandahar, take on fuel, and go right back to their RAF base in Lyneham, England. Enough about that." Summers kicked the explanations back to Double-Oh.

"For the jump, I decided to go with equipment that Coastie is familiar with," he said.

"Coastie?" Beth arched an eyebrow. "That's my code name?"

"No. It's what we called you behind your back when we didn't know you. Now we say it to your face, because we like you. You got a problem with that?"

"No. I guess you have to call me something, and Marines are not big on creativity. Coastie it is."

"Anyway, instead of the new T-11, we will use the older T-10 chute that she learned on. Straight rig, parabolic canopy, and a twenty-foot static line."

"I've done the T-11," she said. "I could handle it. A jump is a jump."

"I didn't ask for your opinion, Coastie." Dawkins glared at her. "Remember, I'm the jumpmaster. You just listen."

"Touchy, aren't we?"

"Damn. Anyway, you'll thank me later because the T-11 would require a couple of more seconds of free fall, and you won't have much airspace to begin with. It would be helpful if you did not hit the ground before your parachute opened."

"I'm light as a feather. You would fall faster than me, you big lump." She knew that she almost had him grinding his teeth.

Summers broke in. "Quit teasing, Coastie. Get serious and listen."

"Now. Weapons and gear. Although you're both snipers, there is no need for a long rifle on this little job. So you each will have a sidearm and a CAR-15 with retractable butt stock and two hundred and ten rounds of ammo. Kyle's has an M-203 grenade launcher, with a vest of seven high-explosive-dual purpose rounds. A few hand grenades, sat phones, some extra ammo, three days of MREs, video and still cameras, binos, maps, GPS, compass, protractors. Not a combat load, but you are not there for a gunfight. Questions? Nothing?"

Sybelle handed them plastic-covered maps. "You go in at zero-one, with this plateau at the end of the valley as your drop zone. Then you will be on the ground for twenty-four hours. Patrol up the valley and find a hide before dawn." She pointed to a red circle on the map, then handed over a photograph of a field that seemed relatively flat. "See what you can see during the day, then finish up at dark and make your way to this landing zone. We'll pick you up there at exactly oh one hundred. Two alternate LZs are marked. Got it?"

"How old is that download?" Kyle asked.

"About five hours," Sybelle answered. "Our boy the Lizard back in Washington will be laying all kinds of havoc on the electromagnetic fields in the area, and he's already throwing spoofs and flyovers throughout the region to draw attention away from the bridge. They may be defending, but they will not be expecting you, and even if they were, they probably would not be able to see your plane. You two just focus on the mission. Leave the rest to us."

Beth Ledford realized that all three of the Marines were looking at her, as if she were going to break under the building pressure of going into a dangerous clandestine mission. She took a step to the table and picked up her pack, then pulled a Snickers candy bar from a jacket pocket and stuffed it in among the bullets. "Emergency chocolate ration," she said. "Now I'm ready. Let's go."

The three Pratt & Whitney Canada PW307A engines kicked the Dassault Falcon 7X off of the apron and into the night sky without a strain, although with enough power to push the three passengers against their seats. The plane seemed to climb almost straight up to thirty thousand feet before leveling off and settling into a gentle cruising speed of five hundred miles per hour. Up front in the cockpit, Major and Captain constantly monitored the Honeywell Primus EPIC avionics suite, but the fly-by-wire aircraft was basically running on its own.

Cousins of the smooth Falcon tri-jet were plying the skies over peaceful countries as fifty-million-dollar luxury long-range business jets, but this one had been converted for special operations, and creature comfort was low on the list of priorities. The six-foot-two cabin ceiling prevented Double-Oh from standing erect. He had to hunch over.

The ride to the target area seemed short to Beth, but then Double-Oh was shaking her shoulder. She had been asleep. He looked at her curiously, then tapped his round black bubble helmet. "Get ready, Coastie," he said.

Swanson was already on his feet, rocking comfortably with the motion of the plane, his face hidden behind the clear plastic mask. A one-pound bottle of oxygen was beneath the right arm of his olive coveralls, with a hose feeding the cool air into the closed jump helmet. The parachute pack was on his back, a day pack around his waist, and the weapons were in a drop bag between his legs.

Looks like he's done this before, thought Beth as she struggled with her own bulky equipment, sucking in the clean oxygen and huffing it out again. The plane was tilted, coming down to seven thousand feet and shaving off speed.

Double-Oh listened to a verbal radio message from the cockpit and held up a palm toward them, all fingers extended. Five minutes.

Beth waddled into place behind Kyle, using her hands to adjust the shoulder straps. She leaned around him to see Double-Oh squatting beside the door, motioning to his face to make certain they were on oxygen as the cabin depressurized. Two fingers were held up. Two minutes.

Normally, the hatch on the Dassault would fold outward and become a stairway. With the modifications, it would come inside. Double-Oh, secured by a safety harness, unlocked it, grabbed the rails with his beefy hands, and pulled it free, then stashed it behind him. He held up one finger. One minute. Both responded with a thumbs-up.

They shuffled closer and hooked their twenty-foot-long static lines to a special ring welded above the hatch. Kyle stood in the open doorway, grabbed each side, and stared down at Double-Oh, who was listening to the reports from the cockpit and held up three fingers: thirty seconds.

Beth looked past Kyle and saw nothing, just blackness beyond the door. The wind tugged at her coveralls and helmet, and the deck seemed to dance beneath her feet as the plane slowed almost to stall speed. She gulped.

Double-Oh had made a fist and pumped it ten times to signal the final seconds. On the last movement he thrust it toward Kyle, and Swanson was out the door. Beth immediately moved forward, saw the big fist thrust out toward her, and dove into the night of howling wind and nothingness.

Swanson steadied up quickly and worked the risers of his parachute so he could look around. He could not see Coastie, who should be floating above and off to his right, and he didn't bother looking for the airplane, which was already out of sight, gaining speed and altitude. It was good to work in the dark, because if he could not see much, neither could anyone who might happen to be looking up. Silence meant safety.

Ribbons of light marked the far end of the valley where the bridge work was under way, and a cluster of illumination showed the location of the village to the northeast. Those were his two biggest markers and were right where they should be. He mentally estimated the vector. There was little wind to shove him off course, so he should be near the unseen drop zone. Down he came, starting to feel the pull of the ground as a little bit of moonlight coming through the low clouds reflected dully off the water, as if bouncing back from a dirty mirror. He adjusted his descent angle, and the flat plateau came up fast. Swanson bent his knees slightly and hit standing up, with a near-perfect parachute landing fall.

Working to release the harness as the canopy collapsed softly on the ground, he looked over in time to see Coastie come to earth about a hundred meters away, hitting hard and doing a rough roll. *Welcome to our world.*

She must have been tracking him all the way, watching the top of his chute and steering to his position, and had done a good job for someone with her skill set. She continued to impress him, although he would never tell her that, for while standing in the doorway of the plane, he had wondered whether she would jump or choke and rated the odds at fifty-fifty. Now here she was, already scrambling to her feet.

He rolled up his chute and went to her. Last thing he wanted was for her to break an ankle on landing. "You hurt?"

"Just my ego," she said quietly, reeling her own canopy together into a tight ball of silk. "That was a rush, dude." She took off the jump helmet and oxygen mask, shook out her hair, and put on a soft, black wool beanie.

When they had their weapons out, chutes off, and packs on, Kyle said, "Follow me, and stay quiet." He headed uphill, into the moonscape left behind by the receding floodwaters, a treacherous jungle of rough terrain and jumbles of debris, downed trees, and boulders that had been brought downriver. The area had dried well, but a swampy pit of sticky mud thick as molasses was just below the surface.

A ten-foot piece of rough concrete slag was mostly buried in the muck, with a low hole created beneath the tilted side where the water had washed around it. Kyle dumped his parachute and helmet into the depression, and Beth added hers as he set a demolition charge that would explode in thirty-six hours to erase that evidence of their landing. They stacked stones to cover the hole, then headed higher up the hillside, neither slow nor fast, blending with the shadows, disappearing.

In the control room at the bridge, two red dots began to blink on a map of the valley, displayed on a flat-screen monitor, where motion sensors had detected movement on the wide southeastern end of the funnel-shaped terrain. The computer slaved to the map automatically registered the coordinates of the intruders and marched the positions across the bottom of the screen. The round cover of a pipe set vertically into the ground popped open, and the long-range video camera nearest to the target automatically hissed up from its nest and swung toward the correct azimuth. Two figures were portrayed on a portion of the screen in the control room, heat signatures of glowing green, yellow, and red blobs. A narrow rectangular lid hidden in the hillside slowly opened, and the barrel of a machine gun nosed out, gyros guiding it to face the threat.

The overhead lights were off in the control room, but tiny lights shone on the servers and computers to confirm they were receiving power. The place was empty of humans, off-limits until another qualified chief engineer could take over. No one was seated at the console to monitor movement in the field. This electronics wonderworld was the lair of the Djinn, who was again lashed down in the infirmary, and he had trained no deputies to sit in his chair, so his lethal hardware sat forgotten and useless for the time being. It was stiflingly warm, and the hum of the cooling fans was the only noise, other than a low but insistent *beep-beep-beep* coming from one control panel.

The door was closed and locked.

Twenty minutes since they had jumped at one o'clock. Good time. No hitches. Kyle checked to be sure Coastie was right behind him, and she was on his heels, step for step, as if on an invisible leash. Dark shapes were all around, and it looked more like a junkyard than a lush forest after a flood. Trees had been torn out by their roots, limbs chipped into sharp splinters, gullies and hillocks gouged by the force of water and boulders that scoured the floor of the floodplain. It reeked of damp and rot, but the area was strangely dry since the sun had baked the mudflats left behind by the river's rampage.

He found a hide beneath a large tree that had been partially uprooted and slanted to one side at about a thirty-degree angle. Ropes of big roots thick with dried mud hung from it like a heavy curtain, and brush had caught against it as the water passed. Kyle stuck his head inside and turned on his flashlight for two seconds, shielding the light with his hand. About six feet wide and five feet long, low overhead. Invisible from outside. Safe. He wiggled in. "Come on in, Coastie. We're home."

17

Swanson settled onto his belly and pawed between the roots to clear a line of sight. Coastie was another set of eyes and was responsible for watching their six, the way they had come in, to be sure no one was following. While rear security was necessary, the real unknowns lay ahead, in the places he had not yet seen. He did not even need his night-vision gear to see the fire below. It flared brightly in the darkness about a thousand meters down from their hide. "Check this out," he said, rolling away so Ledford could look through the opening. "There's your little bridge, Coastie, and what looks like an enemy patrol is camped at the high end."

Ledford scrunched closer. "I can't see much from up here. My brother was down a lot lower when he took that picture. Down by the riverbank."

"Yeah. What do you make of that campsite?"

"I see what looks like some guys sleeping near the little fire. One of them is standing, drinking from a cup, and looking around. Weapons on the ground. "

"Right. So two questions: Why are they out here at

all? And why aren't they patrolling instead of catching z's?" Kyle had his binos focused. "They're just hanging out there like a bunch of clowns."

"Isn't that good?" she asked. "Since they aren't looking for us, our insertion wasn't compromised."

Swanson slowly examined the entire area. Something about it seemed wrong, like a framed picture hanging at an angle. "Nobody is moving anywhere down there. Kind of weird. They should be roaming around, but the campsite is as far out as they go."

"So do you think it would be OK for us to go down closer? Get a better angle?"

Swanson did not reply. He moved his glasses up to scan the larger, newer bridge two thousand meters away. That canopy of bright work lights gave it the look of a carnival, and he could see workmen and vehicles moving about. Sheets of dust blew in the night wind, and the rumble of heavy equipment could be heard in the distance. Seeing it from the ground was totally different than viewing it from an overhead satellite picture. It rose like an old-fashioned castle of stone, dominating the upper end of the valley. "That's a big damned bridge," he said.

"So let's go look around. We have tons of time. Go check it out and be back up here before dawn."

"Take it easy, Coastie. We have to be very careful, or else we can stumble into an ambush or a mine field. This ain't no walk in the park. Overconfidence can get you killed. We will go soon, but we move quietly and slowly."

Ledford chewed on her lower lip. She knew she was

anxious, while Swanson had done this kind of thing before. "I know that," she said.

"Then shut the hell up," Swanson told her. "We go when I'm ready." He looked at his wristwatch. Less than an hour ago, they had still been in the plane, and now she wanted to sprint down into bad-guy country. Rookie nerves. He went back to combing the area with his night-vision binos, checking the map and making notes with a ballpoint pen in his pocket notebook.

"Are you ready yet?" Fifteen minutes had passed, and Ledford was impatient. There was nobody down there but those few guys at the fire.

"Keep your voice down. Sound carries," he said.

"We can't just stay here. What do you want to do?" She was exasperated. The answer to what Joey had seen was right down the hill.

Swanson switched off his flashlight, put away the notebook and binos, took a sip of water, and rolled onto his back. "I'm going to sleep for an hour. Stay awake and don't say another fucking word."

Two thirty in the morning. Sergeant Hafiz stifled a yawn as the need for sleep pulled at his eyes. The radio on his belt buzzed, and he acknowledged the incoming call, listened carefully, and terminated it. The convoy of visitors was only two miles away now, paused on the roadway, ready to come in. Before giving the signal, Hafiz made a quick call to the replacement patrol that was now down in the valley. "What's going on?" he asked the leader.

"Nothing. Very quiet." The voice was calm, which

was good. Hafiz did not want anything else unexpected happening.

"Keep it that way. We're going dark up here for a few minutes. Keep those people alert and spread out. No errors, not now."

"Yes, Sergeant. I'm at the old bridge if you need me."

"Very well. Base out." Hafiz changed channels on the portable radio and inhaled deeply to steady himself. The vehicles, carrying the party of Ayman al-Masri from the New Muslim Order, were waiting nearby, ready to come in. At the sergeant's order, sirens along the bridge whined to life. All engines shut down, every light was turned off, and when the sirens stopped thirty seconds later, the area was enveloped by total silence.

At the campfire beside the old bridge, the patrol leader sipped his tea and stared back toward the massive bridge that had just vanished before his eyes, as if it had been sucked into a hole in the night. The wail of the sirens bounced off the sides of the valley, bringing curses from the Taliban fighters trying to sleep on the ground. They were hard men but had refused to go any farther than this point. He was going to accuse them of being afraid of the Djinn, hiding like scared children, but they probably would have killed him on the spot for insulting their manhood. Better to leave them alone. A relief patrol would come down at dawn. Maybe the Taliban would be braver in the daylight.

Up top, three sports utility vehicles sped onto the bridge with their lights off and were guided into the underground garage by men carrying soft red lights. When large doors to the outside slid closed, all of the

lights came on again, work resumed, and Sergeant
Hafiz approached the middle vehicle. Guards with machine guns pounced out of the lead and trail SUVs and
formed a perimeter; then the door of the middle Ford
Excursion opened, and a slender, bearded man in the
rugged clothes of a mountain dweller stepped nimbly
onto the concrete. His dark eyes rapidly swept his surroundings, and then he exchanged greetings with Hafiz.
Ayman al-Masri, the head of personal security for
Commander Kahn, did not smile. He seldom did.

When the first siren began to turn over with its slow
growl, Beth Ledford jumped in surprise. Instantly,
there was a hand resting softly on her back. "Steady,
Coastie. Keep sharp while we see what's happening."

"All of the lights on the big bridge just went out,"
she said. Her voice was as tight as a piano wire, as was
the rest of her body.

Swanson grunted in acknowledgment. He could see
that, and therefore no words were needed. "Get into
your sniper mode. Loosen up so that if you have to take
a shot, you can make it count. Alert, but don't engage.
Scoot around so you're still covering our six, and have
your weapon safety off and ready."

The sirens grew to a full howl, the volume at earsplitting decibels as it echoed through the long valley.
Swanson propped his CAR-15 beside him and checked
the load, then went to the night-vision goggles. The
only available light was the campfire, which was still
flickering merrily down below, and it did not seem that
any of the men around it had even changed position. So

whatever was happening at the top of the valley had not disturbed them: It was expected. The alarm sirens were turned off, and the shrill whine spun back to silence; then the lights came back on.

"No movement here. You got anything?"

"No. Just darkness back this way." Beth kept her eyes on the hillside. "That was all kind of spooky. You think an electrical failure?"

"More likely, they were doing something they didn't want anybody to see." Kyle smiled at her. "It doesn't matter to our mission. These things always have unexpected wrinkles. Stay cool."

"I am cool, Gunny." She shuffled back away from the entrance.

"OK. Your turn to catch some sleep. We'll pull out in about another hour. At around four in the morning, the biorhythms of those guards will be dragging them down like anchors. Their heart rates and blood pressure will be so low they might as well be offline. Even whoever is standing watch will be about to fall over with sleep. That's when we go. You take a combat nap now, so you can be fresh."

"I don't think I can sleep," she said, lying back. "Too darned tensed up."

"Coastie, you sleep when you're told. So rack out." He turned away and watched the empty valley, wondering about the momentary blackout.

Ayman al-Masri walked with Hafiz to a row of brightly painted golf carts. "The last time we met, Hafiz, I be-

lieve you held the rank of colonel. You have been se-
verely demoted."

"I wear whatever rank my orders tell me to wear,
although I prefer no official rank at all." Hafiz motioned to the lead cart. "I need to show just enough to
get the job done."

"And is the job done here? Is this place safe for the
Commander?"

"That's for you to decide, not me. All I can tell you
is that I like what I have seen. It is a virtually impenetrable place with an automatic defense umbrella the
likes of which you have never encountered. Even most
bombs would just bounce off. When fully online, it
would take a long, all-out assault by a determined enemy to defeat it."

Al-Masri got into the cart and settled his robes.
"Frankly, I find such claims hard to believe. I saw what
the Americans did to the caves of Tora Bora with their
devil bombs, and believe they can do the same here. I
will not put the Commander in jeopardy."

"I had a lot of doubts, too, when I arrived. Now, after studying it, I cannot think of any better place to ride
out a storm. There were no defense systems at Tora
Bora, just caves. Surely this place could eventually be
taken down—history has shown that no defensive position can hold out forever—but to do so would extract
an enormous cost, and become a gagging bone in the
throat of any attacker." He pushed the accelerator,
and the battery-powered cart jerked forward. "This is
only the prototype, the first of many, each to be stronger

than the one before it. We are drawing a line which the Americans and their allies will think twice about attempting to cross. They are not used to fighting against technology and modern defenses that match or surpass their own, and the sort of little Special Forces raid that took the life of Osama bin Laden could simply never happen here, my friend. However, before dazzling you with the missiles and guns and electronic wonders of it all, I want to get some bad news out of the way. The genius who created this has gone totally insane. I have him secured in the infirmary, and I'm waiting for final orders from the ISI about what to do with him. You should see him first."

"To the infirmary, then, Hafiz. I need to inspect it anyway." The string of carts buzzed down the wide main tunnel.

WASHINGTON, D.C.

It was five in the afternoon in Washington, nine hours behind the time at the bridge in Pakistan, and the small staff that worked at the Bureau of American-Islamic Affairs building on Observatory Circle was shutting down for the day. Undersecretary Curtis tidied up his own desk and left with them, courteously calling the clerks by name as everyone headed for their cars, joking that thankfully there would be no receptions or official dinners tonight. Everybody deserves a night off now and then.

The day in Washington had been a scorcher, with

high humidity adding to the misery of being outside, even for a little while. Only tourists braved the heat. Curtis's personal automobile, an elegant metallic red BMW M3, was parked beneath cover in a reserved space, but even so, a blast of roasted air rushed out when he opened the door. He opened the passenger door to let the furnace heat dissipate with a cross-draft. Out in the parking lot, others were doing the same. No true Washington resident would get straight into a car on an afternoon like this. Let the trapped hot air escape, then jump in just long enough to turn on the engine and get the air conditioner pumping on high, then get back out. It took at least two minutes before even the most anxious commuter would slide onto the hot seat and grip a steering wheel that had been baking for hours.

Curtis removed his coat and tie and folded them carefully while he waited for the powerful BMW V6 engine to cool the interior down to a comfortable level. In another minute, he was motoring away from the BAIA, enduring the rush hour traffic northwest around the Beltway to McLean, where he peeled off onto State Route 267, the Dulles International toll road. Once on the long straightaway, it was almost impossible to get off of that road until you hit the airport exit, and Curtis had to fight the urge to let his machine really run, to set free the 414 horsepower as he passed the Leesburg Pike and Wolf Trap, and the pavement unrolled ahead. Instead, he stayed in the slow lane, moving in behind a small hotel bus. He would get the chance to open her up on the return trip.

Once settled into the pack, he activated the automated

built-in cell phone and instructed it to dial a number in New York. The big ears of the National Security Agency constantly swept international conversations in the D.C. area, but Dulles was almost a dead zone; there were so many calls going on between thousands of passengers and their homelands that even the NSA system was overwhelmed. A carefully conducted call to a foreign mission at the United Nations would hardly be noticed if the words "terrorism" and "bomb" were not mentioned.

Cultural attaché Mohammed Javid Bhatti had been expecting the call and he answered on the third ring. They chatted aimlessly for a full minute. Was it hotter in New York or Washington. How the traffic was. How the UN was empty in August, and how they were both looking forward to the weekend. The attaché confirmed that he would be attending a reception the following week.

"Will you be bringing your guest?" Curtis asked.

There as a pause. Javid Bhatti deliberately gave the response that he had memorized. "No, I will arrive alone. I have communicated with my home office, and the guest will not be able to make it. There will be no one sent to replace him." He meant that the Pakistani ISI had decided not to risk having one of their trained assassins being captured while operating on American soil.

Now there was a longer pause. When William Lloyd Curtis asked a favor, he normally got it. He swallowed his disappointment and kept his voice even. "That's fine, then. So I will see you at the reception."

"I'll be there. You furnish the blondes."

Curtis laughed and closed the call. The attaché

loved to party, and getting women and booze for him had been a good investment. No need to be angry at him. Javid was just a messenger boy. Curtis was peeved, however, at having his request rejected by General Gul at the ISI. With so much at stake, and the days counting down toward a major attack, was the ISI getting cold feet, playing him?

Curtis no longer had to paddle along the Dulles road like some grandma in a used Honda. He cut out from behind the passenger van and into faster traffic, ignoring the horn blowing and finger waving of other drivers as he stomped the accelerator and the BMW responded with a burst of blurry speed that catapulted him to ninety miles per hour. The speed limit was sixty-five, but Curtis had not spent sixty-five thousand dollars on a luxury muscle car to do the speed limit.

18

THE VALLEY

Kyle Swanson let the night speak to him. He was fully alert, all of his senses constantly bringing in and updating information, but those people down below, except for the one guy who had stayed up and was walking around, were at the low point of their entire day: bored, tired, and hard asleep. The darkness felt heavy, and the steady grinding of big equipment up on the bridge was almost like white noise, lulling the brain into restfulness, assuring everyone that things were normal.

"OK," he said, giving an easy shake to Beth Ledford's arm. "Time to move out. Police up your trash. Leave no target indicator. No one should ever know that we were here."

Beth sat up and arched her back to work out the kinks. The hump of a thick tree root had been digging into her shoulder while she slept, but there had been little room to shift positions. "Anything going on?" Half of the Snickers bar was still uneaten, so she wrapped it tightly and put it into the pack.

"Same old, same old. Most of them seem to be getting a good night's sleep. They're not professionals, that's for sure. Hopefully, they won't bother us, and we won't bother them."

Beth checked her CAR-15, made sure the flash suppressor had not been plugged by dirt, then slid down the night-vision goggles. "Ready. Are we coming back here?"

Kyle shook his head. "All hides are temporary, Coastie. We go down and look at the fallen bridge, then find another place. There will be plenty of opportunities in this junkyard. Remember what I told you earlier. With the cover of the night, we don't have to crawl. Step with your toe down first, then ease your weight onto your heel. Toe-heel-toe. There is no hurry. Slow is smooth, smooth is fast. Got it?"

"I remember that lecture from the first time," she griped. "Quit treating me like a baby. Let's get out of here and take care of business." She squirmed onto her knees, facing outward.

He left the hide without another word; one step, then another, then stood upright. The direct available light from the campfire was amplified further in his goggles by the faraway illumination at the big bridge, and Kyle took his time to do a 360-degree scan. Nothing was moving. Bizarre shapes and shadows were cast by rocks and brush and trees. Two more steps and he stopped again to wait for Ledford to emerge. When she stood, he held up his right hand and waved four fingers, motioning her to follow him downhill.

He covered the first ten meters in just a few moments and heard her moving behind him, trying to be quiet but sounding to him like a marauding buffalo.

Remembering that she had a smaller stride, he shortened his own step. Yeah. That was better. They settled into a tandem glide.

The first hundred meters went by quickly on the gently sloping ground, and they worked around a couple of minor obstacles without incident. The dirt was hardened mud, and the flood had sluiced away most of the usual scree of little pebbles that would coat a riverbank. Swanson held up his fist and took a knee. Coastie did the same. They had a clear view of the old bridge, and he saw her lips tighten as she studied it.

The stubby old truss span was still firmly anchored at the end where the campsite was, but it buckled sharply downward about fifteen feet from shore, pulled by the weight of the steel after the far supports had given way years ago. The other end rested beneath the surface of the sluggish water. Most of the flooring was missing, and the bumpy rivets stood out clearly. It was a bridge that went nowhere, useless.

It was also an uncanny replica of the bridge from Beth's childhood, the place from which she and Joey and their parents had gone fishing and swimming on hot summer days. She tried to visualize something she was overlooking, but there was nothing unusual about it at all. Not a thing other than its eerie familiarity.

"Is that it?" Kyle had kept his own eyes on the unstirring camp and was whispering into his throat microphone.

She nodded her head. "That's exactly it, just as in Joey's picture. He must have been standing about right here. I don't see anything else. Can I move a little closer?"

"Low-crawl down another fifteen meters while I stay here and cover. No farther than that. No noise." He put his rifle to his shoulder, pointing toward the sleeping patrol that dozed on unperturbed.

Beth eased into a prone position, cradled her weapon in her arms, and then propelled herself carefully forward on knees and elbows.

Kyle heard her breathing harder. No movement in the camp. Then his peripheral vision caught something changing. Coastie stiffened and froze, burying her face into the ground.

As Kyle watched in astonishment, a dark metal tube rose from the ground only a few feet to her right, a pipe of some sort that emerged ghostlike in the gloom with a soft, hydraulic hum. He quickly went flat, as still as a rock. The cylinder came up higher, the top covering slid back, and Swanson saw the reflection of light on glass. It looked like a submarine periscope, and it mechanically rotated twice to scan the entire area, then stopped and automatically closed its lid and slid back into its hiding place with a hiss.

The device had to be a remotely controlled camera, Kyle thought, which meant he had to assume their mission had been compromised. The idea of a soft infiltration had just changed. Not knowing precisely what had happened, he called for Beth to return, and she came back, low but fast.

"What the hell was that?" she whispered.

"Camera," he said. "Must have been triggered by a motion detecting sensor around here. Just be glad it wasn't a mine."

"A camera? That doesn't make any sense."

"Some kind of high-tech perimeter security system, but it doesn't matter to us. We have to assume that we've been spotted, and that changes everything. We probably don't have much time before an alert is sent out and wakes up those dudes on the patrol. Our mission plan changes."

"What do you want to do?"

"Get ready to fight, Coastie. We're ninety-seven meters from that group right now, no wind, downward angle, but I want to close to about thirty to make it point-blank. If the guy with the radio gets a call, we put them down right then. You take the two on the left, and I'll do the two on the right and the guy in the middle. One center mass shot each."

"We're going to shoot them while they're asleep?"

"No. We're going to *kill* them while they're asleep. Don't wuss out on me now, Coastie. Remember what these assholes did to your brother. They are no longer human beings. They are targets, and they have guns." He gave his magazine one final tug to make sure it was secure, then rose to his feet.

Beth Ledford did the same. "What did he see, Kyle? What did Joey see?"

Swanson exhaled and sucked in a deep breath, ready to move. "He didn't see anything at all at this bridge, other than it being a curious reminder of when you were kids, Coastie. So he went deeper up the valley toward the new bridge before they stumbled into trouble. His team probably did not even realize they were tripping hidden sensors as they went. Someone was watching."

THE INFIRMARY

Sergeant Hafiz escorted the New Muslim Order—the NMO—team into the sick bay area, their footsteps hushed by soundproofing. The place was clean, with pure filtered air, the room temperature kept low by a thermostat on the central air and heating system. The almost sterile environment bore no resemblance to the outside world. Ayman al-Masri walked directly to the narrow bed where Chief Engineer Mohammad al-Attas lay tied like a goat, dirty and bloody, his eyes closed. "What happened?" he asked Hafiz.

"This little man escaped last night and killed some of our people before being captured. He was once very important, but something happened in his head."

Al-Masri bent over to put his face near that of the engineer. "That is a shame. From everything we had heard, the man was brilliant." He tapped the chief engineer on the skull. "Can you hear me in there? You did some wonderful work. Even the Commander knew about you, and sends his compliments."

The dark eyes of al-Attas flew open, so wide that the NMO inspector stepped back in surprise. The whites shone bright around the pupils, which darted everywhere, taking in his surroundings. "I'm thirsty," he said weakly.

Hafiz moved closer. "Don't be fooled by this mild manner. He is a heartless murderer when the other personality, the one he calls the Djinn, seizes him. Then he is uncontrollable."

"Sergeant Hafiz! My friend!" The grating voice of al-Attas grew stronger. "Why am I still a prisoner?"

"See?" Hafiz said. "He remembers nothing of his murderous actions."

The inspectors gathered around, examining the engineer as if he were a specimen on a laboratory table. "So he cannot be used at all?"

"No. The breaks in memory and behavior have become too erratic and sharp and are increasing in frequency. In addition to the danger he poses to anyone around him, his work would be suspect, too."

"What a shame," said al-Masri. "*Insh'Allah*. God's will."

"*Insh'Allah*," Hafiz agreed.

The inspectors, having seen enough, moved away at Hafiz's suggestion that the infirmary staff guide them around the elaborately equipped medical clinic. Wounded fighters might receive attention on the operating tables, but the infirmary had been specifically built to serve the special needs of Commander Kahn.

Hafiz glanced back and saw the hot eyes of the Djinn boring into him. He filled a cup with water and helped the bound man sip the liquid. Then he laid the head back down, pulled a cloth screen around the bed, and returned to the tour.

"When you've seen enough here, we can go to the control room, and then the communications suite, so

you can see the heart of this place," he suggested. "Then
we can do the tunnels, the living quarters, and the individual defense systems."

The inspectors moved to their carts, none giving a
second thought back at the screened-off chief engineer.
He was already dead to them. The infirmary was
deemed more than adequate for the needs of the Commander and his senior staff.

THE VALLEY

Beth Ledford's heart was pounding so hard it seemed
that everyone around could hear the thumps. She kept
her eyes glued on Swanson's back, not the targets, and
he moved like a panther through the half-buried boulders and over tree stumps, silent and swift and determined, as they closed on the campsite. Her CAR-15 was
pressed against her shoulder, the safety off. Coming up
on sleeping men who were about to die was a lot different than shooting a boat from a helicopter. It didn't
seem right. Maybe they should just capture them instead. She instantly banished those thoughts. Fairness
has nothing to do with it, Kyle had told her during their
brief training. *Stay focused, girl. Follow the Gunny.
Don't think about Joey or helicopters or anything else.*
The greenish images in the goggles grew in size. The
man standing by the fire had not heard a thing. *They
are targets, not people.*

Suddenly, she was totally in the moment, and nothing else existed in her life. Back a few steps, confidence

had replaced nervousness, and her training kicked in. She knew she could depend on the gunny to do his job, and she was as good with a rifle as he: Annie Oakley in combat boots. In the zone. Can't miss. *You bastards are going to die.*

Kyle slowed and stopped, and she came up beside him. "On my count," he said quietly into the mike. Both had their guns up, and the flames of the fire glowed on the sleeping faces. "Three . . . two . . . one . . ."

They fired simultaneously, with no more sound than a pair of cricket chirps, and two bodies on the ground twitched under the impact. By then, they had tracked to their second targets and squeezed off another pair of silenced shots, and they both hit the standing man at the same time, and he bucked backward and fell away from the fire. Five men lay dead in less than three seconds.

Swanson moved forward, dropping his rifle, which dangled from a D-ring on his harness, while drawing his silenced Colt .45 from its holster. He stalked into the semicircle of downed men and fired one shot into each head. The center mass hits had all been accurate, but the head shots provided total insurance. He put the pistol away, then unsnapped his canteen and took a long drink of water.

Beth stepped near the fire and felt its warmth. She had been so wrapped up in the mission that she had not noticed the night had gotten chilly. She wrapped her arms around herself, rubbing to get warm.

"Grab one of these blankets if you're cold," Swanson said. "Matter of fact, let's take several of them to throw over any more cameras that pop up." He knelt and rolled a body over, snatching out the bloodstained blanket beneath it.

Beth balked at the idea, and Swanson threw the blanket at her. "Use it!" he snapped. "It's too late for second thoughts, Coastie. We are in a fight now, and the bad guys know where we are. The blankets can also cut down on our heat signatures if they are using thermal sights. Get down here and check them for anything else we can use. We've got no more than a few minutes, then we head up the trail, so get your ass in gear."

THE CONTROL ROOM

Hafiz deftly steered the cart down the broad light blue hallway that was lined on each upper corner with fluorescent lights. Color-coded arrows and signs were painted on the walls at every intersection and branch to guide traffic, and he followed a wide green line that led to the control room. The guard at the sealed door snapped to attention.

So far, Hafiz had no doubt that Ayman al-Masri of the NMO was impressed with the tunnel complex, and he had yet to show him the weapons, the mess facilities, the troop barracks, the repair shops, and the private living quarters. "After this stop, we'll take a break and go to the dining hall. I'm certain you and your men could use some hot tea and some food after your long journey."

"How much more time will the official tour take?" asked the al Qaeda man.

"Another hour or so. Then I'll just leave the carts with you, along with a guide, and you go anywhere you want, ask questions of anyone. There is no time limit and no restrictions as far as I am concerned." Hafiz swung the cart into a tight little circle and stopped. The three other carts, two men in each, followed his example.

Hafiz stepped into a white square painted on the floor outside the control room and pushed a button to activate the entrance sequence. A shimmering bright white halo appeared overhead and slowly descended all the way to the floor, taking biometric and facial recognition data, running it through the computer, confirming the findings, and changing to green before snapping off. The door unlocked automatically, and Hafiz pulled it open.

Al-Masri was astonished when he stepped inside, and absently reached out and touched one of the many racks of equipment. His team members came in behind him and gaped like children. The room had the look of an empty financial brokerage, with large screens on the walls, desktop computers, indirect overhead lighting, and several chairs in low cubicles filled with electronic displays. One bigger chair was perched on risers near the back, with a pair of screens right in front of it, a joystick on each arm, and a keyboard beside a panel of switches and knobs. The air-conditioning hummed in its ongoing fight to control the heat churned out by the electronics within the enclosed space.

"What does it do?" he finally asked.

"Everything," replied Hafiz. "I don't understand

even half of it, but from that big chair, the chief engineer had everything at his fingertips. Watching him
work it was like seeing a conjurer doing the impossible.
Despite the wonder, these are not toys for children but
a real war-fighting center. Cameras and sensors everywhere, map overlays, holographic projections, and automatic weapons adjustments. Just imagine; one man
holding off anything the enemy could throw at him, and
doing it in air-conditioned comfort. A bomb hit up top
might not even be felt down here. Giant springs beneath
the floor would soak up the impact."

"Then why is it not filled with technicians right now?"

"Well, the truth is that the chief engineer did not
think about other people running his system. He must
be replaced before it can be truly functioning. Islamabad is putting together a qualified team; no one man
could do what he did. They will be transferred in to
take final control within a week."

Al-Masri walked around, looking, and was drawn
toward the one flat screen that showed some activity
and was giving off a steady beep. The flare of a campfire showed clearly, and several shadowy figures moved
around it. "What is this?"

Hafiz glanced over. "Some of my security people. Just
a routine patrol down in the valley by the old bridge," he
said. "Taliban. They may be good fighters, but not very
disciplined. We are bringing in regular troops to take
over as soon as possible, a whole platoon."

"A lazy patrol does not inspire confidence," said al-
Masri.

"Nothing ever goes totally smooth in bringing a

huge project such as this online, transitioning from construction to operational," said Hafiz, trying to sound casual. "A lot of pieces are yet to finally be in place, including a final security protocol. When everything is up and running, it will be a wonder. The Commander will be quite safe here."

"That is for me to determine," said Ayman al-Masri.

Hafiz laughed. "Wait until you see the guns. Now, let's take a break and have some tea." He led them away and relocked the door. Inwardly, Hafiz was embarrassed that the latest patrol had been seen taking their ease down by the old bridge. The poor quality of the Taliban was reflecting on him personally, and he would not tolerate that. When they reached the dining hall, he took a minute to radio orders to move out the reserve unit immediately. The sergeant planned to kick some sense into that first group when it returned.

19

THE VALLEY

"Now what?" Beth Ledford whispered, staring out beyond the campsite.

"We keep going," Swanson replied, unfolding a map he had found on the man who had been standing up. Taking a compass reading and shielding his flashlight with his hand, Kyle studied it for a moment and determined the landmarks of the old and new bridges. *Bingo. Good intel.* It was a detailed rendering of the sector.

"Things are changing fast, Coastie, but that always happens after the first shot is fired, and our plans have to change to meet the new circumstances. This is just the start of the game, and we have to do a lot more. Get one of the blankets." Among the contour lines on the map was a scattering of bold blue dots, including one about ten meters from the campsite. He pointed and said, "Walk slowly directly west and see if one of those camera pipes comes up. About a dozen steps."

She shook out a sweat-stained blanket and held it before her like a shield. After only three steps, she said, "There it is. Already coming up and pointing at the camp." She tossed the heavy cloth, and it settled like a tent around a center pole, blinding the camera.

"OK. I think every camera in this sector is marked with the same symbol, which is good for us. I'll take point. Follow me up this trail."

Ledford brought her rifle to a ready position and stepped out behind him, changing magazines as she walked. She had reloaded without being told.

So far, Kyle had been satisfied with her work. Started out a little nervous but adjusted well. She had not freaked out in their ambush and was able to pull the trigger, but he anticipated that stronger opposition lay ahead, and the hardest part of the three tiers of reaction was to keep calm when someone is shooting back. She would face that test soon enough.

"We have to believe we have been compromised, but it's too early to leave, because things don't make sense yet. Whatever the secret may be lies up at that big bridge, so we have to move closer. Keep your head on a swivel. And don't worry if you feel scared. You're supposed to be scared. It helps you pay attention."

"In that case, Gunny, I'm paying a lot of attention."

Darkness closed around them again as they left the campsite on the well-traveled trail that ran along the west bank of the river. A treeline started at the top of the ridge. Below, Beth could hear the forceful rumble of water working around smooth boulders, uprooted trees, and the debris caught around the submerged eastern end of the old span. She wasn't really scared, and reminded herself that the Coast Guard preached that you have to go out, but nobody ever said a damn thing about having to come back. Same thing, different place.

The radio Swanson had taken from the patrol leader squawked. Somebody angry, speaking fast Arabic. He caught the drift, that the dead man was being chewed out for not making a scheduled radio check. Swanson turned down the volume but listened carefully. A relief patrol was being sent out. He did not try to reply. The call puzzled him, for it sounded like the headquarters dude was unaware that they were around. Perhaps they had not been badly compromised after all.

THE BRIDGE

Spikes of noise echoed through the corridors, and Sergeant Hafiz had to find a quiet place before trying to raise the second patrol by radio. He pushed open a steel door painted light green and stepped inside a low bunker where an Iranian SPG-9 antitank gun squatted on its automatic mount. The room smelled of oil. Hafiz pushed a control switch on the wall, and the cover of the firing slit hummed open, allowing direct line-of-sight radio transmission into the valley. Beyond the hearing of the al Qaeda inspectors, he now unloaded his pent-up frustration into his radio. The patrol had not checked in, and he had even *seen* them on the control room monitor, loafing and asleep at the old bridge. There was still no response. Hafiz closed the firing lid and stormed out of the gun pit, his face dark with anger.

The barracks was up one flight of steel steps, which he took two at a time, then marched quickly past some startled workers until he was in the troops' sleeping area. "Everybody get up!" he shouted, grabbing the closest man and pulling him hard from the bunk. Taliban fighters understood force a lot better than words, and all of them scrambled to their feet, barefoot, bearded, and dazed. Partially eaten food was scattered by the bunks, along with dirty clothes and empty plastic water bottles. Dirty, worthless scum. "Get ready to move in ten minutes! Your patrol leader will come get you and take you out to the valley. Your friends went to sleep on sentry duty and are out of radio contact! Inexcusable! You go to sleep out there and I will crucify you and let the birds have your worthless bodies." He spun around and stalked away in a fury, out of patience with these people.

He went back the same way he had come up, down the steel circular staircases and once again into the gun bunker, closing the outer door and opening the firing slit. He put his face up to the cool outside air and sucked in a lungful, exhaled, then took another deep breath. Hafiz had retreated to the solitude of the pit to regain his composure and reassemble his outward image of total confidence and competence. Everything on the inspection tour was going well so far, except for that outside security detail. Ayman al-Masri had not seemed disturbed by the condition of the chief engineer in the infirmary, but Hafiz had seen displeasure momentarily cross his face when he had also noticed the idle patrol. That lapse was damaging and required a tough response, but Hafiz still needed those morons for guard duty until the regular troops could arrive.

All he could do at present was to continue the tour and let the mighty bridge fortress sell itself, without him having to say much at all. Answer any questions that he could immediately. Admit no weakness. The message was to be *All is well here; it is safe.*

THE VALLEY

Swanson stopped, reached down, and brushed the dirt beside the trail until he found a patch of smooth ground right where the map indicated. "Another blanket," he whispered over his shoulder, and Ledford unfurled another cloth. "These are little paths that have been tramped down by maintenance workers who serviced the cameras," he said. "The map shows a whole network of them coming off the trail at various points. Go up about twenty meters, find it, and cover it."

Ledford shook out the blanket. Now that she had done it once, her confidence had soared, and when the camera stalk came rising out of the ground, there was no surprise. It wasn't some mighty alien erupting from the flood-scarred mud. Just a dumb machine. She flipped the cloth over the lens. Through her night goggles, she also now could recognize the slightly flattened area around the device where service crews had been working, pulling weeds, clearing obstructions, and keeping the magic eye functioning. Then she saw a longer strip of discolored earth, running straight as an arrow. She dug her fingers into the muck, pried away a few rocks, and touched plastic. Some things are so basic. Beth returned to Swanson on the main trail. "Done," she said. "The cameras are hardwired by landlines running through PVC pipes. We can just disable them with our knives."

"We don't have time to do them all, Coastie. It's enough for now that we know where the cameras are so we can dodge. We've got bits and pieces of information, but we still don't know what's behind it all. I want to get to that bridge. We only have about an hour of darkness left, and weather's moving in."

"I can't figure it out, Gunny. Why all this security to protect a danged bridge?" she asked as he got up. Above them, the sky had filled with troubled clouds, knotting and shifting, blotting out the stars and entirely hiding the moon.

"Nothing out here makes much sense, Coastie. It's a quacks-like-a-duck thing. There is a reason, but we just haven't found it yet. My opinion, worst case, since this is Pakistan, they might have stuck a nuke in there. Let's go. Stay quiet."

A single raindrop touched Beth's hand, and a quick wind swirled through the valley to drop the temperature a few degrees. It was followed by a powerful peal of thunder, and lightning sparkled in jagged sharpness overhead, rendering the nightmare landscape even more misshapen. Then the hard rain slashed down, and the first drops changed to torrents. She hunched up her shoulders and moved on.

The mission had never been considered to be a long-duration job, and they had packed no rain gear other than the special blankets in the survival kits, which they would not use as raincoats. Their uniforms were formulated to retain body heat and not encumber movement, and the goggles still worked, although they had to wipe them. Rain would have gotten into their exposed eyes just as easily, so wearing the NVGs continued the advantage of being able to see in the dark.

Kyle already felt the dirt beginning to mud up beneath his boots, because the area had been so drenched by the recent floods that it still had not deep-dried, and the water saturated the land and rushed down toward the river. On the plus side, the deluge added concealment and deflected noise. The storm and lightning would help protect them from the nosy cameras and motion detectors, so he considered it an even trade.

Kyle heard them coming. The members of the third Taliban patrol were bitching and complaining loudly over the sound of the falling rain about how that dog of a Pakistani sergeant had forced them out of the dry and comfortable barracks and into the foul weather, and now their clothes were weighed down by water, sticking to their skin, and they were growing colder with each step. They cursed the first patrol that had gotten carelessly ambushed, and the second for failing to do its job and making it necessary to be relieved early. There was nothing tactical about their approach; they were just rambling down the trail with a mob mentality, disinterested, angry, ignoring their leader, and wanting to get to the fallen bridge where they could put up some shelter. Each man had an AK-47 over a shoulder or slung across his chest.

Swanson, with the NVGs, had a couple of seconds to react when he saw the smeared images approach, because they could not yet see him. He went to one knee and softly said to Beth, "Contact, front. Five targets, twenty meters. I take One, you got Two, just like we drilled at Quantico." She locked into a firing position, ready to shoot over Swanson's head.

The Taliban came hurrying forward in a ragged line, their eyes on the trail, bodies bent against the slamming rainstorm. Kyle fired when the first man was only twenty feet away, but the target's forward momentum kept him moving even after he had absorbed a bullet in the chest. As he fell, Beth Ledford's CAR-15 spat a silenced round into the center mass of the second man. Swanson, a moment later, downed a third one.

The fourth man in line realized something was happening and began to crouch. Ledford's round smashed into his face and spewed bits of bone and brain onto the fighter behind him.

Because of the melee in front of him, the final fighter had a chance to react and was about to jump from the trail when Swanson shot him; the bullet penetrated under the right arm, and the round bored through the chest cavity, tearing up vital organs as it went. He died as he hit the mud.

"Cease fire," Swanson said, waiting to be sure Ledford was through pulling the trigger before he stood up. Drawing his pistol, he advanced to administer the necessary final head shots. Then he just said, "Let's go."

Beth was breathing heavy, her breath puffing little clouds in the chill and rain. She had felt nothing for these people she had just killed; nothing at all. This time, it was almost like a video game, for the poor visibility and their positions had shielded their faces from her view, so they didn't even look like real people. She just took the shots. Quick and easy, like clockwork; like Swanson.

WASHINGTON, D.C.

Undersecretary William Lloyd Curtis was still working through the shock of having his request turned down by the ISI. Such a simple thing! The secret police apparatus of one of the world's most paranoid nations had refused to let him borrow one of their men for a special mission of mutual benefit at a critical time. A favor, refused. He needed a drink, but not at one of the usual Washington watering holes.

Instead, his BMW M3 seemed to find its own way out of the metropolis, away from the government, as the flush of embarrassment turned to anger. Fuck 'em. Requests for favors were seldom refused in his world, and he would remember this insult. For now, he just wanted to blow off some steam. He could do that during his next appointment. Just outside of Williamsburg sat a tired building that had obviously been a working man's tavern for many years, and a big American flag hung listlessly in the August heat. His kind of secret place, where he could revert to his old self, the rough construction boss, Big Bill Curtis, and have a conversation that he could never have in some fancy Georgetown watering hole. He parked in the broad lot, where several pickups and Jap cars sizzled in the afternoon sun.

He rolled up his sleeves two laps to display the faded tattoo of a rather pitiful-looking dragon that he had picked up one long ago evening in Singapore, then walked into the bar and straight to a stool. "Gimme a cold American draft, pal," he told the bartender, who brought him a Budweiser in a chilled mug.

"Ya know why them Muslim fucks don't drink?" he asked out loud, turning heads. "They don't know shit about making real beer. How long they been sucking up air on this planet? A couple of million years, or something, and they still haven't figured out how to make beer?"

That drew a few laughs and started the conversation. Bill Curtis joined in as he let the back part of his brain deal with the problem. The Diplomatic Security Service had told him to go screw himself. Then the paramilitary tough guys chickened out after two of their punks got popped by Kyle Swanson. Now the damned, camel-screwing ISI decided not to get involved in a job on U.S. dirt, although he was about to pull the trigger on a big operation of which General Gul was intimately aware. Gul was creating some distance between them because of the investigation that was sure to follow.

"Can't depend on the muzzies," he told his new group of friends after ordering a pitcher of beer and joining them at their table. "You understand, don't you? They have money out the wazoo, they have the oil, but they can't buy respect. Ever see one of those Saudi princes' homes, where they paint the statues around the swimming pool with big red nipples or gold cocks?"

A fellow in a checkered shirt, with dirt under his nails, added, "Rodney Dangerfield had it right. Can't get no respect."

"They don't deserve any," Curtis declared, emptying another glass of Bud. Damn, it felt good to be in an out-of-the-way bar with a bunch of strangers, just to be able to bitch and moan without consequence. Everyone in there had a story about their wives, their trucks, their bosses, or politicians. His was different, and he could not share it.

"Want something done right, you got to do it yourself," he said. It was that thought he would take back to Washington. Curtis called for another pitcher.

"You got that right," agreed another man.

Curtis laughed. Now to business. He turned from the bar and walked toward a corner table where a man sat alone, sipping a Corona beer. He wore clean jeans and boots, a sweat-stained golf shirt, and dark aviator-style sunglasses. His brown hair was short and neat. "Buck?" he asked.

Astronaut Buck Gardener acknowledged him, and Curtis slid into the other chair at the dim corner table. "Where's the money?" the astronaut asked.

"In the trunk of my car outside. Is the gizmo finished?"

"Ready. At a hundred thousand feet, it will automatically pop a spark to jump between two wires in the propellant feed system, and the whole flammable vehicle will blow up."

"And you're sure you can get it aboard? Absolutely?"

"Yep. I'm on the support crew and will make the final safety inspection before the bird is ready to fly."

Curtis stared at Gardener, who did not blink. He was not backing out. A hundred thousand dollars was waiting in the parking lot, walking-around money, a million more coming when the device was planted, and four million more when his astronaut wife, Erin, her spaceship commander lover, and their fucking Mars rocket were blown into tiny pieces. Damned straight he would do it.

20

THE BRIDGE

Ayman al-Masri of the NMO and Sergeant Hafiz stood on a discreetly designed terrace in what was to become the new residence for Commander Kahn. Overhanging rocks made the deck invisible from curious satellites, and it provided an expansive view of the valley below. The leader could take fresh air here. "Savage weather," al-Masri commented as the thunderstorm pounded the surrounding mountains. "So mean outside, but dry in here."

"Another special touch from the chief engineer," replied Sergeant Hafiz. "I'm glad you approve of the living quarters. Rather bare and Spartan, but it can be organized in any way that the Commander would like."

"He prefers a very simple lifestyle, actually. Even a fast hare gets tired after a long chase. He needs rest, lots of rest, but he won't slow down."

A snap of lightning was followed by a tremendous crash of thunder. "Work topside has been suspended because of the weather," said Hafiz, pleased that the security inspection was almost done. "The interior work continues. I propose as soon as the new engineers arrive, they concentrate on finishing out the living quarters and adjacent corridors and rooms. The other work can proceed then, with the Commander already secure, with everything he needs."

"Listen to that roar," al-Masri said, deftly changing the subject. "Is the river going to flood again?"

Hafiz gazed out into the thick curtain of falling water. "I doubt it. This storm is just passing through. The big typhoon system that caused all of the trouble had stalled in the mountains and rained like this for almost three months. This should pass on about dawn."

"When we were young soldiers, you and I spent a lot of time out in these typhoons. I would hate to do so now." The al Qaeda man shuddered at the memory of those cold, forlorn conditions.

"It is better to be inside." Hafiz agreed, but a second later he caught the real meaning of the man's words. "Yet someone must stay out on guard."

Al-Masri glanced over, and the dark eyes were piercing. "Have you heard from your patrols? Either the one down in the valley or the one that you sent out in relief? It has been some time."

Hafiz was honest, knowing a lie would be detected immediately. "Not yet. The storm is playing havoc with the communications, but if you are set for the evening now, I will get back to my other duties. I want to get some of the chief engineer's assistants into the main control room to see if they can get it up and running again, at least on a minimal basis."

"That would be excellent, Hafiz. My own people are ready for some sleep after our long journey, and we can finish the inspection tour tomorrow. I readily admit that I have been most impressed with what I have seen so far."

"Well, I shall leave, then. Sleep well."

"And you will check on those patrols?"

"Yes, of course. I was planning to do that immediately," Hafiz said.

"Leave me a radio. I would appreciate you contacting me as soon as you discover what has been going on out there. Let us hope the problems are just due to the bad weather." The sergeant placed his own handheld radio on a table and left the New Muslim Order security chief standing on the overlook, his hands buried in his sleeves for warmth.

THE VALLEY

Kyle Swanson plodded up along the trail, his brain turning over possibilities while mud sucked at his feet and rain whipped his body. The storm was a tactical blessing, providing both some concealment and cover, but it was fucking miserable, and moving forward felt more like swimming than walking. He did not look back for Coastie. It was best to leave her alone with her thoughts, handing over an implied shame if she did not keep up.

Behind him, Ledford doggedly kept putting one boot in front of another, moving blindly in the curtains of wind and rain, fueled only by pride. She had not cracked yet, and she would keep going no matter what.

Her mind pushed the physical discomfort and the aching muscles to a place where they did not matter, so she could get on with the job. Despite the cold, the muck, and the danger, she was excited. Some reptilian part of her brain was actually enjoying being a predator out stalking prey in the storm.

They were now within a hundred meters of the big bridge, and it towered above them like a medieval castle on a mountaintop. Huge slabs of stone had been set and locked into other monstrous rocks to form sheer, high walls that rose about ninety feet above the valley floor at each end and supported the massive arch over the swollen river. Waterfalls poured off of it in thick sheets. The lights high up top burned brightly and reflected through the spray to reach the churning clouds.

Swanson kept moving his head back and forth, checking for outside security and any dangerous areas. He no longer worried about the camera stalks and electronic perimeter devices. If they had not been activated in the past hour, either they had not been triggered or something was wrong in the circuitry. He slowed the pace to look around more closely, trying to find the entrance at the base of the bridge. Despite the map's indication of such an opening, he saw nothing but bushes and solid rock. He removed the night-vision goggles for a better look. The muddy trail led straight into a thicket, which hugged hard against the wall. That last patrol had come straight down the path, so this had to be their route. There was no other way. He held up his fist, and they came to a halt, Beth moving up close.

"Straight ahead," he said quietly. "What do you see?"

Ledford also removed her NVGs and stared hard at the terrain, each side, and up and down. "Nothing. Nobody."

"The path disappears right into that line of bushes. Have you seen any other major trafficway? Something I might have missed?"

"Just rain, Gunny. That's all."

"OK." He made up his mind. "You hang here and give me cover. I'm going forward and look around in that brush. There's got to be some kind of entrance hole around. Those guys didn't pop out of nowhere."

"I've got your six."

He grinned at her through the downpour, reached out, and slapped the top of her black beanie, a rolled-up knitted ski cap. "I know you do."

As Swanson moved closer, he could make out more detail. The brush was almost like a fence that stretched some thirty feet across, and the spacing indicated they had been planted instead of just growing wild out of the weeds. Thick foliage in the middle, a tangled mass ten feet high, was reacting differently to the rain than did the brush clumps on either side, which were crushed down beneath the onslaught of the storm. This section remained firm, indicating that it was somehow anchored in place. He removed the glove from his left hand and reached out: plastic. It looked almost perfect from a few feet away, but it was as phony as a movie set.

Kyle put the glove back on and plunged both arms into the thicket, grabbing handfuls of plastic with each fist and pulling hard. It gave way so easily that he lost his balance and fell backward into the slime as the brush, mounted on a swivel, swung free.

Beth rushed forward as soon as she saw him go down, her rifle swinging in a 180-degree arc. "Gunny?"

"I'm OK," he replied, rolling to his knees and then standing. "This stuff is just plastic. Realistic as hell, but only a special effect that no satellite camera would ever detect. The gate swings open, then closes tight again."

"And there's a door!" she said.

An opening in the rock had been machined to be almost perfectly square; it reached back about six feet into the slab, where a solid metal door with a big lever handle blocked the other end. With no light, it had been invisible behind the bushes.

"Yep." He was on a knee now, studying the area for possible booby traps or other surprises. A camera was secured by a wall brace, and he smashed it with the stock of his rifle.

"We're going inside?" Beth asked.

"Yep."

THE BRIDGE

Sergeant Hafiz decided to go out himself. Two patrols were now out of contact, and he was out of guards. The three corporals who had led the patrols were absent—he did not know where they were—and all of the Taliban security forces were either dead or unaccounted for. All that was left was the approximately one hundred civilian workers on the night shift and the ten men of the NMO security team. The civilian construction workers would be even more useless in the valley than the Taliban roughnecks, and Hafiz would be damned before he begged help from Ayman al-Masri. By the process of elimination, that left it on his shoulders.

That was probably best, he thought, as he walked to the western end of the bridge, descending stairwells along the way because he could move faster on foot than waiting for an elevator. Getting around the complex reminded him of being within a big ship, where multiple levels were woven together for a common purpose. The comm operations were near the top, on the east end, but he did not want to call Islamabad again. General Gul would want answers that he did not have. He had already given cause for concern by pestering them for the regular troops.

The defense control system was housed on the eastern side, deeper into the mountain. It would have been nice if the chief engineer had picked some other time to go crazy, so he could have been in there to work the fancy defense suite and its deadly electronic network. Hafiz brushed the thought aside. He had to deal with reality, not fantasy.

He came to his own small quarters, a single square in which were a small desk, a few shelves, a single bed, and a bathroom. His gear was folded in neat stacks, and he pulled out a rubberized poncho, then retrieved the AK-47 beside the bunk and headed toward the lower exit, pulling on the rain gear. The weapon had been cleaned the previous night and had a full magazine, but

Hafiz checked it anyway before slinging it across his shoulder.

A little room just off the entryway contained supplies for maintenance workers and people heading outside, including a rack of rechargeable battery-powered lanterns. Hafiz chose one that threw a powerful beam. *I really don't want to go out into this mess,* he thought. *What excuse could they possibly have for not reporting in? When I find them, I will put my boot up their backsides hard enough to rattle their teeth.* He picked up a fully charged radio, then headed for the main hatch.

Hafiz pushed down the lever to unlock the main door and gave it a shove.

Beth Ledford was flat against the wall on the right-hand side of the door, reaching out with her left to push down the lever. Kyle Swanson was on the opposite side, also with his back to the wall, weapon poised and his finger on the trigger, ready to charge in as soon as she yanked it open far enough. You never knew what was behind any closed door.

Hafiz registered that something was not right as soon as the door had opened just enough for a strong burst of fresh wind to hiss in, indicating the outer gate at the other end was open to the storm. The door continued to swing outward, seemingly on its own, for unseen by Hafiz, Beth Ledford had grabbed the handle on the other side and was pulling on it. Hafiz dropped the lantern, which bounced on the concrete slab floor and sent the beam of light dancing in the darkness. He fumbled to pull the AK-47 from the shoulder sling as a shadowy figure appeared in the open space, with a rifle already pointed at him. Hafiz did not panic, although he realized that his opponent had the advantage.

Swanson had stepped forward and saw a large man bulked up in a poncho, unlimbering a weapon and staring straight at him. *I see you, you see me, but I saw you first.* He fired a three-round burst, then smashed shoulder-first into the big man and stepped over him to clear the rest of the room.

Sergeant Hafiz felt the impact of the bullets. The shock of the attack masked some of the pain; then his head collided with the floor and his face came to rest with his eyes staring directly into the fierce glow of the lantern. He tried to make his hands grab the rifle so he could fight back. His body would not answer his brain's command.

Hafiz could detect the nearness of his attacker, but there was nothing he could do. There was a brilliant flash, but he did not hear the rifle fire when Beth Ledford pumped a final shot into his head.

21

Beth and Swanson each grabbed a wrist of the lifeless, heavy body of Sergeant Hafiz and hauled it outside to dump it in the soggy brush beside the trail. Returning through the gate that camouflaged the entrance, they swung it closed behind them and were in the tunnel and shut the inner door. Smeared blood streaked the smooth floor, and it was eerily still. Swanson pulled Ledford by the collar and put his mouth close to her ear.

"You stay on my six at all times, Coastie. Do what I do. No questions, and don't hesitate," he said. "We have to push forward as far as possible. If we get contact, follow my lead."

She gave a quick nod but did not reply. That life-taking bullet she had fired point-blank into the big soldier's head was something that she had watched Kyle do to the targets they had downed on the patrols, so she had copied the same move, pulling the trigger without emotion. Once it was done, the man was surely no longer a threat to them. It may have been standard operating procedure in special operations, and she had learned it in a violent way on the job, but she was not yet to the point that it would have no effect on her.

When she removed the night-vision goggles, Kyle saw tears welling in the blue eyes of his baby-faced assassin before she wiped them with her dirty sleeve. Because she had been going along so well, he had momentarily forgotten that she had not been trained for these gut-wrenching missions, that her surge of adrenaline had limits; she was running on fumes, and they had a long way to go. He pulled her into a hug, just as he would soothe a thoroughbred horse, or any first-timer getting a taste of close-up death. "You're doing great, Beth," he said. "As good as anybody, and better than most. Now let's do this."

The first steps were the hardest as they moved into unknown territory, but they had no choice. They were totally exposed in the hallway, which measured about six feet wide, big enough for a small tractor to pull a trailer of material or supplies. The ceiling was about seven feet high and supported by webs of metal girders. Neat clusters of pipes hid the electrical wiring, and long fluorescent bulbs glowed with a bluish tint. The low hum of electrical generators could be heard from elsewhere in the complex, and the constant vibration was transmitted through the stone walls.

Twenty feet down the hallway, on the right-hand side, was a closed door, and they crept toward it, stacking against each wall. Swanson saw it had no lock, just a knob, and he motioned for Beth to give it a slow turn. She opened the portal into a small room that was filled with neat stacks of cardboard and wooden boxes, routine supplies that probably serviced nearby facilities, including the entranceway. He motioned her inside, closed the door, and turned on the lights.

Mops and brooms stood around like spindly sentries, radios and flashlights were recharging on a long metal rack, and a pile of fresh towels lay on a shelf. The tangy odors from the jugs and bottles of various disinfectants and cleaning fluids assaulted their nostrils. A bin of dry rags occupied one corner. Kyle tossed a towel to Beth and used another to rub away the mud that was thick on his boots.

Beth took off the black beanie and shook her blond hair, then worked the towel into it hard and wiped her face. She tossed the hat aside, then also went to work on her boots. "I don't think it matters any longer if they happen to notice I'm a woman," she said. "I'm good to go, Gunny. Just some nerves."

Kyle peeled off his own wet wool beanie and dried the top of his head and his face with a soft towel. It felt better. "This place is incredible. From the outside, it seemed like part of the mountain, but inside, it is something else entirely."

"You think my brother got this far?"

"Probably. Even farther. Maybe the door had been left open to bring in supplies or something and they stumbled upon it and just came on in to explore, like kids on a holiday hike."

Beth looked around the room. "There's nothing here that would be worth killing them. That's not it."

They walked to the next room, and the next, working steadily until they cleared the lower corridor, but still found nothing of interest other than the sprawl of the subterranean labyrinth. Some areas were still under construction, with tools, wiring, and lumber strewn about.

An unexpected, high-pitched whine was barely audible in the silence. "We've got contact," Beth said while Swanson was opening still another storage room. They both ducked into the darkness and closed the door, keeping their weapons ready. The whining came closer and passed them by, then stopped. A door opened down the hall; there were slow footsteps, and a grunt and a scrape as something was moved. Ledford flicked on her flashlight and shone the beam around. Boxes were everywhere, and she knelt to read the black printing. She took a quick, sharp breath, then snapped off the light when the whine resumed, suddenly closer and louder.

It passed by again, heading the other way, and Swanson eased the door open and spotted the disappearing rear end of a blue golf cart with a couple of boxes stacked in the rear. The driver wore brown coveralls, but there was no weapon visible. Some civilian worker who had not been looking for anything unusual in this netherworld and had paid no heed to the mixture of grime and blood at the entrance. That sort of luck would not last.

"We're clear here. Ready?"

"Wait, Kyle. Take a look at this first. Boxes of ammo." She flashed her light toward the door, found the light switch, and clicked it on, flooding the room with fluorescent brightness. Swanson immediately saw a box with stenciled markings that identified it as a case of 7.62 × 39 mm ammunition. The room was filled almost to the ceiling with ordnance of various kinds, not just the 7.62 bullets common to the AK-47 but canisters of machine-gun belts, rockets for grenade launchers, and heavy weapons shells.

He took off his pack and placed it on the floor. "This is more like it, Coastie. Your brother and his friends at least discovered storage rooms crammed with ammo and weapons. That alone would prove that this bridge is not just some benign structure built to hurry traffic along the road. If word got back to the U.S., then Washington would start asking uncomfortable questions that Pakistan would not want to answer."

"Would that really be worth killing them for? Maybe just shoo them away with some cover story, like being a storage area for ammo needed to fight the warlords."

"Whatever. It's too good for us to pass up," he said. "You keep watch while I bury some C-4 in this pile. We can command detonate it later on if we need a diversion."

While he planted a brick of explosive and readied the detonator, Ledford stood facing the door, and her eyes came to rest on a square metal frame around a piece of paper encased in plastic. She stepped closer. It was a computer-created image that looked like the layout for a subway. "Here's some kind of map," she said.

"Grab it," Kyle said, and Beth used her fingernails to pry the map from its frame, then dropped it beside Kyle to keep her hands free on her weapon.

"I'm done with this," he said, then shouldered into

his pack again and spent an extra minute studying the paper. "It's a map, all right, like the kind a hotel puts in guest rooms to show escape routes in case of fire. It diagrams the entire floor that we're on, and it looks like there's nothing down here but supply and storage areas and that outside exit. An elevator is at the far end of the corridor to ferry things up, and there's a stairwell just down the hall from here. OK. We'll head up one level."

Ayman al-Masri did not go to bed. He would not consider doing so until he heard from Hafiz that all was well. As a veteran security specialist, and responsible for the safety of the Commander, he was uncomfortable with the performance of the Taliban, and Hafiz had seemed uncharacteristically unsure of himself. The odds against two patrols being simultaneously stymied and one destroyed were enormous. Nothing had been heard from them, and now Hafiz himself had not reported in. Thirty minutes had passed. A vague sense of unrest was bothering al-Masri, a feeling that had served him well over the years as an early warning that something was happening; something much worse than a storm.

He left the living quarters to awaken his small group of inspectors and guards and told them to arm themselves. "Troubling things are happening," he said. "We must not allow ourselves to be lulled into carelessness by the sheer size and apparent strength of this huge fortress, or its electronic wizardry, or the promises made by others that it is safe."

He paired up bodyguards with each specialist. The

structural engineer was ordered to secure an overall detailed map of the maze of tunnels, and the tactical officer was instructed to inspect some gun positions. Al-Masri took the information technician under his own wing. "We are going to find that defense system control room and try to get it back online. If we can get those computers running, they may help us solve the mystery. Hafiz was supposed to do that, but I think he went outside the bridge first and has not returned."

The team's physician was instructed to go to the infirmary and make an independent examination of the chief engineer to see if the lunatic might be of any use at all.

Al-Masri's mood grew more sour with every passing minute that there was no word from beyond the facility. Hafiz might have stammered a bit in their meetings, but there was no doubt of the man's capabilities; he was one of the best operatives in the ISI, a trained and ruthless fighter with years of experience. So why had he not put this right? The only conclusion was that things must have somehow slipped beyond his control. Some external force was pushing events.

He steered the battery-powered cart, questioning the IT specialist sitting stiffly at his side as they rode along. "I don't know if I can bring the facility fully online immediately," the man admitted. "I suspect there are difficult security passwords and firewalls. That biometric scanner means there will even be a problem just getting into the room. It would help if I had access to the chief engineer's journals and logbooks, for then we could hope that he has written them down. If everything

is in his head, as I suspect, we will have serious problems."

They scooted onto a freight elevator and went down
one level to the third floor. The wide doors slid apart,
and al-Masri thought he recognized the color codes.
"Do you remember how to get to the control room? Isn't
it off to the right from here?"

"Yes, sir. Down at the end of the blue hall."

The cart accelerated again, but it was still slow. "So
instead of getting the entire complicated machine running, I want you to concentrate on the controls needed
to shut this place down, just as if it were under attack. I
want some way to lock this place up tight."

The IT man rode silently for a moment. "That also
will take some time. Why not just signal that there is a
fire, sir? That would not seal off the facility, but it
would empty it of all civilian workers."

Al-Masri smiled. A brilliant idea. He yanked his foot
from the accelerator and slammed the brake so hard
that the IT man was almost thrown overboard. The cart
stopped beside a red box on the wall, clearly marked as
a fire alarm. He jumped out and yanked the handle.

Swanson and Ledford were barely at the top of the
stairwell when the fire alarm screeched, and the shriek-
ing startled them both. Kyle ran to the first door he saw
and burst through it, quickly quartering the area with
his weapon although he could see nothing but darkness.
Beth came in fast behind and shut the door, breathing hard. The smell of gun oil hung thick in the small
space.

In the corridor outside, people ran past their hide-out, shouting in various languages. Boots thumped in the stairwell as workers bolted for the exits.

"Did you smell any smoke before the alarm?" Kyle asked.

"No." She leaned against the wall in the darkness, catching her breath.

"Exactly. Neither did I, so there's no telling where the fire may be, or even if there is one. Maybe on the far side of the bridge." He made the decision. "We stay on track."

He unhooked his flashlight, flicked it on, and pointed it at the wall by door. "Hit the switch, Coastie. Nobody will be looking in here for a while."

Beth flipped the switch, and bright light immediately bathed the room. "Holy cow," she stammered, looking past Swanson's shoulder. "What is *that* doing here?"

Swanson spun, almost tripping over an Mk-19 grenade launcher mounted on an adjustable platform that was locked in place on a short set of rails. Affixed to the weapon was a forty-eight-round can of 40 mm high-explosive grenades, and the weapon appeared ready to fire. He gave a low whistle of surprise and ran his hand over the familiar shape. Kyle had run thousands of rounds through similar Mk-19s, the reliable American-made grenade launcher that was a staple of the U.S. arsenal because of its heavy firepower and adaptability to various platforms. "This baby can do some damage," he said. "One of those grenades can punch through two inches of armor, and it's an infantry platoon's worst nightmare."

Beth had to raise her voice to be heard over the alarm. "Yeah. I read the manual, too. But what is it doing in here?"

Instead of answering, Kyle unloaded the launcher and emptied the chamber, then stood in front of the muzzle, facing away from it. The firing slit was closed but parted easily with the press of a nearby knob. Fresh air rushed in, and Swanson leaned closer to the opening. From this vantage point, he had a clear view of a broad section of the long valley. "This could have blown us apart on approach," he observed with a voice as dry as that of a scientist reciting an unpleasant fact.

"So why didn't it?" Beth moved closer to also get a look from the opening. Dawn was approaching, and the darkness was fading fast.

"I don't know, and don't really care right now," he said. "Let's think about this, Coastie: We overcame a lot of heavily armed guards, then found the motion sensors and the cameras, and then once we broke into this rock castle, we found crates of stored ammunition." He tapped the big gun. "Now this: a straight-out-of-the-box Mk-19 that has been turned into a robo-warrior. Open this little slot, slide it out on those rails, shoot for a while, slide it back, close the door, reload, and do it again—and it looks from the wiring that most of it can be done by remote control."

"Then that's what my brother and his team came on, something like this. I remember how Dad drew pictures for us of the Cu Chi tunnels and how gun positions were so cleverly hidden that Americans would walk right over them and not even know they were there.

It was a nightmare to root them out. This looks just like that; this one looks ready for a war all by itself."

"Yep. I agree." A cold feeling washed over him. How many rooms like this were there? How many weapons? What kind? Why? It was a honeycombed defensive position built into solid rock, but with an offensive purpose. All Marines remembered Iwo Jima and the deadly bunkers of the Pacific islands of World War II, and this bridge might be covering the granddaddy of them all. "This could be more than enough reason to kill some curious foreigner intruders. And it means that I was wrong."

"About what?"

"I thought they might be hiding a nuke in here, but that would not explain all of this fancy hardware and the engineering. With a nuke, they could just drill a hole and hide it. But why put a nuke underground at all, because you would want to inflict maximum damage, not to confine the blast. I don't know the reason for this secret place, but our intel people have not picked it up, and Washington cannot allow it to exist."

The alarm ground down from its hellish howl, and stillness settled in the room. Kyle took out his knife and sliced through a handful of wires. "They can repair this, but I don't want to leave it working, in case we have to come back this way."

Beth Ledford turned out the light and gently opened the door.

22

William Lloyd Curtis sped back to Washington with the windows down, letting the wind drum hard into the car. His head still felt cottony, the sluggishness that usually resulted when he drank too much beer, but the howling wind and an espresso macchiato from a Starbucks drive-through had helped cut through the mental fog. He was not drunk, not even tipsy. He licked some of the steamed milk foam from his upper lip.

The chance to let his frustrations run free and bullshit with strangers in a bar where he was unknown had been cathartic, a needed winding-down from the unexpected ISI setback. The roughneck part of his own life, when he had built his construction empire, was truly in the past. For a moment in the bar, he wondered if he could recapture the flavor of those exciting years when he wore dirty jeans and Grateful Dead T-shirts and could use his fists as well as his brain. All the while, he knew that was only a fantasy for a middle-aged man who now wore expensive suits and was an undersecretary in the U.S. State Department, the man who ran the U.S. Bureau of American-Islamic Affairs.

Ah, Raneen. I miss you so much. I have never stopped loving you, and soon your death will be avenged. America will long remember the evil day you were murdered.

By the time the Beemer M3 hit the Beltway after the drive from Williamsburg, Bill Curtis had regained control of his emotions. Everything was still on track. The sprawling intelligence network within the countries of the BAIA was intact, and he really could harbor no lasting resentment against General Gul for not wanting to send a professional ISI killer onto American soil; the general was simply protecting his own agenda, and Curtis never burned such a valuable source over any single decision. They could work together on other projects.

Still, it was clear that he was on his own in containing the nosy Coast Guard woman and her Marine protector. He did not know where they had hidden, but his wide web of contacts was alert, and when they surfaced, he would be waiting.

By the time he drove over the Lion Bridge, he had rolled up the windows and turned on the air-conditioning, and the interior of the luxury automobile had become a comfortable cocoon in which he was shielded from the noise and the smell of the traffic. Washington was still alive with activity, and the streets were busy with pedestrians, from tour groups to workers. Men in running shorts ran laps on the Mall, and young women spoke urgently into their cell phones.

Women, Curtis thought. They always had to stay in

contact with their girlfriends and their mothers and their distant cousins and friends from the second grade, as if they were all stuck together by verbal glue. They all had to know what each other was doing at every moment. A woman might hate her mother, but that did not mean they would not talk on the phone for hours. That was why cell telephone companies were part of his financial portfolio.

Then it hit him. The obituary of the slain American doctor from the bridge incident had included the names of his only two relatives: the Coast Guard sniper and their mother. He had been from somewhere out west, some farm state: Indiana? Iowa? Yes, Iowa. If it was a fact of life that daughters stay in touch with moms, then it would logically follow that this Ledford woman out in the land of alfalfa and cows might have some information that Bill Curtis needed. He suddenly smiled and honked his horn once in celebration. He would go and see her.

"Do we get pieces of cheese when we get out of this maze?" Beth Ledford was only half kidding. The long corridors, side hallways, and vacant rooms still under construction seemed endless, like a high school science experiment to train mice. The fire alarm had emptied the structure, allowing them more freedom of movement, and they had taken advantage of the opportunity to uncover and clear more gun positions, storage areas, support centers, even a mess hall and living quarters. The place seemed endless.

Kyle admitted, "We're just seeing more of the same shit. It must have a purpose, but I don't see it."

"It's just a big bridge."

"With a ton of remote control armament. It burns me that we can't find what they think they are defending in this pile of rocks. There's nothing of real value here. Nada."

"So we can go home now?"

They were in a yellow hallway, before a bright red cross with the word INFIRMARY printed neatly in several languages. "Let's duck in here while I call the extract team."

The solid door to the medical facility was unlocked, and when they stepped inside, it automatically closed behind them. Swanson momentarily felt claustrophobic, as if trapped underground, but six feet away stood another secure door, and he realized they were in an airlock chamber. Blasts of cool, filtered air were pushed in by fans near the floor and slid along their clothing before being sucked out through vents in the ceiling. After ten seconds of the high-pressure sweep, the fans stopped, and the second door swung open silently on its oiled hinges.

They moved into a room that looked in every way like a modern medical clinic, with spotless floors and furnishings. Equipment was neatly stored in cabinets. At the rear of the long room were two empty metal-framed beds covered in white sheets with tight hospital corners, and on each was a blanket folded in half. A frame on rollers supported a head-high curtain that partitioned off the far side of the beds.

Kyle motioned Beth to cover him as he moved forward, pistol drawn.

Ayman al-Masri climbed onto a spool of wire cable beside the road topside and spoke to the approximately fifty workmen who had evacuated the facility. When he identified himself as representing the NMO, there was a shifting of feet in the crowd, and an averting of the eyes. "There is no fire," he said to calm them. "It was necessary to sound the alarm because there has been a serious breakdown in security here. The entire guard force has either been killed or is missing. You, too, may be in danger."

Now they were paying attention to the bearded man. "I do not yet know the extent of the problem, so my team will go back to determine what has happened. I need a few volunteers to stay out here, men who have had military experience to act as guards at the entryways, and let no one in or out until I say differently. Who will help us fight the infidels?"

A few men raised their hands or stepped forward, then more followed. Although they were only construction hands finishing the midnight shift, it would not be wise to be known as an enemy of the NMO. Al-Masri had counted on that fear. He put a volunteer who said he had once been with the Pakistani military in charge and ordered that weapons be issued to the men on guard duty, for he did not want any of them having second thoughts about their loyalty.

Most of his team had also run topside when the alarm sounded, leaving behind only the computer specialist who had the original idea for the alarm. He was still down in the tunnels trying to find the defense systems control room. When they all had weapons, and the entrances and exits were effectively cut off, al-Masri gathered the others and went back inside.

On the elevator ride, he joined the doctor and his bodyguard, who were heading for the infirmary to determine if the captive chief engineer might be able to divulge some of the secret passwords needed in the control room. If necessary, he could be forced to talk. Pain could do wonderful things for a memory.

Tangled, interesting images had been wafting through the brain of Chief Engineer Mohammad al-Attas when the fire alarm sounded, the shrill noise penetrating the last barriers of the sedative he had been given. He came awake slowly with a series of blinks, yawned, and smiled to himself. *Still alive.*

He wondered only momentarily about the fire, because there was nothing at all he could do about it. Burning to death or a bullet in the head would have the same result. Instead, he ran a mental diagnostic of his body. His arms and legs were all still secured by straps, with two more bands of strong woven plastic running across his hips and his chest. For some reason, the clamp around his head had been removed, or perhaps it had slipped off while he thrashed about in the nightmares. Irrelevant. At least he could see around him now.

He surveyed his situation. He was still in the infirmary, with the rolling curtain hiding the rest of the room from view. The usual hospital apparatus was near the bed but was not connected to him. He sucked in a deep breath, then blew it out hard to expel the old, stale air from his lungs. When he did it again, the heartbeat slowed to normal as his mind shifted from a place of uncertain fright to cold analysis. Al-Attas was not afraid. He just settled in for the long wait, until whatever was to happen happened. *Insh'Allah.*

He wondered about Sergeant Hafiz and the al Qaeda inspectors who had examined him like a goat. There was no doubt that he was tagged for death, but then everyone is, and there was no need to fear it. The chief engineer understood that if he had been an ordinary man of ordinary skills, he would have been dealt with some time ago. Since he wasn't, his guardians in Islamabad and Washington were still protecting him, at least for the time being, but he could not count on that.

The alarm was irritatingly loud, and he wished he could shut it off. He wanted to be back in the chair in the defense systems control room, operating his digital domain, supervising the workers to finish the bridge project. Everyone wanted it completed, and the pressure was on him to get it all running. No one else could do it! Another part of him, the invisible part, wished he could be outside, running free beneath the bridge, loose in the valley.

His thoughts were interrupted by the opening of the infirmary door. It closed quickly, and the lock snapped into place. Soft footsteps, not the usual stride of normal workers, came from the far side of the curtain. He saw the silhouette of someone cautiously approaching, and the curtain was thrust aside.

* * *

Kyle Swanson pushed the curtain back with his left hand and brought up his pistol with his right, pointing it straight at the startled face of a dark-haired young man lashed down to a bed. The decision not to shoot was made in a split second, and Swanson moved around the bed to be sure the rest of the area was clear of potential threats. Satisfied, he holstered the pistol, ignoring the bound figure, and removed a satellite phone from his pack. Beth covered the front of the room with her finger resting on the trigger guard of the CAR-15.

"Trident Base, Trident Base. This is Bounty Hunter." His voice was unhurried and clear. He heard only static in return and tried again. "Trident Base. This is Bounty Hunter. Do you read me? Come in." Still, only the hiss of interference.

"Your sat phone won't work down here," said the patient on the bed. "You're beneath tons of rock. The signal can't get out."

Swanson was startled. The words were clear English with only a slight accent. Ledford pointed her rifle at the man. "Who the hell are you?" Kyle asked.

The man shifted the weight of his shoulders, as if trying to get comfortable, but was held tightly by the chest strap. "My name is Mohammad al-Attas."

"Why are you tied down?" Beth Ledford had not lowered her guard.

"They are going to kill me," the young man said.

"Who is? Why?"

"I am considered a security risk by the New Muslim

Order. I suppose I am, because I know too much, and don't say my prayers all the time."

"The Order?" Swanson put away his radio and sat beside the man. "You're saying the NMO is involved here? How do you know that?"

"Oh, they surely are involved," the man replied, with a small, sly smile. "I know that because I am the chief engineer of the entire project. I know everything about it." He relaxed even more. "Other things as well." This encounter was going better than he could have dared hope. Americans: one the usual hard-case commando type, but the other a pretty young woman.

He asked Beth, "I assume you people are the reason for the fire alarm? Did you set it off?"

"We don't know anything about that. Where did you learn English?" She was fascinated. A man tied to a bed in the infirmary of a hostile facility, and apparently under a death sentence, was carrying on a casual conversation, as if he had not a worry in the world. His clothes were bloodstained, and his face and hair were filthy.

"Boston," al-Attas said. "Actually, across the river over in Cambridge, at the Massachusetts Institute of Technology. Picked up my master's degree there. Trust me, your sat phone is useless in this location."

"Can you make it work?"

"Of course. Let's do a deal. Like I said, I know everything about this place, including how to get out. I will be a gold mine for your intelligence people. Take me back with you."

Swanson was still hesitant. "You talk a good game, dude, but why are you so messed up?"

"Basically I outlived my usefulness, and they really did not like that I helped some strangers, particularly an international medical team that wandered in here by accident a few weeks ago. I tried to help them escape, but they caught all of us. It was horrible; they killed those unfortunates after torturing them for sport for a while. They made me continue my work, and when I tried to escape on my own, they put me in here to await execution, probably tomorrow. We're wasting time, sir. Help me get out, and I'll help you in return."

"You built all this?" Kyle knew the man had potentially vital information.

"Yes. I designed every inch."

"Why? For what purpose? All the weaponry?"

Al-Attas shook his head. "At first, I thought that I was just building a bunkered and well-protected bridge. Then it turned out that the New Muslim Order plans for this to be a new hideout for Commander Kahn so he can carry out his attack on *America* while protected against reprisal."

"What new attack on America?"

"It's complicated," he said, "but I know everything. I listened to a lot of conversations that I was not supposed to hear."

Swanson began to unlash the patient. "Let's get the sat phone working," he said.

Al-Attas sat up and rubbed his wrists, then pointed toward a nearby door that was set meticulously into a steel frame. "Sure. Right this way," he said.

23

The elevator made a smooth descent that ended with a slight bump and opened onto a pale yellow corridor with directions painted on the walls in bloodred lettering pointing to the infirmary. After the fire alarm had cleared out the workers, an unusual stillness had settled throughout the big project, where the deep rumble of construction work had been such a constant noise to the ears of Ayman al-Masri that its absence now was startling to the inspector.

He recognized the area and led the other two men directly to the outer door of the airlock that shielded the sterile clinic. "Come," he said. "We can all go through it at the same time." The three stepped inside, the door shut tightly behind them, the rubber seals locked into place, and the automatic fans blasted them for ten seconds. Al-Masri closed his eyes against the force of the wind and remained immobile until the fans cut off and the automatic inner portal opened with a hiss to admit them into the infirmary.

The startled inspector came to a halt. The cloth

screen at the far end had been pushed aside, and the bed behind it, where the chief engineer had been subdued, was empty. The restraints hung down to the floor like sleeping snakes. There was movement at the far doorway, through which a figure dressed in black and carrying a weapon was disappearing. Al-Masri shouted an order to stop, fumbled out his own pistol, and snapped off two shots. The bullets flew wide and chipped the wall.

The unknown figure immediately spun back and answered with a hard rip of automatic rifle fire, a raking stream of bullets that crashed through the room left to right and hip high. The three New Muslim Order men went sprawling on the floor, hugging the cool tiles as a hail of glass and wood and plaster chips splattered into a rising cloud of debris and dust, while ricochets sang wherever the slugs hit metal. When the firing stopped, al-Masri looked up again, pointing his weapon over a flipped table, but no one was there. The door was closed, and the empty room smelled of burned gunpowder.

He eased his weapon down, and they all got to their feet, shaking off the surprise assault. There had been no forewarning of any danger. Both of the others had their own weapons out, too late to join the fight. "Who was it?" the bigger one asked.

Al-Masri surveyed the wreckage, taking quite a bit of time to process his thoughts before speaking. He knew what he had seen clearly before the shots were fired: the diminutive size, the white feminine face, and the short blond hair were unmistakable. A woman had made him cower like a whipped dog. *Impossible*. It could only be a little Satan from the Zionists, who were the only people that used women to actually fight their battles for them. He would never speak of it, at least until after he killed her; slowly. "It is a Jew special operations team," he concluded, walking to the bed where the technician had been strapped. "The Zionists have stolen the chief engineer. They must not leave this bridge alive."

Where was Sergeant Hafiz?

"Dammit, Coastie! Don't do that." Swanson barked at Beth, who was changing magazines. She had emptied a full clip into the room when the man fired at them and had seen three of them dive to the floor as she hammered away with long bursts.

"They were shooting at us," she explained, a calm, empty voice. She had not given the possibility that she had killed anyone a second thought. Worrying about that sort of thing was part of another life, a distant memory of an Iowa farm girl who no longer existed.

"We have limited ammunition, so stop hosing down things like this is some action movie," Kyle said. "Be selective. Short, targeted bursts."

"Huh," she said, turning away, angry. She had just saved their asses and all he could do was bitch, although she knew he was right. There had never been a shortage of ammo in her HITRON helicopter, but they were using NATO 5.56 mm rounds today and only had what they carried. She would not make the same mistake again.

Beth made a mental note to pick up the next AK-47 she saw and a bunch of magazines. There was certainly no shortage of AK bullets in this place.

Swanson found himself in a large, well-appointed suite that would have fit in well at the Ritz-Carlton in Boston: walls of finished wood, well-made furniture, and an open balcony that extended outside. "Will the satellite phone work out there?" he asked their new guide.

Mohammad al-Attas shrugged his shoulders. "Perhaps. No guarantee. May I make an alternate suggestion?"

"Sure." Kyle was ready to try anything. The mission had been blown, and the bad guys knew exactly where they were. It was time to call the birds and get out.

The engineer moved to a small desk on one side of the room and pulled open the center drawer to reveal a computer keyboard, then unfolded a seventeen-inch flat-screen monitor. "This has a separate hard drive but is wired into the main computer system to get a clear wireless link. Can you send an e-mail, or do a Skype face-to-face video connection?"

For a moment Kyle considered Commander Kahn of the New Muslim Order sitting before this keyboard, playing chess by himself, adding new friends on his Facebook page, updating his MySpace profile, checking out porn sites or launching an attack on the United States. The beauty and the bedevilment of social media was its anonymity, and it was so simple that a caveman could do it.

Swanson grunted assent. The control room of Task

Force Trident was manned 24/7 when an operation was in progress, and Commander Benton Freedman would be plugged in, constantly trawling his electronic universe. Kyle shifted his gear so he could sit at the desk, pulled the keyboard close, and sent a quick note to lizard@lizard.com. "Liz?" He signed it "Bounty Hunter."

There was a brief pause; then a pop-up window appeared in one corner of the screen to show the Lizard had created a point-to-point connection. "Yo," came the response.

Kyle typed, "Launch extract."

"Confirming extract, Bounty Hunter. Cords?"

Swanson referred to his map and typed two groups of numbers, and the Lizard confirmed.

"When?"

The engineer had been watching over Kyle's shoulder, impressed by the knowledge being demonstrated at the other end of the conversation. Whoever it was had cracked his security wall with ease and put up a private window that no one else could control. For the first time, he entertained a doubt about the security of the entire project. There were other smart people in the world.

"How long will it take for us to get from where we are right now up to the top of the bridge?" Kyle asked the engineer.

"Maybe ten minutes," al-Attas replied. "If we are not slowed down too much by fighting."

Kyle knew that was unlikely. The battle had already begun and would only get worse. "T-minus-twenty," he wrote. "Start time now. Hot LZ."

"On the way. Lizard out." The image of a green gecko scurried up the screen, ate the window and the words in it, then crawled off the screen, leaving it blank.

Swanson ripped out the hard drive and checked his weapon. Another problem solved. A pair of Boeing V-22 tilt-rotor Ospreys had been orbiting safely out of harm's way and beyond radar range since Kyle and Beth had parachuted into the night. With in-flight refueling and relief crews aboard, the high-speed, long-range birds could remain on station almost indefinitely and were perfect as an exfiltration vehicle. They could take off and land like helicopters, and the large turbofan engines on each wing could rotate to provide conventional flight, which made them much faster than a chopper. The Lizard was even now alerting them to break out of orbit and head in. One would supply covering fire while the other did the pickup.

A new checklist was forming as he surveyed the room one last time. "What are the exits here? Just the two doors and the ledge? Is there an emergency way out?"

"Of course." Al-Attas remembered the original instructions he had been given to design the living facility so that the resident would never be trapped, no matter what. "The easiest way is a long rope that can be snapped to that big ring secured into the rocks out on the balcony."

"Too exposed." Kyle did not like the idea of dangling from a rope over the side of a cliff with people shooting at him.

"Then there are hatchways in the floor and ceiling of the closet over there. The top one leads directly into a gun bunker, and the lower one is a service tunnel for wiring and maintenance. From either one, you can get into the tunnels and go anywhere, even beneath the river to reach the east tower, or out into the valley."

Pounding was heard at the door to the infirmary as the NMO security men shook the handle and tried the locks. Kyle knew they would not stay there long, and the other door would soon be under attack. He had no idea how many enemy troops would be involved.

"Beth, listen to me. The Ospreys are inbound and will land on the helicopter LZ up top, beside the road, in exactly twenty minutes. You know the place?"

Ledford nodded. She had studied the bridge minutely during the recon, and Kyle had pointed out the large flat area. They were going to run into opposition on the way out, but she was confident that she and Kyle would be more than a match for whoever it was. "I'm ready."

"We split up now. You take this guy and the maps and go through the lower hatch; get to the east tower and go up and out that way. I'm going to stick around and cause some diversions to draw them off."

"Shouldn't we stay together, Kyle, to increase our firepower?" She didn't relish the idea of being on her own.

"Trust me, Coastie. In a few minutes, they will be coming after me with everything they've got. The main mission now is to get this guy and his information back to base. Now move. You have twenty minutes, and that's all. Remember Quantico; don't miss the pickup, and you go with or without me."

"Kyle—" she started again, but he cut her off.

"Shut up and do what I just fucking told you. Get him and the intel out of here. If an attack on America is imminent, we've got to get him back safely. I'll run interference. I trust you."

She looked at him with steady blue eyes, wanting to stay in his zone, while knowing it was inevitable that she had to go out on her own. She wasn't afraid but had to push down the troublesome question of what she was doing here in the first place. *Three weeks ago I worked for the dang Coast Guard, but now Kyle Swanson trusts me!* That changed everything. "Come on, Mohammad," she finally said. "Into that service tunnel."

Al-Attas bristled and turned to Kyle. "I do not take orders from women," he said.

"In that case, I will just shoot you right now and make our egress a lot easier. We will settle for the information that we already have, that hard drive, and the maps. Don't think for a moment that you are indispensable. If you give my friend any macho shit on the way out, she has my permission to blow your head off. She never misses."

"Very well, but I intend to report this rudeness to your superiors."

"You do that. If any of us live that long."

Ayman al-Masri left his doctor at the infirmary door and sent the bodyguard around to the second entrance, returning to the elevator alone and rising back to the surface. His eyes glowered like burning stones as he looked out at the vastness of the construction area. It was all such a sham, such a waste. The Pakistanis and the Taliban had both promised that it was a fortress for the new age, a place in which Commander Kahn would be totally safe, because no enemy force could possibly breach the bridge and its mighty array of techno-weapons. Those promises were worthless. They had planned on methods to turn away massive assaults, yet a small special operations team had breached all of the security devices and snatched the man who had put it all together. That chief engineer should have been disposed of immediately, for disaster seemed to follow in his footsteps. Now he and his secrets were in the hands of the infidels.

All of the workers were called together again, a mob of shuffling construction men who were physically fit, although most of them were militarily untrained. To motivate them, he announced that the enemy had penetrated deep into the bridge, intending to destroy it and then kill everyone on the site. The suddenly excited men were divided into teams and provided with weapons and radios. There were upwards of forty of them, which should be enough, so he culled out a few European technicians, who were bound and left under guard because they could not be trusted. The rest surged into the tunnels, starting the search at the top of the bridge, then flooding down through the stone passageways. They were already familiar with the maze, not least because they had helped build it. They did not need maps, only leadership.

Al-Masri organized his command post topside, then drank an entire bottle of water while considering his next move. *Play this backward,* he thought; *start at the end, not the beginning.* The ultimate goal of the raiders, now that they had been uncovered, would be to escape, and that probably would involve a helicopter. By studying a topographical map and walking the area to peer down the valley, he was able to identify several likely landing sites within a two-kilometer radius of the bridge. He gave a quiet curse. With the morning light growing brighter, it would be an easy thing to shoot them down with the proper weapons. However, the antiaircraft cannons he needed were located deep down within the bridge, anchored on mounts in the gun rooms, useless, unless his tech specialist could get things running again. Men would be required to cover each potential landing zone, and he would send one to scrounge for some rocket-propelled grenades in the storerooms.

Once his teams were on the move, and with the likely landing zones pinpointed, al-Masri finally went to his secure radio link to report back to the New Muslim Order headquarters. The conversation was short, and he was firm. Commander Kahn was not to be brought to this bridge, no matter what promises were made. The bridge, he declared, was not a safe digital fortress but little more than a sand castle.

24

Kyle Swanson was finally alone, and his chances of living beyond the next nineteen minutes rested solely on his own shoulders. All he had to do was master a varying formula of time, space, the number of tangos, distance, and direction. The time could be pinpointed, and the opposition force would be adjusted as he went along. Space and distance were unknown factors, because of the labyrinth of confusing corridors and pathways, but he did not need any special talent, not even a compass, to keep going in the right direction; up was always up.

He had total freedom of action and would consider anyone he encountered to be a hostile. Although he knew little about his enemy, they knew less about him, and they would be in his free-fire zone.

There was noise and movement on the far side of the infirmary door, indicating an assault was being prepared. They would probably blow the door and rush into the room. Kyle intended to be long gone by then, although he would leave a clear trail to be followed. He dragged a chair into the closet, pushed open the ceiling hatch, grabbed the edge, did a chin-up, and chicken-winged his elbow into the opening to gain more leverage. He climbed up and out, leaving the chair standing in place over the lower hatch through which Ledford and the engineer had gone. The natural choice for the chasers would be to follow him.

Swanson came up in the dim light of a bunker, beside another fully loaded heavy machine gun affixed to the usual mechanical arms and anchors. He closed the hatch, unsnapped the box of ammunition from the big weapon, and rested it carefully on a fragmentation grenade the size of a baseball. With the box holding down the safety spoon, he pulled out the pin to arm the grenade. Moving the hatch would jar the box, which would detonate the booby trap.

He touched his throat microphone. "Coastie. Can you read me?"

"Barely," came her huffing reply. "We're on hands and knees, but the opening to a corridor is just ahead. Mohammad says it will take us under the river. No opposition so far."

"Eighteen minutes."

"We'll be there," she said and then lowered her voice. "Kyle? He is starting to growl."

Swanson walked to the exit hatch of the gun bunker, suppressing his natural sniper instincts and training. On any ordinary mission, stealth and hiding were the keys to success, so he would have remained invisible. This time, he not only had to expose his own position but also initiate a running gunfight. That meant sending an invitation that could not be ignored.

The usual laminated map on the door revealed the layout for this section. Elevators were at one end of the main corridor, and the broad main staircase at the other, about a hundred meters away. Five hallways branched off at irregular distances, and each terminated at a set of steel spiral stairs. At first he had worried that he might be cornered like a rat in a trap, but in reality, his situation was much better. The ten spirals, two elevators, and main stairway connecting each level were all designed to ensure easy movement of men and materiel within the bridge, to resupply and help shift forces during a battle against a force attacking from outside. The whole thing was built to keep people out, not to keep someone inside. From Kyle's perspective, that system presented the defending force with a significant problem, for they could not possibly cover all of the choke points. Time to go hunting.

He slowly opened the gun pit exit and peered into the hallway. It was empty, so he stepped outside and kicked down the doorstop to hold it open when he left. Swanson moved like a shadow to the far corridor beside the main stairs and into the intersecting hall, where he backed into a doorway. The frame was only about seven inches deep, but it also was the only available cover, so he wedged in tight, happy that he was only five foot nine and slim instead of six foot plus and bulky. Anyone rushing down the main hall from either the elevator or the staircase would run right past his hiding place.

His muscles were rigid, so he commanded his body to relax, and the heart rate immediately obeyed; he breathed steadily, his eyes cleared to razor sharpness, and both the world and time began to slow down, as they always did before he let all hell break loose.

He removed the remote control detonator from his pack, clicked off the safety, and pressed the button. In an instant, the brick of C-4 he had placed in the ammunition storage room at the lower entrance to the tunnels exploded with a booming, furious crash that challenged the thick rock. The walls channeled the concussion along like a flood of water surging through giant pipes, and only two floors above, Swanson pulled his head down into his shoulders and braced in the door frame as his entire world twisted and groaned. *That should get their attention,* he thought. Secondary explosions cooked off and added to the bedlam.

The heavy stone was part of an entire mountain range and soon ate the blast effects. The lights that had blinked off sparkled back to life, and only a mist of dirt seeped from the ceiling. Swanson stepped into the empty main hallway and laid down a long and loud burst of automatic fire that rippled and ricocheted, and the bullets tore at doors and walls, pocked the elevator, and smashed the lights. The doorway to the gun pit remained yawning open, and he put a few rounds in there for good measure before ducking back into his narrow hide and reloading. He looked at his watch: seventeen minutes before pickup.

Beth Ledford and Mohammad al-Attas were thrown off their feet when the explosion shook the mountain. They were halfway through the big tunnel beneath the river, and she momentarily wondered if the blast might crack a seam that would drown them beneath tons of churning water.

"Get up! Get up!" she screamed at the engineer, who was still on his knees, dazed and shaking his head. A small cut had been torn in his scalp, and blood flowed on his cheek. Beth grabbed his sleeve and hauled him up from the floor.

There wasn't much to this guy, she thought. No muscle tone, uncoordinated, and weird eyes that spelled geek. She yelled, "Now run. Run like your life depends on it."

Al-Attas shambled forward, smelling the dank surroundings as his mind processed some formulas about pressure limits. He was pleased that the structure had held so well against the force of the unexpected explosion, just as he designed it to do. There had been no serious damage. The chief engineer smiled at the woman. He got another hard push and moved a bit faster.

"I didn't say jog. I said *run*." This dude was slowing things down. "We've got to reach the other end of the tunnel and then get topside. If we miss the extraction bird, we're dead, because it won't wait. Come on. Just follow me. You can do it." Her boots beat a steady tempo on the cold stone floor.

The engineer was breathing harder, panting. Running felt good. It made him remember being outside and free, trotting lazily around in the darkness, and feeling cool wind on his body. The tunnel took on the appearance of a big hole to him, which it was, and he imagined a wolf chasing a rabbit, closing steadily.

Beth slowed at the end of the tunnel and stopped at the bottom of the metal staircase. When she turned to check on the engineer, his fist came flying at her face, so unexpected and fast that she did not have time to block it. The impact was followed by a terrible yowl, and then the engineer leaped and knocked her flat. She rolled her head away from the blow, moving with the punch to dissipate its force, although the knuckles smashed her left cheek hard enough to make her see stars. While she spun downward, a second blow smacked the top of her head; then the tackle put her down totally. Her rifle was still firmly attached to her harness, but she felt the attacker's hands grasping for the knife on her belt, and the man's hot breath on her face.

"What the hell are you doing?" she shouted. With his hands going for the knife, he had no way to block her palm strike at his nose, and she punched in hard. The nose broke, and al-Attas's head flew back, leaving the neck unprotected for her to drive three stiff fingers into the trachea.

The wild-eyed man deflated like a balloon. He grabbed his throat with both hands, gagging to try to get air, and rolled away. Beth turned around on the floor, kneed him in the groin, then clocked him on the temple with the butt of her rifle. Mohammad Al-Attas was down and out, blood pouring from his nose.

Ledford got to her feet and lifted her fingers to check her face. She tasted blood and felt the pulsing ache by her eye. Nothing serious. She kicked him in the ribs, and he emitted a long groan that indicated he wasn't totally unconscious. "I really want to shoot your sorry ass, but you apparently are a valuable target," she said and secured his wrists with plastic flex-cuffs. Unbuckling his belt, she tightened it into a noose around his neck so she could pull him along on a leash, then cut away the top button on his jeans and slit the waistband. "You can use your hands to hold up your pants. Come on." She yanked the leash and hauled him upstairs.

The explosion far belowground had spent its force by the time the concussion wave reached the main roadway topside, where it had hardly made the rocks grumble. Ayman al-Masri figured it was just the opening of the battle against the Zionist raiders and continued to study the maps of the complex that he had spread on a table. A tinny voice on his radio broke into his thoughts, and one of his bodyguards who had broken into the infirmary stronghold reported, "Gunshots on the third level, directly above us." Gunfire was different than the explosion; someone had to be present to pull a trigger. He decided to tighten the hunt by surging everyone into the one area where he knew the enemy was located.

"What is your status?" he asked.

"We are inside the infirmary," said the bodyguard. "No one is here, but we found a hatch that leads to the floor above, where the shooting is."

"Pursue them. I am sending help immediately."

"Yes, sir. We're going up."

Al-Masri's palms felt wet with perspiration, and he wiped them on his robe. This might be over quickly if they could lock the commando team into that one space. Al-Masri could make up for their lack of training by using the advantage of sheer numbers. He gave a quick order to everyone. "All teams converge to the third level of the east tower. There are probably not more than three or four Zionists to fight. We will have them trapped there. Use your combined firepower to keep their heads down, then wipe them out."

Men who had just entered the west tower responded and came back out in a rush to cross the broad bridge and descend into the east-side tunnel. More would advance through the access corridors just below the roadway.

The bodyguard who lifted the hatch cover above the infirmary had to push hard against the unexpected weight, and the grenade booby trap detonated in the gun room bunker with a harsh *craaack* that covered his agonizing scream as he caught the full force of the explosion in his head and chest. A coil of thick smoke oozed through the open door into the third-level hallway, and single rounds of machine-gun ammunition ignited with a clatter in the intense heat.

Swanson heard men running down the main stairwell and entering the hall, and he shoved himself back deeper into his door frame. Four went past his corridor without glancing at it, firing blindly into the smoke ahead. When they were beyond his position, he came out and lit them up from behind with short bursts, using more bullets than actually needed for the job, but wanting to use the surprise effect of a noisy firefight on the oncoming force.

The next batch paused and slowed their advance; then Kyle triggered a burst that chipped the lower steps, and drew a barrage of automatic fire in return. He bellowed as if he had been hit and ran back into the churning smoke, dropping flat at the corner of two corridors to watch them come down. They shot wildly around the first intersection until they discovered no one was there, and the easy capture of that little bit of territory gave them a false feeling of victory, emboldening them while at the same time making them more careless.

Kyle held his fire, using the time to rig another grenade booby trap and string a tripwire low across the hallway. The group moved closer down the main hallway, laying waste to the next intersection of corridors, gaining even more confidence when no fire was returned. They had captured two intersections without incident and stepped up the advance, talking loudly and with confidence. He leaned out and buzzed them, then ducked back after the single long burst and took off for the nearest spiral stairwell.

He paused halfway up to fire again as the more aggressive pursuers came charging around the corner. He wanted them to have their eyes locked on him, rather than where they were going. The lead man cleared the tripline without even seeing it, but the toe of the fighter behind him hit the taut wire, which yanked out the pin, and the grenade exploded, filling the hallway with flying shrapnel, confusion, blood, and terror. Swanson dashed the rest of the way up the stairs, taking them two at a time.

25

The opening steps of his violent choreography to reach the top of the bridge had gone as smoothly as a waltz on *Dancing with the Stars*, a series of well-drilled maneuvers so common and practiced that they even had names. He had opened with Excessive Force, to lure the curious enemy into a kill zone, and followed that with a Flash Attack to stun them. Now he was falling back in a controlled Australian Peel.

The Peel was a sniper's protective game of leapfrog on defense. After an attack against a larger force, the sniper would stay put and lay down suppressive fire while his spotter fell back twenty meters, hit the ground, and took up the firing to allow the sniper to bound back another twenty meters, then repeat the process. The difference today at the bridge was that Swanson had to perform both roles: fire, then give up some ground to his pursuers to make them think they were making progress, with no idea that it was being given to them. Kyle did not want to break contact, and so far, it had worked. He was picking apart the opposing force.

He found no one waiting when he emerged up on the second level, so he ran to another doorway and squeezed in tight again, thinking of what to do next. He was uninjured and still had plenty of ammo if he was careful, some C-4, several hand grenades, and a bandolier of five grenades for the launcher that hung beneath the barrel of his CAR-15. There were plenty of moves left, although he was feeling the press of time. Eleven minutes.

He could hear the pursuers milling around below, an indication of a lack of discipline, training, experience, and leadership. He fired a single shot back down the stairs to focus their attention again, and the bullet struck metal stairs and zinged away like the clanging of a bell. The enemy fighters realized their quarry was waiting for them up on the next level, still ready to fight.

Kyle intended to make the most of his clear advantage in this small underground city of channels and burrows. Rooting out a skilled defender required patience, determination, luck, and skill, and the butcher's bill was usually high. An untrained force such as he was facing today had little choice other than to pour in a lot of bodies.

"Ahlo?" A strange voice from the radio was tinged with despair, even as the caller said a universal form of "Hello."

Ayman al-Masri of the New Muslim Order responded without introduction. "Who is this? Where are you?"

"We are on the third level, mister," said the nervous

voice. "There has been a horrible battle down here. The casualties have been heavy."

"How many of the Zionist raiders have been killed?"

"None that I have seen, sir."

"Well, how many are there?"

A pause. "About six?"

"Can you actually see the enemy from your position?"

A long pause. "No, mister."

"Then how do you know there are six?"

"Ummh. That is just my estimate, mister. So much damage. So many men are down and badly hurt. Please send medical help."

Al-Masri knew the pleading coward on the radio was hiding, not advancing.

"What is your name?" The demand was almost a snarl.

The radio went silent. Bonte Ibara had no intention of giving his name to the terrorist leader and possibly being singled out later for blame, or worse, to be appointed leader of the other men down in this hellish battle. The fifty-one-year-old Congolese man, with weathered dark skin and sprinkles of white in his black hair. was a month from the end of a one-year contract as an electrician subcontractor with a Saudi construction firm. Bonte looked over at his friend Guychel Mouko, a heavy equipment operator who had come north with Ibara as a contract worker. They had lived for months on meager rations, sending almost everything they earned back to their families. Both had come to work on a bridge, not to fight soldiers. They were not even Muslim.

Having survived civil wars in Africa, both had seen many times what bullets and explosions could do to the human body. Let the young hotheads who had never tasted a real fight do whatever they wanted, like that boy who had run forward without looking and stepped on the booby trap. The blast had torn the torso in half, painted the walls with blood and purple intestines, and clouded the corridor with smoke. Only a fool would want to be the first to go into that kind of death trap against an Israeli raiding party. Bonte and Guychel had lagged far behind coming down the stairs and were the only members of their small group still standing.

"Can you hear me?" The radio squawked, the New Muslim Order man obviously angry. "Give me your name!"

Guychel shook his head. "No." He gently removed the radio from the hand of his friend and hurled it far down the corridor, where it smashed into pieces as it bounced and slid along the rock floor.

Bonte pushed open a door and went inside, and Guychel followed, closing it behind him, then turning the lock on the supply room. They put their AK-47s aside, sat on the boxes, and lit cigarettes. "It will be over soon. Fights this intense never last too long," Bonte said. "What do you hear from home?"

Elsewhere in the complex, other workers were making similar decisions to let sudden, deadly violence pass them by.

Ten minutes remained before the inbound extraction birds were due topside. Kyle Swanson could not waste time hanging around in the second level of this subterranean maze. Nothing of value would be gained by forcing another firefight, but he had to do some damage before leaving.

The pursuing force was already in disarray, and their firing had momentarily ceased, so Swanson intended to make his next move as horrific as possible before they could shake off the feeling that certain death lurked around every corner. Mobility and his pitiless attacks had tilted things in his favor, and he needed to capitalize on that. His brain told him to be patient, to work it through step by step. *Slow is smooth; smooth is fast.*

He pressed the latch of the grenade launcher slung beneath his rifle, slid its barrel forward, put the weapon on safe, and removed a stubby, low-velocity 40 mm high-explosive, dual-purpose grenade from his bandolier. The golden dome and olive green body slid easily into the chamber, and Swanson pulled the barrel toward the rear to lock it. Then he broke cover and ran to the corner where his latest corridor intersected with the main hallway. Leaning around, he saw it was clear, and he moved his finger to squeeze the launcher's separate trigger.

The weapon bucked with a firm *bhoomp* as the M-433 HEDP grenade fired, and Kyle spun to the floor behind the concrete wall, curled into the fetal position, closed his eyes, and covered his ears as the grenade hit the stone steps with a stunning explosion and a blinding flash. The earsplitting blast tore a deep gouge into the stairs, spraying out a thick circle of shrapnel and de-

bris that would have killed anyone within fifteen feet.
With that echo still vibrating and smoke boiling, Swanson loaded a second HEDP round, moved to the other side of the auxiliary corridor, and took aim through the leaf sight in the opposite direction down the main hallway. When he was sighted on the midpoint of the big doors of one of the elevators, he fired, then again dove to the floor against the near wall as the grenade penetrated the thin-skinned door. A long tongue of red and yellow flame jetted out of the elevator shaft, the aluminum doors blew off, and heavy shards of rock and shrapnel ripped and tore at the cables supporting the elevator. The high-pitched squeal of tortured metal pulling against metal rose above the din of the explosion, and the heavy elevator was twisted and pushed with ever-increasing force against the braided steel cables that had been chipped and sliced. It did not fall but was jammed so hard between the walls and the support girders that it could not move.

The concussion slammed through the corridor like a broadside from a battleship and bounced Swanson like a ball. Even after the wave passed beyond him, he remained curled up, disoriented, certain that he had been deafened and blinded by his own doing. *I was too close!* Acrid smoke made him cough, and that automatic physical response brought the rest of his senses back online. The eyes blinked, but his ears were popping like little firecrackers. Nature of the business; part of the game. Spitting out dirt, he shook himself free of layers of debris, and junk fell from his clothing and gear. Using the wall for support, Kyle pulled himself back to his feet, peeled away from his position, and moved out. It had taken three minutes.

In the east tower, Beth Ledford had made good progress, towing the young engineer along behind as she advanced through the levels. In fact, the prisoner—she no longer thought of him as an ally—had been the only real opposition since she had separated from Swanson. She was almost to the top now, in the first basement level, and the main entrance was less than fifty meters away, framing a bright square of light outside. She could smell the fresher air. With less than seven minutes remaining before extraction, she had never felt so totally alert and sharp. There was no sense of panic.

An unattended line of little golf carts was parked along one wall, with slack cables plugged into power sources to charge the batteries. The corridor seemed clear, and distant explosions told her that Swanson still was going strong over in the other tower; it sounded like a war. She felt she probably could have walked out of this corridor in a miniskirt and high heels and nobody would have paid any attention, because everyone was at the party next door.

A silhouette crossed at the entrance, and Beth ducked out of sight between the carts and the wall, pulling her prisoner to his knees. He grunted, and she held a finger to her lips to shush him. They were long past the time where he might have anything to say that would be of interest to her.

The figure at the entrance passed through the cone of light and vanished again. Beth assumed it was a guard who had been left behind to secure that tunnel mouth while the hard fighting raged elsewhere. She could easily shoot him from this angle, but the retort of a rifle would be amplified enough in the tight confines of the corridor and might be enough to draw unwanted attention. She could not expect to just walk the next two hundred feet unobserved while pulling a man along on a leash.

"Get in this cart. Left side," she whispered. "Call out or try to escape and I'll shoot you." Mohammad al-Attas nodded that he understood, and she dropped the end of the leash but unholstered her pistol. There was a rag on the floor, and she tied it like a kerchief over her blond hair.

She yanked the cable on the cart from the power strip and climbed in. It was just an ordinary golf cart with a light blue fiberglass body, no more complicated to drive than a child's wagon. When Beth pressed the accelerator, the vehicle moved forward on a battery-powered engine that was virtually silent. She steered with her left hand, with the pistol in her right, resting out of sight in her lap.

The guard might have been curious had he seen two people walking out, but he hardly noticed the approach of one of the buglike carts that constantly roamed the bridge and tunnels. Beth shot him with two point-blank taps to the head without even taking her foot from the accelerator.

NEW YORK

It was night in Manhattan. The neon signs around Times Square took on a bright life of their own, the tourists flocked to the theaters, the Royal Shakespeare Company was doing *Julius Caesar* at Lincoln Center, the Rockettes were stretching out prior to another high-kicking show at Radio City Music Hall, and Jimmy Buffett was jamming with Neil Young in a Village bar. After another workday in the canyons of office buildings, millions of people were on the move again, hungry for entertainment and personal contact, going to restaurants or to their apartments or to the saloons. In midtown, a few blocks from the United Nations tower, three men were seated around a table in a luxury hotel suite that was protected by bodyguards with small machine guns. They all wore serious game faces. "I think we've got a Fish," said one. "Not just a Fish, but fuckin' Moby Dick."

Fred Ellison, chief of the State Department's Diplomatic Security Service, sipped some sweet lemonade before continuing his pitch. Andy Moore of the Central Intelligence Agency and David Hunt of the Federal Bureau of Investigation listened with growing astonishment as Ellison spun his tale of how Undersecretary William Lloyd Curtis of the U.S. Bureau of American-Islamic Affairs had recently stepped far beyond his pay grade and used DSS assets to track an American citizen. "I put a stop to it as soon as I found out, then I read Curtis the riot act," said Ellison. "At the time, I chalked it up to a mistake in judgment, although he was no glad-handing rookie diplomat. I underestimated him."

"Is he a heavy hitter in the administration?" asked Hunt.

"Absolutely. Former ambassador to Kuwait and Egypt. Heavy campaign contributor to both parties as a civilian, with lots of experience, contacts, and knowledge about the Sandbox countries. He hosts swanky parties that cover as a backdoor channel for communication between Washington and the Islamic world."

"Man, we could probably send him to prison just for that security breach, but it's pretty thin. No real red flags that I see," said Moore.

"It became a burr under my saddle," admitted Ellison. "Not so much that he did it, but why would he do such a stupid thing? So I started showing a special interest in him."

"So, since we all work in Washington, why are we here in New York?" Hunt leaned forward and rested his elbows on his knees.

Ellison drew out a photo of a middle-aged fat man with dark hair and passed it around. "This man is Mohammed Javid Bhatti, who works for the Pakistani Foreign Office right over at the UN, and he has been showing up frequently, either in person or by phone or e-mail, with Undersecretary Curtis. I ran him by our resident security officer in Islamabad, who got back to me this morning. We're here because there are too many leaks in Washington. I've known and trusted you guys for years, and want to keep this on the down-low."

"Javid Bhatti is your Fish?" Hunt looked curiously at the photograph. "Pardon my French, Freddy, but this guy ain't no Moby Dick. More like a fat flounder."

Ellison rapped the table with his knuckles. "No, Dave. Undersecretary Curtis is the Fish. My RSO in Pakistan reported that this flounder, Mr. Bhatti, really works for the New Muslim Order."

Moore and Hunt exchanged frowns, and Hunt cleared his throat. "You think this Bhatti and the NMO are trying to manipulate or blackmail a ranking American diplomat?"

"Worse. I think Curtis is working for them of his own free will. My opinion, the son of a bitch is a closet jihadist."

"Why? He had to have gone through a complete security clearance just to get his job"

There was silence in the room, and the noise of New York drifted up to the fifteenth floor, a muted burble of yells, taxi horns, and a siren from a traffic accident. "I want to do another one, deeper this time. All the way down to the bone because I missed something the first time around. I propose a full-court press on this, guys, but keep it quiet. All three of our agencies have to be involved and cooperate."

"What about Homeland Security?" Hunt asked with a slight smirk.

"Who?" laughed Moore, removing a white legal pad from his briefcase to draft a game plan.

26

Security Chief Ayman al-Masri of the New Muslim Order remained confident of the outcome of the fight, despite the setbacks. The untrained rabble at his disposal was clearly outmatched by the professionals of the Zionist raiding party, but the trail of bodies on the lower levels and the battle noise in the east tunnel indicated the raiders were still headed topside. If they expected a ride out of here, at some point their rescue helicopter had to arrive, and the enemy would have to emerge from the tunnel to board it.

In the distance, he had watched a blue golf cart carrying one of his teams emerge from the east tunnel and zip across to where heavy earthmoving equipment was parked. Good men. Finally, some of these cowards were showing the aggressiveness needed to overcome the flaws in the general attack. They had taken a good defensive position behind the big machines without being told, and that action gave him an idea for a final strategy.

Instead of wasting his fighters belowground, al-Masri

decided to reorganize into a pair of strong defensive positions around both main entrances, and simply wait for the targets to present themselves. When they did, he would finish them off.

"Leave the guard and those other two down at the west tunnel mouth, but gather the rest here," he told his bodyguard, who radioed the instructions to the other teams. "I will instill the fear of Allah in them, and they will fight!"

About thirty men had gone into the tunnels, but fewer than ten came out and drifted over to him. Twenty dead? Al-Masri snorted; some of the foreign contract workers were hiding down there to save their skins. He would deal with them later. There was still some shooting below, so others were still engaged and unable to break contact.

"Now listen carefully, you worthless dogs," he shouted and took a deep breath to begin explaining his trap. He never finished, because he heard the pounding thrum of approaching aircraft.

It is hard to kill someone behind a wall, and Kyle Swanson huddled down tight in a small alcove on the first basement level while a tight curtain of bullets whizzed by him. Finally, he had run into someone who knew how to fight.

Swanson was bottled up in the wide tunnel that sloped up to the main entrance, and he had about a minute and a half left, with the seconds falling rapidly away. Soon, the bird would touch down for a moment and then be gone.

If he missed the extract, he planned to haul ass back downstairs as fast as possible and crawl out of a firing slit in one of the gun pits. Once in the valley, he could evade, find a new hide, and arrange another pickup.

He would stick here for a few more seconds and raise some hell to divide the attention of any topside fighters and help the Ospreys come in safely. He could only hope that Coastie and the engineer were ready, although he had not heard from them for several minutes.

Another fusillade of bullets buzzed his way, sliding and bouncing along the wall, gnawing at his hiding place, and he stuck the CAR-15 out and returned a burst. The other guy was shielded at a corner and was cold locked in on Kyle. There was too much open space to rush the gunman, and if reinforcements came in to help, Swanson would have a real problem. The one thing he could not afford to do was nothing.

The bright glare of the sun had made Beth Ledford shade her eyes with her palm when her cart swept out of the tunnel and onto the bridge. Free of the tight confines of the subterranean levels, she found herself in the open, driving across a wide roadway that had broad aprons spread on each side, with high guardrails along the edges. To her left were the cloth cubicles of the bazaar, although the hawkers had abandoned the area when the shooting started. Far to the right at the other end of the bridge, she saw a group of men gathered in a circle.

She swerved to the apron and parked between heavy excavation equipment, then shoved the engineer out, grabbed his leash, and hauled him down beside a huge bulldozer. As she checked her weapons, she heard the planes and pressed her radio earpiece hard, calling for help, praying for a response.

"Limo Three-Two. Limo Three-Two. This is Bounty Hunter Bravo."

During years of controversial development, the Osprey had gained such a bad reputation that Marines assigned to fly on them grimly called themselves death crews. As the bugs were finally worked out, the twin tilt-rotor aircraft became a gem of the fleet and far surpassed the capabilities of the old medium-lift CH-46 Sea Knight helicopters. A pair of them were a minute out from the bridge.

Major Sam Jameson, at the controls of the lead bird, was just popping up over the final crest of hills when he heard the message. He responded immediately. "Bounty Hunter Bravo, this is Limo Three-One. What's your traffic?"

"Roger, Limo Three-One," Beth confirmed, trying to control her voice to filter out the excitement and relief that flooded through her. "We're at the LZ. What is your timeline?"

The Ospreys clawed for a bit more altitude as the high ground unrolled beneath them, then dropped away into a valley, where a huge man-made structure dominated the far end. "We're one mike out, and I see the LZ." The friendly Kentucky twang of the Marine aviator made Beth feel more comfortable. *We-uh one mack out, an' Ah see thuh LZ.*

Ledford, kneeling behind a Komatsu lowboy flatbed

trailer, smiled when she was finally able to see the pair of planes. "Limo Three-One. Bounty Hunter Bravo. I see you now. Popping yellow smoke." She threw the grenade as hard as she could. It hit the roadway, bounced and rolled, and belched a spreading cloud of bright color.

"Roger, I see yellow," confirmed Jameson. "Where are you?"

"Bounty Hunter Bravo and one pax are behind the earthmovers at the west end, next to a blue golf cart."

Major Jameson altered the angle of approach and set the computers to perform the almost magical transition from airplane to helicopter. The speed fell away from cruising at 277 miles per hour as the nacelles on each wingtip elevated in slow motion up to a sixty-degree elevation, cut to about sixty miles per hour. Then the props were pointing straight up at ninety degrees, and the plane was at a complete hover, hanging in the sky, balanced by multiple computers of the fly-by-wire systems. Jameson nudged the stick to make minor adjustments.

The second Osprey remained in airplane mode to fly cover. Captain Les Richter banked slightly as the bridge came up fast. "Bounty Hunter Bravo, this is Limo Three-Two. Any friendlies down there?" Richter was not worried about small-arms ground fire, which was almost inconsequential to an Osprey, but if he had to make a gun run, he did not want innocent people caught in the .50 caliber shit storm. There was a village several klicks beyond the east end of the bridge, and that was far out of the danger zone.

Beth paused before answering. Better to be honest.

"I have no contact with Bounty Hunter Actual," she said. "I don't see him topside. Everyone I see on the bridge has a weapon."

"Good enough," said Richter, whirling his big plane in closer. "Limo Three-Two will make one recon pass, then cover your extract. If you need help, we'll hose the place down."

Kyle heard the transmission. If he could get the Osprey to sweep the bridge, he still might get out of this mess. "Break! Break! This is Bounty Hunter Actual. Consider the entire bridge a free-fire zone!" He was still too far underground for his little radio to transmit properly, and no one heard him. Then another blast of gunfire erupted from down the hall, and he pressed his back into the alcove.

First things first. He had put up with about as much of this being pinned down crap as he cared to endure and was flat out of time. Swanson grabbed his last round M-67 hand grenade, holding it in close to his belly, simultaneously securing the safety lever with his right hand while picking out the pin with his left. He heard the covering Osprey roar by just as he released the safety spoon to activate the four-second fuse.

Instead of stepping out into the line of fire to throw the grenade, Kyle underhanded it across the corridor, where it clipped the opposite wall at a forty-five-degree angle and banked back toward the corner where the gunman was shielded. The metal baseball skittered across the stone and exploded at the man's feet, blowing him backward, lacerated with metal shards.

Kyle had turned from the blast, but as soon as the concussion passed, he was out of his hideaway, charging for daylight.

Al-Masri was momentarily frozen. At the west terminus of the bridge, a blossom of yellow smoke had flashed on the road and was expanding into a thick cloud that hung like a curtain. Then a plane with propellers like giant windmills dashed overhead, and its prop wash kicked up such a storm of dirt and debris that everyone around him hit the ground, and he turned away, covering his face. Americans! Ayman al-Masri recognized the aircraft as being one of the futuristic Ospreys, and the Americans were the only ones who had such aircraft. It was not Zionists after all.

"Get up and shoot at them," he yelled to his small group. "Kill the Americans. Fire at them, damn you. Shoot." He swatted the nearest one on the head. "Get up and fight or I'll kill you myself." The man he slapped got to his feet with his weapon, but his eyes were wide in fright. Al-Masri moved to the next one, screaming over the sound of the aircraft.

A second Osprey had appeared and was gently lowering itself toward the flat surface of the bridge, and he momentarily wondered why the team that he had seen take position down there was not shooting at it. Instead, he watched the two figures emerge from among the heavy equipment and hurry toward the hovering aircraft.

"There they are!" Two of the Americans had somehow gotten into the western column but were finally out in the open. "Kill them now!"

His men were responding, although sluggishly, and a few were snapping off some shots. Al-Masri had a vision of actually destroying an Osprey and watching the Americans burn to death in the wreckage. He pulled his own pistol and ran forward, firing at the big plane. If they could get close enough, there might be a chance.

Beth stumbled to the rear of the Osprey through the hard wash of the propellers, hauling al-Attas along. The gunner behind the ramp-mounted .50 caliber machine gun jumped down to help her wrestle the prisoner inside. He was used to surprises on these special missions but had never before encountered an operator who was a beautiful, almost petite, woman with short blond hair, and especially one who tossed him the leash to a flex-tied captive whose blue jeans were falling down over his skinny legs.

Ledford gained her footing and ran through the fuselage as fast as she could, feeling the vibration as the Osprey's rotors turned. Since the machine had never actually touched down, it was already flying, and Major Jameson was just waiting for confirmation from the gunner that the two passengers were safely aboard.

Beth Ledford plunged onto the flight deck and grabbed the pilot's shoulder. "Don't lift off yet," she screamed.

"What?" he yelled back.

"Don't lift off!"

"We have to. We've made our pickup, and now we are getting the hell out of here."

"You hang right here. Bounty Hunger Actual is coming."

"Sorry, but he's on his own."

"Like hell he is." She jammed a pistol hard into the ribs of the pilot. "That was not a request. We wait."

Swanson bolted from the tunnel in a full sprint. The attention of everyone was locked on the aircraft, allowing him to run up unseen behind them. Within ten meters, he was in the middle of the group before someone finally noticed him.

Ayman al-Masri saw movement at his side, thinking that it was one of his men, but when he looked, he was staring straight into a face he knew well from studying intelligence photographs: The strong jawline and cheekbones, the hard gray-green eyes, the light brown hair, and the lithe body matched the characteristics of the infamous American operator Kyle Swanson, who had been causing trouble for years. At that moment of recognition, Swanson punched him in the face with the butt of a rifle and sent the New Muslim Order security chief crumpling to the roadway.

Now he was in front of the crowd, and Kyle knew the rest of them would start shooting at him. He dodged into a zigzag to create a moving target and flung a green smoke grenade back over his shoulder. Not far away, the Osprey was still hanging there, waiting for him, against orders and operational practice.

He saw someone leap from the rear of the plane, go to a knee, bring up a rifle, and start firing. A man to his right keeled over into the spreading emerald smoke, his face a mask of blood, and then a second man rolled forward in a somersault, hands grabbing at the bullet wound in his stomach.

He had only thirty more yards to go when he recognized that it was Coastie covering his approach with methodical bursts, and he couldn't think of anyone he would rather have doing the job. She fired, and another man fell, then he ran past her, patting her shoulder to signal that it was time to leave.

Swanson jumped into the Osprey and pulled Beth up right behind him. Both had big smiles on their dirty faces.

"Everybody's aboard," the gunner called to the pilot, who had been balancing the Osprey in a delicate position as he watched the show from the cockpit. The swirling cloud of yellow and green smoke had covered the enemy, but he had seen at least four of them fall, and the only person who had been shooting was the girl who had threatened him. They could talk about that later. He fed the Osprey power, and the machine lifted off in a typhoon of wind, climbed rapidly on the rotors, which were already moving back to airplane mode, and banked away from the bridge.

27

Swanson and Ledford dropped into canvas-strap seats, side by side, as the Osprey curved away from the bridge that could have been a death trap for both of them. They were filthy and stained, streaked with sweat, but their eyes still glowed with excitement from the action. Beth had a fresh purpling mouse beneath her left eye, and her lower lip was split, seeping blood. Kyle was bruised and scraped from being slammed about by explosions. They smiled, then broke into peals of laughter and slapped their palms together in a high five. They had made it.

"What's with the kid?" Swanson asked, shedding the now useless combat gear and taking a long drink of water.

Across the aisle, Mohammad al-Attas had been lashed into a seat, his hair matted and tangled, his eyes rolling wide, and his head twisting all around. His nose was bloody, a big bruise colored his left forehead, and his pants were around his knees. Plastic flex-cuffs bound his wrists, and when he kicked at the gunner who fastened the seat harness around him, the gunner spun a few turns of duct tape around the ankles. The belt was still looped around his neck. He tried to bite the gunner and was put to sleep with a strong sedative injected with a syringe in the medical kit.

"He went weird about ten minutes after we left you. We were running along just fine, and the next thing I knew, he was snarling and snapping like a dog, punching and knocking me to the ground. It was like he was flying on some super coke high. I had to slap him about a little bit and hogtie him."

"Shoulda just shot him." Kyle shrugged.

"Yeah," she agreed, "but you said bring him back alive, and his intel might be worth trying to save. Maybe the shrinks can straighten him out."

"Whatever. Just glad you made it out with the extra luggage."

Kyle waved to the gunner, who was seated near the engineer, facing them. "Hey, dude, thanks for waiting for me."

The big man looked out beneath his olive drab helmet and pointed at Beth. "Didn't have much of a choice," he yelled over the noise of the churning propellers. "We were ready to haul ass until your friend pulled a gun on Major Jameson, the pilot. He ain't none too happy about that, neither. You ought to have heard him cussin'."

Beth leaned back and closed her eyes, lacing her hands behind her head. "Won't leave my BFF behind."

"What?"

"Girl talk. Best Friend Forever. I'm probably going to get court-martialed, huh?"

"Naw. They'll make you stand at attention and gnaw on you for a while, but if you don't laugh in their faces, you'll walk away OK. General Middleton protects the Tridents, and you done good. We're bringing back a hell of a lot of information. We tend to piss off some people, time to time." Swanson looked at her face. Ten minutes after coming through a major action, she was damned near asleep.

"I'm not in Trident," she said, somewhat wistfully, lifting her chin in defiance of the fates.

"I am, and I would have been in a world of hurt back there if this bird had left without me. Then you jump back out there and do your Little Sure Shot routine on the guys chasing me? Outstanding, Beth. What was that you just said? BFF?"

"Yeah."

"BFF it is, then." He reached over and playfully mussed her dirty hair. "I owe you. Go to sleep."

KANDAHAR ARMY AIR FIELD,
AFGHANISTAN

Lieutenant Colonel Sybelle Summers and Master Gunnery Sergeant O. O. Dawkins led the debriefing of Swanson and Ledford, with a half-dozen specialists from various intelligence agencies making notes and asking questions. The Lizard was patched in from Washington on a secure video link. A large screen on a wall of the room glowed with a map of the region, with the grid location of the bridge painted in red.

Kyle was hydrating with a cold fruit juice, while Beth sat quietly with a fresh bottle of water. Her tongue felt glued to the top of her mouth. "We never did determine exactly who was fighting us, but one of the guys that we brought down was wearing the uniform of a Pakistani army sergeant."

"That doesn't really prove anything," observed one of the nameless men at the table.

"I'm not here to prove shit to you, Suit. Just telling you what I saw and showing you the pictures we took. The bridge is in Pakistan. That proof enough that they are involved, or at least knew about it? Of course they will deny it. No different from their denials of hiding Osama bin Laden in a mansion by an army camp."

"What about you, Petty Officer Ledford?" the man asked. "Did you see anything that could be incontrovertible proof that the Pakis were in on it?"

She shook her head, and her voice was soft. "No. Just the guy the gunny mentioned, and a whole bunch of guys with a lot of guns. We didn't exchange business cards."

Sybelle steepled her fingers. "Side issue. The prisoner confirmed the ISI, the secret police, was involved, and as Swanson said, the thing is inside Pakistan. There is absolutely no way they weren't in on it."

For an hour, the questioners picked the brains of the two tired warriors, and Summers let the topic ramble but always brought it back to the bridge. The maps and papers the team had gathered, the computer hard drive, plus their personal on-site observations, photographs, and sketches, gave the situation a tight focus.

"So as high-tech as this place is, the purpose was simply to be the new, protected lair for Commander Kahn. It was created for the New Muslim Order. Are we agreed?"

"Looks that way from back here in Washington," said the Lizard. "I will pull some intercept logs to see what the boys in Islamabad have been talking about. It would be a big help if that captured engineer could give us details on the bridge itself, the weaponry, and that array of sensors and cameras in the valley."

"Don't count on that, Liz," said Kyle. "The man has definitely slipped into his own scrambled little world. The shrinks will have a hard time separating fact from fiction with him, because he apparently believes everything he says is real."

Freedman chewed on a thumbnail. "General Middleton wants to get that guy down to Guantánamo as soon as possible and turn the experts loose on him. Chemistry can do wonders."

Sybelle Summers cut in and pointed to the Central Intelligence Agency representative. "That will take too long. My friend here says they have much of the same capability right here at Kandahar, primarily used for time-sensitive, tactical interrogation."

"That's correct. Let's see what we can do to supplement the information about the bridge and its defenses, and then ship him to Gitmo for deeper work."

"Fine," the Lizard replied. "Colonel Summers, the general also wants your report and recommendations ASAP, so he can take them to the White House. He gave them a heads-up that he's coming over."

"I'll get him a summary within the hour; then we can link up again and do the details."

"Sounds good. Oh, yes, the general wants to pass along his compliments to Petty Officer Ledford for her outstanding work."

"What about me?" Kyle laughed. "I was there, too."

"He didn't mention you."

THE OLD EXEC
WASHINGTON, D.C.

The president of the United States, hands in the pockets of his dark suit, strolled nonchalantly out of the basement door of the White House, beneath the maroon awning, between some parked cars, and across the narrow street to a similar basement entrance to the Old Executive Office Building, a baroque gray giant. At the moment, the entire news media corps was corralled in the White House Press Room for the routine daily briefing by his press secretary, who was giving an update on the upcoming Mars mission and confirming the president would be at the Cape for the historic launch. Camera crews were at their tripods on the front lawn, preparing for the stand-ups by the TV correspondents. No one noticed the sudden unannounced departure from the president's public schedule, and he was in view for less than a minute, alone, as he crossed the protected street without obvious Secret Service protection.

The tall Californian was alone in numerous ways on

this day, for he was facing one of the toughest decisions of his presidency—the absolute need to order a direct military attack on Pakistan, an allied nation that was an anchor in the overall war on terror in a fiery region. Only someone who knew him well could discern that the slightly hunched shoulders were actually bowed with worry. He had been pacing the Oval Office, trying to walk off the fury of once again feeling double-crossed by the Pakistanis—Osama's compound all over again, but bigger and better—but he had calmed little by the time of this meeting just after lunch.

Members of the Secret Service detail that had unobtrusively shepherded him across the street met him at the door of Old Exec and gave verbal confirmation of the handoff to the agents at the seldom-used White House exit and to agents in the parked cars that he passed. He led the way to the second floor of the musty building, and another agent opened a normal-looking door into a comfortable large room that was thoroughly soundproof. Several easy chairs and two large sofas formed a large, loose circle. Senior administration officials had come in earlier through various entrances and were gathered in small groups. They turned to face him, and a repeated murmur of "Mr. President" acknowledged his presence. He did not shake anyone's hand and did not flash the famous smile but proceeded to an armchair, sat, and crossed his legs. The others took seats. All eyes were on him.

There was no preamble. "Each of you has been privately briefed within the past few hours concerning this latest event in Pakistan. It is an intolerable situation. A vital ally that already had given shelter to our single biggest enemy, Osama bin Laden, has been busy creating a new and possibly worse threat to our security, and as usual, intentionally keeping it secret from us.

"There is no way to sugarcoat my decision. As you were briefed, I intend to launch a military strike to wipe out that new sanctuary, and by doing so, to send a clear message to our friends throughout the Middle East. Any new terrorist leader will never be beyond the reach of the United States, and neither will any country that gives him sanctuary." He paused, hands clasped before him, looking from face to face.

"We will hit it hard—very hard—and that once again includes boots on the ground for a short window of time, for I consider this to be a matter of utmost national security. Our military leaders predict that if all goes well, we will be in and out of there within three hours, leaving behind nothing but a smoking ruin. Consider it to be a surgical operation to remove a deadly cancer. Pakistan has to learn that this must stop! Before I give the final order, I wanted you all together to thank you for agreeing that this course of action is necessary. Any further discussion? Questions?"

"I don't see how we can do anything else," declared the vice president.

"Pakistan is going to be outraged," Secretary of State Mark Grayson added, "but that's to be expected, and you pay me the big bucks to take the heat."

"This time, you don't have to," said the president, finally falling into a smile. "To further demonstrate how pissed off we are, they don't even get to complain to you or to me about it. Give that job to Undersecretary Curtis of the Bureau of American-Islamic Affairs, along with my order to rudely brush them off."

"They will consider that to be a great insult," Secretary of State Grayson replied.

"Good, because that is exactly what is intended. If they are smart, they will grab the opportunity to let the whole sleazy incident disappear instead of flying into meaningless outrage. They got off easy with the surgical SEAL Team Six raid that did bin Laden. This time, not so much."

The president turned to the chairman of the Joint Chiefs of Staff. "There it is, General Rauch. You have a go. Give the orders. And let me remind everybody here: no leaks, or you might be visiting Guantánamo Bay for a while. Friend or not, you must believe that I am serious."

NORTH WAZIRISTAN,
TRIBAL LANDS,
PAKISTAN

Ayman al-Masri was puffing with exertion as he climbed the final stretch of stairs that led to a square and unassuming block building that served as the local mosque, carefully working his way around pecking chickens that darted underfoot and seemed determined to hurl him off the cliff to his death. The only door was on the west side, so that all who entered would be facing east toward Mecca, the birthplace of the Prophet.

At the end of the room was a window with a startling

view of a fertile valley shielded by steep mountains, where ridgelines gave way to terraced gardens that were still green, even this far into autumn. Monstrous boulders the size of trucks stood out like ragged statues. Shaggy buffalo, a commodity so valuable that they lived indoors with their owners, hauled huge loads of goods and produce along the dirt roads. The mosque overlooked a busy little village of adobe-style mud and log homes, and on one flank of the town was a special cemetery reserved for fallen warriors of the great cause. Long sticks marked each grave, and from each stick waved a piece of cloth made from the garments worn by the dead fighter. Al-Masri was pleased that nothing at all had changed since he had left the village a few days ago.

He bowed and touched his head to the warm burgundy carpet, then announced himself with one word. "Commander."

Kahn was at the eastern window, looking down on the village, and out to the spectacular view of the rugged tribal lands of Pakistan, where he had built his reputation as a fearless military leader and a smart political star in the terrorist firmament. He had seen his security chief arrive by automobile, be checked out at the guard post, and start the long climb up to the mosque. He was eager to hear the report.

Ever since the death of his rival Osama bin Laden, Commander Kahn had been interested in the bridge scheme that could become a safe and secure headquarters for his New Muslim Order, and a more permanent residence for him. It bore the promise of a better life for the next few years, with a sophisticated communications suite. Kahn did not buy the old saying by Mao Tse-tung that political power grew out of the barrel of a gun; in the twenty-first century, such power also grew out of microcircuits and the so-called social media. He led a new generation of terrorists, the invisible man behind the curtain who stirred the revolutions that were hammering the Middle East and accumulating power for himself and the NMO.

He turned from the window and made himself comfortable on his favorite resting spot of thick, soft cushions. Kahn was in his late forties, of medium height and a solid build, with only a stubble of a beard that was trimmed once a week. He smiled at al-Masri as a servant served tea and a plate of breads and cheese. "I understand that your trip was quite eventful," he observed.

"Yes, Commander." He gave Kahn a folder containing a two-page written report and a number of photographs. "The Pakistanis failed badly with the bridge project. Security was laughable. I could never allow you to be placed in such jeopardy."

"That is too bad. It seemed like such a good idea, and the Pakistanis were being extremely cooperative. Maybe they were too cooperative?" The terrorist mastermind flipped through the folder, then handed it back to his bodyguard. He was not interested in such minor details as why it had failed. Only the fact that a few American commandos had once again penetrated security screens gave him pause. *Will they never stop?*

"Then I agree with your decision to discard it. This is a pleasant village. We should spend the winter here. My computer works from anywhere."

As if in answer, a gust of cold wind spun through the nearby mountaintops and curled a chilled blast over the village and the mosque. The servant hurried back and wrapped a blanket around the Commander's shoulders. Despite the confident tone, winter would be hard here.

Ayman al-Masri cleared his throat, then spoke. "Among those photographs is the American who led the raiding party. He almost killed me during his escape, so I came face-to-face with him; there is no question of his identity."

Kahn reopened the folder and found the picture. He studied it and the identification tag. "Kyle Swanson. A United States Marine. I know this name."

"Yes, Commander. He has long been a constant thorn, from raiding our training camps to destroying entire operations. He is a very lethal enemy, and the time has come to remove him."

Kahn closed the folder again. "Have you found a weakness to attack?"

"Yes. The man is not really a machine. His soft spot is his heart; a killer with a conscience. You recall that he was captured in Islamabad a few years ago and foiled an al Qaeda coup attempt there?"

"And then escaped." The dark eyes were now drilling into al-Masri, showing interest.

"The reason he was captured was that he stopped to save a woman and her two children from a collapsed building. He gave himself up for total strangers who were Muslims. That humanity is his weak point."

"So you plan to exploit that?"

Al-Masri was ready with an answer. "According to our sources, Swanson came on this mission apparently as the guard for a woman soldier whose brother, a doctor, was killed at the bridge. Once they discovered what the bridge was about, Swanson tore the place up and left a lot of bodies behind."

"I see."

"I want your permission to activate our highest-ranking friend in the American government, William Curtis. He must find the woman soldier and use her as leverage to draw Swanson to him, and then kill him."

"Bill Curtis is a strong man, but he is not capable of defeating a Satan like this Kyle Swanson alone."

Al-Masri's stone countenance broke into a slow smile. "It would be a suicide mission, Commander. Curtis will wrap his arms around the girl soldier and Kyle Swanson and blow himself up. There will be no question."

"A new martyr."

"Yes. To rid us of an old enemy who has done great harm."

Commander Kahn weighed the scales for only a moment. Curtis was extremely valuable in his position in the State Department, and the source of important advice, but striking back directly against a Special Forces operative was a great opportunity. "Will doing so harm the Mars mission attack? That is more important. We have put a lot of money into that."

Al-Masri had thought that one through during his

long drive back from the bridge. "Curtis will not be anywhere near the rocket in any case, and his man carrying
out the sabotage reports nothing unusual at this time.
It's still on, and we will claim responsibility as soon as
it happens. The two plans are independent."

Kahn was quiet, thinking. The one thing that he still
lacked in trying to take over the Osama bin Laden legacy was a signature strike of huge proportions against
the United States. Bin Laden had brought about 9/11
and had killed thousands; Kahn was still relatively unknown, which was both a blessing and a curse.

The destruction of the Mars mission would put him
on the throne of terrorism. When the space vessel died,
credit would fall to him through a computer-powered
campaign of publicity. Now he was being given an opportunity to make his claim even stronger. An American suicide bomber with a widely known political name
would kill other Americans within the United States'
borders. The double assault would resurrect the fear of
Islamic attacks, a fear that he wanted to permeate the
United States and establish his supremacy as the new
terrorist chieftain. And the troublesome Marine, Kyle
Swanson, would die in the bargain.

"Very well, my friend," he said. "You have my permission. Give Curtis whatever help we can."

28

THE *VAGABOND*

Lord Jeff, Lady Pat, and Beth Ledford were at the table in the spacious dining salon, digging into the chef's presentation of fish that had been caught only a few hours earlier. A pinot noir had been chosen from the wine locker to complement the meal, the French bread loaf was fresh and warm, and the vegetables and fruit tasted straight from a garden. No place had been set for Kyle Swanson, who had disappeared into his stateroom almost as soon as the helicopter landed on the fantail of the long white yacht that morning. Pat had gently told Beth to just leave him be and not spend any time worrying. Kyle had some odd ways.

The Cornwells were old hands at settling down warriors after a fight. Jeff had gone through the same decompression process while he was an officer in the British SAS and had developed a habit of hauling home young men who were stressed out and struggling. His leadership never stopped at the front gate of the base. Pat had watched them come and go, all thoroughbreds who needed some quiet time and a warm cup of tea, a mug of beer, or a bottle of whisky and a nonjudgmental ear. Gradually, most would climb out of their mental foxholes, reassemble their thoughts, and stop dwelling on the grinder of death and destruction they had survived, perhaps while some close buddy had not. Some soldiers had not been able to handle it, and Jeff helped them move on to civilian life.

Beth was now being led through the same recovery exercise, without realizing it. They spoke of little things at first, such as raising cattle and the coming interplanetary launch; then she opened her soul. *Everything happened so fast!* She had been on the yacht, then jumped from an airplane, then ran into the patrols, and then, and then, and then. With only an occasional question from Jeff or a prod from Pat, the small woman spilled out the bloody story. The words came faster, her voice rose, and the thunderclap of realization hit her.

"When I went in, I knew I could shoot, but I did not know if I could kill like that," she said. "Then I discovered that not only could I do it, but it was easy. Even that wasn't enough. I learned from Kyle to give them a head shot, a coup de grace, to be sure they were dead. Then that became easy, too."

She crumpled the napkin and pushed away from the tables, with sudden hot tears bursting from her eyes and streaming down her face. "My God, what have I done? What have I become?" She ran from the salon.

Pat unobtrusively wiped some tears from her own eyes, then met the sympathetic stare from her husband. "Should I go and fetch her?" she asked.

"No. Not yet. She'll be back. Our pretty petty officer has finally seen the elephant." Sir Jeff wheeled his chair out and around to where Lady Pat was seated, then reached out and poured some more wine. "Our only job is to let her know we are here, remember?"

"It is easier when we're dealing with a man," she replied. "They have that whole special ops fraternity thing to help them adjust, other men who have been through hell. Beth is almost alone as a woman; much more fragile, and this could tear her apart."

Jeff moved around and hugged his wife. "The hardest part is yet to come. She's standing at the gateway, deciding whether to pass through and join an elite club of operators or stay out on the safe side, where apple trees grow and ponies frolic in the pasture."

"I know. I saw it in her eyes, too; the gleam."

"Right-o. Deep down, she enjoyed it."

"Yes. Oh, without a doubt." He placed his hand on Pat's forearm and dropped into a booming stage voice to recite a favored fragment of *Henry V*: "And gentlemen in England now a-bed/ Shall think themselves accursed they were not here/ And hold their manhoods cheap whiles any speaks/ That fought with us upon Saint Crispin's day."

"So we should not hold her back?"

"No, my dear. We cannot. If anything, we must help and encourage her. She is what she is, and she wants more. This time, the elephant has met its match."

KANDAHAR ARMY AIR FIELD,
AFGHANISTAN

Chief Engineer Mohammad al-Attas, clad in cotton pajamas and a bathrobe, smiled broadly, a picture of cooperation. A cold soft drink in a bottle stood on the small table in front of him. His arms were free, but he was handcuffed and firmly belted to the chair. He lifted the soda bottle, examined it, then took a long pull.

Steve Longstreet, a longtime interrogator with the CIA, was struggling to remain pleasant and unruffled. He had been talking with the young man for almost an hour during this latest questioning session, and the conversation ebbed and flooded like the tides as the severe psychiatric disturbance surged back and forth within the captive's brain. Looking into the bruised face, Longstreet was reminded that serial killers look just like everyone else.

When Longstreet had first met al-Attas earlier in the day, it was with an absolutely blank slate. The prisoner was allegedly the designer who had built a superbridge in Pakistan, and there was no doubt that he was capable of doing that. A few elementary tests indicated that the young man was a brilliant mathematician and engineer, a savant with numbers who freely gave details of the sophisticated construction design, right down to the weight-bearing girders, and then would describe weaponry and optics and communications. However, al-Attas was also something else. He had been found tied to a hospital bed and had unexpectedly attacked those who had rescued him.

During the first session, Longstreet had listened with stoic, professional patience when the engineer would stop spouting numbers to start shouting nonsense about being an Arabic fairy-tale demon that he called "the Djinn" and give an evil sigh when describing how it felt to look into the eyes of his victims as he cut their throats. The bridge was not a fortress built by man but a digital castle that the Crusaders would never conquer; or he might describe it next as a portal to the red planet, where the Djinn would wield his bloody sword for Allah, then return to earth to slay all of the infidels. In those moments, Longstreet was glad that the prisoner was secure. When that mental storm would pass, the engineer's thoughts would return, and he would reach out and calmly snare another cookie. He had eaten almost the full pack.

The CIA man had interviewed hundreds of patients during his long career, sometimes resorting to extreme measures of physical punishment, and felt he had seen it all. He had been told to get as much information as possible from this captive about a possible attack on the United States, and to uncover details about this strange bridge, then also to delve into his mental history, political beliefs, and feelings toward the United States, plus his personal background. Easy enough. A standard assignment.

Once the conversation began, however, things quickly crossed the threshold of being standard in any way. Dealing with a brilliant mind that was also totally mad was tiring Longstreet, while the engineer seemed ready to chat about his evolving nightmare world, quite pleasantly, all day long—but he would not stick to the priority list. He wanted to share his personal information, and only reluctantly was he even willing to move away from talking about himself long enough to discuss the bridge. The possible attack drew only a blank stare. It was time for the CIA man to decide about the next step.

"Mohammad, you must excuse me for a few minutes. I have to use the restroom. If you have to go, I can have a guard take you, and we can start again in fifteen minutes."

"You know, that is probably a good idea, Mr. Longstreet." He patted his stomach. "Too much Pepsi and Oreos."

Longstreet called for a guard from outside the door and watched as al-Attas was taken away. He got up and paced the room, and a voice came over the speaker hidden in the ceiling. "What about it, Steve?"

"This guy will take months of work and still leave us in the dark," Longstreet said, looking at a one-way mirror set into one wall. "You heard what he is doing. Yammering all over the place."

"Any conclusions so far? Anything hard that we can pass along?"

"Only that we can't really believe a damned word he says. Is it real, or some fantasy, and does he know the difference? One moment he hates the entire human race, and the next second he wants to marry the woman soldier who captured him. He confirmed my queries about Commander Kahn and the New Muslim Order, but can we believe him? Some waterboard sessions or other stuff might tighten that up, but how could we trust the information? This guy would tell us what he thought was true, or whatever we wanted to hear to make it stop, and he would be quite believable."

Longstreet stretched his arms and twisted his torso as he thought. Sitting too long in that damned chair was slaughtering his back. "So far, I gotta say the only new gem of information is this name that he keeps mentioning, apparently a former employer named Bill Curtis. Let's find him and see if he can give us some personal background on this nut."

"OK," said the voice on the speaker. "I'll send it on up the line."

Steve Longstreet headed out for his own bathroom break, taking the black notebook from the interrogation room. Stopping back in his office to check the e-mails and phone calls, he took another look through the early part of the questioning and made a note to himself. The special operators who brought him back had mentioned that the engineer had spoken of a coming attack on America. Enough of the bullshit. Longstreet knew that was the top priority for the next questioning session, and things might get rough.

THE *VAGABOND*

Moonlight checkered the restless sea with rolling shadows as passing waves rose and fell, and the big vessel slid through the water. Beth Ledford was at the bow, staring out at the blackness, and the cold spray that flew up every time the bow cracked open another wave made her shiver, and she eventually decided to find a more sheltered spot. She walked down the starboard side, got out of the buffeting wind, and found some deck chairs that were lashed to the bulkhead. She unfolded one and moved it close enough to the railing that she could put up her feet. No stars out tonight. Her whole world seemed black and bleak, and her future even worse.

Kyle Swanson had watched from the deck above. He had awakened an hour ago, tangled in his sheets after another taunting dream visit from the Boatman, his own personal inner fiend, but things had been squared away between them. The Boatman did not have a lot to say that night and laughingly paddled off in his rickety boat to cross the final abyss with another load of Kyle-killed souls. Swanson was once again told to go back to work. That was their deal: Kyle kept the supply coming, and the skeletal Boatman hauled away the corpses, along with Kyle's shame and the guilt.

He put on a gray sweatshirt and black sweatpants and went outside, barefoot on the damp deck, blending into the evening mist and standing invisible in the cool air in the shadow of an overhang. The action was done, the extraction was done, the debrief was done, and even the inevitable reckoning with the Boatman was done. He felt good. So why was his spider sense tingling, as if something had lightly touched his protective web? He stretched and scanned a three-sixty, checking off everything as normal, and then saw Beth, alone in a deck chair, in the dark.

No one knew any better than he what Beth was going through. He went down to the armory, checked out a large gun case of polished aluminum, and returned to the deck softly, barely stirring the air.

Swanson was good at waiting. He stood about ten feet behind her, balanced with the slight roll of the yacht, looking out at whatever she was seeing in the blank space beyond the stern. Then he spoke. "Beth, the common wisdom is, give these things time and you'll get over it. I call bullshit on that, because it's advice that is usually given by people who have no idea what it's like. Truth is, you're not going to get over it. The best you can do is to learn to accept it."

She didn't turn around. "How long have you been there?"

"A while. Just finished adjusting my own attitude. You ain't the only one who killed people back there."

That made her turn and look over her shoulder. "I can't believe that it bothers you."

"I'm a professional, and I still have to process it. Otherwise, it stacks up to be so much baggage that it can crush you." He moved forward, put the gun case down, and leaned against the rail to face her. "Tell you a secret. My nickname in the Corps is 'Shaky' because someone—General Middleton, actually—one day found me shaking after a firefight. I never lived that down. The older jarheads still call me Shake. I hate it."

Beth chuckled. "Hard to believe, Kyle. Can I call you Shaky?"

"No." Swanson took a moment to make sure they were alone. "Don't look at the lives you took as being innocent victims. Every one of them would have killed you first if they had the chance. We had to stay focused and committed to our mission, and they were in the way. Bad juju for them. There is always going to be another mission, and another one after that."

"But—"

"No. Listen to me first. I'm playing schoolteacher right now, giving you all of the information you need to process where you are. I was very reluctant to take you along on the mission, because another professional scout-sniper would have been a more experienced and reliable partner. You won me over, probably saved my life. I had a long talk with Sybelle Summers before we left Kandahar to come out here, and she agreed to recommend you for a Silver Star. Problem is that you can never talk about it because this was a secret mission."

"Kyle, I don't deserve that decoration. You did most of the work."

"Oh, I'll probably get another medal to throw in my footlocker, but it's unimportant. Let me finish. We are offering you an opportunity to earn your way into Task Force Trident. Only two other candidates, both men, are in the pipeline at present because we're so selective, and there is no favoritism. You would officially slide off of the Coast Guard books to become a special liaison within the Pentagon, and your records all go into General Middleton's private safe. We operate at the pleasure of the president and answer to no one else. As for rank, that disappears, too; you will be whatever you need to be, a Navy commander or an Army sergeant or a civilian, like a retail clerk, depending on the mission.

"It will take approximately two years to finish the training, and you can be tapped for missions throughout that time. You will attend a wide spread of schools, many of them not on the books. The teaching ratio is usually one-on-one. Among other things, you would shoot at the Ghost House with Seal Team Six, learn IEDs from demolition experts, study forensics with the FBI, and learn to fly a helo. All kinds of other stuff, because the training never stops. Your expense account will be virtually unlimited, and the pay will be substantial, out of a black budget."

"And in return?"

"Outwardly, you will look and act the same, but inside, it will be the end of cute and demure Beth Ledford, the ever-popular Little Sure Shot. Personal relationships will be hard, if not impossible. Without putting too fine a point on it, you will be a highly skilled killer who will do whatever is necessary, including sacrificing your own life, to protect your country."

"Be like you?"

"God, let's hope not. This is not a decision for you to make immediately. We want you to take some time off. When we finish in Washington, you go home and kick back for a while and think it through. Long as it takes."

He shoved off from the rail and went to the gun case, which lay flat and gleaming. "Come here," he said, and Beth followed him over. "You're a farm type, so what's the best thing to do when you fall off a horse?"

"Get right back on?"

"Exactly. Conquer your own fear, and also let the sumbitch horse know who's boss. That's where you are now, Beth. You need to shoot again, just to let your body and your brain know that you can and will pull the trigger." He unfastened the snaps and lifted the lid. A lone rifle with a big scope lay in a nest of foam. "Behold."

"Good God, Kyle. It's beautiful."

"It's the Excalibur 3GX—third generation, experimental. We've been working on it for more than a year, and I'm taking this one back to 29 Palms for field tests. Pick it up."

She did, and the weight felt good. She pointed it out to sea and peered through the scope, which came alive with color and numbers and surprising clarity from its enhanced abilities. "Can I fire it?"

"That's why it's here." He opened a box of bullets that rested in one corner of the case. "Here's the biggest part of the experiment. What do you estimate would be the range for this weapon?"

She guessed: .50 caliber, all the bells and whistles. "Up to sixteen hundred meters, a mile?"

Swanson laughed. She was talking about their skilled craft again, and already the worries about the death she had wrought were fading. "Nope. More than two miles, plus, with accuracy."

Beth looked up at him. "You're kidding. That's impossible."

He handed her one of the long bullets. "Here's the secret. Instead of the normal round, this weapon fires a rocket-assisted projectile, a miniature artillery shell. Titanium tip for individuals, depleted uranium for vehicles."

"A RAP bullet?"

"Yes," he said, holding up a heavy brass cartridge and rolling it between his fingers.

"Gimme. Gimme." She was smiling as Kyle handed her the RAP round. No more tears. He knew they had her.

29

Congolese contract workers Bonte Ibara and Guychel Mouko cooked up a hot and spicy stew and ate it hungrily while strips of goat meat sizzled over a small fire. After emerging from their hiding place belowground and seeing the carnage of the battle, they decided to leave. The wide eyes in worried faces of other workers indicated they would not be the only ones abandoning this sinking ship of stone.

While everyone else was still out on the bridge, the two Africans moved fast. First, they slipped into the administrative office, where Guychel ransacked the desks until he found the combination for a small safe. He removed their passports and several hundred euros and American dollars.

Meanwhile, Bonte pecked out a letter on the computer and printed it out on the embossed letterhead of the company that had hired them. It stated that his contract had been fulfilled and he had permission to return home. He signed with a ballpoint pen in the unreadable flourish of a busy, self-important bureaucrat and carefully folded it into an envelope, then did an identical letter for Guychel.

Next, they raided the mess tent and found the pantry stocked with everything they needed. Extra potatoes, a few loaves of bread, some cheese, rice, and even a bottle of wine each went into their sacks. The two men did not return to the workers' barracks but retreated to a single room attached to the garage where the heavy equipment was serviced. It was a good temporary shelter, and they rested there with full bellies, waiting for the hours to pass.

At two o'clock in the morning, they ventured out, each carrying a canvas bag slung across a shoulder. It was silent all along the bridge, one of those rare moments when all construction had been shut down. They hoisted the gear into the bed of a battered white Toyota truck that Guychel Mouko had hidden among the earthmovers. "I want to put as many kilometers behind us as possible before daylight," he said, starting the engine.

Ibara climbed into the passenger seat and laid his AK-47 across his lap. "There is no choice. Fucking New Muslim Order!" He spat from the window. "They were probably going to kill all of us workers to keep the secrets of this bridge. The Paki army is going to be arriving tomorrow morning, and all exits will be closed. Then escape will be impossible. On top of that, the Americans will probably be back. They will never let this place exist."

The truck lurched into motion and left the big garage, passed through a big puddle of light, and crossed the bridge, slowing as it approached the checkpoint at the west end. The guard hut was empty. "We are not the only ones leaving," Bonte commented.

"Then they are wise, too. Only dead men will be here tomorrow night." Guychel nodded toward the edge of the road. "These rocks will be slick with blood."

"Not ours." The two friends settled into silence and drove away.

Lieutenant Khalid Athar Farooq of the Pakistani Army stood in the gun turret of a Humvee, leading a small convoy of Mercedes-Benz Unimog 1300/L trucks packed with a full platoon of soldiers, with another armored Humvee bringing up the rear. Farooq was tired of sitting down and could get a better view and some fresh air by standing behind the mounted machine gun.

His unit had moved out of its encampment a hundred miles away when orders had come to help with a security problem at the mysterious bridge that was nothing more to him than a location on his map. No urgency had been attached to the instructions. A plan was drawn up as Farooq began the complex task of readying his men for the move; there were a thousand items to check before the wheels could roll. As the hours had passed, newer reports came in about a major battle at the bridge; then all contact was lost. A flyover by a Pakistani air force plane at first light showed that the place seemed abandoned.

Twenty-five-year-old Lieutenant Farooq was an experienced officer, a combat veteran of the lawless tribal areas, and as his convoy neared its destination, he felt a familiar prebattle prickling of the hair on his neck. When his Humvee led the trucks around still another hairpin curve in the mountain road, the entire bridge complex came into view about three kilometers ahead. It was huge, precisely carved from layers of stone at the back of a broad valley, and seemed ghostly still. Farooq brought the convoy to a halt, unwilling to take his platoon farther before some reconnaissance. They could use a brief break to prepare for whatever lay ahead, and the lieutenant climbed out and walked forward a hundred meters, accompanied by his platoon sergeant.

"Nothing is moving down there, sir," said the sergeant, scanning his binoculars over the entire area.

"Put together a small patrol, Sergeant, and send a Humvee down for a quick look," the lieutenant replied. "Let the rest of the men get out of the tracks to stretch, then make them ready, weapons locked and loaded. I don't like this place."

"Yes, sir." The sergeant turned away but stopped when the lieutenant, with his binoculars still at his eyes, grabbed him by the arm.

"Hold on, Sergeant. Look at the far end of the valley to the south, just above the hills."

The sergeant no longer needed the big glasses. Two fast-moving F-18 fighter-bombers were streaking in low, and large canisters were tumbling free beneath them, glinting in the early sunlight. Both soldiers spun away and broke into a run back toward the trucks, screaming at their troops, "Take cover! Incoming!"

The pair of U.S. Air Force F-18s from Kandahar peeled out of their run, the thundering engines roaring off the cliffs and mountains. Another strike set was coming in right behind them, already toggling their switches when the first large napalm containers slammed into the valley and exploded, splashing out tidal waves of the incendiary fuel-gel mixture.

The first bombs struck near the old fallen bridge, and each of the others marched just a little farther up the valley, cooking it with immense heat and roaring flames that rolled forward in swaths of orange, red, yellow, and black. The mission was to turn the valley into a wasteland by saturating the hillsides with the hellish brew that would burn out the motion sensors and cameras and anything else that the deadly fingers of napalm could touch.

After the second set of F-18s banked out of their bomb runs and screeched away, Lieutenant Farooq peered from his hiding place in a ditch and saw that the valley had been turned into a charred and burning wilderness that stank of jet fuel. Then he looked at the bridge, which seemed untouched, still dominating the area. His men, emerging from their cover, were also staring at the balls of fire still lashing the valley. "Hold up on that patrol, Sergeant, and set up defensive positions here until we can figure out what's going on," Farooq said. "I've got to report this." He took his time getting to the radio, trying to keep his hands from shaking, thankful to still be alive. The mighty crush of the napalm had fallen almost two miles away, and he still had felt the flash of its heat, as if it had landed right on top of him.

Three B-52H Stratofortress bombers that had been

around longer than the men who flew them had taken off hours before from the isolated secret base on the island of Diego Garcia, a thousand miles from the coast of southern India. Eight engines hung below swept-back wings with a span of 185 feet carried the large planes at a very high altitude with ease, unseen by anyone below.

In what was no more than a routine milk run for the biggest bombers in the U.S. arsenal, the triangle of three aircraft reached a plotted GPS location only thirty seconds after the F-18 napalm strike. The large doors on the bottom of the planes opened with the hiss of hydraulics, and every B-52 spilled out fifty-one Mk-82 general purpose bombs, each weighing five hundred pounds.

Lieutenant Farooq was recovering from the shock of the napalm attack, and leaning against his Humvee, smoking a cigarette, while his superiors processed his new information. He looked around to satisfy himself that everyone was in position and the road was blocked. Nobody would leave or enter the area at his end until they could assess what was going on. The fires were out in the valley, but smoke still rose like thick mist from the earth.

He heard a high-pitched whine in the heavens, no louder than wind whistling through trees, and for the second time that morning, his world erupted.

The B-52 bombs hammered down just far enough away to give Farooq a chance to actually see the explosions blossom in towering spouts of earth and dirt before the sound reached his ears and the concussions slammed him. He staggered and fell, and his men again dove for protection. The vehicles rocked on their suspensions and the 153 bombs strolled along, punching the ground and gouging out craters in ragged, side-by-side lines that stretched more than a mile. A dust cloud rose like a curtain and drifted toward the soldiers. Farooq's ears were ringing, his jaw was sore from gritting his teeth, and he pulled a scarf across his nose and mouth so he could breathe.

He had never experienced anything like this. What was it? He had never even seen the planes that dropped the bombs, and looking up now, he still could not find them. Rising to a knee, he pulled his binoculars to his eyes and was finally able to spy the flight of three bombers disappearing on a steady northward course. Turning back to the damage, the young officer realized the target had once again been the valley, which was now twisted and pulverized. After being scoured by napalm and crunched by bombs, it was a no-man's-land. The bridge was still untouched, but he doubted that would be the case very long. He reached again for his radio to alert his superiors, knowing that they still would not believe that the Americans were actually attacking in Pakistan with a full military strike, not with unmanned drones or a team of special operations soldiers, but in force, with the heavy, frontline weapons that had been in use since the Cold War. If they didn't believe him, he would invite them to come and see for themselves, for he knew this party was just starting.

Even as the shaky lieutenant was updating his report, he heard the throaty sound of a multiengine airplane approaching and saw an AC-130 coming up the valley, low and slow and ominous. "Now a Spectre gunship is coming in," he yelled. "It's going after the bridge."

The lumbering plane climbed for some altitude and banked to the right as the sensors precisely computed the target and the side-firing gunners opened up, raining 40 mm and booming 105 mm cannon fire. As the aircraft flew past the bridge, left to right, the shells started at one end and walked all the way across, tearing up the surface and destroying almost every vehicle and piece of equipment on it. It made three passes before departing, leaving the surface in smoking ruin.

Farooq had fallen speechless. The voice on the radio was calling for him to answer, but words failed him. The destruction he had witnessed in the past few minutes was beyond imagination. He heard someone yelling, "Lieutenant! Lieutenant!" in his face and felt someone shaking him hard, but Farooq was too dazed to answer until his platoon sergeant finally slapped him and poured water onto his face.

"Helicopters, sir," the sergeant shouted. "I hear helicopters."

THE OVAL OFFICE,
WASHINGTON, D.C.

Secretary of State Mark Grayson was the youngest son of a judge in Oregon, and both of his brothers were lawyers. It had been pounded into his head during family dinners for as long as he could remember that there are two sides to every story, even when pictures and witnesses and evidence pointed to a slam-dunk conviction of an accused person. Presumed innocence was the foundation of the American system of justice. Now he was seated on a sofa across from the president of the United States, having to accuse one of his own trusted advisers of treason, based on flimsy, circumstantial evidence gathered by the national intelligence community. They had been wrong before.

The president had come up from the Situation Room, where he had been monitoring the attack in Pakistan, because Secretary Grayson had said he had a matter that needed his urgent and immediate attention. The president listened to Grayson and to Andy Moore of the CIA with an expression of disbelief.

"Let me be certain that I understand you, Mark," he said. "A senior diplomat, the head of the Bureau of American-Islamic Affairs, a man who had cleared the most stringent background checks, actually has been working with a terrorist organization dedicated to destroying the United States? Is that even possible?"

Grayson thought he saw the president's eternal air of absolute confidence deflating. "I'm afraid so, sir. The intel community has been onto him for a couple of days. There's no doubt in my mind that Bill Curtis has for some time been aiding the New Muslim Order and its leader, Commander Kahn. Unbelievable and unproven, but an apparent fact."

The president slid his half-glasses down his long nose and read the one-page report again. He asked the CIA briefer, "You're sure about this one, Andy?"

"Yes, sir. We had hacked the e-mails of Mohammed Javid Bhatti, a Pakistani at the UN, who is his main contact. Bhatti received an encoded message a few hours ago from Pakistan, and we back-tracked it to the security chief of the New Muslim Order, a man named Ayman al-Masri. Bhatti passed it on, word for word, to Curtis."

"What did the message say?"

"We're still breaking it down, sir, but one of our specialists in Pakistan has been questioning that prisoner picked up during the raid on the bridge, the guy who built it, and he confirms the bridge was to be a haven for Commander Kahn. He repeatedly coughed up Bill Curtis's name as an old friend. If the bridge was being built for the New Muslim Order, and the e-mail is directly from the NMO, then Mr. Curtis has some explaining to do."

"You bet he does." The president laid the report on a small table, took off his glasses, folded them and put them in his shirt pocket, then looked at his watch. Almost midnight. "I remember once a long time ago when I actually wanted this job, even went out and campaigned for it. I don't know if I would do it again. Your recommendation on the Curtis situation, Mr. Secretary?"

"We should take him into custody immediately and quietly," said Grayson. "Do it under Homeland Security provisions and declare him an enemy combatant, so the case will be under a military tribunal. I can't believe I'm saying this, but the burden will be on Curtis to earn our trust. At present, although he is an American citizen, he cannot have an open trial in a public courtroom."

The president looked steadily at both Grayson and the CIA man, Moore. "Well, Mark, it looks like you've got to take on the Pakistani complaints after all. Our guys are kicking butt over there on that bridge. It is hard to imagine having a mole this high in the government. Good job digging this guy out. Go get Curtis, and find him a cot in Guantánamo."

"Yes, sir." Grayson sat back, glad that his part of this meeting was done.

The White House chief of staff picked up the ball. "One more thing, sir. We have to consider that Curtis may be orchestrating some kind of high profile strike against the Mars mission. The Pentagon, Homeland Security, and NASA are already on it."

The president closed his eyes and pushed his head back against his tall chair, stunned. "How long do we have before the *America* launch?"

"About seventy hours, sir. No need to scrub it until we find out more. There are always threats before a mission, and this one is from a man who is already known to be mentally unstable. We will stay on it. Meanwhile, security is being increased at the Cape. If there is any confirmation, we will stop the mission. Best for now to keep this information under wraps, and just stay alert."

30

THE BRIDGE

Had Mohammad al-Attas been in his control room to steer the battle, the American aircraft would never have gotten close. Part of his design was to funnel such attacks into killing corridors protected by his automated shield of missiles, fast-firing cannon, clouds of masking electronics, jamming, directed electromagnetic pulses, and pinpoint fire control. Effective aerial attacks would have been almost impossible, and extremely heavy losses to the attackers would have been certain. However, there was no genius in the control chair to orchestrate the elaborate automated defense systems, nor were there troops around to maintain the computers and service the weapons. With much of the interior badly damaged, the bridge now stood empty and vulnerable. It had been on the edge of being fully operational, but now it had already ceased being a threat. Instead of being an impenetrable anchor for an imagined chain of virtual fortresses, it had reverted to a useless pile of rocks.

Lima Company (Reinforced), out of the 3rd Battalion, 7th Regiment, 1st Division of the United States Marine Corps, landed on the long, wide level bridge in a carefully timed series of deliveries by a covey of tilt-rotor Ospreys. AH-1Z Viper helicopter gunships flew figure-eight patterns to provide low overhead cover, and fighters orbited at ten thousand feet. Not a shot had to be fired as the squads charged out of the Ospreys and established a perimeter defense.

The only people around were a halted small military convoy of trucks and Humvees some three klicks away on the eastern approach road, and a pair of Vipers hovered at each end of it.

Company commander Captain Richard Mendoza was able to report back to Kandahar that the bridge was secure within five minutes of the first boot hitting the ground.

"Lieutenant Connelly, get the engineers and ordnance teams down into those tunnels. I want to drop this span and be out of here as soon as possible," Mendoza ordered.

"Aye, aye, Skipper," Connelly said, then passed the orders to the waiting sergeants. Men immediately began to disappear underground.

"Ever see such a chunk of chopped-up real estate, Captain?" asked Gunnery Sergeant Hale Dinsmore, looking out over the destroyed valley below them.

"I have not, Gunnery Sergeant, and we are going to make this bridge look just as attractive. What are the Vipers saying about that convoy?"

"Pakistan army, sir. Just sittin' there. The Snakes are all over 'em."

"If they move, light 'em up."

"Yes, sir."

* * *

Lieutenant Farooq had no intention of moving, and in fact had ordered his men to stack their weapons in the beds of the trucks and leave the Humvee machine-gun positions empty. The radio link back to headquarters, he decided, had been damaged by the B-52 strike, which meant that he could make on-the-spot commands. His sergeant agreed the radio was inoperative and turned it off. Farooq then had his platoon brew tea and make themselves comfortable along the road for a while, walking around in the open, presenting no threat that could ignite a fight. At the pace the Americans were moving on this violent morning, their operation would not take much longer.

Helping make his choices easier were the two Viper attack helicopters that hung noisily a hundred feet above the roadbed, hemming the vehicles into place as carefully as dogs herd sheep. The stubby wings of the narrow helos held pods of 70 mm rockets, while 20 mm Gatlings were mounted beneath the noses. After what he had already witnessed, Farooq understood that on this day, it would not be a smart thing to get in the way of the Americans.

His sergeant brought him a canteen cup of hot tea, and the lieutenant blew on the liquid a few times before taking a sip, trying with all his might to maintain a sense of dignity. The pilot of one of those Vipers was staring at him through tinted goggles. Farooq smoothly raised his tin cup in a silent salute. The pilot nodded ever so slightly.

We understand each other, the lieutenant concluded, and he climbed atop his Humvee to watch the show. He felt almost privileged to be an observer at this demonstration of unlimited firepower.

WASHINGTON, D.C.

The arrest of Undersecretary William Curtis was assigned to the Federal Bureau of Investigation, with Special Agent David Hunt in charge, and his orders were to carry out the apprehension with utmost care. To ensure radio silence and avoid tipping off the media, the D.C. Metropolitan Police were not alerted, nor were any Virginia law enforcement authorities. The Secret Service detail guarding the vice president's residence on Observatory Circle was incorporated into the plan, since the FBI would be hitting the nearby BAIA office. As soon as the arrest was accomplished, the FBI was to turn Curtis over to the CIA for some serious questioning.

Hunt put two-agent teams to each corner of the BAIA property, then went up to the front door himself. He rang the bell, and a bewildered security guard opened up, his face dropping when Hunt flashed his creds and two more agents walked past with their guns drawn.

"Is Undersecretary Curtis here?" asked Hunt.

"No, sir," said the guard, a bald giant who worked for a private security company contracted to provide overnight protection for a number of government buildings. "The place is empty, except for me and the two housekeepers who are asleep upstairs. Want me to call them?"

"No. Give me your weapon with the fingers of your opposite hand, and stay right here with me while the agents check things out. Have you seen Curtis tonight?"

The guard slowly removed his pistol from the holster on his right hip with his left hand as more FBI agents came into the building, also with their guns out. "I haven't seen him, but I just came on duty at midnight. If you'll let me look at my logbook over on the desk, I can give you the time when he left."

"OK," Hunt said. The guard nodded, happy to be part of whatever was happening, and showed the logbook to Hunt. Curtis had not been in his office since leaving for lunch, and the guard printed out a list of ranking bureau officials, with their addresses and telephone numbers. "Maybe one of them can help," he said.

Hunt cocked his head to listen to the voices in his earpiece as the reports flooded in from agents clearing every room, and finding nothing. The housekeepers were awakened, came downstairs in their robes, and were questioned. Neither had seen the undersecretary.

Hunt ascended the curving staircase to find Curtis's office. Everything he saw bespoke quiet elegance, with a distinct sense of Middle Eastern culture in the vases, paintings, ornate tile work, and lush carpets. The office itself was a dazzling display of artifacts that had been presented to the BAIA and Curtis by officials throughout the Arab world. The veteran agent had the feeling he was walking through some special exhibit at the Smithsonian, or a bazaar in Istanbul. Rubies and emeralds, intricate gold work, and shining silver winked beneath small spotlights, as if the objects knew something that he did not. A big picture window opened out on the darkened lawn.

Dave Hunt was suddenly tense and nervous. It was just too perfect. This was no soft diplomat they were after, and if Curtis was in the wind, then maybe he had left something behind to delay his pursuers. Something else was in play.

"Everybody stop in place. Don't make another move," he ordered on his radio. "Get the civilians out of here, then rendezvous back at the rally point. Touch nothing. Retrace your footsteps. Watch for possible booby traps."

Just before he could repeat the order for the agents who had entered Curtis's empty home, one of them turned off a dripping faucet in the kitchen. That closed the circuit for a dynamite bomb hidden in a wall of the foyer where several agents had gathered. The following explosion blew apart much of the ground floor, and the rest of the town house collapsed in a fireball.

THE BRIDGE

The Vipers had given up watching the idle convoy, settled down on the bridge, and shut off their engines. Lieutenant Farooq thought that was wise; no use wasting petrol, dangling in the sky watching him do nothing but drink tea. The only thing bothering him was whether the busy Americans were going to leave any witnesses, but he reasoned that if they had wanted him dead, he would already be dead. They probably wanted him to report exactly what had happened, and he would.

"Sergeant? Are the radios working yet?" Play the game.

"No, sir. A lot of static." The sergeant pointed to the sky. "Probably one of their electronic warfare planes is up there, jamming everything."

Farooq shielded his eyes and looked up the road. He threw out the remains of his cup and climbed from the Humvee. "We have company coming, Sergeant. Form the men in ranks. No visible weapons," he ordered, straightening his uniform.

A little blue golf cart carrying two men in camouflage uniforms with protective vests and helmets was humming toward them from the bridge, an enlisted man driving an officer. Farooq's men were in formation by the time the cart pulled to a halt and the passenger got out. "Captain Richard Mendoza, U.S. Marines," the man said.

Lieutenant Farooq saluted and introduced himself.

The salute was returned. "Well, Lieutenant, I'm paying a courtesy visit to thank you for not interfering with our work today."

"Those were my orders, Captain. Observe and report only."

Mendoza knew that was a lie. The Pakistani officer had made the smart move to stay out of the way when he discovered he was so outmatched. No use for either one trying to keep secrets at this point. "We're about done down there. I want to advise you that when we depart, it would be best for you to wait right here, or even pull back. We're going to blow that bridge apart. My engineers estimated how much explosive would be needed, then doubled that amount. It would be a great risk to try to defuse any of it, because the clock is already ticking."

"I understand, sir. Thank you for coming up."

"Fine-looking troops you have here, Lieutenant. I would hate to have anyone needlessly injured at this point. Good luck to you."

"And to you, sir." Salutes were exchanged again, and Mendoza climbed back into the cart, which began the trip back to the landing zone. The Vipers were already winding up their engines and lifting off to make room for the Ospreys to retrieve the Marines. It appeared that the entire force was out of the tunnels and leaving. Farooq watched the departing captain, sorely tempted to grab a rifle and blow him to pieces.

As if hearing the thought, the cart stopped, turned, and came back. This time, Mendoza did not get out but just called to him. "Lieutenant, I forgot to tell you; two cruise missiles are on the way, one targeted on each of the support towers. That'll be the end of it." He cheerfully waved, and the cart buzzed away.

THE PENTAGON

Kyle Swanson was back in front of General Middleton's office window again, relaxed, watching the tourists. He asked, "We ready to go after Charlie Brown now?"

"No. You just got back, and things are in an uproar

over at the White House," the general replied, leafing through a stack of colorful brochures. "This isn't the time to drop another Green Light request on them."

"Best time to do it, General, while everybody in the Sandbox is trying to figure out what happened at the bridge, and why we were so out front about it."

Sybelle Summers was half-watching some talking heads on television discussing that very subject. "If the president's goal was to send a message that we won't ever stop hitting the terrorists, no matter where the chase leads, then he was successful. The TV people are constantly playing the videos of the center span dropping like an old Las Vegas casino being blown up, and then the missiles hitting the support towers."

"It has everything the TV requires but a shower scene and a car chase." Double-Oh Dawkins sipped from his ever-present cup of coffee. "Where you going on vacation, General?"

"I'm picking up my daughter and the grandkids in Richmond tonight and making the long drive down to the Cape to watch the Mars launch. That will be something they will always remember. After that, we're going to Disney World. Then they go home and I break away for some deep-sea fishing." He put the brochures in order, squared the edges, and put them aside. "What about our Coastie, Kyle? Did she make a decision before going on leave?"

"Not officially, sir. She'll do it, though. The kid was made for this stuff, and she did great in Pakistan. Not only that, but she worships Lieutenant Colonel Summers."

"As do we all." The general chuckled.

"Fuck you very much, sir. *I'm going to Disney World.* Jesus," Summers shot back as she changed TV channels, stopping at one on which the political talking heads were barking about the cost versus value of the Mars mission. She turned off the set and called loudly toward the door, "Liz? You got that FBI stuff?"

Benton Freedman walked in, carrying a handheld computer. "Got it all right here. You want a hard copy? I can send it to your BlackBerry."

"Not yet." She didn't want him spinning off into techno-talk. "Talk to us."

"Right. That Undersecretary Curtis fellow has disappeared, leaving a bomb in his residence, two agents killed and four wounded, another bomb found and defused at his office, his car abandoned in Maryland, la-da-da-da . . . and, uh, that's it from the FBI."

"Liz?" General Middleton arched an eyebrow.

"Sir, Lieutenant Colonel Summers asked for the FBI material. I was being specific, but the CIA has some interesting new stuff. You want to hear that, too?"

"Yes, Commander Freedman. If you please." The general sighed. The Lizard could be a curse.

"They're no longer sure he is a mole for the New Muslim Order at all, sir. He has strong connections with them, but there's no evidence that he actually is like a soldier or a guerrilla. More likely, he works with them on some things but also is a lone wolf, carrying out his own agenda. He was married to a Muslim woman, and they had a son, but both were killed during the U.S. bombing of Baghdad during Desert Storm. The CIA believes personal revenge to be his motivation. Financial records show his construction company had a stake in building the bridge."

Double-Oh interrupted. "He sounds like one helluva disturbed creature. A facilitator doesn't booby-trap his house and office. Too bad about his wife and kid, but shit happens in war. Anyway, what about right now? Is he on some mission here, or is he flying down to Rio?"

Freedman's round face lit up. "*Flying Down to Rio*. Ah. That was the first time Fred Astaire danced with Ginger Rogers. Black-and-white film, 1933. Neither of them was the star; that was Dolores del Rio."

"Back on track, Liz," Summers coaxed.

"From everything that has been dug up so far, I believe that Mr. Curtis is still within the United States, because everybody is looking for him, particularly along the borders and at the airports, commercial and private. He will be too busy staying ahead of the folks with badges to do any more mischief."

Swanson walked away from the window and filled a cup with coffee. "He's not done," Kyle said. "This all started with him, when he put the DSS onto chasing Beth Ledford, and he probably hired the two characters who attacked me before we left for Pakistan."

"That is correct," Lizard said. "Because the petty officer's brother found the bridge in Pakistan, and was murdered there, she wouldn't leave it alone. As long as she fought the system, the involvement of Undersecretary Curtis and the New Muslim Order was at risk. She is a brave young woman."

Swanson smiled. "So it is going to have to end with him. He's not done yet."

"Which is why our Coastie should have an FBI escort for a while, particularly when she goes out to California with her mother to visit San Diego," Summers said. "What about you? You want to go to Disney World, too?"

"I will leave Mickey Mouse to our esteemed general. Beth will be fine, because Curtis has bigger problems, like staying alive. I'll be spending some time running tests on the new Excalibur rifle, so I will be out at 29 Palms in California in the middle of thousands of Marines. Good luck to Curtis on coming after either one of us."

"Feebs will probably have Curtis soon, but you stay in touch with Coastie and keep your eyes open anyway, Kyle."

"I always do, sir. Always do."

of their coveralls, each had some unauthorized items, from nude pictures torn from *Playgirl* magazine to pink jockstraps to a Slinky toy, and those would be stuffed in nooks and crannies throughout the vessel. The jokes always helped break the tension on a flight.

The final vehicle and facility closeouts were a frantic period, with checks being conducted on everything from the flight deck to navigational control software, and Buck had responsibility for final check for loading the power reactant storage and distribution system. It took him less than a minute to peel off the panel and exchange an already installed circuit board with the one he had retrofitted to include a tiny battery, a bit of wiring, and an altitude-sensitive ignition switch. He put the real one in his pocket and closed the panel, studying his work. Nobody would detect anything.

He rejoined the rest of the support crew, and as they finished the day's tasks, the spaceship was less than a day from launch. The countdown clock stood at T minus twenty-three.

Joke's on you, my dear Erin, he said to himself as they reboarded the elevator and descended through the open web of the support tower. At T minus three, Buck Gardener and the closeout crew were to return to the rocket for final checks of the crew module and to assist the astronauts into their positions for the launch.

Gardener planned to be long gone by then. After the support crew reached ground level, he reported to the flight surgeon and complained about a mild headache and nausea. His temperature, blood pressure, eyes, and throat were normal, but the doctors would not chance the introduction of flu-like symptoms into the spacecraft. Buck would be replaced for the final closeout by a member of the backup crew, and he was soon on the road out of Merritt Island, heading toward Orlando, only forty-five miles away.

A final meeting and status report, another payday, and then Buck Gardener would board a flight at Orlando International Airport and jump over to the Bahamas, and further destinations unknown.

SAN DIEGO, CALIFORNIA

Beth Ledford had to leave her rented town house in Alexandria, Virginia, before dawn, but it still took an hour to get up to Glen Burnie, Maryland, in time to park in the long-term lot, then get through security and aboard the flight from the Baltimore Washington International Thurgood Marshall Airport to San Diego. She pulled a blue blanket and a small pillow from the overhead, and just after takeoff she was sound asleep, her head on the pillow against the window.

She awakened an hour later, went to the restroom to freshen up, then got a cup of coffee from the attendant's station and returned to her seat. An egg-and-cheese croissant that she had made and left in the refrigerator the night before, then put in her bag that morning, had warmed during the flight, and she ate it slowly, enjoying the flavor. That drew a disapproving glance from the man beside her, who was making do with airline food, a combo bag of pretzels and peanuts.

As the sun rose behind the plane, Beth was alone with her thoughts, eagerly anticipating spending a few days with her mother, playing tourist in southern California. See the whale jump, shop in La Jolla, get some quality beach time by the cliffs in Del Mar, enjoy spicy Mexican food, and drive up the coast. After Pakistan, doing nothing but hanging out with Mom sounded pretty good.

The flight crossed the country and several time zones in only four and a half hours, touching down at Lindbergh at 10:50 A.M., Pacific, which was almost two o'clock in the afternoon back on the East Coast. It felt like she had been given three hours to live all over again, and she smiled as she came out into the California sunshine. The iPod stack she had chosen for the long trip was on the *Chicago* sound track, and while she gathered her suitcase and waited in the cab rank, she jacked up the volume for the incredible jailhouse tango number. How she would have loved to see that on Broadway. Her fingers tapped her luggage in time with the music.

Her private cell phone chirped, and she dug it out of her purse to look at the calling number. Mom. She softened the music and took out a bud so she could press the phone to her ear. "Hi, Mom. I just got in. Are you at the hotel?"

"Beth?" Margaret Ledford's voice trembled, and her mom never got nervous. Something wasn't right.

"Yeah, Mom?"

"Can anyone else hear this conversation?"

"Not really. I'm in line for a cab. What's up?"

"You have to talk to this man. I've been, uh, kidnapped, and he wants to talk to you. I'm OK, Beth . . ."

Ledford tensed, and had to fight not to stagger and fall. *Kidnapped?*

The voice of a man took over, serious and calm. "Petty Officer Ledford, listen carefully to me and your mother will not be harmed. You are unaccompanied, are you not?"

"That's right."

"Don't try to be a hero. You and Kyle Swanson did enough of that at the bridge in Pakistan."

"OK. I understand. Who is this?" Someone got into a taxi, and the line moved forward. She shuffled along with it.

"I have been trying to find you for some time, but you and Swanson are quite elusive. Now do you know who I am? Do not say my name out loud."

Undersecretary Curtis had rejoined the game, despite being the most hunted man in America. "Yes. I know."

"Good. Then follow my instructions, and do not vary at all, because there will be no second chance for mommy dearest. For now, proceed to your reserved room at the Hacienda Hotel in Old Town. Do not contact law enforcement. I'll call you there and give you more directions."

"Let me speak—"

"You want to hear her? Listen." There was the startling sound of a loud slap, followed by a woman's scream. "Did you hear that well enough, bitch? Don't even try to think you're going to control this situation. I will call you at the hotel."

The connection was broken, and Beth Ledford just

stood there momentarily, staring straight ahead, listening to the buzz, before folding it up and putting it away. She stepped out of the taxi line and moved to a quieter zone, thinking hard while the tango girls sang low about how the men they had murdered had it comin' and only had themselves to blame.

Well, Mr. Curtis, you should be careful of what you wish for, because you might get it. Lay a finger on my mother and your worst dream will come true. She made a decision. *As a matter of fact, that nightmare will come true anyway.* Beth rummaged around in her purse and found the slightly bigger, more complex, and totally secure cell phone that Trident had issued her, scrolled to the frequent numbers, and hit the SEND button.

29 PALMS, CALIFORNIA

It was late morning on Range 400 at the sprawling Marine Corps Air Ground Combat Center in 29 Palms, and Kyle Swanson lay sprawled on his belly, slowly taking in the slack of the trigger, bringing it straight back. The big Excalibur was resting on a bipod, trailing lines of wires that linked it to sensitive computer-monitored data collection gear lined up on a small table. Seated in a chair was J. Horace "Verify" Wellington, a short, bespectacled man buttoned up in a scientist's white frock coat, with thick earmuffs to protect his hearing. He looked like a clockmaker, had never served in the military, and still was recognized as the best gunsmith in Great Britain. In the old days of swords, a blade forged of Birmingham steel was considered the ultimate weapon. In the modern day, a rifle bearing Wellington's imprint had the same value. He was called "Verify" because he tested and retested and retested before clearing anything on which he worked. The Excalibur 3GX had not yet earned his stamp of approval, although he had been on the project from the start.

"Ready," said Swanson.

"You may fire," replied Verify Wellington, and Kyle finished the trigger pull. The big gun bucked with a burst of high energy as it spat a .50 caliber round downrange. Swanson took the big recoil but did not reposition the gun. Instead, he moved away as Wellington approached with more measuring instruments.

Kyle removed his soft utilities cap and wiped his brow. He had chosen Range 400 on a weekend when there were not too many other people about, but had to piggyback on a previously scheduled live-fire exercise. Rifles, heavy machine guns, and mortars all banged away at targets.

Private Jerry Hubbard punched an elbow into Private K'Shan Lincoln. "Hey, K, ain't that the Ghost over there?"

Lincoln squinted. "I think so. Look at the freakin' gun he's got."

"Holy shit, dude, did you hear the sound of that thing? Sounded like a cannon!"

"Let's go say hello. The LT won't mind, and we're on a ten-minute break anyway."

The two young Marines moved before they had

second thoughts and trotted the twenty-five yards to where Kyle Swanson was watching Verify do his thing. They stopped, came to attention, and gave sharp salutes. "Gunny Swanson? Privates Lincoln and Hubbard, sir."

Swanson returned the salute. "Don't call me sir, privates, I work for a living. And I don't like being saluted."

"Aw, c'mon, Gunny; you're a living Medal of Honor winner. Even the commandant has to salute you." Lincoln smiled broadly. "Wow, man, this is an honor."

Kyle had won the nation's highest award for bravery by saving General Middleton from terrorists in Syria, but Middleton insisted that Kyle was just lucky—it was an accident of fate, and he had been about to escape all by himself when the sniper showed up and ruined everything. The general knew that wasn't the way it happened, of course, but he felt bound to needle Swanson at every opportunity.

The Medal could at times be a heavy weight to carry, and Swanson felt a duty to play the role when necessary. This was one of those times that he had to be an ambassador, take the opportunity to teach some young Marines about respect and the meaning of the Corps. They were good kids, and since Verify was still probing and measuring and taking barrel temperatures, Swanson walked with them back to their group, shook hands all around, and talked for a while about the big Excalibur without revealing its secrets. They would have to graduate from Scout Sniper School before they could ever touch that weapon.

When his cell phone rang, he gave them a wave and a Semper Fi and went back to his position. He recognized the number. "Beth," he said. "Wassup?"

CARLSBAD, CALIFORNIA

Bill Curtis checked Margaret Ledford's bindings once again. A strip of silver duct tape covered her mouth, and flex-ties were on her ankles and wrists. "Sorry about the slap, but I had to make sure that your daughter understood that I was serious," he said.

It had not been difficult to take her as a hostage. A knock on the door of the big red-roofed hotel in Old Town that morning, a pistol jammed into her ribs, and a quick trot to the van in the upper parking garage. No one noticed them. Finding a truly isolated area was just as easy, for Californians hugged the coast, paying to get as close to the Pacific Ocean as they could afford. He drove up to Carlsbad, then bent inland twenty miles, and he was soon parked off of a twisting side road in the dry mountains, beside a forgotten grove of gnarled manzanita trees.

"Now let's get you all set up," he said and pulled a green tarpaulin from a large cardboard box. "I fixed all of this yesterday, Margaret, just for you and your pesky daughter. Got the vests from a sports equipment store. The stitching is a little rough, I admit, but an old construction hand like me never forgets how to handle dynamite."

Her eyes grew wide in terror, and she struggled against the restraints as she recognized what she was seeing. The man was going to wrap her in a vest of explosives.

"I figured you were both about the same size, small, so that made things easier. See? Matching outfits." Curtis opened the van door and pulled her outside, then cut the flex-cuffs, forced her arms into the vest, and put new plastic ties on her wrists. "Be still! Don't make me slap you again, and there is no one around to hear you scream." With a few more moves, he secured the vest tightly. Sticks of bound dynamite covered the back, the wiring was in the generous pockets, and a detonator was on her right shoulder. He put her back into the van and removed the tape from her mouth only long enough to give her some water.

Curtis climbed into the driver's seat, turned on the ignition, and flipped the air-conditioning on high. It was noon, and the August temperature was climbing in the open chaparral country. "OK. Let's go pick up Beth now."

As he drove back toward San Diego, he kept the radio on, listening to the news from the Cape about the Mars rocket. The reporter, lapsing into space talk, said it was "T minus nineteen and counting."

Curtis was satisfied, for things were in motion. Tomorrow would be a very Black Sunday for the United States, with simultaneous terrorism strikes on each coast. One would be payback for Raneen, and the other would be payback for the bridge.

32

"I am on vacation. I am wearing a mouse-ears cap and a flowery blue Hawaiian shirt, baggy cargo shorts, black socks, and sandals. Why are you bothering me?" General Brad Middleton growled into his cell phone.

"Weren't you going to watch the rocket launch before going to Disney World?" Sybelle Summers was in Washington and had not thought twice about interrupting Middleton's schedule.

"My bug-dumb grandchildren made it very clear on the way down that they did not care about seeing any stupid rocket, which they can watch on YouTube if they ever want to. Now they are bankrupting me in this pleasure dome. Never mind. Why are you calling?"

"Undersecretary Bill Curtis is back on our radar, General. He apparently has kidnapped Beth Ledford's mother, presumably with the intent of drawing Beth and Kyle into his web and taking them down face-to-face."

"Then he is a stupid fellow. Why do you need me?"

Sybelle was smiling. "I wanted to touch base on whether to bring in the FBI or the locals."

The general grabbed his grandson with one big arm and held him motionless. "What does Kyle want to do?"

"He wants to keep it within Trident. Let him handle it."

"Well, I trust the skill sets of Swanson and Ledford more than those of the Feebs. Notify the White House chief of staff that we're going after the bastard, and give Kyle permission to light him up."

"Yes, sir. Have a good time."

"I'm going to drive over to the Cape tomorrow morning for the launch. Leave the rest of them here with the rat. It's my vacation, too, and I'm a general."

"Now, now, sir. Think of the children."

SAN DIEGO

Bill Curtis wrapped a colorful Mexican serape over the shoulders of Margaret Ledford, adjusted the front, and took her by the arm. "Scream or try to escape and I will shoot you dead where you stand," he warned. "Now let's go see Beth."

The small woman and the tall man pulling a little suitcase left the parking garage aboard an elevator that took them up to the top level of the Hacienda Hotel. The hallway was empty except for a service cart at the far end, where two Mexican room attendants were finishing up a room. It was two o'clock in the afternoon, and most of the new guests would start checking in about four. By then, the huge hotel would sparkle.

Curtis stopped at a door, knocked, and called out, "Beth! It's us, dear. Open up."

The white door opened quickly, and he shoved Margaret inside, into the arms of her daughter, and shut the door as they stumbled back. A pistol was now in his free hand. "Hello, Beth," he said. "I've been waiting a long time to meet you. You have caused me a great deal of trouble. Before you try to do anything, look beneath the serape your mother is wearing. You will find a vest filled with dynamite, and I have the trigger."

Beth gave Curtis a measured stare: tall, strong, with desperate eyes. Play along, Kyle had said, and find out what he really wants. "I understand, and I'm not going to cause any trouble that might get my mom hurt. Just tell me what you want me to do."

Keeping the pistol pointed at her, Curtis said, "First, go over to the window and close all the blinds and curtains so your sniper buddies cannot take an easy shot."

"There's no one out there." She twisted the plastic knobs and the blinds closed, and then she pulled the heavy dark drapes together. The room went almost dark.

"Lock the door and push the straight-back chair from the desk under the knob." Curtis turned on the bathroom light, as she did as she was told. He sat in an easy chair in the corner. "Now, open the suitcase. There's another vest in there, just like the one your mom is wearing. Put it on. Once we get you all strapped up, I will cut the flex-ties on your mother's wrists. The rules are simple: One of you will remain in my sight at all times, so you can even use the bathroom in private. Any attempt to escape or call for help, or any hand-to-hand combat shit, and I will be forced to do something very unpleasant, and a lot of innocent people in this fine hotel will get hurt. Understand?"

Both of the women nodded. "Then make yourselves comfortable, ladies. I will order up an early dinner from room service, and after that, I suggest you try to get some rest. I want to watch the TV special tonight about the Mars launch tomorrow. Now, Beth, I assume you have been in touch with Kyle Swanson, correct?"

"Yes," she answered.

"We will call him at midnight and give him his instructions. I want him to be part of this package, too."

"Gunny Swanson will eat you alive," she said in an almost threatening tone and wrapped an arm around her mother's waist. "You don't know him."

Curtis stuffed the pistol into his belt. "I know that some very important people want him dead. I know that I hold all the aces in this game. He will come to me, and he will die. All of you will."

ORLANDO, FLORIDA

Linda looked sexy and exquisite in a lightweight white dress, the lobster at Primo's was sublime, and astronaut Buck Gardener was a happy man. "I'm going to miss you," he said, raising a glass of white wine. "Wish we could spend the night together."

"It won't be for long," she responded with a smile. "I'll join you in Italy in ten days."

"You and me, rockin' along the Italian Riviera, with money to burn." He patted his chest pocket, which contained an envelope she had delivered containing nine thousand dollars. Ten thousand in cash leaving the country would raise eyebrows at customs. Nine did not. Millions of dollars were waiting on the other side of the pond, to be released to his numbered account when the rocket blew.

She crossed her arms, and her dark eyes sparkled. "You look good in civilian clothes. Nice new suit, comfortable shoes, expensive tie. No longer like an astronaut at all."

"Thanks. I feel really different, like reborn. This has been a rush, Linda." A mild look of concern crossed his face. "Be glad when it's all done, though."

Linda reached across the table, put her hand on his, and gave it a squeeze. "I know. Just think of the future, Buck. All that money stored in Switzerland, and a lifetime to spend it any way you want. That's a dream come true, isn't it? Now, let's get out of here, grab one more drink in a nice place, then get you on that last plane to Nassau, sweetheart."

"Yeah," he said. The good spirits came surging back, and he looked at his watch, a sleek JeanRichard model with a black face and slim leather band that had replaced his enormous fighter-pilot watch. Seven o'clock. Fifteen hours before liftoff.

KANDAHAR ARMY AIR FIELD,
AFGHANISTAN

Steve Longstreet of the CIA was sweating in the tight room that was eight feet long by eight feet wide and eight feet high, but Chief Engineer Mohammad al-Attas was wide-eyed in exhaustion and stank of fear. The CIA interrogator had pushed the young engineer hard for hours, waiting out the pauses when the Djinn personality arose, and fighting to keep al-Attas going in the right direction. The lights were bright, and the air-conditioning was off, so the two of them sat stinking in the box.

The news that Curtis had gone on the run, was wanted for murder, and would not be speaking in behalf of al-Attas had shocked the engineer, who picked at his fingernails as his face twisted in confusion.

"Give me something, Mohammad," Longstreet nudged, keeping a command edge on his voice. "Think hard about all of the traffic you saw exchanged between Bill Curtis and Commander Kahn. Try to visualize it. Think of where you were when you read it; pretend that you're there right now, reading those messages you were never supposed to see."

"I have given you everything I know, sir. Everything. I need rest and sleep, and medication. Let me have a pill to sleep, and maybe I can remember something tomorrow."

Longstreet slapped his palm on the tabletop, and al-Attas jumped. "There may be no tomorrow for you,

Mohammad. There is only *now!* Tell me about this attack!"

"I will then die as a martyr?" The proud Djinn voice. Crazy eyes. He jerked at the restraints but could not move.

"You will not die at all, boy. You will live a long life in our version of a dungeon. Twenty-three hours a day in a room smaller than this, no computers or books to distract your mind, blistering heat or freezing cold, and surrounded by the worst criminals in America. You are not strong enough for that, and you will go mad within a month. Talk to me."

Al-Attas squinted his eyes hard, picturing the scrolling screens of communications that he had intercepted and read. "New Muslim Order. Commander Kahn. Undersecretary Curtis. The bridge," he murmured. "Something about Columbus and America."

"Whoa." Longstreet stopped the thought. "Columbus and America? That's good, Mohammad. You're doing good. That is new. Think hard now. Keep going." Christopher Columbus discovering America? That made no sense.

"No. No." The engineer was trying to find a single piece of information that was itching in his brain. "Not Columbus. Columbia?" A smile creased the sweaty face. "Yes. Something about Columbia and America."

Longstreet got up and leaned over the table on stiff arms, but trying to look peaceful and put al-Attas at ease. "And Challenger. Did they mention the word 'Challenger'?"

A long moment passed before al-Attas nodded and spoke almost obediently, as if wanting to please his teacher. "Yes. I think so. Challenger, Columbia, America."

Both *Challenger* and *Columbia* were space shuttles that blew up, one on takeoff, the other on landing. It wasn't America that was to be attacked, it was THE *America*, the Mars mission. "Oh, my God," Longstreet shouted as he bolted from the room, doing the time adjustment in his head: It was about three o'clock in the morning on the East Coast of the United States, T minus four.

ORLANDO, FLORIDA

The Parramore section of Orlando was a distressed area that was as far as the imagination could reach from the magic of the frolicking Disney characters and the glitter of Universal Studios. Police patrol units cruising the alleys and checking the dark corners were constantly alert, particularly in the wee hours when the night creatures were out and fights, dope, and whores were a normal morning menu.

"Over there," said Officer Brandi Sharpe, and her partner, Jake Young, yanked the patrol car to the curb where a disheveled man was waving at them at the mouth of an alley on Church Street. Young flicked on the blinking lights, painting the area with flashes of blue and white. Sharpe got out first, followed by Young. "What's the problem, dude?"

"I found a dead man!" The wrinkled old wino pointed at a Dumpster. "He's in there."

As Young pulled his pistol to cover her, Sharpe slid her hands into rubber gloves. She hated Dumpster diving, but if the victim was truly dead, she could leave that for the crime scene techs. *Please be dead.* She raised up on her toes, hands on the edge of the Dumpster, and gave a low whistle. "Hey, Jake, come take a look."

The victim was a white man in a dark suit, with two gunshots in his forehead. "I don't think he's from around here," he said, as Brandi called in the apparent homicide. Jake Young told the wino to sit down and stay put.

Technicians hauled the body onto the cracked concrete of the alley, took some pictures, and looked for ID but found no wallet, although an expensive watch was still strapped to the left wrist. Deep in the right front pants pocket, a tech discovered an unusual small gold pin, a star above three columns rising inside a circle, with a name etched on the reverse.

A detective at the scene was connected by phone to the security office at the Kennedy Space Center over at the Cape. "I think we've found one of your people over here, dead in a Dumpster," the detective said, looking at his notebook. "Gunshots to the head. No positive identification yet, but there's a name on an astronaut lapel pin we found on him. Guy named Buck Gardener. Ring a bell?"

The duty officer in the security office sat up straighter. The alert status was already at the top of the scale because of the threat picked up in Pakistan, and now an astronaut on the closeout crew had left the base the evening before launch and had been murdered? Not just anyone, but Gardener, whose wife was to fly on *America* within a few hours. Without wasting further time, he set up a conference call with his boss and the *America* flight director. In five minutes, a hold was put on the launch while officials at the Cape, and in Washington and Houston, were rousted from bed to emergency meetings to decide: Go or no go?

33

Kyle Swanson had not heard from Beth Ledford for twelve hours, which indicated that she had also been taken by Curtis and wasn't allowed to communicate. That had not particularly bothered him, for it had been anticipated in some form, ever since her mother was captured. Curtis used Margaret as bait to get Beth, and intended to use both of them to get to him. Beth's job was to stay cool, stay focused, and keep Curtis from doing something in panic.

The silence had allowed Swanson some unexpected time in which to prepare for the unknown, and with the assistance of the Lizard and Sybelle from Washington, the giant Marine base at 29 Palms geared up to offer Gunny Swanson whatever and whoever was needed to take down this new terrorist. A major from the base commandant's staff, a light colonel from the Marine Special Operations Command, and a master gunnery sergeant had been on deck with him since late afternoon, prepared to expedite matters. Sybelle and the Lizard were ready to work in Washington. All they needed was a time and a place.

"You still awake back there?" he asked the Lizard via the live video hookup, as he took a seat before the laptop computer.

"Yes, of course I am. The signal from Petty Officer Ledford's sat phone has not moved. It is still in room 310 in the Hacienda Hotel. The tracer button on her belt shows that she is still there, too. This fellow is taking his time."

"He is waiting on something specific. We'll know soon."

Kyle's sat phone finally buzzed, shortly after two o'clock in the morning, startling everyone. They looked at it as if it were a live thing, and Kyle picked it up. "Swanson."

"Take down these coordinates," came the harsh order from a male voice; Curtis.

"Go," Swanson said, flicking his eyes to meet the others. Bill Curtis read off a string of numbers, then Swanson read them back. "What now?"

"You get in a Humvee and drive down from 29 Palms and arrive at that position at exactly 5:42 A.M. The approach is a narrow road in an ocean of sand, and I will have a perch with a clear view for miles around. Come alone, and stop when I call and tell you to. Then get out of the car, take off your shirt, and walk up the path that you will find marked by flags directly in front of you. It will take you east, up the ridge where the women will be strapped together, wearing dynamite vests, with my finger on the detonator. One suspicious move by you and I press the button. Clear?"

"Clear." There was no use asking the condition of the two captives; either they were alive or they were not.

"Give me a cell phone number to call," Curtis said, and Swanson did so. "You have about three and a half hours to drive there from where you are in 29 Palms, so I suggest that you get on the road. That time is absolute, drop-dead certain. Don't be late."

"OK. I'm on the way," Kyle said, keeping his voice level. He had every intention of being on time.

They closed the connection.

There was no flurry of action, or jumping for guns or cars, or a yelling of orders. In this moment of stress, the professionals took time to exchange glances, and all around the table the faces looked like a bunch of hungry wolves that had just found a rabbit. Bill Curtis had made his first mistake, allowing his adversary too much time to plan a response.

Swanson spoke to the Lizard in Washington. "Can you bring up a map of those coordinates, please, Liz?"

Almost instantly, a detailed map of Southern California came on the big screen against a wall, and Commander Freedman zoomed in on the specific numbers Curtis had given; a desolate desert position near the Arizona line, just north of the U.S. border with Mexico. "Imperial Sand Dunes Rec Area. Dune buggy heaven," observed the master gunny.

"How about matching that with the three-and-a-half-hour drive he mentioned from the Stumps."

The map expanded in size, and a straight blue line bloomed from 29 Palms to the desert location south of the Gordon Wells exit on Interstate 8. "Almost perfect, based on driving sixty miles per hour," the Lizard said.

"And the time, precisely at five forty-two?"

"Dawn."

"Ah."

"Gunny?" the Lizard called out. "The tracking signal on Petty Officer Ledford's sat phone is still stationary in the hotel room, but the one on her belt shows movement. I hacked into the hotel's security cameras and have a visual on all three of them leaving. The women seem to be OK."

"Roger that, Liz. Keep us in the loop. How far does he have to travel?"

There was a clicking of a computer keyboard before Freedman answered. "About one hundred and twenty-five miles to El Centro, then add another half hour to that exit. Say two and one-half hours, plus or minus. Which would put them on the spot about an hour before you, if you drove from 29 Palms."

"Thanks."

Now the men at the table changed from watching the screen to facing each other and writing on the legal pads. The MARSOC lieutenant colonel said, "The first thing is pretty obvious, Kyle. This guy doesn't want to go face-to-face with you. He would be a fool to let you within fifty feet."

"So the instruction to take off the shirt and walk up the path is bullshit?"

"Probably just a distraction, to keep you thinking that you can go up and rescue the hostages."

"And the daybreak time? What's that about?"

"He wants you coming from the west, looking into the rising morning sun."

The master gunnery sergeant wrote the capital letters *IED* on his pad. "I agree. It will be an ambush of some sort. From the file, this Curtis dude was a construction roughneck back in the day, and in Washington, he booby-trapped his home and killed those FBI types. My guess is he will make up for his lack of military skill with weapons by staying with what he knows: dynamite. He most likely will sprinkle an improvised explosive device or two along the road, and certainly mine up any marked path."

"Ouch." Kyle agreed with the possibility and turned to the staff officer. "We need a hero, sir. A volunteer who is an IED expert, someone with experience, and about my size. If he wears a full body armor suit, and can use an MRAP, he could soak up the explosion and walk away. Take some balls, but it can be done."

"I'll shop it out with the engineers," the major said. "They actually enjoy this sort of thing. Driving a blast-resistant V-bottom truck that weighs fourteen tons through a mine field helps measure the size of their dicks at beer call. We can lift one of them straight down to the El Centro Naval Air Station by helicopter, along with the driver."

Kyle turned to the master gunny. "That works, and I need to chop a pair of sniper teams to me. Not for shooting unless I give the call, but to flank the position and feed me information. Let's go ahead and do their insertion by air right away. Take along their ghillie suits, establish hides, and report. Sooner the better."

The MARSOC officer had a question. "You think this Curtis guy understands that we do desert warfare training up here all the time? What edge does he possibly believe he can obtain just by going into the dunes?"

"It's probably based on his planned egress route," answered the master gunny. "This is only a few hundred yards from the international border in the middle of a wasteland, so once he does the deed, he hauls ass across the line. Obviously he has been there before to stake it out and plan this, and he thinks he has control; he has the hostages, the dynamite, and a handpicked position and is calling the orders. Want to bet that he's got an off-road vehicle stashed nearby?"

The staff officer made a note. "We can lay on an Osprey right now to take you and the sniper teams down so you can all can hump in, and it can hang around out of sight, then be a medevac when it's all done."

"Sounds good, sir, but I'm not going in with the sniper teams. I've got to invade Mexico first, and faster than an Osprey can move. Time is critical. Can you line me up with a Citation down to Calexico?"

As the other three men were running checklists through their heads, Swanson called for the Lizard again. "I'm out of here, gang. See if Sybelle can arrange a priority call for me with the Fuerzas Especiales unit of the Infantería de Marina in Tijuana; particularly I need to talk to Capitano Miguel Francisco Castillo. Last I heard, he was running a platoon of Special Forces against the cartel in Sonora, right along the area where we will be working. I'll be in the air, but the Stumps can patch the call through."

The master gunnery sergeant gave a wicked grin. "We trained those Mexican marines. Good, solid fighters, although they do prefer that piece of shit Heckler & Koch MSG-90 for a sniper rifle."

Swanson was up and moving. "I helped train Mickey myself, back when he was still an enlisted man, so he can be my spotter. His weapon, Master Gunny, doesn't matter, because I'll be taking my own."

Captain Mickey Castillo was waiting at the Calexico International Airport when Kyle came in aboard a Cessna Citation V; he escorted Swanson through the border crossing with his gear, then drove to the Taboada International in the mirroring town of Mexicali. In minutes, they were aboard a Eurocopter Panther AS-565 helicopter churning east along I-8, paralleling the border, and were dropped off three miles south of the line. A following helicopter dumped out a dozen Marines who spread out to form a broad half-moon defensive position and protect the rear of the position for the unusual sniper team of Swanson and Castillo.

Kyle knew he had won the race. Curtis would still be on the road, believing he was ahead of the curve and would have about an hour to set up his trap atop a giant sand dune. Swanson, meanwhile, would be in a hide two and a half miles away, in Mexico, watching.

He and Mickey made quick work of digging a comfortable hole in the loose sand at the top of a huge dune, covering it with boards, then stacking the dirt back on and plugging in chunks of local vegetation. "This will be a very long shot, Kyle. I hope your special rifle can even make the shot at this range," Castillo said.

"It's not just the rifle, Mickey. I'll be using a rocket-powered titanium bullet that is still in the experimental stage. We were testing it at 29 Palms when this mission popped up." He arranged his radio, made the Excalibur ready, and covered it with a clean, soft cloth to keep out the fine dirt until it was time to use it. "I appreciate you taking time off from your druggies to help out this morning."

"Always happy to help kill an American terrorist." The Mexican captain in the black beret grinned, and his bright teeth flashed beneath the mustache. "The guy sounds like a real asshole."

"That he is, my friend. That he is. But he has two women, one of whom is Beth Ledford, a good friend of mine, and we have to rescue them."

"Aha. A pretty señorita?"

"Actually, she is pretty. A little blonde with a nice figure, but we're just friends. Beth is a helluva fighter, can shoot better than you, and is going to join Task Force Trident."

"Then she certainly sounds worth saving. Afterward, we can perhaps have a celebration?"

"You always have women on your mind. Just concentrate for now on popping this tango, OK?"

"Of course. Or course. This Beth Ledford; she is a little blonde, did you say?"

EL CENTRO, CALIFORNIA

Bill Curtis kept his van within the speed limit on the interstate highway as he passed through the agricultural fields of the fertile Imperial Valley, and the smell of fertilizer and chemicals hung heavy on the night air. Huge sprinkler systems hissed from pipes. He was in control. The women were immobilized in the back, wrapped in dynamite, and gagged, behaving themselves. He would have the sun at his back when Swanson came through the big dunes and into the kill zone. He would be up high, with the advantage of looking down on the approaching man, who would be helpless. The explosive device was buried at the turnoff where he would leave his van, and Curtis had planted two additional dynamite caches along the little path up the steep, shifting side of the sand dune. At that point, there would be nothing Swanson could do to stop him.

He looked at the digital clock on the dashboard and saw that it was almost four thirty in the morning, which meant it was seven thirty at the Space Center; according to the published schedule, the Mars astronauts would be boarding the command module of the rocket about now. Coming up on T minus three hours. He pressed the scan button to see if a news report might be picked up out in the desert night. Radio reception was tricky in this bowl of desert that was below sea level, and getting clear signals from commercial stations was erratic.

Curtis found a talk show whose host specialized in

the weird and bizarre, including coverage of aliens and UFOs, for his listening audience of night owls. He had been refereeing an argument for the past hour between experts about what kind of life existed on Mars, and if it might be hostile to humans.

"Well, guys, this is really interesting, and our lines are on fire, but I want to bring everybody up to date here. The wire services are reporting from the Cape that the Mars launch has been scrubbed!" Excitement rose in his voice. "A NASA spokesman has just announced that during the final safety check this morning, several heat-resistant tiles on the reentry vehicle were found to be defective, and the *America* will not fly until the problem can be corrected. A news conference will be held later. Well, guys, this is a stunner. No launch this morning! What do you think, Dr. Lerner?"

Bill Curtis slammed on the brakes, and the tires locked and the van skidded to a jerky halt with the right wheels off the pavement. He bashed the steering wheel with both hands and shouted every obscenity he could think of, got out and stormed around, waving his arms in frustration, then beat hard on the side of the van. A passing motorist gave him a curious look, then sped away. The damned Mars mission was off! How? What? They would go through the rocket piece by piece now and find the detonator. *Ohhhhhh, damndamndamn.* His groan was deep and guttural, and his stomach was in such sudden pain that he leaned over and vomited bile onto the pavement. He collapsed beside the back wheel, leaned back, and drew in deep breaths. Failure again. First the bridge, then his exposure as a traitor, and now this. The tiles story had to be a lie. He didn't know how but was certain that Swanson was involved in foiling the rocket plan, too. The double strike on the United States had evaporated. Blood surged through his veins, and he felt like killing somebody.

Kyle Swanson swept the 40-power spotting scope slowly over the empty sands that would turn into a cauldron within a few hours as temperatures soared to over 100 degrees, occasionally kissing 120 plus. On most summer days, the cooked little towns in the Imperial Valley were among the hottest places in the United States. The dunes folded away, one after another for forty miles to the north, and when the hot, heavy winds kicked in, the incredibly wrinkled landscape would rearrange itself into brand-new trackless, bumpy wastes, and sand would fill the air and turn the world tan and blot out the sun.

"Headlights," he said and handed the scope to Mickey. Without the increased magnification, the lights were a mere dot in the darkness to the naked eye, but when Kyle brought up the Excalibur, its 20-power scope brought everything back to clarity, adjusting to night-vision mode. "He's late. Only thirty minutes until sunrise." The darkness was already thinning as a new day crept toward the valley.

The hump of the huge dune hid the new arrivals, but the flanking teams had clear views and gave step-by-step reports as Bill Curtis parked south of the small bridge at the intersection of the All-American and New Coachella canals, part of the desert aqueduct system. He killed the engine and pulled his two hostages from the back of the van, cut the manacles on their ankles, and made each carry some gear as they climbed the dune, following the little flags dimly visible at their feet.

The snipers had all lasered the top of the target dune earlier with infrared beams, and Swanson had locked the exact distance into Excalibur's internal computer. "Windage?" he asked and was told there was no change. A recurring light breeze had been recorded sweeping through the valleys between the dunes every seven minutes, and the timing had remained constant. Mickey was keeping track of the time, and just as expected, the faint wind eased down through the depressions right on schedule.

"We've got another seven minutes of clear air," he whispered, as though his voice might be heard two and a half miles away. In the big scope, he saw the man come to the crest of the faraway ridge with the women beside him. Then the women sat down, and the man stood tall. "Everybody stay still," Mickey called. "He's doing a sweep of the area with binoculars. Good. He's done. Jesus, Kyle, he didn't even look this way."

"Of course not. He's overconfident and careless. This is Mexico, and he drew a mental boundary on threats at the border. He has not factored in the danger to himself. What's that he's doing?"

"Shit. It's a beach chair! The son of a bitch has unfolded a beach chair and has plopped his ass down in it, like a king on a throne. A hostage is tight on each side."

Swanson brought the picture to perfect clarity in his own scope. Hunh. The elevation calculation was still good; Kyle's hide was fifty feet above the target, and he figured a plus three. His aim point would be the base of the neck, right above the shoulders. Not much wiggle room left and right, but better margin of error up and down, and Swanson did not plan on missing anyway. Not this morning.

While Curtis was seated, Kyle could only glimpse the head itself, which was moving back and forth, either talking to the hostages or looking for the expected vehicle. "Stand up, you fucker. Stand up." The rifle was ready, the shooter was ready, and the target had about a minute to live.

At precisely 5:42 A.M., the final wispy gray fled the sky and the fiery rim of the sun seemed to leap up with a blinding light. Curtis would not even try to look backward now, and right on time, the huge Marine MRAP armored truck surged out of the west, the big engine shattering the stillness, as if the world's biggest dune buggy had awakened. The driver jammed the accelerator down hard so the noise could help complete the distraction, and he was confident the beast would do no more than rock a few times on its protected springs if a couple of sticks of dynamite exploded beneath it. It ate big bombs for breakfast.

Curtis saw the MRAP coming, put aside the detonator for the vests, and picked up the one for the explosive package that he had buried at the wooden bridge. The truck was rushing nearer by the instant, Swanson hurrying for his doom. In the building excitement, Big Bill Curtis stood up, and Kyle took the shot.

A twin instantaneous explosion tore through the daybreak; a *ka-pow* . . . *POW* thunder as Excalibur fired. The huge .50 caliber bullet erupted from the barrel with a deafening *crack* and instantly covered the first thousand yards on its own power; then three microscopic fins popped open and a tiny solid-fuel motor ignited with a roar of its own that kicked the bullet forward even harder and multiplied its normal effective range without altering the spin. The bullet became a missile.

It struck Curtis with such brutal force that it ripped his head off at the neck, and the impact hurled the body forward as if it had leaped ten feet. The corpse hit the slope hard, and it cartwheeled hideously down the length of the high dune, leaving behind a splattered trail of blood and gore that shone brightly in the sunlight of the new day.

Lance Corporal Jim "Boomer" Carpenter saw the head fly off of the man at the top of the steep dune before he heard the double-whammy of the shot. As the body tumbled down the sharply angled slope, he kept up the speed of his MRAP and dodged it, letting the truck's Caterpillar turbocharged diesel engine churn the strong Michelin tires until it could go no farther. Sand and gravity stopped it about halfway up. Boomer was a little disappointed that he had not run over any booby trap. He grasped the microphone from the dashboard and flipped on the loudspeaker. "Ladies up there! It's all over! Stay calm. The helicopter is inbound from the south." Then he unbuckled the four-point safety harness and climbed up behind the machine gun in the turret, just in case.

The Eurocopter Panther did not touch the ground

when it swirled in to let Kyle and Mickey jump aboard, and then it covered the two and a half miles to the dune in a flash. To keep from creating a sandstorm with its rotors, it hovered above the crest and the two Marines fast-roped down, crouching beneath the blast until the bird flew away.

Kyle ran to the hostage on his left while Mickey sprinted to the other woman. Margaret Ledford's eyes were tightly shut, and tears tracked from the corners; her body shook with sobs. Kyle knelt down and propped her into a sitting position against his left arm and leg. "It's OK, Mrs. Ledford. Everything is under control now. My name is Kyle Swanson, and I'm a friend of Beth's." He gently peeled away the duct tape gag, and she hauled in deep breaths and gagged a bit while he used his Ka-Bar knife to slice away the ties at her wrists and ankles, then closely examined the dynamite pack. "I don't see any triggering device on this vest, Mickey. He probably wanted to command detonate after he got away. I think we can just cut them off."

He looked over to where Mickey and Beth were, less than ten feet away. She was sitting up on her own, and Mickey had removed the tape from her mouth and cut away the bindings. He had his black beret low over his forehead, and somehow his desert camo uniform looked clean and sharp. They were looking directly into each other's eyes, dark Latin brown and bright Iowa blue, and Mickey lifted Beth's right hand to his lips to give it a light kiss. "I am Captain Miguel Francisco Castillo, Infantería de Marina, señorita. At your service. Please, call me Mickey."

Swanson shook his head in wonder as Beth gave Mickey a ten-thousand-watt smile that erased the dangerous past hours as if they never had happened. *Damn,* he thought, *she never smiled at me like that.*

PEARL HARBOR,
HAWAII

Two weeks later, Kyle Swanson was wrapping up some leave time in Hawaii before heading back to Washington. He had spent long days on the beaches of Oahu, hanging out with the surfer crowds and even now and then catching an empty wave where he would find himself alone with his board atop a surging mountain of water. As much as the waves called to him at Makaha and Waimea and out in the Pipeline, he tore himself away from the lure of the breaking surf for his final evening in Hawaii, had his hair cut, shaved, and donned his full evening dress uniform. For a change, he wanted—needed—to look sharp. Even the Medal of Honor would be worn around his neck on its silken blue ribbon.

At 1700 hours sharp, Swanson strode up the gangway to the mighty battleship USS *Missouri,* anchored at Ford Island, saluted the flag and the welcoming officer of the deck, and stepped aboard to join a private reception being hosted by the U.S. Pacific Command. A new admiral was taking over, and this party was the last hurrah for the departing commander. Major General Brad Middleton of Task Force Trident had been invited to the change-of-command ceremony because he was an old friend of the incoming admiral but could not get away from Washington, so he sent Medal of Honor winner Kyle Swanson as a consolation prize.

Kyle spent an hour of meaningless mingling to make sure that Middleton would be informed that everything had gone off well; then he casually drifted away from the herd of dress uniforms, stars, and tuxedoes, and the women in gowns that seemed to glow in the bright lights. The cocktails would be followed by dinner and dancing, but Kyle wanted some alone time aboard the Mighty Mo.

The ship was huge, as big as a small city, and he wandered freely beneath the big guns, from the stern to the bow, which was pointed directly at the *Arizona* memorial. The positioning represented the alpha and omega, the beginning and the end, of World War II for America, since the *Arizona* was sunk when the Japanese attacked Pearl Harbor in 1941, and the surrender documents were signed aboard the *Missouri* almost four years later in 1945 in Tokyo Bay.

Alone at the bow, Kyle came to attention and saluted the *Arizona,* which entombed most of the 1,177 crewmen who lost their lives that day. The memories were as fresh as the oil that still oozed from the bunkers of the dead battlewagon.

Closure. That was what Kyle wanted on this latest war, but he knew he would never live to see it. The War on Terror had already lasted twice as long as World War II and showed no signs of really stopping; there would never be a signing of a peace treaty with the shadowy jihadist religious fanatics and their supporters in so many countries. They would never stop trying to attack the United States.

Kyle would never stop going after them.

He turned back to where the ladies and officers and gentlemen were gathered on the deck beneath a new and cloudless Hawaiian night. He would go back to them now, tolerate the speeches, enjoy the lavish buffet, but pass on the dancing and get back to the hotel. There was a flight out early the next morning that would take him back to Washington, where he would report for duty at Task Force Trident and then go kill Charlie Brown.

Read on for an excerpt from the next Sniper Novel

TIME TO KILL

by Gunnery Sgt. JACK COUGHLIN USMC (RET)
with DONALD A. DAVIS

Coming soon in hardcover from St. Martin's Press

1

NEWPORT BEACH,
CALIFORNIA

Kyle Swanson leaned on the white railing of the deck on the second floor of his house as the sun edged down toward the horizon, and wondered if he had time to get out in the surf one last time, paddle down to the Wedge, ride a few sets, and get back before it got too dark. Madeline, his girlfriend of the past two weeks, was coming over after her shift in a beachfront restaurant and was expecting him to grill some tuna while she whipped up a salad. They would drink cold *cerveza*, eat on the open patio with the glass doors all the way open, with fresh ocean breezes coming in while music spilled into the night. They might take a midnight dip, and he would be dazzled by her body in that red bikini with her blonde hair reflecting the moonlight. After that, a strategic retreat to the big bedroom to make love while boarders, bladers, dog-walkers, tourists, and other lovers strolled the boardwalk out front, unable to see them.

No, he decided as he rubbed the freshly painted railing. He didn't have time for one last swim, and he and Maddy would have to part in the morning, but it had been a hell of a leave. The United States Marine Corps wanted its top sniper back on duty.

His telephone rang, as if it had been waiting for just the right moment to ruin the idyllic mood. A glance at the screen showed Lieutenant Colonel Sybelle Summers was calling from Washington. "Hey," he said.

"Are you out of the lazy vacation mode yet?"

"Did I ever tell you that you have a sultry voice?"

"I am your superior officer, Gunnery Sergeant Swanson."

"But we slept together once, Sybelle," he said. "Remember? A rainy night in France?"

"I've never been to France. You must be thinking of your current chippie, what's her name? Michelin, like the tires?"

"Her name is Madeline, and your memory is slipping. I thought you and I had a deep and special relationship."

There was a slight, pleasant change in her tone. "Some people are just not that memorable." They both laughed.

"Sybelle, why are you bothering me on my final evening of leave? Gimme a break, girl. The sun is just about down, I'm drinking beer, watching the beach, getting ready to grill a dead fish, Maddy is coming over, and the California weather is perfect. Washington, is clogged with snow, according to the Weather Channel. I don't want to come back."

"Quit whining, Kyle. You built that big house and now you start acting all rich instead of like the raggedy-ass jarhead you are. Maddy, is it? Maddy? Is she out of the high school yet?"

"Here's a suggestion; why don't you come out here instead? No snow."

She said, "Miss Maddy Michelin would be upset if I did that. Let's get to business. You are wanted back here right away."

"I'll be there tomorrow afternoon anyway, Sybelle, and I can't get back any faster than that." He tilted back the long-neck bottle of Corona beer, which was getting warm. The sky had deepened into a band of solid orange that was being chased by the heavy purple night coming from the east, and the sun was moving so fast that it seemed to be falling.

"Change of plans. A plane will be waiting by the time you get out to John Wayne. I'll meet the flight here, then we go directly to a meeting. Take this thing off speakerphone."

He closed the speaker and picked up the receiver. "Okay. I'm listening. This line is not secure."

"Really? I had no idea. Does Maddy know that?"

"Can you get to the point?"

"Some of your father's friends have contacted the boss, and they want us to talk to a guy who lives out on the Maryland shore. We'll drive out from Andrews."

That was a jolt. It was her way of advising him that

Sir Geoffrey Cornwell in Great Britain apparently had pulled the original string to start this ball rolling, and that was Kyle's real other life. The man had been a colonel in the British Special Air Services Regiment before a broken leg forced him into retirement. Refusing to be shelved, he had set out to design technical applications and new weaponry for the military, and was on the cutting edge when War on Terror dollars started to flow like cheap wine. Eventually, he persuaded the Pentagon to lend him a sniper for technical assistance on a unique project to develop a new kind of long-range rifle, the *Excalibur.* They had sent Kyle Swanson over to England, and before long, the project was successful, and Jeff and his extraordinary wife, Lady Patricia, who were childless, had found a new friend in Kyle Swanson, an American orphan.

Over the years, through some very good times and some very bad and dangerous times, they had unconsciously knitted together as a family. Sir Jeff branched into other fields and had a golden touch for business, and although Kyle remained a Marine, he was brought into the business, too, for the Pentagon liked having its own liaison man in the thriving Cornwell pipeline. It had been a special day for Kyle when the Cornwells adopted him as their son.

So if Sir Jeff, who was always helping out clandestine operations for the U.S. and Great Britain, was behind this thing—Kyle still didn't know what it was—then Swanson would consider it important and worthwhile. The problem had probably gone from Jeff to his friends within the British Intelligence Service and perhaps even into the Prime Minister's office before leaping over the pond to the White House. That was enough for Swanson, but a last night with Maddy would have been nice.

Kyle paused. "So General Middleton himself is ordering me back?"

"Not that boss, Swanson. The *big* boss. Anyway, Task Force Trident is now involved."

That more than aroused his curiosity, but he couldn't swallow it whole. "You want me to give up my final night, fly coast-to-coast, get off the plane a few hours before I would get there anyway, and go straight to work in Maryland? That urgent?"

"Damn straight, Gunny. Consider yourself back on the government dime." She ended the call.

"Aw, man." Kyle folded his phone and took it and the remains of the beer out to the deck. The rim of the sun was almost totally gone, sinking into the Pacific Ocean. It was the moment he always watched for, but usually missed, because it happened so quickly. Then, there it was, for only a heartbeat, a brilliant sparkle of emerald as the final rim of the sun disappeared. Maybe it was an omen, he thought, an official ending to his two weeks of peace and quiet. Now it was back to being the trigger-man for Trident.

Reluctantly, he hit the speed-dial number to give Madeline the bad news of the broken date.

Two hours later, he was the only passenger aboard a small executive jet that was hauling him from John Wayne Airport outside of Newport, heading to Andrews Air Force Base, just over the Maryland line outside of

Washington, D.C. Swanson was in the wide, soft seat and had already finished reading the *Time* and *Newsweek* magazines that were in the seatback. It was a government plane, so there was no flight attendant, but he could fix a drink on his own in the galley, and somewhere over Missouri he would probably test the shrink-wrapped turkey and cheese sandwich.

Both magazines had covers showing the mobs demonstrating in the cities of Egypt, and their lead articles were about the latest treacherous political storm that was roiling that ancient country. The situation was deteriorating, just as it had been when he began his leave thirteen days earlier, just as it had been doing for years, if not centuries.

He tossed the magazines onto the empty seat across the aisle, settled back, and tried to puzzle together why he was being called back so suddenly. Sybelle's guarded conversation had given him only some very broad parameters for consideration, but they were startling. First of all, she had mentioned Sir Jeff, and had also said it was the big boss calling him home, and emphasized "big." His actual commander in Task Force Trident was two-star Marine Major General Bradley Middleton, and the general's only boss was whoever happened to be the President of the United States.

More than a decade had passed since terrorists had flown fuel-packed civilian airlines into the Twin Towers in New York, the Pentagon in Washington, and the Pennsylvania dirt. In response, the entire U.S. government had reshaped itself both at home and abroad to make sure such attacks never happened again and that gave birth to the behemoth Homeland Security Department. Even that wasn't enough because the inevitable bureaucratic friction soon appeared along the seams of the various departments. Numerous plots had been foiled since 9/11, involving crude devices like explosive shoes and underwear, which proved the system worked as long as people remained alert and paranoid enough to maintain their vigilance.

There were always going to be maniacs out there who would try to kill Americans, but airplane hijackers had lost their advantage. The nature of air travel had changed dramatically, from the tedious searches by TSA workers before boarding, to the flight attendants who would willingly die rather than open the cockpit door, to every passenger on the plane, from a semi-pro athlete to a college girl, being willing to jump on a hijacker like a pack of crazed dogs. The willingness of a terrorist to give up his life to achieve his goal was of no use when his targets were as equally willing to die to stop him.

The military had also finally changed to accept the talents of special forces, and elite operations like the Army's Delta Force and the Navy SEALs, and the futuristic technology of remote-controlled drones had changed the landscape of the battlefield. The Pentagon had met the challenge of terrorism head-on, as had the CIA, the FBI, the NSA, and the rest of the alphabet agencies.

Nevertheless, there were still holes in the protection net, for publicity, budgets, congressional oversight, and the huge numbers of people supporting and carrying out any operation always tended to multiply over time. The heroes had become *known*. It had been a short step from the increased exposure to the creation of Task Force Trident by people who still cared fervently about secrecy.

Trident was invisible by military standards, with a total roster of only five people, including General Middleton, who ran the show. The offices were in a hard-to-find area of the Pentagon, and the budget came out of Homeland Security via the Department of Agriculture. The team was far outside the chain of command other than Middleton's reach to the President.

Sybelle Summers was the ops officer, and Master Gunnery Sergeant O.O. Dawkins handled the administrative end, working the inner paths of Pentagon power. Double-Oh could borrow anything in the arsenal, from individual troops to Stealth bombers for a Trident mission. The team's only non-Marine was a squid, Lieutenant Commander Benton Freedman of the Navy, a quirky geek whose proprietary electronic net could kick the combined computer butts of Google and Facebook without breaking a sweat. They called him the "Lizard," a corruption of his college nickname of "Wizard." Swanson handled the wet work. Few people even knew about Trident, but the president always knew where they were, in case they were needed. Like now.

He left his seat, went to the head with his Dopp kit, and studied his reflection as he shaved. Only yesterday, he had been a beach bum wearing baggy board shorts, and now he was back in his Trident uniform of jeans and a dark blue sweatshirt. His Marine dress blues were on a hanger in Washington, and carried the three gold stripes and two rockers on the sleeves to denote his USMC rank of gunnery sergeant, with rows of ribbons and awards, including the Congressional Medal of Honor. He loved the uniform and the Corps, which had been his home during long years of training, field work, assignments around the world, and taught him the trade of the sniper. In doing so, they had honed him into a fierce weapon.

He seldom wore the blues these days; he worked in places where he dressed the part he was playing. Jeans and sweatshirts today, maybe a business suit tomorrow, with authentic credentials to match the character.

Swanson cleaned his face of leftover lather, replaced the razor, then picked up the alleged sandwich and a can of tomato juice on his way back to his seat. The sandwich was tasteless. He took a few deep breaths and his mind continued the shift back into the counterintelligence mode. It was like time travel, bridging the freedom he had enjoyed during the past few weeks back into the complex and deadly world of Trident, where only the mission existed.

He went to sleep to the hum of the dual engines, flying backward in time as the plane subtracted time zones from his life. The four-hour flight would arrive in Maryland about the same time he left California, and he could live the time all over again.

The descent to land at Andrews was swift. The plane circled quickly and dropped into the approach path of the most exclusive airport in America, the one that Air

Force One, the President's official plane, called home. It was too dark for Kyle to see the trees when the little jet's tires squealed as they caught the runway. The front tilted down until the forward wheels made contact, the reverse thrusters screamed, and the brakes clamped hard to slow the bird.

"We're here, Gunny," said the co-pilot as he stepped out of the cabin. "Snowing out there. Watch your step going down, it'll be slickery."

Sybelle Summers was waiting on the tarmac nearby beside an old Ford Crown Vic with a single blue light blinking brightly atop its roof. She was as tall as Kyle, with a classic face that never carried much makeup, and snowflakes were catching on the black hair cut to collar length. The only woman ever to pass the Marine Recon course, she had become a special ops and counter-terrorism expert and was on a fast track to someday become a general, if she lived that long. There was nobody Kyle would rather have at his side if the going got rough.

Tonight, she had her game face on. A worn black leather gun belt was buckled around her waist, and a big gold badge flashed on her right hip, just in front of the holstered Glock19.

"Working undercover, Lieutenant Colonel Summers?" he asked.

She thrust a padded nylon briefcase at him. It was zipped closed. "Homeland Security creds for you tonight and your .45 Colt ACP, loaded and racked with one in the chamber. Grab your gear and get in the car."

"What's going on?" he asked.

"This guy we were meeting tonight? He's dead."